WAGES OF WAR

IMMORTAL REALMS

BOOK 3

ELLE BEAUMONT
CHRISTIS CHRISTIE

Midnight Tide
PUBLISHING

To my siblings—
For every battle and war we've fought together—thank you for being
there. Most importantly, thanks for dealing with my insanity.
**smooches* ~ Elle*

For Scott—
Thank you for your continued support and interest in this crazy
endeavour of mine. It means more to me than you could ever know.
xoxo ~ Tiss

Prologue

Zryan

"Sire, your griffin has arrived." Amyntas appeared in the study, suddenly at Zryan's side, as if out of nowhere. His chamberlain had a tendency to do that. Simply *being there* when needed and yet never in the way when he wasn't.

He was a tall, lean figure with straight blond hair an›d moved with an elegance that was reminiscent of a dancer. Zryan had jokingly asked him once if he did performative pieces in his spare time, and Amyntas had only gazed back at him, no humor showing, and said simply, no.

"Fantastic. A day early!" Zryan rolled up the scroll that he had been reading, a new law for parliament to ceremoniously pass once he'd finalized the wordage. Some would like it. Some would hate it. But Zryan would enact the law just the same. Something to prevent any one noble or fae of wealth from owning too much property in Lucem. Even himself. Land meant more farms, which meant more earnings. Beyond titles, land meant power.

For as long as he was ruler, tyrants would not be able to keep Lucem in a monopolistic hold.

"Papa." Kian popped his head out from under the desk where he had been playing with a little spot of gold, molding it by hand into a lumpy butterfly. "Can I come see the griffin too?"

Zryan pushed back his chair, stood, and held his hand out to his youngest son. "Of course, Kiki."

His heart swelled as the little hand slid into his. Fatherhood was truly the greatest gift life had bestowed upon him. Which made it even harder to understand the male his own father had been. Ludari hadn't loved his children; he'd seen them only as growing threats to his own supremacy.

There hadn't been a single day that Zryan had received a look of love, respect, or pride from Ludari. Every word had been filled with degradation and scorn. He should have feared fatherhood considering the example he'd had; instead, the moment Alessia had told him she was expecting their first child, Zryan had been filled with a sort of elation he'd never felt before. He had impatiently awaited Ruan's arrival.

He squeezed Kian's small hand, and together, they left his office, heading through the brightly lit hallways of the palace. Creams, golds, and soft whites encased them in a warm glow that was both welcoming and elegant. Zryan and Alessia had built their own palace. Once everything had been settled between himself and his brothers, he and Alessia made the decision to destroy the monstrosity of tyranny his father had built. And in its place, they made their home.

On their way to the stables, Ruan found them. He was turning into a strapping young lad. Tall for his age, already showing the way his adult form would bulk out into strong muscle and agile limbs. For now, he was on the cusp of adolescence growing into young adulthood, and his eagerness to grow up warred with the childlike nature of his remaining youth.

Ruan was turbulence to Kian's serenity, and Zryan found it amazing how he could love both so immensely for entirely different reasons.

"Papa?" Ruan asked, looking between them.

"The new griffin is here!" Kian was quick to chirp, bouncing excitedly as he walked, his hand tugging lightly at Zryan's.

Ruan's eyes lit up with interest, which he quickly tried to mask. Zryan hid his knowing chuckle. "Come along with us, if you wish." He said it nonchalantly, so that Ruan wouldn't feel pressured to pretend he wasn't as excited to see the creature as they were.

The trio left through the east entrance of the palace, walking the crushed gravel walk that led to the stables. From behind the large structure, the sound of an agitated griffin could be heard.

"Oh, I think someone is excited to meet us," he said to Kian, looking down at his upturned face.

"Let's hurry, Papa!"

Chuckling, Zryan picked up his pace, Kian already tugging at his arm in an attempt to run them through the stables more quickly. He swept his youngest son up, resting him on his forearm to trot through the stables, trumpeting like a griffin. Kian squealed in happiness, his arms tight around Zryan's neck.

The back doors of the stables were open to the paddock where his new griffin was penned, a gold cuff around its neck chaining it to a post at the center. The beast had yet to be broken; still wild and untamed, it tugged agitatedly at the chain, wings beating harshly to keep it aloft. The post, embedded deep in the ground, did not give.

Zryan trotted to the fence, stopping before it with a little slide that made Kian giggle happily. A grin on his own face, Zryan plopped the young child down on top of the fence to face the griffin. "Look at him, isn't he magnificent?"

Kian nodded quickly in agreement, eyes big in wonder.

The griffin's coat and feathers gleamed in the sunshine, outlining the corded muscle beneath. Its eyes were piercing and filled with determination and fury. Strength and ferociousness poured from every sinew, and Zryan could tell it would make a worthy steed for any king.

As Ruan stepped up beside them, Zryan looked down at him. *By the sun, he's nearly as tall as I am.* Twenty years, but still a boy; so long yet to manhood, yet wishing so badly to be there. Zryan saw it more every day, how Ruan fought his child form, so eager to be seen as an adult. It would be a battle for him, for all of them. They had eighty years still until he would be a grown man, but already Zryan could see the way those decades would disappear like smoke. Gone before he'd truly had a chance to appreciate them.

"What do you think?" he asked, trying to mask his own excitement.

Ruan showed little emotion, but his brows lifted a fraction, and there was a hint of a crinkle at the corner of his dark brown eyes. "He's so powerful," the boy whispered, his eyes lighting up in awe. "And wild."

Zryan smiled, a happy tingle traveling through him. "Yes, it's our job to tame him. Earn his loyalty. There is no greater thing in life than having the respect and loyalty of something as ferocious as he." His thoughts flickered quickly to his wife. She had been the epitome of ferocious when they first met. A creature who would rather strike first than allow anyone too close. Earning her love had been the greatest feat of his life, even beyond helping to slay his father.

"Your Majesty," Chariloas called. "May we speak with you a moment?"

Zryan looked to his stable master and nodded. "Boys, stay put. I will be right back." Both Ruan and Kian simply nodded, their focus on the griffin rather than him. He pressed a kiss to the top of Kian's head and ruffled Ruan's hair, to the boy's chagrin, before stepping away from them and heading over to Chariloas and another male.

"Your Majesty." The other man bowed.

"This is Euclid, sire."

"Ahh! The skilled griffin breeder!" Zryan held out his hand, and Euclid accepted it, dipping forward to press his lips to his knuckles. "While I haven't had a chance to ride him yet, the beast appears to be everything you promised."

"Thank you, sire. I pride myself in breeding worthy animals and have offered you the best of my brood. He comes from a long line of alphas within my pride, and his dam was from another long line of fierce griffins. He is the accumulation of many generations of choice breeding," Euclid explained with pride. "My females are allowed back into the wild to birth and raise their young. This way, they are imbued with the natural instinct to hunt and protect."

Zryan rubbed his palms together in jubilation. "I cannot wait to strap a saddle to his back and break him in." His eyes met Chariloas', and the stable master shared his sentiments.

"If he is everything you claim him to be, we will talk about additions to our infantry pride."

"I would be honored, Your Majesty, to provide you with more steeds."

An ear-piercing wail of pain shattered their conversation, making an instinctive part of Zryan prepare for battle as he spun toward the source of the sound.

It was worse than he could have imagined.

Kian lay on his back in the center of the paddock, a bright pool of blood surrounding him. To Zryan's horror, a tiny child's arm hung from the griffin's beak until the beast tossed its head back and swallowed it down. Ruan clung to the griffin's back, his arms around its shoulders, fingers tight in its feathers as the griffin began to buck, doing his best to wrestle the beast away from his little brother.

"No!" Zryan screamed, terror the likes of which he had never felt filling him to the point of nearly exploding. Grabbing the top of the fence, he leaped over it. He threw himself at the beast's neck, arms circling it before he had time to think. Muscles straining against the power of the animal, he looked to Ruan still clinging to its back. "Get off it and run!" he growled at his firstborn, whose brown eyes were wide with fear and pain.

As the sharp talons of the griffin tore through Zryan's side, Euclid rushed up, at once moving in to pull Ruan to safety.

Zryan dropped himself into a roll, pulling the griffin down to the ground with him, and from the corner of his eye saw Chariloas scoop Kian's small body up into his arms. His sons safe, Zryan drew electricity out of the air around him, the tingles curling around his arm and up to his fingers, and he zapped the griffin. It was just enough of a spark to startle the animal into regressing, and Zryan tore himself away from its clutches.

He hurried to the edge of the paddock, climbing over the fence and rushing to Chariloas. Zryan pulled Kian from his arms, clutching him to his own chest as he ran for the palace, heart pounding in his ears. He hadn't dared to look at Kian yet. To see if his face was slack with lifelessness or if there was simply an immeasurable amount of pain visible there.

"Find the healer!" he yelled, tearing into the palace. The servants paused, eyes widening at the sight of their king and prince covered in so much blood. *"The healer!"* he screamed with insistence, and they leaped into action.

Zryan raced down the hall, kicking open the door to the nursery and gingerly laying Kian on his bed. Blood flowed freely from the garish wound on his shoulder where his arm had been torn free. A sob lodged itself in Zryan's throat as he gathered the bedding and pressed it to the wound.

Kian screamed in pain, his bright blue eyes shooting open, filled with agony, confusion, and tears. "P-papa!" his little voice warbled, and his free hand clutched the hair at the side of Zryan's head, pulling him close.

"Papa's here, Kiki. You're going to be okay."

All at once, chaos filled the room as the healer arrived, shoving Zryan's hand out of the way. A harried looking Alessia appeared, her face paling as she saw their youngest child.

"Zryan! What has happened?!" She raced over to the bed and pushed him aside. She fell to her knees at Kian's head, her hands slipping around his cheeks, and pulled his face toward her. "Oh, my love."

"Mama?" Seeing her, Kian began to sob, his little hand, coated in blood, gripping her wrist tightly. "I'm sorry, Mama!" he cried. "I'm sorry."

"Shhh, shhh. No, baby. This is not your fault." She pressed a kiss to his forehead, then glared at the healer. "Fix him, and fix him *now*." She whipped around to Zryan, her brown eyes darkening to near black. "What *happened*!?"

"I don—"

"It was my fault," Ruan called from the doorway. His features were strained, wet tracks visible on his cheeks.

"What do you mea—"

"Out, now!" All three of them turned quickly to look at the healer. "In the hall," he insisted firmly, his hands pressed to the open wound on Kian's shoulder. "I need quiet, and I need serenity." When they didn't move, he pointed to the door. "*Now*."

There was hesitation in both Zryan and Alessia, but for the sake of their son, they stood and left the room.

Once in the hall, Alessia whipped around to pin both him and Ruan with a harsh look. "Explain to me right now why my baby is lying in there bleeding to death!"

Ruan swallowed roughly and sniffled back any more tears as he straightened his shoulders. "I dared him," he whispered, then cleared his throat to speak louder. "I told him he wasn't brave enough to touch the griffin. I didn't . . . I didn't think he would *do* it!"

Alessia growled. "He is just a child, Ruan. He looks up to you! Of course he would do it!"

Zryan moved to speak, but instead, he found himself silenced by the look of pure fury and—his heart faltered— loathing on Alessia's face.

"And you," she whispered with deadly force. "What were you doing while our youngest was being mauled by a wild beast?"

Zryan swallowed, stomach sinking with guilt and sorrow. "I was just a few feet away." By the sun, how had it all gone so wrong so quickly? One minute, his boys were giggling, and now . . . "I was just talking with Chariloas and the breeder. I didn't think—"

"You never do!" she snapped, her words a dagger beneath his ribs, directly into his heart. "By the sun, Zryan. How could you let this happen?!" Alessia shook her head and spun on her heel, storming back into the nursery.

Zryan slipped his arm around Ruan's shoulders, pulling him into his side, and watched his wife kneel by Kian's bed once more. Her hands took his tiny one within them. He watched her murmur tenderly to him, and his heart clenched. She was correct; this was all his fault. He had taken the boys out to the paddock and should not have left them alone. Even to only walk a few steps away. Had he not been distracted, this never would have happened.

He stayed in the hall, pacing back and forth, while he waited for the news of how Kian would fare. Ruan had moved to lean against the doorframe, staring into the room. As close to his brother as he could get.

When at last the healer came to the doorway, Ruan stepped back, and Zryan moved over to Pokrates quickly. "How is he?"

"I've healed the wound, but it took a great deal of repair. There were also numerous bones broken in his chest and legs, I can only assume from the weight of the beast's attack. He's lost a great deal of blood, and I've used my ability to encourage more production in his body, but the rest is up to him. Some will simply need to be naturally replenished over the coming days. The next few hours are critical, but I believe he will be just fine." Pokrates pressed a reassuring hand to Zryan's shoulder, then looked down at his own seeping wound.

Zryan had thought little of it as he'd paced the halls. His toga and leg were drenched in blood, red footprints left as a sign of his distress.

"Perhaps we should get you patched up as well, Your Majesty?"

Zryan, too, looked down at the wound, which his hand had naturally covered to staunch the blood as he waited. He only nodded and let the healer do as he needed. Warmth filled him, pain barely breaching the fog of his worried thoughts as Pokrates called to the muscles in his body, slowly stitching the claw marks back together.

When he was finished, Pokrates bowed his head and left his king to his thoughts.

Zryan stepped gingerly into the nursery. Alessia lay on the small bed, her arms around the now sleeping Kian, who was tucked into her chest. His skin was still gray, dark hair matted to his forehead and black circles under his eyes. But his chest lifted with each breath he took, a sign that his Kiki was still very much alive.

Alessia looked up. Her face hardened, and her eyes shifted from soft, motherly concern, into anger. "Don't even," she hissed.

"Less, please. I just want to be with him."

"Get out." Her eyes remained like flint. Harsh and cold. "I am going to stay in here with him tonight."

Zryan's eyes fell to Kian. He needed to be in here with him. To quench the fear inside himself that his son wasn't going to be okay. To at last soothe the terror that had filled him since the first blood-curdling scream had sounded.

But he had failed them both. Kian and Alessia. And his wife was right; he didn't deserve to be in this room.

Zryan nodded. "If he wakes, please—" His voice broke. "Just tell him I love him."

Alessia bobbed her head with a single, sharp movement and didn't look at him again. Silently, and filled with regret, Zryan left the nursery.

Alessia

Present Day.
Two and a half weeks after Midniva's battle.

Lucem's midday sun beat down on the white-stone walls of the palace, bathing Alessia in its warmth as she paced across the highest battlement on the structure. A soft breeze whispered across her face as she gazed down at the greenery below, watching for movement, for a foe to dare approach her home.

Wherever they may be.

Up here, she was away from the training soldiers, away from the ever-growing tension between her and Zryan. Alessia needed the quiet to still her ever-chaotic mind, more now than ever.

War was coming to Lucem.

She didn't know when or what it would entail, but it was coming. Rage flared to life inside of her whenever she recalled the delighted expression on Phaedora's face, especially when she'd locked eyes with Zryan.

At that moment, Alessia had wanted to sprint across the cathedral, embed a dagger in Phaedora's heart, and revel in the light fading from Phaedora's eyes.

But she hadn't. None of them had. And why was that? Too shocked to see Phaedora again after thousands of years? Or did they not want to shed blood on sacred ground—tarnishing Travion's union with Sereia?

Midniva's recent victory was hardly that. It was a battle won, but not the war. And she wanted victory for the realm—for her family.

Alessia sighed in frustration, crossing her arms. The green gauzy fabric of her gown brushed against her legs as a breeze swept by. Below the palace, the land sloped downward, giving way to a kingdom alive, flourishing, and preparing for what lay ahead of them all.

Carried on the air was the scent of fragrant gardenia and jasmine blooms, but it did nothing to soothe Alessia's ire. "By the sun, when I see you again, Phaedora—"

"Mother?" Brione's soft voice called from behind her.

She turned in time to see her youngest and only daughter cross the threshold and onto the battlement. Brione's hair, like hers, was worn in a long plait that draped over her shoulder. Her clever green eyes locked onto Alessia, then her brows furrowed.

"My sweet child, what is the matter?"

Brione strode forward and cocked her head. "I should ask you the same." She looked as though she wanted to press and ask more but sighed before continuing. "I am worried about you. With the return of Phaedora—"

Alessia flexed her fingers, fighting against clenching her teeth at the mention of that damnable female. Phaedora wasn't simply wicked with her desires for Zryan. She was power hungry and sought what she believed was her rightful place in Lucem—in the three realms.

Again, that worried glint surfaced in Brione's gaze, and Alessia had to look elsewhere. "Where is your father?"

"The last I knew, he was in his study."

"Thank you." Alessia closed the distance between them and leaned her forehead against Brione's. Her daughter was only a hair shorter than herself, but both were sleek and tall. "For always being there."

Brione offered a small smile. "Always." She withdrew but didn't turn away. "If you need me, I'll be training with Demos."

Alessia lifted a dark brow. The captain of Brione's personal guard was more than adequate when it came to fighting, but she wondered how much training went on. Alessia wasn't oblivious to the lingering stares, the flirting when Brione thought no one was watching. It was harmless, for now. And when the time came, when duty called, Brione would have to brush aside her entertainments.

She was a princess, after all.

"Have a care with him, Brione." Though she spoke the words, Alessia knew that her daughter lacked the sharp edges her mother possessed. That she was kind, thoughtful, and capable.

"Caring is what I do best, Mother." With that, Brione turned down the battlement's path and disappeared into the palace once more.

Once upon a time, Alessia had openly cared as much as her daughter, but her marriage to an unfaithful male had put an end to that. *No.* Ludari had put an end to that when he had slain her parents for acting out against him and imprisoned Alessia because of her affinity to manipulate and torture a being's mind.

She raked her fingers along her forearm, reminding herself that she was no longer in the pit of a dungeon but basking in the rays of the sun.

Since Travion's wedding, Alessia had done well to avoid Zryan. Seeing Phaedora in the cathedral had ripped a centuries-old bandage off of a festering wound. Still, she needed to speak to him regarding their kingdom. She would brush aside her frustration because the realms depended on it.

Alessia took one last look at the land, then made her way back into the palace. As soon as she was inside, the aroma of rosemary and mint tickled her nose, reminding her of freshly washed linens. It must have been laundry day; had she paid any mind, perhaps she would have seen flapping sheets from her bird's-eye view.

She descended the stairwell, not seeing a soul until she reached the bottom landing. Servants bowed before hurrying to the shadows where they'd been before. She was neither kind nor unkind to them, but depending on her mood, her temper could flare, and she had been known to grow impatient and shout.

Down the hall, Alessia continued, maintaining silent footfalls. She dreaded these moments when she had to hunt down Zryan unannounced. There were too many times she'd found him, arms twined around another female, her lips touching his skin, hands traveling beneath his toga. Tarnishing what belonged to Alessia.

Time after time, he'd sworn it would never happen again, but his words were nothing more than empty promises.

Sometimes, Alessia could trick herself into believing none of it had ever happened. She would brush away the bitter memories and allow herself to claim the male that she had chosen as her partner. Those days were dangerous and threatened to melt the protective ice she'd formed around her heart as the wildfire blazed within.

But as with most things, those moments never lasted.

Zryan had a tendency to wound her, as much as she was loath to admit it.

Even after all these centuries.

Alessia stopped against the wall outside of the study. She swallowed roughly, listening to see if he had a guest. No sound of lips clashing or clothes falling to the floor; all she heard was the scribbling of a quill on paper.

She snaked around the doorframe, leaning her torso into the room. Against the far wall, Zryan sat, frowning as he wrote. To most, it was a rarity to see such an expression on his face. He would have preferred for the world to see him as carefree, but Alessia knew better. He was no different from his brothers, carrying the weight of the realms on his shoulders.

Except, Zryan lied.

He lied to himself.

He lied to others.

Zryan pushed his chair back, standing as he folded the letter. He rounded the desk, spotting her leaning against the doorframe, and his demeanor changed at once. His eyes lit up, and his lips twisted into a playful grin, masking whatever plagued him moments ago.

Still, that grin and his vibrant green eyes were enough to cause her heart to trip.

Alessia rapped her fingers against the wall and then entered the room.

"Hello, Less." He rumbled her name, but it almost sounded like a question too. As if he wasn't sure whether or not her being here was a good thing.

She wasn't certain either.

"What is that?" She stepped closer to him, pointing to the paper.

He arched a brow like he'd forgotten about it. "Oh, this?" Zryan twisted it in his grasp as he closed the distance between them. "I believe they call it a letter. This particular one is addressed to Lord Spiros regarding his son's passing in Midniva." The storm clouds that had been there moments ago rolled back in, bringing with them every line of exhaustion that he hid well.

Despite not wanting to care how Zryan felt, Alessia *did* care, and she hated herself for it. He didn't deserve her sympathies, didn't deserve a speck of affection from her. Besides, the loss of one of their own was tragic and was akin to an arrow straight to her heart. Lucemites were her people, her responsibility, just as much as they were Zryan's.

She frowned. "When it is safe to do so, we should see to the families who have made the greatest sacrifice."

"We?" Zryan's lips curled at the sides, and he moved forward so that his chest pressed against hers. As far as being a unified front, the two of them had been lacking. Too caught up in battle, too distant from one another aside from those heated moments when she'd give in to desire.

The scent of him—fresh air, a hint of citrus and musk—

invaded her senses. He brushed a loose strand of hair out of her face and tucked it behind her ear. "As king and queen."

He purred the words in a way that brought a smile to her face. She didn't want to give him that, but he was trying, and she supposed she could too.

"I came here to discuss the security measures we're taking. I don't trust that snake's deception. We saw what she did with Naya and Taimon." She frowned as she stared into his playful green eyes.

But Zryan didn't want to discuss battles. At least, that was what she garnered, for his fingers coasted along her chin and into her hairline, sending goosebumps along her skin. She loathed that he could pull such a reaction from her still, but he knew what she liked, and by the great sky above, knew how to sate her.

Alessia lifted her hands, letting her palms rest against his firm chest. His heart hammered wildly beneath them, and she didn't stop to consider why. She gave him a firm shove and flicked her gaze toward the desk.

Zryan didn't need a word. He backed until he could sit on top of the mahogany desk and spun so he could sprawl onto his back.

Alessia crawled on top of him but didn't let her body lower. Beneath her, he body responded to her in a way that stirred heat low in her belly. His member stiffened under his toga, rising to the point it brushed against her mound.

"All for me?" she murmured and scraped her nails along his hip, eliciting a soft hiss.

A moan escaped him as her hand traversed along his thigh to grip his shaft. She dragged her hand up, running her thumb in a slow circle.

"You shouldn't tease me so, not when my beautiful wife could walk in at any moment . . ."

Alessia's hand stilled. It was a jest; she knew that. But Zryan's words were much like plunging in to the icy sea of Midniva. *My wife could walk in.* They cooled her down to her marrow, and Alessia narrowed her eyes, hopping down from the desk. Ill-chosen words on his part, for it pulled her out of the moment so quickly, she was nearly dizzy.

Surely he meant nothing by his words, but that was it—he never meant anything with his words. His actions spoke volumes. And she was tired of him never caring enough to notice how much it wounded her.

"Alessia! I didn't mean—"

She didn't bother to look over her shoulder as she stormed across the room. "You never do, Zryan. You never *mean* it. Except this time, I think you do. Is that what you say to all your paramours? That I could walk in at any moment?" And with that, she fled into the hall. What did it matter if he chased after her, pleaded with her to stay, when he'd only be in someone else's arms by the end of the day?

She scowled as she breezed through the hall, venturing toward the stairwell that led to her bedchamber.

Shadows danced on the wall as the wind shifted the trees outside, distracting Alessia from her inner turmoil. There was no room for her to dwell on an age-old wound, not with a looming threat to focus on. When her thoughts should have been on the approaching war.

She paused outside of her room, uncertainty caressing her mind.

An armor-clad guard stood at her door. His aquiline nose was as sharp as every other feature about him. But there was one thing wrong. "Who are you?" She didn't recognize his face, and she made it a point to know who served her.

He brought his gaze to hers; two bottomless pits of darkness framed by thick lashes stared at her. "I am Loukas, Your Majesty."

"Where is Tobias?"

Loukas' eyes shifted for a moment. "Eating lunch. Is there a problem, Your Majesty?"

"None at all." She pressed her hand against the door. "Please make sure no one disturbs me."

He nodded.

It wasn't a rare occurrence to have a changing of the guards, but not knowing someone, that *was* odd.

For a moment, she thought to pry into his mind, see what he saw. Then again, if Tobias approved of him, she ought to as well.

She shook her head and stepped into her chambers. The sun spilled from her balcony onto the floor, reflecting onto the white walls. Accents of deep green drapes with golden embroidery offset the brightness of the room.

A trumpeting peacock let all in the vicinity know of his presence, then shortly after, he flew toward the balcony, perching. She was surprised they hadn't flown inside her room, as it wasn't a rarity. Although she didn't mind, it upset the servants who had to clean feathers and feces.

She bent down, unlacing her sandals, and a moment later, a soft scuffling noise sounded from behind her.

Alessia drew in a breath and reached up the skirt of her dress until her fingers found purchase on the hilt of a hidden dagger.

She twisted around just as a blade lunged toward her.

Rising, she batted the sword away from her and realized who her attacker was—Loukas. Alessia spat at him as he whirled around to face her. "I knew you were no ally."

Rage contorted Loukas' expression, and his full lips twisted in disgust. "I may be a traitor, but you are a termite, eating away at the structure of the realms." He raised his sword again. This time, Alessia didn't wait for him to lunge. She dove low, knocking away the blade with her dagger, and landed a solid punch to his face.

Pain radiated up her fist to her forearm, but she pressed on as Loukas nearly tripped over his own feet.

Not a fighter.

He steadied himself, lowering, and when he popped back up, he growled and charged forward.

Alessia attempted to block his foot as he kicked out, but there was enough force behind him, and she hadn't had time to steady herself, so she fell to the floor. Her head smacked the stone, and Alessia's vision flickered in and out.

Loukas towered over her, stomping on her hand with the dagger in it still.

She gritted her teeth, glaring up at him.

"You should have run, Queenie," he taunted her.

"Loukas," Alessia said lowly. "You must not be from Lucem, because if you were, you'd know that I never run." A wicked smile tugged at her lips as she stared up into his eyes. "And I don't need a sword to end you."

Fear flickered in his eyes, and doubt too. He was no Lucemite, for he would have run or tried to shield himself from her. "It's time you died." Loukas lifted his sword, intent on landing the killing blow. It arced, then, as it lowered, Alessia reached out to his mind, probing for a barrier. He was weak because there was no resistance. Not even the slightest of barriers for her to trespass on.

Loukas exhaled, dropping the sword behind him. Then he feebly flapped his hands to the side. His fingers flexed and tightened. "No," he stammered.

"How do you feel about scorpions?" Alessia slid back, slowly rising the moment she implanted the nightmarish vision of thousands of scorpions crawling over him. He could live in his misery until a proper interrogation was performed.

She wavered on her feet, still dizzy from knocking her head on the floor, but with Loukas in her grasp, she moved forward, toeing the sword onto her foot. She kicked it up into her hand and held the tip to his throat. "You made a mistake."

Loukas screamed, clawing at his head as invisible foes crawled along his skin. "M-may the Old-d Ways R-Rise." Loukas screamed again, then clenched his jaw, and when he did, Alessia heard a faint snap. A rush of white foam escaped from his mouth, and he convulsed and fell to the floor.

"By the sun! You bastard!" She knelt before him, grabbing him by the chin. His eyes rolled back, and he gasped for air, but it was too late. The poison had taken him.

A moment later, the door opened, and Tobias rushed in, blood dripping down the side of his face. "My deepest apologies, Your Majesty." He stepped closer, then knelt next to her. "Are you all right?"

Alessia took a moment to assess him. Although his skin was darker, she could still see the bruising around his temple and where fresh blood oozed from a cut. "By the sun. Are *you* all right?"

He frowned. "Physically, I'll be fine, but I'll not forgive myself for this."

"There is nothing to forgive." She hissed as she stood and glared at the doorway. "There are snakes among us. And I'm afraid we have no way of knowing who is a friend and who is a foe."

Tobias had proven himself long ago. When he was only a little thing, with dewberry juice smeared across his lips, he had vowed to serve Alessia as his father had done before him. He may as well have been one of her children too, for she cared for him as much as she did one of her own.

"We must keep this quiet. Do you understand?" Alessia whispered.

"Your Majesty?"

"No one can know there was an attempt on my life, Tobias."

Not even Zryan, if she could help it. The last thing she needed was him interrogating the entire palace. While he was clever, Zryan wouldn't be discreet about punishing offenders. The entire realm would know before the day was done.

And while she wanted to thwart every threat before they had a chance to harm anyone in her family, Alessia was of the mindset this was no more than a distraction. A game for the royal family to focus their efforts on while the real events took place. That was something she didn't want to happen.

Alessia would handle this herself.

2

Zryan

Sexual frustration was a heady thing, but worse was the look of dying passion on Alessia's face replaced by cold aloofness.

Zryan should be used to the aloofness now; it had been his true partner for more centuries than he could count. There had been days when he thought she would get past it. Years when he thought perhaps Alessia could forgive him for what he had done, and he could stop seeking solace in the arms of someone else. But there was so much pain, betrayal, and separation between them now, he was certain there would never be a way to repair it.

He pushed aside the notices from the treasury and adjusted himself beneath his toga once more, cursing the heat that still raged through his blood. Village repairs had finally been completed after the attack Naya had brought upon them, which Zryan was happy to note, but he cared not for how much coin had been spent to see it completed—and couldn't really focus on numbers at the moment as it was.

His people had suffered due to a grudge Naya Demaris,

Eden's mother, held against him over the death of her husband. It had been a senseless act, something that could not have been anticipated in his wildest dreams.

Lelantos Demaris had been one of Zryan's best advisors, skilled in diplomacy. When a situation arose with an angry noble, he had been Zryan's first choice to send to deal with the matter. It had been a shock and horror to learn the noble had lashed out in anger and killed Lelantos where he stood. The citizens of Lucem had paid for the fallout of that death with their homes, and for others, their own lives. It was Zryan's duty to right the wrongs however he could.

It hadn't ended there, however. Naya had not been the only one involved in the plot against Lucem and the three realms. In the end, Phaedora had been behind it all. She'd enlisted Travion's steward, Taimon, into the fight against Zryan and his brothers. Midniva had suffered the worst, the entire middle realm falling under attack by giant sea monsters that had left Travion's kingdom in ruins.

Phaedora was not done. She had made sure to appear after Travion's wedding to let them know she had only just begun her true assault on the realms. As he was the main target for her anger, Zryan could only assume soon she would be bringing the battle here, to him.

"Your Majesty, I have brought you some refreshments."

Zryan looked up to see Talia, a young maid in their service. In her hands, she held a tray which bore a goblet, decanter, and plate of food. She was new and eager to prove herself amongst the palace staff.

He nodded and motioned her in. Talia crossed the study in quick, careful steps, setting the tray down on his desk and unloading the items.

"Shall I pour your wine, Your Majesty?" she asked softly, glancing toward him.

"Please." Zryan settled back in his chair, lifting his hands behind his head to stretch out his aching shoulders. When was the last time he had ceased feeling so tense? Surely not since the debacle with Naya.

"Sire?" Zryan glanced at Talia at the uncertainty in her voice and found that her eyes were upon his nether regions. "Should I . . . Should I aid you, sire?"

Zryan's brows lifted at her forwardness. "Excuse me?"

She had the good grace to blush. "The other maids . . . they said that, at times, they are needed to help relieve you of"—here, she faltered—"tensions."

Zryan paused. A part of him wanted to say yes. If she was pliant and willing, why not seek some comfort in caring arms?

He stretched out his hand to take hers, holding it gently. She trembled lightly beneath his touch. Frailty and innocence. Malleable and tender.

It left him cold.

Zryan turned her hand over and pressed a soft kiss to her palm, then patted the top of it. "No, Talia. Such services will not be required of you."

She blanched a little, pulling her hand back quickly to tuck behind her back. "Did I say something wrong, Your Majesty? Did I misstep? I am so sor—"

He cut her off. "No, you did not." He sighed, shaking his head. "You were merely misinformed." Zryan stood and pressed a hand to the small of her back, guiding her back toward the door. "Thank you for being so . . ." He hesitated, trying to find the right word to both soothe her concerns and also halt any future conversation of this. "Dutiful. But rest easy, you are only needed for your maid services."

Talia nodded, curtseyed, and left the room.

Zryan sighed roughly once more and brushed fingers through his dark brown hair. Hair that set him apart from his brothers, along with his green eyes. He resembled their mother, or so he had been told, while Draven and Travion were nearly spitting images of Ludari. Perhaps that had helped to keep him from the dungeons; some small spot of mercy due to his likeness to the queen.

Yet, had that been a blessing or a curse?

Freedom from the horrors of the dungeon had also meant constant visibility. Ludari's keen and judgmental eyes ever upon him. Zryan, the eternal whipping boy.

Zryan moved back to his desk, picking up the goblet of wine Talia had poured for him, and downed all of it in a well-practiced gulp.

There had been many days when he had accepted the advances of the maids. Many days when he had sought them out himself. And they talked; he could not begrudge them that. Swapping stories, showing off gifts meant to silence them. Encouraging others to find "favor" with their king, and with it, perhaps, advancement to more important roles within the palace.

The weak part of him that always sought instant gratification and approval from others wanted to call Talia back. To hide away from what plagued him by dissolving into pleasure for a bit of time. It was an old habit. A yearning for the affection and approval of others that he constantly chased, whether it was real or not.

But the stark emptiness of his own life had become so

very apparent in the last two months. Watching both of his brothers find and wed the loves of their lives had only made his own tragic marriage seem more broken than ever. Zryan had been forced to acknowledge just how much he truly loved his wife. Even after all of these years. And the rabid, painful cry of his heart to have her back in his arms. To have her love and tenderness directed toward him once more.

Above all else, Zryan needed Alessia back.

A curse outside his study pulled him from his thoughts, and Zryan stepped out into the hall in time to see two soldiers carrying a stretcher pass by. On top of the stretcher lay a body wrapped in linen.

Zryan frowned, uncertain of just what he was seeing.

"Please explain to me at once what exactly you are doing," he called out to them.

The soldiers froze, both shifting uncomfortably. There was a shared look that passed between them and did not go unnoticed by Zryan, as if they weren't sure of what to say. Zryan cleared his throat irritably.

The tallest of the two soldiers straightened his shoulders and met his king's gaze. "An assassin broke into the palace and attempted to kill Her Majesty, the queen."

Lightning crackled along Zryan's fingertips, traveling up his arms to tickle at the back of his neck, highlighting the rage coursing through his veins. "Why was this not brought to my attention immediately?" he growled.

The tall soldier bowed. "We apologize, Your Majesty, the queen told us not to."

Zryan did not wait around. He stormed past the two of them, roaring Alessia's name through the halls as he searched for her. Finally, a frightened looking servant pointed him toward Alessia's quarters. He managed to smile through his anger, lightning now crackling along his cheeks and through his hair. "Thank you."

The servant bowed, a tremble visibly taking over her body.

His steps carried him quickly down the marbled hall to Alessia's private suite. Once upon a time, they had shared quarters. But sometime after Kian had been injured, she'd begun decorating quarters for herself. Her shift into staying there at night had been gradual, but eventually, it had become a permanent thing. He wasn't sure when it had happened, perhaps just after Brione had been born, but at some point, the fracture between them had split wide open, causing a divide that only dramatic things could momentarily span.

Alessia's door was open. She sat on the edge of a chair as the palace healer dealt with an angry looking wound at her temple.

Zryan growled at the sight of the injury.

"Were you even going to tell me someone had attempted to *kill* you?!" he roared.

Everyone in the room straightened up. Tobias, one of Alessia's private guards, motioned to the others in the room. En masse, they left, all except the healer, who finished her work before standing.

"You should be fine, Your Majesty." As she turned to Zryan, she curtseyed, head bowed, and murmured a soft "*Sire*," then left the room as well.

When the chamber was empty of everyone except the two of them, Zryan repeated himself. "Were you going to tell me, Alessia, that someone had made an attempt on your life?"

By the sun, what if they had succeeded? What if they'd caught her completely unawares and killed her?

Zryan's blood pounded furiously in his ears, the lightning tangled around his body beginning to make the carpets beneath his feet smoke.

"Eventually," she said. "I took care of it." She was aloof—always aloof—and stood, fingers gently prodding her temple to test for any further soreness.

"Took *care* of it?!" Did she not understand? "Alessia, I need to be aware of these things!"

"I am aware, but at this very moment, this isn't what we need. What our *palace* needs." She raked her gaze along him as if to say, *My point precisely.* "The threat to me is dead, but the bigger one still remains. We need to focus on finding Phaedora."

"And in order to deal with the bigger threat, I need to be aware of all the other threats that come in!" It made him want to scream. Just another way that she cut him off, kept him out in the cold concerning what happened in her life. "How can I protect you, or our children, if I am not aware of what is going on in my own palace?"

But this went beyond her, and beyond him; this was a matter of the kingdom at large.

Alessia spread her hand out as if to say, *What can be done now?* Instead of replying further, she simply moved to straighten a few things in the room that had been disturbed by the struggle.

"Where was Tobias during all of this?"

"He was struck down from behind. The assassin stole guard clothing and was waiting outside my room for me. I knew something was off when I didn't recognize him."

Zryan nodded, taking all of this in. This unknown assailant had managed to walk past all of their other guards without issue. Sneak through the palace without raising any alarms.

He moved without thought, turning Alessia slowly to face him and cupping her cheek in his palm. "Are you okay?" he asked softly. "Truly?" He searched her eyes, wanting to check for fear, hidden pain, anything that he was missing.

"I am angry," she stated, her warm brown eyes turning fiery. "She sent them into *my home*. I will not stand for this, Zryan." What she did not need to say was that he had brought this upon them. That he should have handled the dissolution of his engagement to Phaedora in a much better way all those millennia ago.

"She will pay," he vowed, and before she could pull away, he leaned in to kiss her forehead.

Zryan left the room, pausing only to turn on Tobias, who stood just outside, along with several other soldiers. "Follow me," he growled. "And you!" He pointed at another. "Find Ruan and send him to my study."

The trip down the hall was quick, with Tobias just behind him. When Zryan stepped into the study, Tobias moved to stand off to the side, allowing room for his sovereign to begin pacing back and forth. Which he did, anger flooding his bloodstream and making it difficult for him to think. He kicked his chair out of the way as he came around the side of his desk, leaning forward to press his hands into the surface of the solid oak. He didn't say a word until Ruan joined them.

"We have a problem."

Ruan scoffed. "That isn't news, Father."

Zryan looked at his eldest irritably. "A *new* problem. An intruder has managed to sneak his way undetected through the palace, knock young Tobias here out, and then make an attempt on our queen's life." Ruan had the decency to look both ashamed and furious, his dark eyes narrowing. "Please make me understand *how* this could have happened."

Ruan's gaze shifted into a frown, which soon morphed into a full scowl. "My men and I failed."

Zryan sighed. Could he have corrected him, he would have. But there was no other word for it other than failure. "Tobias, please explain fully to both of us exactly what happened today. Tell us every sweep you did through Alessia's quarters and the halls leading to her wing."

Tobias nodded, standing with his back straight and hands folded behind his back. "I woke in the barracks as usual, sire. There was no one there that was not familiar. My rounds started just after daybreak when I relieved Eskros." He kept his eyes on them as he spoke. "I did a sweep through the halls of her quarters, checking every room in her wing, and spoke with the guards patrolling outside her windows."

"Antonian and Hercela," Ruan cut in, impressing Zryan with his knowledge of who was on patrol and where.

Tobias nodded in agreement. "Once Her Majesty was awake, I did my check through her rooms. Nothing out of the ordinary stood out. Everything was as it should be."

"When did the intruder take over your post?" Zryan asked.

"I think it was shortly after I did my noonday rounds. I was relieved by Galentas to have my noon meal. At some point on my return to Her Majesty, I was struck from behind. When I woke, I was bound, and my mouth covered. I had been left in one of the spare rooms. Had I not been discovered by a servant, I'm not certain when I would have gotten to the queen."

Zryan frowned as Tobias finished, and he and Ruan shared a glance.

"I will speak with Captain Stianos, and we will increase the guards at each entrance," Ruan announced.

"Increase perimeter walks as well. I don't want there to be a moment when an inch of this palace isn't being covered. Do you understand?" Zryan eyed Ruan, who simply nodded . He knew that his son would take this as a personal failure. "Anyone entering the palace must be thoroughly vetted by our top security." Ruan nodded once more. Not only had it been an attack on his mother, but it had been a breach of his own well-maintained security. Ruan did not accept defeat and would not allow this to happen again. "Go and see it done. You're both dismissed."

The two males left, leaving Zryan to think of how close he had come to losing his wife today.

Phaedora, when at last she was found, was not likely to survive this.

Before he had a chance to settle, Amyntas was in the doorframe. "Sire, Lord Seducere is here."

Zryan frowned. "Was that meant to be today?" He had forgotten he'd sent word for the nobleman to meet with him. It had been before the wedding and Phaedora's appearance at the ceremony. Now, the security of the kingdom had overtaken his thoughts on settling Kian into happy, wedded bliss.

Though the day-to-day dealings of his kingdom did not

disappear simply because there was a threat looming at his door.

Amyntas was good at hiding his own opinions, for his brow did not rise in surprise. Instead, he said, "Yes, sire. Today."

"Bring him in, then."

Amyntas nodded, and stepped away, presumably to fetch the nobleman.

Zryan brushed his hands through his hair, straightening it, and moved to pick up the chair he'd kicked over. He then took a seat, preparing himself for Severance Seducere.

When the lord entered, his blond hair looking like spun gold and his crystalline eyes bright and worried, Zryan was ready for him. He waved to a vacant chair before his desk. "Take a seat."

Lord Severance Seducere bowed upon entry, then moved to the indicated chair. "Greetings, Your Majesty, and thank you."

Zryan smiled and folded his hands over his abdomen, relaxing into his seat and lifting his feet up to the edge of his desk. For all the world, he looked casual and at ease, not like a man whose wife had just been nearly killed. "I've heard tales, Seducere."

"Tales, sire?" The courtier gave nothing away except for a slight tick at the corner of his right eye.

Zryan's lips twitched at the man's mounting nervousness. "Yes. Tales of what a beautiful, extraordinary daughter you have." Seducere stiffened, his back straightening. "Alvia, correct?"

"Yes," Seducere murmured. "That is my daughter's name." Suspicion grew within the fae's gray eyes. Was he wondering if his king was looking to make a conquest of his child?

"Is it true about her abilities?" Zryan asked. "Is she able to . . . *influence* . . . desire?" His brow lifted.

Seducere shifted in his seat, many thoughts filtering through his eyes. He didn't know whether to be honest or lie to his king and risk the chance of being called out for his treason.

"She's a beautiful fae, sire. Of course she stirs interest."

So, he's going for a diplomatic answer, Zryan thought with amusement. Though he couldn't fault him for his attempts to protect his daughter. "We both know it's more than that." Zryan's eyes narrowed on Seducere, and he dropped his feet to the floor, leaning forward to rest his elbows on the desk.

Seducere, to his credit, held himself well in check before his king's studying gaze. Remaining silent.

"I am interested in making a new family connection, Severance. What are your thoughts on a betrothal?"

Lord Seducere blinked. "A betrothal, sire?"

Zryan nodded and leaned back in his chair once more. "A betrothal between my son and your daughter."

"Prince Ruan and Alvia?" The lord's eyes brightened, features shifting in surprise. And perhaps a flare of greedy excitement as well.

Zryan laughed and shook his head. "No, no, no. Not Ruan. My eldest is not in the mindset to settle down right now. If ever." He spread his hands out wide. "He has wanderlust deep in his soul, if you understand my meaning."

He was too much like his father in that way. Ever seeking satisfaction in the arms of someone new. It was a shame he had taken after Zryan's faults rather than the deep well of love he still held for his wife and the utter devotion and loyalty he longed to give her. If only he could get past his own fears and hang-ups.

If only she'd let him.

"Prince Kian, then." The light in Seducere's eyes dimmed, a slight frown pressing at his lips. It awoke a dark and angry part of Zryan that wanted to protect his youngest son at all costs.

Lucem was a society of beauty and light. Perfection. Kian was seen by many as having been tainted by his accident. Somehow, despite his amazing abilities to bring molten gold to life, his gleaming arm marked him as damaged.

It was a way of thinking left over from Ludari's days, one that Zryan had not been able to burn out of the highest levels of the aristocracy.

"Yes," Zryan said slowly, a steely tone in his voice. "Kian. My second born, crafter of my golden armies and heir to Midniva's throne."

Seducere made a soft noise, something between a snort and a scoff. "A title that he holds only until King Travion's new bride bears a child."

Zryan's face hardened. "Am I to understand you foster ill thoughts of Prince Kian? That you are in disfavor of him marrying your daughter? Might I remind you of your own low standing in the courts? That I have taken note of you and your family at all is a miracle."

Seducere's eyes flamed. "With all due respect, Your Majesty, may I be so bold as to say that it is my child you are wishing to add to your family. She has powers that can help raise me through the ranks of your aristocracy."

Zryan leaned forward once more, a low snarl slipping

from his lips. "Caution, Severance, you're treading the line of treason." Seducere paled a little. "Let me be frank with you. I don't trust Alvia's abilities running unchecked over my kingdom. The fae she could sway into doing her bidding. Lest you've forgotten, we're already dealing with a power-hungry fae wielding more power than she ought to have. So Alvia can marry my son, become a princess of the realm, and live a life of spoiled delight, or she can spend her days in a cage."

Seducere looked stricken. "You're no better than your father," he rasped.

"Oh, I am much better than my father. I came to you with an offer of friendship and family, which you wanted until you knew which son it was I offered." Seducere's face was hard. "So, what will it be? Marriage? Or a gilded cage?"

"I look forward to us being family," he said through gritted teeth. "Your Majesty." Lord Seducere bowed his head.

"Fabulous!" Zryan clapped his hands. "She has two days to prepare herself and come to the palace. We will give her and Kian a period of courting first."

"As you wish, Your Majesty." Seducere nodded.

"Until then, be well." Zryan motioned for him to leave, and Lord Seducere stood, exiting the room quickly.

That hadn't gone the way he'd intended. His anger over Seducere's opinion of Kian had brought out his protectiveness. However, he'd spoken true when he said he didn't trust Alvia Seducere's ability being out there for anyone or anything to take advantage of. Mortal and immortal alike would do many terrible things for the sake of desire.

But not all of his plans came from wishing to control the power wielded by the Seducere girl. He also desperately wanted to see Kian happy. To know that he was loved and cared for. That he had a partner in life to be ever by his side. And what could be better than the proclaimed most beautiful female in the realm?

He would make up for the damage he had done to his son. He would give him this gift. Now, to give him the news.

Alessia

Zryan deserved to know what had transpired. As king—as her husband—but Alessia knew him as though he were an extension of herself. No one needed Zryan rampaging like a bull bent on smothering an offender. Nor did they need his rage getting the best of him.

Most saw the aloof, playful king, but his temper flared to life when his family was in danger, and his wrath was an unforgivable force. Lucem could not afford the distraction of a failed assassination attempt, not when it could mean assailants moving deeper into the castle.

Angry footsteps pounded on the marble floor behind Alessia. She turned to see her daughter approaching. Brione's face had a sheen of sweat, and her eyes blazed with a mixture of fear and anger. "Is it true?"

Alessia lifted her chin and nodded. Lying or denying it would only incite Brione's temper. "Yes."

"Mother!" Brione hissed and rushed forward, giving her a once over, as if she wasn't certain if her mother was whole.

"We don't have the luxury of time to fret over the what-ifs, my darling. All that we can do is being done right now. Increase security and trust no one." She rubbed between her brows. "I never thought my children would have to live through this, but here we are."

Brione closed what little distance lay between them and pressed her forehead against Alessia's. "We are grown and have lived if not a millennium, close to it. You have seen to raising capable children, so don't for one moment worry about us needing to live through *this*."

Alessia smiled wryly and brushed her knuckles down the side of Brione's face. In her daughter's time, she'd seen relative peace. Upheaval was one thing, but the mayhem that was no doubt soon to be released was another thing entirely.

Phaedora would see to that.

Alessia was no stranger to her sordid mind, and that female would bend reality to her whim to get exactly what she wanted. Which was precisely what the realms had fought against for so long.

Alessia had endured time in the pits of the old palace, prior to taking down Ludari, where she could hear the screams of a boy and the shouts of a grown male. She didn't know at the time that it was Draven and Travion, but she was there too. Held captive for no other reason than her affinity to taint and warp a mind. Otherwise, she would've met the same fate as her parents, slain and nailed to a post for any passersby to see.

And that was precisely what Alessia feared would return. Tyranny in its vilest form.

"Be strong, always, my darling." She pulled back and pressed a kiss to Brione's nose. "See if your father needs any soothing."

Brione sighed and cast her gaze toward one of the marble pillars. "I am not the one he wants soothing him."

Alessia clenched her jaw. "He saw that I am well. I cannot offer more than that right now." There was nothing else to say, so she turned away from Brione and continued down the hall. If this were another era, she would've soothed Zryan, reassuring him she was there and well until both their bodies were spent and coated with a sheen of lovemaking, but time was an unkind mistress, and betrayal was her ugly accomplice.

Every time she closed her eyes, there were the eyes of all the lovers he'd ever taken, taunting her, whispering that he didn't belong to *her*.

Alessia walked down the corridor until she reached a guarded door. The guards bowed to her, then opened it. Aside from the scent of flowers in bloom, there was a smoky-metallic fragrance clinging to the humid air.

Kian. He was the only one who likely didn't know what had transpired. Guilt gnawed at her, and she stepped onto the stone landing, fully intent on heading to his workshop.

"Mother," Kian's soft voice called from behind.

She turned on her heel and furrowed her brows. "I was just coming to see you."

He sighed and stepped forward, shifting his jaw in slight annoyance or perhaps stress. "Why am I always the *last* to know everything?" Kian looked her up and down, as if searching for a wound that wasn't there.

Oh.

"I was coming to see you. To tell you." Alessia wouldn't be lectured. "Need I remind you that you'd know if you were in your shop less and in here more." She lifted a finger to silence him as he opened his mouth. "I never cared how much time you spent in there, but that is a fact. I am glad you have an outlet for your ability, and one that everyone benefits from. However, you're tucked away."

Kian's mouth twisted, then formed a thin line. "Fair enough."

She glanced outside to the gardens and inclined her head. "Come with me," she said and walked down the stairs, hoping that he would follow, but she didn't check.

The sound of his boots landing on the stone steps brought a smile to her face. As she walked down the white-washed stone path, a peacock trumpeted from its perch, and a moment later, a shadow passed as it flew over and landed on the lawn. The male's tail fanned out in a beautiful display of green-painted feathers with sapphire eyes glistening in the sunlight.

Alessia stopped in front of a golden bench, one that Kian had crafted in his younger years. He'd wanted to make something to add to the blooming flora, and what better than a place to rest. It was the first of many additions. She motioned for him to sit and waited.

When he walked by, the aroma of fire, sweat, and metal breezed by her. He impressed her—always—with how he could bring to life creations that were born of flame and metal.

"Yes, there was an attempt on my life, and if the whole palace doesn't know by now—courtesy of your father—it soon will." She pinched the bridge of her nose in frustration. "I want to keep it quiet in case it was a message to someone other than us." She sighed and threw her hands out wide. "But here we are."

"I see," he murmured and tucked away some strands of hair that had escaped his small ponytail. "I hope you ran him through a dozen times over." Kian brushed his hands down his thighs, to his knees, and Alessia noticed his knuckles whitening as he gripped them, except for those on his golden arm. Those fingers, though as delicate as flesh, remained their brilliant metallic hue.

Alessia clasped her hands together and forced a smile. "I didn't get the option, sadly." There had been something that nagged at her, though. "He didn't seem to know what would come from close combat with me. What my affinity can do to one's mind. Which is strange." It was unfortunate for *her* that her ability needed a close encounter.

Kian's brow rumpled. "That is strange. Anyone well acquainted with Lucem, with the royal family, would know of your affinity to plague the mind."

Alessia crossed the grass and reached for a fuchsia peony. She snapped the long stem and twirled the flower in her grasp. "He seemed to think I was an easy target."

Kian snorted. "Not a Lucemite then, and not Andherian. So, that leaves one option."

She turned to face him and nodded. "Yes. They're being pulled in from Midniva." She sighed, rubbing between her eyes. "But who is to say more *aren't* being pulled from Andhera?" This was the part of war she loathed. The uncertainty, and not knowing where the danger was coming from. Phaedora possessed The Creaturae, which meant she could tear the kingdom in half if she so wished, but that wasn't what she wanted. She wanted Zryan, and to rule the three kingdoms as one.

There were many holes in Phaedora's plan.

The most noteworthy being that she couldn't have Zryan, for he *belonged* to Alessia.

Kian frowned and folded his arms. He scowled a moment later, which reminded her of a brooding Travion. "Lucem will be ready. We didn't lose as much as Midniva during Naya Damaris' schemes."

"No. We were fortunate, but by the sun . . ." Alessia peered down at her hands and shook her head. "You saw what she did in Midniva."

"I also saw what Uncle did. He nearly tore an island in half."

She hadn't seen the destruction herself, had only heard that Travion wielded the destruction half of the book and, lost in his grief as well as fury for Sereia, used the power of The Creaturae.

Not for one moment would she ever blame him for trading his half for Sereia's life. Despite how much she loathed Zryan, she also loved him, too damn much, and she wasn't certain she would have been able to control her wrath as well as Travion had.

Especially facing Phaedora.

"You know our history—the history of the realms. Access to Andhera and Midniva was designed with The Creaturae. The veils were opened to them with only a few words. Great behemoths were brought to life by that damn book."

"Mother—"

"The entire kingdom of Lucem shook, Kian." She lowered her gaze to the ground, frowning.

It *wasn't* how she wanted to die.

Alessia lowered her hand to her throat, which suddenly seemed dry. "I don't know what you need to make, my darling, but make something capable of taking down a giant. I would rather be overprepared than under."

Kian reached out and tentatively touched her arm. "I know this can't be easy."

It wasn't, and he had only the slightest notion of what it brought up for her. "No, but I will face it." She closed the distance between them and placed her hands on his cheeks. "And I will do whatever I can to protect us all. *Whatever* I must do."

Phaedora's very existence reopened a centuries-old wound that had never quite healed. While Zryan may have spurned the female, Alessia had always wondered if he ever regretted that. Then came his flock of lovers, and she endured heartbreak after heartbreak, until one day it was only a dull throb, an annoyance that angered her.

Kian's brows furrowed, and he shook his head. "Don't start talking as if this is the end," he murmured.

She didn't say it could be, although the words hung on the tip of her tongue.

"I will craft a behemoth of my own without a book."

Alessia smiled at this and dropped her hands. "I cannot wait to see what you conjure up."

He was quiet for a moment, then peered down at his boots. "So, is it true that father wants to match me with Alvia Seducere?"

Alessia bit her bottom lip. The match hadn't just been Zryan's idea, it had been hers too. With one as powerful as that fae, her ability couldn't be trusted to go unchecked. If life had panned out differently for Alessia, it would have been an honor to be presented to the royal family as a marital prospect.

"It's true. Alvia is sweet, and it is a smart match."

Kian sighed heavily and nodded.

A wedding would be a welcome distraction after the dust settled.

When Alessia reached her quarters, she paused outside and placed her hand over her heart. Beneath her palm, her pulse raced violently. This wasn't panic, for that was a steady companion of hers, but rather something else. Perhaps just the rush of adrenaline.

Alessia's stomach roiled, and her skin felt clammy.

Do not be sick, do not be sick.

She swallowed roughly, then again.

"Your Majesty," Tobias' low, calm voice called to her.

Alessia swore under her breath and doubled over, spewing bile onto the marble flooring. She retched until her stomach ached and she was dizzy enough to lean into her guard.

"I can fetch someone," he said, slipping his arm around her waist to aid her into her chambers.

Alessia allowed him to help her, only because her ears rang and her head throbbed. "No. By the sun, Tobias, no. The palace is already buzzing, and Zryan is—"

"Occupied?" he supplied with a hint of a smile as he helped her to the chaise lounge just inside her room.

Alessia sat down and peered up at him. "That is one way of putting it." She pressed her lips together; the sour taste sat on her tongue heavily. "Phaedora's return isn't just that, it's a reminder of everything she tried to do to me. Tried to make me out to be a fool in front of the court, tried to steal Zryan away from *me*. But for Zryan?" She shook her head and glanced up at the ornate, coffered ceiling. "His past is being paraded before him by his demented ex-betrothed, and his family is in the line of fire because of the book she possesses."

Tobias remained quiet but sat down next to her, folding his calloused hands. "May I speak freely?"

Alessia scoffed. "When haven't you?"

He grinned at this, then, "I know you care for your husband, and whether that is love or simply empathy, I cannot say. But for his sake and the kingdom's, don't shut him out. A warrior needs peace, and anyone can see that you offer him that." Tobias sighed. "After, come what may. But by the sun, we need you to rule together."

Part of Alessia wanted to lash out at her guard. For what right did he have to make these assumptions? But he knew her better than most and had been with them for some time. She was tired. Exhausted from their quarrels, the constant drain on her emotions as she had to ponder whether he was tangled up with someone else or not.

Certainly, she'd taken up lovers of her own, and most discreetly so, because Zryan would punish them otherwise. It was not fair that he could have his paramours and she had to suffer alone.

Yet there was always the steady rumbling voice in her mind whenever she thought of leaving Zryan with his dalliances. *Mine, mine, mine*, it said.

And so, she remained. But she could not continue this way anymore.

"For the sake of Lucem, I will remain, for now."

Tobias reached for her hand and gently squeezed. "And with that, Majesty, I shall retrieve one of your attendants, some tea, and let you rest."

Alessia nodded, feeling even more exhausted than she had before. "Thank you."

Come what may, she would fight to the very end.

4

Zryan

Twice, the sun had fallen low in the sky and allowed dusk to settle over the land. Twice, Zryan had lain awake staring at the domed ceiling of his personal chambers, wishing that the soft feather-stuffed mattress of his bed was firmer. Wished that it was softer. Wished that the breeze coming in through the open window was cooler.

Nothing helped. Nothing allowed his eyes to shut and the concerns swirling in his mind to fade away. His family was in danger, had been for months now, and he wasn't sure how he was meant to protect all of them.

Exhaustion weighed down his steps as Zryan made his way down the hall of his palace, barely noting the servants who bowed as he passed. He kept his steps quick despite his weariness and found himself at the door to his study soon enough. He stepped into the chamber and made his way to the back of the desk, dropping into the high-backed chair with a heavy sigh.

Phaedora had worked her way through all three kingdoms,

orchestrating chaos and destruction that had left him and his brothers scrambling to catch up. They needed to get a step ahead of her if they ever hoped to stop her. But how?

He scraped his hands over his face and into his short-cropped brown hair, tugging at the strands as he growled.

His wife.

Phaedora had come after his wife.

Zryan picked up the discarded goblet on his desk and threw it against the wall. The clang of denting metal brought only momentary satisfaction. He needed to tell Draven and Travion what had happened. His eyes dropped to the stone bowl sitting on a pedestal beside his desk. He should drop a speck of blood into it and perform the spell that would call both of his brothers to their own bowls and tell them what had taken place. How he had failed to protect his family yet again.

He took up his gold-plated quill instead, dipping it in ink and scribbling quick notes to both his brothers. He would send the letters by eagle. He didn't have the time nor energy to stare down his brothers' disappointment and irritation at what he'd allowed to happen. Nor did he feel like explaining why it had taken him two days to notify them of the occurrence.

"Amyntas!" he called out, knowing that somehow his Chamberlain would be nearby.

The tall, slender fae stepped into the royal office. Today, only portions of his ash-blond hair fell in straight lines to his shoulders. The rest was tied back from his temples with a cord at the back of his head. His honey-kissed form was dressed in a sheer blue toga, with a swatch of royal-blue velvet attached at his shoulder, hanging down to the knee on either side of his body.

"Yes, Your Majesty?"

"Send these letters to my brothers." He quickly folded the two letters and held them out to Amyntas, who took them with a bow.

"Right away, sire." He turned on his heel and headed for the door, then stopped to look back at Zryan quickly. "Is Her Majesty okay, sire?"

"It will take more than an amateur assassin to startle my wife."

Amyntas nodded. "Glad to hear it. And you?"

Zryan's lips formed a self-deprecating smile. "I will be fine, Amyntas. I always am."

Amyntas gazed at him solemnly for a moment, reading more deeply than the facade Zryan erected around himself. "You will be, sire."

The chamberlain then left the room, and Zryan slumped back in his seat, wondering where to begin in his hunt for his ex-betrothed. He hated that his days had been taken up with security of the palace. Hated that she had effectively distracted him from his goal of finding her with making sure no one could step foot inside the palace without him knowing. With the sheer number of personnel within the palace that had needed to be interviewed.

A knock sounded at his door, and Zryan looked up to see Ruan. His eldest offered a slight bow of his head and entered the study.

"How are the interrogations going?" Zryan asked.

Ruan sighed and moved to stand before his desk. "Currently, we have not unearthed anyone who appears to have had a hand in helping him. He entered the palace under the guise of delivering vegetables to the kitchens. From there, it would seem he slipped down a hall out of sight of servants and soldiers and made his way up to Mother's wing." Ruan's face was pinched with irritation and fury. His son did not like being duped, and Zryan could tell this was one scheme that would haunt him for a long time.

"An absolute waste of time," Zryan growled.

"Excuse me?" Ruan looked affronted.

"This entire endeavor. Phaedora knew we would be taken up with trying to find out how the assassin got in." Just as Alessia had said. "And in the meantime, she's been free to continue on with her plan, whatever it may be."

"We *will* find her. My scouts have not ceased searching. We may have been focused on the palace, but they are out there in the kingdom. Phaedora can't hide forever." Ruan looked fierce and determined.

"I pray we do."

Ruan nodded. "I will report back as soon as we have news."

"Thank you." Zryan watched his son turn and leave the room, seeing the invisible weight that rested on his shoulders. A weight he had placed there when he'd proclaimed Ruan the prince of war. Zryan rubbed at his forehead, then, from beneath a stack of other papers, he pulled out a map of Lucem. From his desk, he picked a few things at random to hold down the corners. A misshapen piece of gold at one corner, which had been a present from Kian in his youth. A portrait of Alessia holding Brione as a mere babe, something he'd commissioned for both of them shortly after her birth. The bottom two corners were weighed down with an old stone Ruan had given him and an empty wine goblet. With the map stretched out before him, his fingers smoothed over the inked lines of each town and roadway.

Where was Phaedora hiding? He draped his fingers along the road that traveled from the city out toward the hills and circled around the mountains. There, Calor had his forge buried deep in the foothills. He had been the one to first fashion Kian a new arm, teaching the young fae how to master the craft until he was able to create his own, imbuing gold with the element of life.

Calor's forge was a place of creation, where The Creaturae itself had been formed. Not by a fae wielding his hammer but by the elemental molten fires within the forge. There was magic there, beyond the beginning of life itself.

"Is that where you're hid—" He froze. There was a sudden pressure on his body, and the hair at the back of his neck stood up. Slowly, he looked around the room.

Was someone here?

Zryan rose from his seat, cautiously walking around his desk. "Are you here, Phaedora?" he rasped. "Let's stop playing these games . . . Let's talk. Just you and I."

A rustling noise sounded behind him, and he whirled around to see a small mouse darting over the tops of books on the bottom shelf of his bookcase.

"There you are!" he hissed, launching himself at the tiny creature.

It darted from his fingertips, leaping to the other side of the bookcase and darting through a small hole in the wood to hide behind it. Growling, Zryan stood, grabbing the shelf and pulling it hard enough to the side that the entire unit shook and tipped forward. A chair stopped it from falling to the floor, but all of the books and items on it crashed to the marble with a cascade of thumps and the smashing of crystal.

The mouse, seeing its giant pursuer, leaped from one side to the other, confusion and fear taking over.

"By the sun, you little traitor, I've got you now." Zryan swiped out toward it this time, but as his fingers closed around the tiny form, they went right through it, and the mouse disappeared as if it never was.

Zryan froze. A chill coursed through him, making the hair on his arms and neck stand up.

The mouse had been there. It had *been* there. He was sure of it. Zryan slowly examined the floor around him, lifting up books and pushing several scrolls to the side just to be certain it had not gotten away. The pest was nowhere.

His stomach turned, and his mouth tasted sour. He was being toyed with.

Zryan looked over his shoulder, startled, as someone rapped on the frame of his door.

"Sire, Lord Seducere and his daughter are here to meet with you."

Zryan nodded at the pageboy and rose to his feet. "Send him in. And please fetch Prince Kian as well."

He looked at the state of his office and silently cursed. He looked as if he had gone insane.

"Did I come at a bad time, Your Majesty?" Severance Seducere asked from his place in the doorway. A beautiful, young fae stood behind him, her hands folded before her.

Zryan chuckled, brushing his words away with a casual wave of his hand. "You know how it is, the best way to rebuild is to first destroy." He winked at the lord and motioned him and his daughter into the room and toward the chairs before his desk.

Casually, as if nothing were amiss, Zryan lifted his bookcase back into place. A number of shattered vases and marble statuettes littered the floor. "Amyntas!" Zryan bellowed, turning to smile at Seducere and his daughter. He winked slightly at the female, who was eyeing him with uncertainty.

The chamberlain stepped into the study, immediately saw the mess, and nodded. "Right away, sire," he said without Zryan even having to ask.

Dusting his hands off, Zryan stepped up to the young Seducere maiden and took her hand between both of his. "On behalf of the royal family, I would like to welcome you to the palace." He kissed the back of it, nodded to Seducere himself, then stepped back around his desk to sit down.

"Thank you, Your Majesty. It is an honor to be here." Her voice was soft. Lyrical. It held a quality to it that told Zryan it could easily grow husky and warm. Smooth like honey that would slip over one's body, caressing and awakening emotions as well as desires.

As he settled into his chair, Zryan let his eyes fall on Alvia Seducere, studying her. Her honey-blond hair fell in soft waves about her shoulders and down her back. Her skin, while kissed by the sun and rosy, was paler than he was used to. Like warm cream, ready to soothe one's frazzled nerves.

Wideset blue eyes stared back at him bravely, though respectfully. They were a light blue, not as deep as his brothers' or even Kian's. Alvia's were bright, icy pools that still held warmth and suggested relief would be found within their depths. She was beautiful, like the fresh start of a new day. Or the first hints of spring in Midniva as the snow melted and new warmth filled the frigid air.

While he had not dealt with the girl firsthand, all those who spoke of her did so quite highly. Her tutors spoke of her intelligence and grace. Those in court spoke of her as graceful and polite yet endearing.

Zryan believed even more fully that she would be perfect for Kian. That with her, his son would find balm for the wounds enforced on him by their society of perfectionism.

"Oh, the honor is all ours, Alvia. It is a pleasure to host you, and I cannot wait for you to properly meet Kian." He smiled at her, well pleased.

At his daughter's side, Lord Seducere shifted, but he nodded. "Alvia has been fully informed of the betrothal and is happy to comply."

Zryan tutted. "Comply? Mm . . . Now, I don't like the sound of that." He looked at Alvia. "I wish to bring you into the fold of my family, Alvia. To welcome you as one of us and give you the place you are due. It is also my hope that you and Kian will learn to love and support each other in a true marriage."

Alvia studied him back, her gaze not giving much away, but something in how she held his eyes told him that she saw more than she tended to reveal. "That is my hope as well, sire."

Zryan nodded, then looked up as Kian stepped in. He grinned at the sight of his youngest son and opened his arms in greeting, rising to his feet. "Kian, come in! I have someone I wish to introduce you to."

Kian's dark hair was pulled back from his face and tied in

a small tail near the back of his head. His face, though no longer sweaty, had clearly been wiped dry by one of his work rags, and just enough water had been splashed upon it to take away most of the dirt and grime, though some remained along his hairline and across one proud cheekbone.

He was dressed in tight brown slacks and a loose-fitting white shirt, its sleeves rolled up to his elbows and the stays at the top loosed, showing off the tanned skin beneath. It was something more befitting Midniva than Lucem. But such were his son's proclivities.

There was hesitation in his eyes and an uneasy smile pasted to his lips as Alvia stood and turned to face him. Zryan recognized the smile. He'd seen it in every instance that Kian was forced to interact with people of the court. A smile. Lovely and kind. But untrue. The one he pasted to his lips when he was trying to pretend to be what he was not.

Zryan felt a moment of doubt, but he pressed forward. He stepped around the desk and took Alvia's hand so he could tug her closer to Kian. "Kian, I am pleased to introduce you to Lady Alvia Seducere, daughter of Lord Severance Seducere."

Kian took the hand Zryan held out to him, fingers clean but showing signs of wear and use as they slipped around the slender, well-manicured fingers of Alvia.

Zryan smiled, looking between them.

While it was true he feared what Alvia's powers being loose and unchecked in the kingdom could mean, he also truly wished to see his son happy. All of his children, in fact, were well within age to be married, and yet none had found the one who fit their soul perfectly. Something he could not explain told him that Alvia was meant to be a part of this family. That she fit perfectly within it. Years of watching his sire's court from the sidelines had made Zryan a good judge of character, and there was an aura of truthfulness around Alvia that Zryan couldn't help but trust.

Kian bowed over the hand, pressing a kiss to her knuckles. "Pleasure to meet you, Lady Seducere."

Alvia curtsied. "The pleasure is all mine, Your Highness."

And then there was silence, the two of them looking back at each other uncertainly, until they looked away.

Zryan chuckled and clapped his hands together. "Fabulous! Kian, why don't you take Alvia into the family wing to show her the rooms that the servants have prepared for her? And then perhaps you could give her a tour of the palace." His son looked back at him, lips opening on a protest, he was sure. "Alvia, I hope you will find your chambers to your liking, but if there is anything that you are missing, please do not hesitate to let us know."

He pressed his hands to their backs and unceremoniously ushered both of them out into the hall.

When they were gone, he turned to face Severance. "Well, she is as beautiful as the rumors say she is."

Seducere nodded, a calculating look in his eyes. "I would hate to step out of bounds, Your Majesty, but I do believe, with a wedding announcement between our two families, an increase in rank may also be warranted?" Seducere's brow lifted.

Zryan eyed him, his lids narrowing a fraction. *Conniving bastard.* Though Zryan supposed he couldn't blame him. "I think we may be able to accommodate that. Once they are wed."

Severance Seducere stood, smoothing out his toga.

"Wonderful." He bowed to Zryan. "I trust you to take good care of my daughter."

"As if she were one of the family already."

Seducere nodded. "I'll take my leave of you then, Your Majesty."

Zryan motioned to the door to give him leave, and the nobleman stepped out of the room.

With a sigh, Zryan stepped back around his desk and sat. Though it could have gone better, and there certainly hadn't been sparks of attraction and instant love flying between Kian and Alvia—unlike when Zryan had first laid eyes on Alessia and simply *known*—it could have also gone much worse.

"I see what you are doing."

Zryan's head whipped around, following the eerie voice that had sounded from behind him. No one was there.

"Zryan . . . my Zryan."

The hair at the back of his neck rose, and he felt a chill coursing through his blood.

"Zryan."

He swallowed.

"Show yourself!"

"Zryan."

"I said, show yourself to me!"

The scent of lilacs and amber accosted his nose, and memories of Phaedora surfaced. The smell overwhelmed him, the voice now seemingly inside his very head, piercing his temples and clamping around his jaw.

Zryan moaned, hands clutching at his head.

And then it was all gone, as if it had never been there. Leaving him to wonder if it had been real at all.

So much of his life hadn't felt real. Under the rule of his sire, life had been what Ludari wanted. Zryan had tried to be someone other than who he was. Someone Ludari would be proud of. He had taken Phaedora as his betrothed, not because he had loved her but because it was what was expected of him. And because it was expected, he had simply lived with it.

Phaedora had made it easy for him. She seemed to worship him, and in many ways, it made him grow to care for her, never having had someone look at him the way she did— like he was worth more than everyone else. It had been a heady experience, and for a while, he'd let himself get swept up in her affection. But it wasn't real. Zryan didn't love her, no matter how hard he tried. She didn't challenge him. She didn't make him a better person because she didn't expect anything better from him than the false front he already showed everyone.

She didn't love the real him.

"We weren't meant to be, Phaedora," he said out loud to his empty study.

As if the world had heard and responded, a deep thrum vibrated through him. It rattled his teeth and wrung a shuddering breath out of him. That was not good, nor was it normal. It felt suspiciously like a vast draw of magic from the earth itself.

Zryan pushed to his feet. He needed to find Ruan. They needed to send men out at once.

5

Alessia

Waves of nausea washed over Alessia, and her head ached from the day's stress. Between the attempt on her life, dealing with Zryan, and the worrying about Phaedora, she'd had her fill. She lifted a piece of candied ginger and placed it on her tongue as she strode through the garden. Daphnes were in full bloom. Their soft pink petals stood out against the dark green leaves surrounding them and the fuchsia center. The fragrant scent of the flora tickled her nose: pepper and soap.

She'd remember this moment, with the peacocks trilling in the distance, bees humming as they lapped up the nectar. This was as peaceful as life would be for however long Phaedora and her lackeys plagued the realms.

It wouldn't make sense to run into battle without knowing who they were truly fighting or who was on their side, but she longed to do just that. To finally put an end to that blasted bitch.

Wherever she was hiding.

Since no one knew her whereabouts, all they could do was send scouts and increase security at the Veil.

Alessia ran her hand down her hip to find the dagger she kept secured there. She tugged it free and bent to cut a bundle of the flowers for herself.

"Your Majesty," Tobias grunted from behind. The sound of his leathers shifting indicated he was bowing.

Not to her, though.

She turned her head just in time to see Zryan padding toward her. His eyes lacked their typical sparkle and looked more akin to his brother's: storm-ridden and unforgiving.

There were times she enjoyed seeing that side to him, where she knew their enemies would pay and they would reign victorious. But then, she wanted it to fade too, because his often ridiculous behavior made her smile and forget the terrors that haunted her.

Zryan's sandals clapped against the white stone pathway, his muscles gleaming in the sun, and had she not been so furious with the current predicament, she may have pulled him into the shadows of the garden.

Yet, here they were.

Phaedora was breathing down their necks, and if Zryan had killed her long ago, this wouldn't be happening.

"I know you want to be alone," he started to say and continued to walk toward her until he was an arm's length away. "But I don't want you to be." Zryan frowned, and his fingers flexed at his sides as if he wanted to reach out for her, but he didn't. "If that's what you want, send me away."

Alessia clenched her teeth as she spun to fully face him. The bundle of flowers was in one hand, and in the other, she held her dagger.

Zryan's eyes dipped to the blade in her grasp. "Out of all the possible ways to do away with me, in the garden with a dagger isn't one I'd had in mind." A spark of humor flickered in his eyes, teasing, baiting Alessia into the playfulness.

But now wasn't the time.

She sighed, tucking the dagger into place on her thigh. "I don't want to send you away, but I won't be playing any games."

"Less," he whispered and edged closer to her. "I won't stop until the wrongs are put to rights. I will end Phaedora." His last words were growled, and whatever light that had trickled into his green eyes vanished at once.

"I believe you, but know this too . . ." She closed the distance between them and shoved the flowers against his chest. Being nearly eye level with him made it easier to glare into his eyes. "If I have the chance to, I will kill her myself, and I will revel in it."

He bent his head as if ready to capture her lips, but she withdrew, pressing her back into the Daphnes behind her.

"I only ask that I am there to watch." At first, Alessia thought he was speaking coyly, but there was no hint of warmth in his voice. "She seeks to ruin what I cherish most. Don't think for a moment I'll weep over her, Alessia." Zryan's brow furrowed, and he looked away.

Just as she was readying to walk away, a pulse that she felt in her very marrow swept through her. It was the second time such a sensation had passed through her, the first happening the day before. She glanced to Zryan, and he looked down at the cobblestone path. Tobias shifted in the distance, and when she assessed him, he looked as concerned as *she felt.*

"What—"

From behind Zryan, someone rushed into the garden.

Tobias drew his sword at once and darted forward, poised to attack. "Don't make another move."

Alessia brushed past her husband and stared as a tanned fae came into view. Dark curls clung to his forehead, and sweat trickled down his rounded face.

Ermis, one of their messengers.

"Majesties," he said breathlessly, bowing. "There is news, but I'm not certain you'll like it." His dark eyes lifted and flicked between Alessia and Zryan.

"Out with it," Zryan ground out.

Alessia stepped closer and folded her arms. "What is it, Ermis?"

The messenger sucked in a breath before speaking. "The scouts have returned, and the ley lines are indeed being triggered. They followed the flow of energy but didn't want to fully act without support." He paused, brushing his fingers along the strap of his satchel at his shoulder. "The surges are heading toward Mount Pyrsos."

"By the sun," Alessia murmured. Was Phaedora in the mountain? Or was this another bloody diversion she'd cooked up?

Zryan swore none too quietly. "You're dismissed."

Ermis bowed and left just as quickly as he'd entered the garden.

Fear crept its way up Alessia's back, and her flesh cooled despite the heat of the sun beating down on her.

Zryan was watching her, and she didn't want him to see her falter. *What is this wretch up to?*

She frowned and turned her gaze to her husband. "Ruan needs to know, he needs to—"

"Not yet," he hissed and strode forward, gripping her by the forearms. "He needs to know, but he will not be going yet. I feared this may be where she was headed. You may not believe anything that I say, but know that I will do anything to protect you and our family."

That she knew. That she believed.

Alessia nodded and slid her hand over his heart. "To the war room."

Zryan abruptly stormed away, and in his wake, she felt the distinct current of electricity. He hated being backed into a corner as much as she did, especially when it threatened those he cared for.

Yet it always awakened something in her, the absolute rage and desperation to live to see another day, and to protect whom and what she loved most.

"I think you should go with him," Tobias prodded from a distance.

"I am." She shot him a pointed look. "Parts of my life may be unsettled, but I am still queen." She flicked her hand. "I'd prefer not to seem unhinged in front of everyone."

His lips quivered, which only made her roll her eyes before she, too, set off to the war room.

A grand round table stretched the length of the room, the dark wood contrasting with the light-colored map. High-back chairs gathered around, but no one sat; instead, Ruan hovered over it, his eyes searching the kingdom on paper.

Annoyance coursed through her, and she clenched her fists. "So, you told him already," she mused out loud, irritation lacing her tone as she spoke to Zryan.

"Yes, Father did. And I'll go with a party of scouts. I don't want to send more than necessary in case this is only a diversion, but I want to be there in case it is a true lead." Ruan swiped his hand across the map, glowering. "I don't like this game of hide-and-seek, it's cowardice."

Zryan's lips were pressed together, and his jaw muscles flexed. He was none too pleased about Ruan's decision to leave. "I thought it would be best to clue in our war strategist, Less."

It was, but he'd said Ruan wasn't to leave yet, now here he was . . .

Alessia laughed bitterly. "Then you are finally understanding Phaedora. She would rather hide behind the pages of a book than confront her foe on even ground."

"If cutting her arm off would benefit her, she would do it," Zryan echoed her sentiments.

Ruan chewed on his bottom lip, and he looked as though he longed to ask the same question Alessia wanted the answer to: Why not execute her?

"Remember, this is a scouting mission only. Do not attempt to instigate battle, no matter what you see. We do not attack until all of us have been made aware of what is going on." Zryan's voice was strained.

Ruan nodded.

Alessia rounded the table and approached her son. He was taller than her, and even his father. Still, she cupped his cheeks. "Return to us safely."

"I will not fail you."

His words twisted her heart. He could never fail her.

Ruan pulled back and eyed Alessia, then Zryan. With a bow, he left the war room.

It went without saying, if anything happened to him—Lucem wasn't ready for what would become of her.

As the sun lost its strength in the sky, signaling evening hours, Alessia knew she wouldn't be able to sleep. Instead, she grabbed her black silk robe, wrapped it around herself, and strode into the hall.

Tobias was there, whittling at a piece of wood. A messy yet endearing hobby of his.

"It's rather late, Your Majesty."

"I cannot sleep knowing Ruan is out there, with *her*."

"The prince of war is more than capable."

Alessia didn't want to doubt her son, and yet . . . when she looked at everything Phaedora had done already . . . "Against nearly any other foe, I would agree, but *she* isn't a common enemy. Phaedora would like nothing more than to pull the skin from my body strip by strip. But if she cannot do that, she will come for my children." Her voice grew quieter, harsher.

Before Alessia had married Zryan, when she was still meeting the courtiers and trying to make a good impression, Phaedora had tried to sabotage her in various ways.

Once, she'd *accidentally* locked her in a small meeting room. It shouldn't have fazed Alessia, or at least, it wouldn't have if her years of imprisonment hadn't washed over, suffocating her. By the time Zryan found her, she'd bloodied her hands and screamed herself hoarse.

Another time, Phaedora had left a missive signed by one

of the officials requiring Alessia to see to them at once, when in fact, she was to remain at the palace.

Each *small* inconvenience added up, and all it did was prove to the council she wasn't a worthy queen and Zryan couldn't wed her. However, Alessia fought to heal and prove them wrong. Prove that she was worthy and Zryan hadn't made a mistake.

Tobias remained quiet, but as she continued to walk down the hall, he followed closely behind.

She rounded one of the white columns and headed toward the marble stairwell, only pausing when the sound of the doors creaking open echoed through the palace.

"Get away from me!" Ruan bellowed, sounding half-drunk.

"Ruan?" Alessia whispered to herself and raced down the stairs, nearly missing a few as she did.

When she reached the bottom, Ruan's voice grew more agitated, and the sound of protesting guards filled the space.

"Ruan!" she called and rounded the corner just in time to see him land a punch to a guard's jaw. He looked poised to attack, his nearly black eyes wild, frenzied. However, Zryan appeared behind him and wrapped his arms around Ruan, securing him in place.

"Enough!" Zryan's voice was forceful yet gentle.

What had happened? Alessia moved forward, motioning for the guards to leave. Her eyes raked over her son. Dust coated him. Volcanic ash? She frowned. There hadn't been an eruption, they would have felt it.

Ruan relaxed only a little. Enough that Zryan relinquished his hold on him.

"By the sun, what happened?"

"Our scouting party . . . obliterated. We arrived on griffin. And from the sky, everything looked normal, we couldn't see anything. So we landed, and as we drew closer to the suspected entry to the mountain, a strange surge of magic occurred. I felt it in my bones. I told the scouts to press on. Oh . . . I wish I hadn't." His voice cracked, and he dragged his hand through his hair, then swore as a cloud of dust came from it.

The way he stared at it was filled with such pain and regret, it was nearly tangible.

Alessia swallowed roughly. "Ruan," she gently pressed, and as he locked eyes with her, clarity filtered back into his gaze.

"One moment, we were standing there, and the next . . . my party was no more than dust. Their griffins, weapons, them . . . gone."

That was the power of the book. The power of destruction, creation, and everything in between. Life could be rendered to dust in the uttering of a spell.

It was why they'd fought so hard to protect The Creaturae, for it was a danger to everyone. Once opened, it released all manner of things into the world.

Alessia's heart thrummed wildly, deafening her. She gently pulled Ruan into her arms. "You did what you had to. And your scouts died honorably."

Ruan embraced her, squeezing, but just as quickly, he pulled away and shuttered his expression. "What honor is there in dying without the ability to fight? We need to come up with a better plan. One that will work against this bitch. I must bathe first, but then we need to discuss some things at length. I need to know everything about her. I need to know what will undo her."

Zryan's shoulders sagged a fraction. "We do, and we will discuss this."

Alessia's anger morphed into something akin to hysteria. Her skin prickled, her head raced with a thousand scenarios of how this evening could've panned out, and she wanted to scream. Wanted to tear Phaedora's smirking lips off her face.

Once Ruan left, Zryan started to turn away, and she grabbed his arm, yanking him.

He whirled on her, eyes narrowed. "Do not beat me when I am already down, Alessia."

She ignored his words and the way they were a knife to her chest. "She is in the mountain." Zryan couldn't know, only surmise as she had. He'd mentioned it earlier, but this . . . it seemed like proof. But for all anyone knew, it could have been someone with a page.

"Not out here," Zryan said, his voice low.

Alessia nodded, then took his hand and led him toward the stairs. He followed closely behind as she reached the top and continued to her door.

Tobias leaned against the wall, knife in hand as he whittled away at the block of wood. As soon as he noticed Zryan storming his way, he lowered his work to the ground and stood at attention.

"Your Majesties," came Tobias' low voice. He swept his gaze from Alessia to Zryan, then bowed his head. "Allow me to search the room first."

Zryan sighed. "No need while I'm here."

"With all due respect, Your Majesty, I insist. You requested heightened security—"

"So be it."

Since the attack, Zryan hadn't been the only one on edge; Alessia had been as well. Tobias had made it his task to search the room frequently, especially prior to her entering. He could not be faulted for being thorough.

Alessia folded her arms as she waited for her guard to search the room. With each passing moment, she could see Zryan's irritation grow. His fingers flexed by his side, and his jaw muscle leaped wildly.

Tobias sauntered out of the room, inclining his head. "All clear, Majesties."

Alessia stepped into her room and waved her hand to Zryan. "Close the door behind you."

He did, and when he stepped inside, he assessed it like he would a battlefield. His gaze drank in every corner, as if he expected a foe that Tobias hadn't detected to leap out at any moment. Not that she blamed him.

"Do you think it's Phaedora leeching off the ley lines?" Alessia crossed her arms and paced at the foot of her bed. It took a great deal of time and energy to tap into the ley lines, pull the natural flow of creation magic from them, and wield it no differently than an affinity. And coupled with The Creaturae . . . Alessia couldn't fathom the possibilities with the two.

"Less, wearing a hole in your floor won't solve a thing. Sit down." He walked to the bottom of her bed and gave the blanket a pat. "Come here."

She hated how her body responded to those simple words. Once, they'd shared a room, and those words had held heat and promise, ensuring her mind and body would be so focused on pleasure that she'd not have a moment to dwell on anything else.

By the sun. Why have we let this go on so long?

She sighed heavily. Zryan was right, though; exhausting herself before they even made it to battle would do them no good. Alessia sat down and stared at her upturned hands, wondering how they'd fight a puppeteer.

Zryan sat beside her and placed his hand on her knee. "I believe she is. But for what, I cannot say. I know this magic, Less. I felt it when the veils were created by Ludari. The same surge of power . . . and I'm certain the ley lines were used then too, since no one is that powerful on their own. Not even with the spells. It drains far too much magic, and an outside source was needed. If this is Phaedora, it concerns me what she could possibly need that much magic for."

Alessia turned her head to study his face. His brows were furrowed, and regret lined his features as much as exhaustion did.

The creation of the veils had been so long ago, but she recalled the pulsation of power as she coiled in on herself in the belly of the old palace. Alessia had learned after that it was, in fact, the creation of the veils, one extending into a land of darkness and another into a realm full of humans, for Ludari sought to rule *all* the realms.

Unlike his brothers and herself, Zryan had been there, had witnessed and felt the brunt of the power. If anyone knew what it felt like most, it would be him.

She reached for his hand, twining her fingers with his and squeezing tightly. "I cannot lose them," Alessia whispered. There may have been a chasm between her and Zryan, but the one thing they could agree on was the safety of their family. She wrenched her eyes shut. "Yet our children are going to be key in this too. We need to infiltrate that mountain without it costing us everything."

Zryan shifted beside her, and when she opened her eyes, he was staring intently at her. "I will not let it cost us everything. I vow it, Alessia. I vow it." His tone was rough but held a promise in it—something she hadn't heard in a long time.

And for as much as she'd tossed his words to the side in the present days, she believed him when he spoke.

She had to, for her own sanity.

6

Zryan

His children were gathered around the war room, staring down at a detailed map of the mountain. Ruan's rugged face was creased with a heavy frown, guilt and fury intermingled in his gaze. Kian's features, which so resembled his mother's, bore the weight of what he'd faced in Midniva. His youngest son may not have been their prince of war, but he had shouldered the burden of protecting an entire kingdom.

His boys.

They may have been well over a millennia old, but they would always be the small children clinging to his hand and looking up at him with trust and love.

They would always be the boys he had failed. Zryan would not let it happen again. He would take down their enemy before she could take them from him.

Brione stood beside Kian, her lovely face pinched with concern and frustration. In a lot of ways, she was the best parts of him and Alessia. All of the good things about themselves had come together to create her before they both forgot what those good aspects were and lost them.

She deserved so much better than the chaos and bickering she had been born into.

By the sun, he would fix this for them. Even if he had to die to achieve it.

At his side was Alessia, and for the moment, they were a united front. For the moment, a common enemy brought them together, but she would be the first one to thrust a knife beneath his ribs should he fail their children once more. She had made that perfectly clear long ago.

"It has been a long day, and we've already suffered great losses." Zryan looked at Ruan, who simply glowered down at the map, his fingers dug into the table before them, white at the tips from the pressure. "But the night is not over. We can only assume, based on the desolation of our scouts, that Phaedora has barricaded herself beneath the mountain and is drawing from the power of the ley lines for some purpose. I am done with her being ahead of us. Ruan, Kian, you will take another faction of our calvary and head to the mountain. I want you camped out on either side watching the tunnels that come from beneath it. Do *not*"—at this, he eyed Ruan specifically—"get close enough to be ashed. This is not a battle; this is only reconnaissance. Once she or someone with her emerges from the mountain, and we know the barrier is down, I want to be notified. Understood?"

He glanced between his sons, waiting for them to respond. Kian nodded solemnly, but it was Ruan who grunted.

"I don't like playing the waiting game," he bit through clenched teeth.

"Neither do I," Alessia inserted. "But either of you dying will not help the situation. Do as your father says."

Ruan's dark eyes lifted from the map to meet his mother's pointed gaze, and he nodded begrudgingly.

"What about me?" Brione asked.

"With both of your brothers gone, I will need you here helping to maintain palace security. A second assassination attempt is always a risk, and I need someone I trust to be maintaining order with the palace guards and watching over all of them." Zryan peered into her green eyes, a mirror of his own. He wanted to bundle her up and protect her from this. To keep her as far away from risk as he could. But despite her tender heart, she was as fierce as any of them.

Brione nodded in acceptance of her role.

"You're dismissed," he told them. "Do us proud."

He wanted to tell them that he loved them. That he would have died here and now if it meant this was all over. But instead, Zryan watched his three grown children leave the war room and felt a large piece of him leave with them.

If Phaedora harmed one hair on any of their heads, he would not need The Creaturae to obliterate her.

"Have you informed your brothers?" Alessia asked.

"Not yet."

"Do you plan on it?"

Zryan nodded, his fingers tapping lightly on the table. "It is next on my list." He glanced her way, so many words on his lips, none of which made their way past the blockage in his throat. Instead, "Shall I send them kisses for you?" He quirked a brow at her, and Alessia rolled her eyes.

"Just get this done and over with, Zryan. I want Phaedora dead." She growled and stormed from the room.

Zryan watched her tall, lithe frame until it disappeared, his fingers itching to hold her once more. To brush through her hair and taste her skin on his lips. His soul yearned for the firmness of her commanding words ordering him onto his knees to service her and the heat of her dominance as she claimed him as hers.

He had never felt as valued as he did when Alessia looked upon him with love and approval.

Shaking his head against intrusive thoughts that had no place in war, Zryan crossed the room, opening a door in the side of the war room that led into his study, which had been put back to rights by servants.

The marble summoning bowl sat on a pedestal beside his desk. Stepping up to it, he used a quill from his desk to prick his finger, letting drops fall onto the surface of the water. Murmuring the incantation, he said his brothers' names.

It took a moment, but soon enough, both Draven and Travion's face swirled into view.

"Zryan?" Draven asked, frowning. "What is wrong? Did they come for Alessia once more?"

He couldn't help but think of the similar scowl his eldest son had borne not too long ago. Did Ruan know how much of a similar demeanor he shared with his uncle?

"Where to begin?" His voice was casual, not belying the stress that radiated through his form. "This morning, the ley lines were activated by someone hiding in the mountain, and when Ruan took a scouting party to investigate, they were turned to ash."

"Ruan?" Travion said. Shock and worry filtered into his eyes.

Zryan shook his head. "No, he is all right."

Draven cursed in a clipped tone, but it was Travion who swore a blue streak. "I'm on my way right now."

"No," Zryan cut him off.

"What do you mean, *no*?" he snapped.

"What I mean, dearest brother—" His eyes flitted to Draven. "Sorry, Drae." Draven brushed him off with the twitch of a brow. "Is that your kingdom was just attacked. It has been a matter of a couple weeks. I will not pull you from your still-grieving kingdom, nor your new bride, until I know what we are up against. Stay where you are."

"What are you doing about it?" he asked irritably, brushing a hand through his auburn locks.

"I have just sent Ruan and Kian back with more of our men to guard the entrances into the mountain tunnel. The moment someone emerges, we will know."

"Do you think it's Phaedora?" Draven asked, his frown deepening.

"I can only assume."

"What is she doing down there?" Travion's face moved in closer as he leaned over his bowl.

"Beyond using a great deal of magic, we have no clue as of yet."

"Nothing good." Draven sighed. "I wish I could assist myself."

Zryan nodded. He knew that it was a great bane on Draven's life that the permanent sunshine of Lucem was a deadly factor for him. While his eldest brother no longer needed to sleep and possessed strength and speed exceeding their own, one mere touch of the sun's rays, and he would burn up like a match put to a tinder box.

"However, since I cannot be there personally, and Travion

is low on troops, I will send Hannelore and a number of other harpies to your aid."

Zryan wouldn't turn the offer down. "That I will accept." The harpies were a skilled group of soldiers who acted as Draven's main army. Once, they had been normal women living in Midniva, but after suffering violent deaths at the hands of men, they had awoken in Andhera, Draven's realm, in newly formed bodies. Towering height, icy-blue flesh, bird-like talons for feet, and large feathered wings on their backs. They were killing machines, and he would most certainly add them to his forces.

Draven nodded and motioned to someone Zryan could not see. "Call Hannelore to me now." His focus was then once more on the bowl. "I will send them right away."

"Appreciated."

"And I will be there the moment you need me," Travion added.

"I will update you both once I know more." With a wave of his hand, Zryan ended the communications. Dropping down into the chair by his desk, he let his head fall back, closing his eyes.

They would be able to do this . . . Would they not?

The hair on the back of his neck rose, and Zryan was aware of someone watching him. Slowly, he opened his eyes to scan the room. Nothing seemed out of place. There were no figures hiding in dark shadows. Something white fluttered on his desk, and he looked down to see a piece of parchment bearing his own scrawling script.

Phae,

There remains only a short amount of time until we are one.

Until then, I wish to get to know you. The real you. Not the

Phaedora society knows, or even the Phaedora your family
knows. But who you truly are inside.
Will you let me in?
Zryan

When he attempted to pick the letter up, same as the mouse, it dissolved at his touch. Furious, Zryan rushed to his feet so quickly, the chair crashed to the floor.

"Where are you?!" he roared to the empty room before him. "Stop hiding like a coward and face me!"

Only silence greeted him. However she had done it, Phaedora was no longer here. No scent of her, no subtle presence. Just gone.

He moved to the door. "You!" He pointed to the guard standing at attention in the hall. "Someone is on our property. Alert the guards and search every corner of the palace."

The soldier looked stunned and then snapped to attention, saluting him. "Of course, Your Majesty." With a click of his heels, he was gone to begin the search.

Unable to stomach the thought of his defenses failing once more, Zryan stormed back over to his desk and pulled a bottle of aged rum from his desk drawer. Unstopping it, he gulped down a large portion. The fiery liquid burned down his throat and warmed in the pit of his stomach.

She was going to drive him to madness. Remind him of all the ways he had brought this down upon them all. How, just as always, he was the one who destroyed the things he loved.

Zryan took another deep drink, until fresh fear settled into his bones. What if she went for Alessia again? If she could make it into his study, she could easily make it into

Alessia's quarters undetected. Shedding his clothes, he pictured the form of a peacock, willing his body to change. Every part of him tingled and itched as the transformation began. His flesh seemed to ripple, and then feathers started to sprout from raised bumps along his arms and back. His body curled, and he sunk to his knees just as his legs shortened and became spindled, leathery sprigs ending in taloned feet. Another shudder coursed through him, and he arched his back and neck, everything cinching inside until he had shrunk and it was a squawk coming from his parted beak rather than words from lips. Stretching his new wings out, Zryan ruffled his feathers and slipped between the doors of his study leading out onto his balcony. He hopped up onto the railing and then glided to Alessia's. Inside, he could see her prone figure lying on her bed. She slumbered fitfully, her own stress and worries keeping her from a deep sleep.

Still clad in the bright, flamboyant greens and blues of a peacock, Zryan nestled down on the balcony floor to keep a watchful eye over his wife. Not even the drink was able to pull him away.

7

Alessia

Palace guards lined the courtyard, their eyes trained forward on the bleached steps as they stood for inspection. Alessia walked down the first row, peering into their faces as if she could determine who was a traitor just by looking at them. Since yesterday, interrogations had been ongoing, and because of the assassination attempt, each guard had been instructed to report to the courtyard and endure the once-over.

Even Alessia didn't know every face, every name, but there were a few who did, and Tobias was one of them.

Captain Stianos led the inspection, but Alessia wanted to see them with her own eyes, watch if their lips curled in a sneer as she drew closer.

Tobias walked by her side, sighing as she wove into the second row. "You don't need to be out here," he whispered.

Although he meant well, the words grated on her. She whipped around to face Tobias, her jaw muscles tightening. "And you need not tell the queen what she can and cannot do. If there is a defector among us, let them show themselves now and be done with it."

Tobias' gaze slid to the nearest male. The other guard's lips wavered as though he were fighting a smirk.

She was ready to throttle the male, but Tobias reached out, grabbed him by the front of his leathers, and tossed him to the ground.

"Do you mind stating what is so amusing?" Tobias' deep voice rumbled in his chest.

"Only that if you believe familiar faces are loyal, you're delusional."

He was right, of course. Still, Alessia glowered at him. "You," she said, turning to a guard who had turned a shade paler than a moment before. "Bring him to a holding cell. I will not tolerate insubordination, and should you—"

"Alessia!" Zryan bellowed from behind her.

This was no excited howling, for his tone was tense, and it was that alone which had her head snapping toward the stairs. Gold shoulder plates clashed with the red cape billowing behind him, and with every heavy step he took, his metal armor shifted. Fury simmered in his gaze, and it was a look Alessia knew well, one that meant someone would pay dearly.

This didn't bode well.

"Edessa is under attack. With Ruan and Kian at the mountain, we need to leave at once with a small infantry."

Every muscle in her tensed. Edessa was only a town over from Celeia, where the newly crowned queen of Andhera's family manor was. Eden was more akin to a daughter than sister to Alessia, but she had been fond of her since she had been thrust into Andhera because of Zryan's foolishness.

Alessia ground her teeth. She longed to hop on a griffin and take to the skies immediately to thwart the enemy who thought to sink their teeth into *her* kingdom.

And now was her chance.

"Who has Phaedora sent to attack Edessa?" At this point, she surmised the cowardly fae wouldn't do it herself but send a lackey instead. She turned her gaze to Tobias, who bowed his head immediately and backed away to aid Captain Stianos.

When Alessia turned her attention back to Zryan, he grimaced. "Not *who*, but what." He motioned toward the stairs, and she started up them. "The civilians who fled and brought word claim there are scorpions the size of the palace assaulting the heart of the town."

Alessia's chest constricted as she envisioned her people cornered by such an abomination. Leave it to Phaedora to create havoc and destroy innocent people to serve her purposes.

She quickened her stride and darted up the stairs. "We are being scattered like fowl!"

"Yes, we are," Zryan paused, then sighed heavily. "Gear up. We leave at once," he called after her as she fled down the hall once they were back inside.

By the time she reached her quarters, Brione was already pacing outside like a mountain lion. She glanced up at her and immediately opened the door. "I already have your leathers waiting."

Alessia didn't spare her daughter a second look as she swept into her room. The door had scarcely shut behind her when she peeled her dress from her figure. Brione had already laid out the thick cotton undershirt for her too.

She quickly dressed and pulled on what armor she could, and what she struggled with lacing, Brione swiftly stepped up to tie for her.

They met one another's gaze, and Alessia lifted her hands, cupping her daughter's face. "When we leave, don't send more troops out. No matter what. You need protection here, and we are being scattered for a reason. But I trust you, Bri. You will do what is necessary here." She bit her bottom lip and shook her head.

"I will do everything I can to protect Celeia." Brione leaned in and pressed her forehead to Alessia's. "I will see you when you return."

If there had been a way to remain behind with Brione *and* join Zryan in battling the beasts, she would have.

Alessia finished dressing and laced up her boots, and aside from her armor squeaking, it was silent in the room.

"Go, Mother. I will defend our home until my last breath."

That was what she feared most.

With one last kiss on her daughter's brow, she turned and left.

There was a hole developing within Alessia; it had started when the boys left for the mountain, and it seemed to grow with every step she took away from Brione. As if this was the last time she'd see any of them. And it very well could be.

For years, she had fought as if she'd come out unscathed, but this . . . this was different.

When she emerged from the palace, Zryan sat on his griffin, waiting with her mount beside him. His features were hardened, and in these moments, he looked the part of Ludari's son: unyielding and cruel.

She scratched Zissi's side, and he lifted his head, crying out in anticipation of flight. He was a deep bronze hue with ivory feathers. Except for his head, where the feathers were black, and in a pointed pattern that made him look as though he were scowling.

"She will be all right, Less. She is your daughter," Zryan offered softly, but it did nothing to ease the unrest in her belly.

"I hope so." With that, she mounted her beast, and together, the griffins charged forward, only to leap into the air and take off toward Edessa. The griffins' wings beat loudly as they trod the air, and below, the palace became a distant, miniature thing.

In their wake, a small fleet of riders followed. She guessed around a hundred.

The harpies had arrived from Andhera, and they flew beside the Lucemites, determination lining each of their dark faces.

"You are aware this is more than likely a trap for one of us?" Alessia shouted over the thunderous sound of wind passing by.

Zryan said nothing, only slanted her a look that said he knew.

And so the ride to Edessa went. Silent and chilled.

So be it.

Nothing could have prepared Alessia for the twin beasts in Edessa. One pincer alone had to be the length of her! And the way they whipped their barbed tails around like a venomous mace had her wondering how in the depths she would conquer one.

Dozens of bodies littered the streets, strewn as if the claws had torn their bodies apart, and dark blood coated the ground.

Her stomach roiled.

"Get down and see to those in need, protect the vulnerable!" Alessia ordered.

"Except the front half of you," Zryan interjected. "We need you. Hannelore, divide the harpies among our groups." What he didn't say was what she *knew*. It was less that they needed them to fight and more that they would be in dire need of a distraction until they figured out how to defeat the beasts.

"Have you ever—"

"No. I tried my best to stay away from Ludari's little creations and his . . . experimenting. I know Draven and Travion have, but their knowledge is of little use to us now." He reached for the sword, tucked away in its scabbard on his saddle, and grimaced. "Alessia, try not to die." This he said wryly but then added in a ragged tone, "No one would be able to contain me if that happened."

Despite the gravity of his words, her lips twitched into a smile because she knew it to be the truth. "Maybe that is the Zryan the realms need."

He hissed, and the air crackled with electricity. She could nearly feel it skimming along her flesh. "No, Alessia, I'd burn the realm down if that came to be."

To that, she didn't know what to say or, in truth, how to feel.

Her griffin dove toward the ground, claws outstretched, and the moment he touched down, Alessia grabbed her sword and charged forward.

A bitter smell permeated the air, threatening to send her stomach into an upheaval. What in the sun's name was that? She peered around the pillar of a home and saw liquid dripping from the barb on one creature's tail. When it touched the dirt, smoke billowed, and the same bitter fragrance wafted toward her.

"By the sun," Zryan whispered near her ear.

She jolted to attention, nearly clocking him in the jaw with her elbow. When she glared at him, he had the good grace to look apologetic.

"The venom is acidic. Don't let it touch you." Alessia pointed to the sizzling ground.

He grunted and darted across the front lawn toward a tall oak. The closest scorpion spun around, its mouth lined with drool as it loomed closer to where Zryan hid.

Alessia was about to rush forward when the sound of stones crumbling behind her forced her to turn around. There, making its way closer to her, was the twin beast.

She raised her sword and dove as the creature slammed its pincers down. It whirled around on its tree-trunk sized legs.

Alessia jabbed upward, but her sword couldn't pierce the exoskeleton. She swore under her breath as she tried ramming it between soft spots.

The beast reared up, and when it crashed down, it sent her tumbling to the ground. One leg punctured the earth mere inches from her head. She stared, sucking in a breath before rolling to the side. Fear lanced through her, but instead of freezing, it fueled the need to move and fight.

The scorpion skittered to the side and whipped its tail around. The barbed end lunged at her. Alessia wasn't foolish enough to think she could block the blow, so she ducked and felt as the rough hairs skimmed her back.

She shuddered and thrust her sword into one of the creases in the underbelly, but the hardened exoskeleton didn't give way.

Thunder shook the earth, but she couldn't spare a glance in Zryan's direction. She could only hope he was holding his own.

Alessia dodged the stabbing legs, stumbled over her own feet as she jumped out of the way of one of them, and as the barb came swinging down at her, a few soldiers clanged their swords against their shields, distracting the beast.

If she'd possessed the ability to leap into the mind of beasts, this would have been over in a matter of moments, but her affinity only reached the minds of mortals or fae—not creatures.

Above, the harpies let loose their arrows, aiming for the scorpion's eyes. They took out two clusters before the beast shrieked and spun away.

Alessia eyed the fallen pillar next to the scorpion as it advanced on the soldiers. There were too many moving parts to the creature, and it was armored, but if they could pin the pincers down, that was two of its defenses out of the way.

The tail swung around, knocking into the side of the building. As it did, Alessia spotted a weak joint. It was fleshy and unlike the hardened exterior of the body.

A barrage of arrows pelted the back, falling away. Alessia

grimaced as she ran forward. "If you have an earth affinity, you'd best use it now!" she screamed. "Use vines to tie the pincers down!"

The scorpion hissed, and a grating shriek cut through the air. One of their deaths was imminent, and Alessia wasn't certain whose it was, but if the fates meant it to be her, she wouldn't go down without a fight.

From behind her, she heard Zryan growling, and something cracked and crashed to the ground. She couldn't look, not now. Her heart hammered in her ears, deafening her as she raced toward the front of the beast.

The soldiers with earth affinity lashed out at the scorpion with long tentacles of greenery. They writhed as if they were alive, and just as the strands ensnared the abomination, the other pincer snapped the vine in two.

Alessia danced between the legs of the creature, slamming her sword against its legs. "Again!"

This time, the scorpion ducked low, as if to bite at her, but the vines circled around the pincers and grew in size.

"Hold as long as you can!" Alessia scrambled from beneath the creature, but one of the legs caught her in the side and sent her flying against a broken pillar. She choked as the wind rushed from her lungs and reached down to brush her side. No warmth spilled out, and she thanked the fates her son had crafted her armor.

She scrambled to her feet, tightening her grip on her sword, and charged forward. The scorpion bucked, swinging its tail around violently until it struck a line of soldiers with a sickening snap.

Alessia waited until the scorpion dove down. Shouts rang

out around her, but they sounded dull to her ears, and in the distance, Zryan roared in outrage.

If this failed . . .

No, she couldn't fail.

She sheathed her sword, grimacing as her muscles screamed at her with every movement. Her eyes followed the swinging tail of the scorpion, but its attention was no longer on her; it was on the caped individual racing her way.

Shit.

"Zryan! The mouth!" It was all she had time to say as she launched herself at its back. As it thrashed around, she yanked her sword out, and with scarcely a moment to spare, she rolled to the side and swung it.

The barb came away with a crunch, and if Alessia had thought the beast would still, she was sorely mistaken.

With a hard buck, it threw her to the ground, and she couldn't gain her breath back.

8

Zryan

The crackle of electricity rolled along his arms, and he called it from the skies only to watch it ripple over the shell of the scorpion and not even faze it. From above, Draven's harpies attacked the tail in compact formations, like a blue fist of rage meeting the giant boulder of shell and venom.

The beast spun, large pointed feet cracking through cobblestone, tail crashing through another home. Stone and glass exploded, raining over the infantry. He raised an arm to cover himself, protecting his head from the debris.

The scorpions were not the size of his palace. They were, however, the size of large manors and had demolished several of the shops and homes at the center of Edessa. Bodies of his people lay crushed and bloodied along the street. Green acid dripped from trees, and bushes were bursting into flames from the heat.

He stepped over the body of a mother who had attempted to shield her child from one spray of it only for it to eat through her middle and move on to the child anyway.

His gut clenched in revulsion and fury. Phaedora would pay for this.

An instinctive feeling caused him to glance over his shoulder to find Alessia. He watched his wife sheath her blade. His heart faltered in his chest. *What is she about to do?*

Zryan didn't stop to think. He turned from his beast, leaving it to the flock of harpies and his own soldiers. Leaping over a large chunk of roof, he called his lightning to himself, gathering it along his arm until it formed a large ball in his hand. His heart leapt into his throat as Alessia launched herself onto the back of the beast, risking herself in a way that was wholly unnecessary.

"*Alessia!*" he screamed as the scorpion began to buck, rising up on its back feet, fighting the weight of her on it.

He watched Alessia roll along its back, swiping at the large bulbous knot at the top of the creature's tail. It roared in pain as the tip of its tail was severed, and then it threw Alessia several yards from them both. Before Zryan could react, the scorpion slammed back down onto the ground, causing it to tremble, and his knees threatened to buckle beneath him at the force.

Its pinchers came toward him, a dark mountain of death looking to cut him in two. The lightning that had gathered in his hand cracked more fiercely, and Alessia's words came back to him. *Zryan! The mouth!*

Curling his arm back, Zryan ignored the pincher hurtling toward him and instead focused on the open maw roaring its outrage. He growled low in his throat as his arm flung forward, releasing the sharp burst of lightning at his fingertips. It soared through the air, colliding with the monster's mouth just as its pinchers fell around him.

The hard shell of the tarsus and manus pressed into his midsection, doubling him over as they squeezed more tightly. Just as the pain grew to unbearable levels, the scorpion crashed to the ground, lightning still crackling around and inside its mouth, steam and liquid oozing from its eye sockets.

Zryan dropped to his knees, gasping for breath as the pincher released him, and fell, unmoving, to the ground. He inhaled sharply, his abdomen and ribs protesting the action. He was fortunate that the gold leather-like metal of his armor had protected him as much as it had. Kian's brilliance in molding the metal into a flesh-like substance that was also impenetrable was beyond understanding.

Breath returned, Zryan clambered quickly to his feet, racing toward Alessia, who was already getting back up. "Are you okay?" he rasped, taking hold of her shoulders to look her over closely.

"I'm fine." Her eyes were hard, but her features softened as she was faced with his concern. "Only had the breath knocked out of me." Alessia gave him a once-over. "Are *you* okay?"

Zryan peered down at his midsection, where her gaze had been trained on the dent in his chest piece. He let out a chuckle seeing it and shrugged as he lifted his eyes to meet hers once more. "Right as rain, darling." Unable to stop himself, he leaned in and pressed a quick kiss to her lips. "Now, let's kill the second one."

Alessia loosed a breath and nodded. She bent to retrieve the sword that had tumbled from her grasp, then darted in the direction of the second scorpion.

Zryan moved to follow—only, a figure caught his attention.

A chill rushed over his exposed skin, lavender and amber tickling at his nose. He didn't think, he merely acted, racing across the street to dart down the alley, following the hooded figure. At the end of the alley, the figure stopped, blue velvet dragging heavily along the ground as the fae spun to face him.

Phaedora.

It had been a very long time since Zryan had seen her.

When he had ended their betrothal, Phaedora had been seemingly heartbroken, though he'd always assumed that had been more about the loss of the throne than Zryan himself. She had remained in Celeia for many centuries. A constant presence, a reminder of his father's reign and tyranny, attempting to somehow wheedle her way back into his life.

He'd almost caved at one point, after Kian's accident, when things had begun to truly get bad between him and Alessia. But there had been something about turning back to a former betrothed that felt like more of a betrayal than a random fae of the court. And so, Zryan had pushed her away, perhaps viciously, a little too cruelly, needing to drive away the temptation before he did something truly unforgivable.

Phaedora was a beautiful woman. Fair skin, rounded cheeks, and perfect heart-shaped lips. There was a sweetness to her face that spoke of wholesome innocence and tenderness. But he had seen beneath the façade to the viper that resided within. The sweetness was false, and the venom in her eyes left him cold.

As their eyes met, she smiled slowly, red lips unfolding

into something resembling a smirk of victory. "Hello, love," she cooed.

Zryan's stomach clenched, and his fist tightened at his side. "Stop this, Phae." He said her nickname in hopes of appealing to her sentimental side. "Leave the others out of it. This is just between you and me."

"Mmm, it is, isn't it?" She smiled, fingers lifting to brush at her lips. "And yet . . ."

"Yet what?" he asked, taking one small step toward her.

"You've brought your family into it, Zryan. Your sons stand guard outside the mountain. You taunt me with them, begging for me to end their lives."

Zryan felt his heart stop as his insides turned to icy dread. "Don't—" he began to whisper.

"And I could," she continued on as if he hadn't started to speak. "With the book at my fingertips, it would take but a snap, and I could explode the very hearts in their chests. No way for them to see it or to fight it."

Bile rose in the back of his throat, pulses of terror throbbing through him and pounding at his temples. *Please don't take my sons.*

He wanted to beg. Wanted to fall to his knees before her and plead with every ounce of desperation within him. But he couldn't give her that satisfaction. Couldn't make this the sadistic game of torment that she wanted it to be. And so, he pulled his own facade on over his features, schooling himself as he had with his father. Aloof. Disinterested. Anything to pretend he wasn't as concerned as he truly was.

"Yes," he said simply. "You could." Phaedora lifted a brow. "But perhaps I would be faster and could end you before you had a chance."

Phaedora smiled slowly, a dark, sick thing that made Zryan's stomach twist and turn sour. "Yes." She paused, copying him. "You could. And then your sons would also die. There is a spell linked to my death . . . if I should die, everyone around the base of the mountain will die." Her eyes pinched with glee, her pretty mouth ruined by the smirk that replaced her smile.

Zryan felt cold, a chill slipping down his back.

"Why are you here? Why risk it?" he asked carefully. Spirits, what if someone else killed her thinking they were helping out? "You want something from me."

Phaedora's slow smile returned, honey-brown eyes warming with amusement. "You're right, I do." She paused, savoring the moment. "A kiss."

"What?" Zryan blinked in surprise.

"A kiss. And not just a simple one, but a true one. A kiss like you used to give me just before you'd take me to your bed."

Zryan laughed, cold and bitter. "You want a kiss?" Disbelief rang in his tone. She had come down from the mountain, pulled him away from the castle with this attack for a mere *kiss*?

"Yes. Give me a kiss, and I won't end the lives of both of your children." Any amusement left her face, and she stared back at him stone cold and bitter, the viper rising to the surface.

Zryan frowned, staring at her. She disgusted him. "Very well." What was a kiss?

Phaedora grinned and lifted her hand to quirk a finger at him.

Slowly, Zryan made his way down the alley toward her,

stopping within arm's reach. Lavender and amber overtook his senses, filling his nostrils and taking him back to the many nights they had spent together when Zryan had attempted to make the best of the life Ludari was forcing upon him.

She didn't move, simply watched him, waiting for him to fulfill his portion of the deal. Zryan reached out to slip his hand around the back of her neck and pulled her in firmly against him. His lips crushed down on hers, a growl releasing from him as he forced her lips open and his tongue grazed hers.

Phaedora murmured, her body softening. Her hands moved to clutch at his hair, and Zryan growled once more, wanting to bat her hands away but allowing it.

She was here, within his arms. He could so very easily wrap his hands around her neck and squeeze until her lips grew blue and the light faded in her eyes. He could end it all now. It wouldn't be that hard; his own affinity by far overtook her own. There were many fae who found themselves with minimal powers. Minor things that helped with day-to-day living but would never make them a fighting force. Phaedora was one such fae. With nothing but the ability to change the temperature of a room, or create a light breeze, she would never win a battle by her own might.

But Phaedora did not rely on her own abilities. That was why she had mastered the use of The Creaturae. Why she had so happily said yes to marrying a prince. A male of power. Because Phaedora schemed and haggled and manipulated others into fighting her battles for her.

Which was why she may have been lying about the spell connecting her death to the destruction of the valley around

Mount Pyrsos. But if she was telling the truth about what would happen if she died, then he would never forgive himself.

Alessia would never forgive him.

Any hope he had of fixing things with her would be gone.

He pulled back slightly, green eyes glinting with fury. "Is that enough?" He rasped, lightning crackling along the fingertips of his hand that lay loose at his side.

She smirked. "Mmm . . . not quite."

"Zryan!"

He froze, Alessia's voice ringing down the alleyway.

Phaedora's eyes glinted with triumph. "Now it is enough." With a hiss, Zryan shoved Phaedora away from him. She only laughed manically as she stumbled back, her hood falling to show off the long tumble of her soft brown waves. "You taste of wine." She licked her lips.

"Zryan?" Alessia's voice came again, then a howl of rage sounded.

Zryan spun to see the rage overtaking Alessia's features. Murder in her eyes and all sense of restraint gone from her.

Phaedora was laughing, her hand lifted in the air, fingers poised for a snap. Zryan's chest clenched. What would she do with those fingers? Which of his family would she take away from him should Alessia attack?

Spinning on his heel, Zryan raced back down the alley and tackled Alessia to the ground. His arms wrapped around her body, his hands moving up to cup the back of her head protectively as their bodies hit the stone below.

Beneath him, his wife raged, an angry scream echoing into the air.

9

Alessia

"What a pathetic sight to see. How anyone thinks *you're* the rightful queen of Lucem is beyond me." Phaedora laughed. "How does it feel, Alessia, to be so weak and *useless*?"

This went beyond the present days and dove deep into their youths, when Phaedora was trying her damnedest to pull Zryan's affection back to her. She hadn't been born with a strong affinity, nor was it very useful. A parlor trick at best. And Phaedora had loathed Alessia even more because it was a reminder of what she wasn't—strong and capable.

Alessia didn't hide behind a book.

"Don't listen to her, Alessia," Zryan rasped as her head crashed into his jaw.

Alessia writhed beneath him, struggling to get out from under the weight of his body. The more she struggled, the more his body bared down on her. "Get. Off." She growled with enough force that her throat ached. Fury rose within her to the point tears stung her eyes. Why wouldn't he allow her to end the bitch? Zryan had even said he'd end her himself. Now, he was letting her live another day to rain torment down on them all.

Phaedora's words echoed in her ears, and Alessia thrashed, beyond enraged with her. There was no word to describe the loathing she had for Phaedora or what she wanted her to endure.

Zryan only pushed her down more, refusing to roll over, refusing to let her attack that wicked bitch.

"Move now, you fool!" she hissed, pounding her fists against his sides with all her strength. *Damn the armor. Damn him.* "Get off! I am going to kill her!" Try as she may, his body didn't shift. It only angered her further.

"No!" Zryan pinned her legs with his, trapping her, then grabbed her arms and held them against the warm stones.

No wasn't the word she had expected from him. This was her chance to see the life drain from Phaedora's glittering gaze, and she could have been the one to embed a knife into her side too. But Zryan was meddling once again and allowing the retch to live, to continue to wreak havoc on their land.

They *both* had mocked her. Phaedora with her hands tight in his hair, lips and tongue melding with Zryan's. And Alessia had seen his tongue caressing hers.

"While I enjoy watching you reduce yourself to a feral idiot, I have plans to see to." With one more laugh in her direction, Phaedora disappeared around the corner.

Alessia sucked in precious breaths, and her chest heaved with the effort, but she couldn't get enough air. Tears of sheer anger and frustration spilled down her cheeks, burning her skin. Her chance at embedding a knife into Phaedora's heart—gone.

Too many damn times had he done this to her. She'd lost count as to how many dalliances he'd had, and when she wanted to retaliate and take a lover of her own, Zryan had punished them by reducing them to beggars.

Alessia screamed in frustration and slammed her head back. "I'm done with you. I am *done!*" Zryan stilled but didn't allow her up. "I will end this one way or another, but by the sun . . . Don't for one moment believe I'll be by *your* side when the dust settles." She sobbed in fury. He'd lied. *Lied again!*

This time, Zryan released her and rocked back on his heels. His jaw was set in a hard line, and she didn't care that she'd hurt him.

He had done it thousands of times to her, and she was done.

Zryan's shoulders slumped as he looked away from her. "Believe it or not, Alessia, I don't care if Phaedora rots. But if you attacked her, she would have killed you or had our boys slain. So there was a reason for me stopping you. As for the kiss—"

"I don't want to hear it." Alessia slid away from him and dusted herself off, but she kept a watchful eye on him as he sulked on the ground.

She loathed the way he looked in this moment—weak and vulnerable. He was more than that. Alessia swallowed roughly and turned on her heel, knowing that now was the time to withdraw from him, to focus on the impending war and the safety of those they loved.

"I hate her. For what she represents and certainly for what she has done. Don't convince yourself of anything else."

Her lip curled at his words. He did not know how much she truly hated that waste of flesh and bone. But now, his words were simply spoken things that meant absolutely *nothing*. For centuries, he had hurled pretty words at her, stroked her ego, and promised he'd change. Promise after promise lay broken at her feet, and Alessia was done with it. Because now, her kingdom was under attack because of his lack of action.

"Get up. We still have one more scorpion to kill—if the harpies haven't managed it already."

Now that the blood didn't pump through her ears, now that her screams had faded, Alessia could hear the cries of soldiers and feel the reverberations of the battle still raging. She didn't glance over her shoulder before she ran out of the alleyway and toward the sound of fighting.

When she rounded the corner, the harpies were in flight, poised with their swords at the ready. The remaining fae with an earth affinity dodged out of the way of the scorpion's lashing tail. They were attempting to replicate the earlier attack, but this beast seemed wise to their tactics.

Steam rose from the acid dripping from the barbed tail, and one unfortunate soldier wasn't fast enough as some of the liquid splattered against him. He shrieked, falling to the ground in anguish—but he didn't cry for long, as one of the beast's legs impaled him.

Alessia raced to the point beneath the harpies. "Draw it to the right so the vines can ensnare one of the pincers!" Zryan bounded into view just behind the thrashing scorpion, his eyes trained onto the sky, and it darkened. Electrical currents raced over her, but she spared no other thoughts as she ran across the gravel ground, this time with the scorpion homed in on her.

By the sun. I'm not sure how I'll get out of this one.

Rocks leaped up as the scorpion raced across the ground, threatening to send her careening to the dirt, but finally, the soldiers grew a vine large enough to smack against one of the pincers. It writhed like a living thing, then grew around the claw, tightening until it was trapped.

The abomination swung its tail, but Zryan called upon the sky, and lightning rained down, not on the shell but the tail. Blue currents licked along the hardened exterior, and Alessia wasn't certain it would do anything until a cry emitted from the scorpion.

She motioned for the soldiers to move to the left, but as they maneuvered around the creature, it lashed out with its free appendage, and when the soldiers scurried back, it attempted to cut the vine from itself.

The harpies dove at once, batting uselessly at the hardened shell, but it was all the time the soldiers needed, for they worked a large, whipping vine from the ground and it grew thicker than its twin. It coiled around the pincers so tightly, Alessia could hear it crunch.

The scorpion hissed lowly, then ran at her with its mouth open wide.

Alessia grabbed her sword from the scabbard and tightened her hold. She drew in a deep breath, and as the beast descended on her, all she heard were the bellows from all around.

She leaped upward the moment the beast crashed down on her, the inky, sour fangs parted, and she thrust her blade deep into the cavernous mouth. A loud pop sounded, then a rush of hot, blue blood coursed down Alessia.

She heard the snapping crunch, and then it collapsed around her.

Unable to keep the weight off of her, she crumpled to the ground.

Light streamed in from the cracks between the pincers, and hurriedly, soldiers rushed forward. The harpies batted them away and yanked away the corpse's pincer.

"Alessia! By the sun." Zryan grabbed her by the arms, pulling her to her feet. Thankfully, he kept a hold on her, for she wasn't certain if she could remain standing. Zryan frowned at her.

She blinked, pain radiating down her wrists, forearms, and shoulders. Despite the discomfort, she regarded the crumbled storefronts. Their once tall and sturdy pillars were knocked over, and the stone walls had collapsed from the beasts ramming into them.

Simple townsfolk lay in the streets, surrounded by their blood. Gaping wounds from where the acid had splashed against them were on display, showing off necrotic tissue.

Several fallen soldiers lay dead on the ground. Falling debris from the buildings had crushed some, and others were victims of the scorpion's tail.

This was all because of Phaedora.

"Are you all right, Your Majesty?" one harpy pressed. Her brow furrowed as she awaited Alessia's response.

"As fine as I can be." She realized Zryan was still steadying her and swiped his hands away. She grabbed his cape and wiped away the blue sludge from her face. He didn't complain, not that she thought he would. He seemed fairly disgusted with the blue slime himself, for he curled his lip as she cleansed her hands too.

With the threat here gone, Alessia needed to know her boys were alive and well. She needed to see them for herself.

"Half of the squadron can follow us to the mountain, but the rest are to remain behind to clean up. The harpies can remain behind too, since Ruan has his griffin forces with him." Just as the words left Alessia's mouth, the ground trembled with enough force that everyone stumbled. When she looked up toward Mount Pyrsos, her heart sank.

"Ruan and Kian!" Zryan roared and brought his fingers to his mouth, whistling for their mounts.

A thick plume of dark smoke streamed from the top of the mountain, and thick ash rained down, coating the tops of the evergreen trees. Some of the oaks burst into flames, their canopies like a torchlight.

The damn mountain is about to erupt!

"Get to your mounts, now!" Alessia cried out, calling for her griffin. Zissi swung his head around in irritation as she climbed on top of him. She didn't wait for everyone to join her; they'd catch up soon enough.

She needed to get to Pyrsos.

If Alessia had thought the sky's vantage point would make her feel any better, it did not. Heavy clouds of ash filled the immediate area, and although they weren't close enough to face the true effects of the eruption, the air tickled her throat and stung her eyes.

Zryan's griffin led the way, with Alessia close behind him.

"We need to get to the ground. The air is too heavy, and

the smoke is going to grow thicker the closer we are," he called to her. His cape billowed behind him as the harsh wind impeded their approach.

Fire snaked through the trees, angry and hungry as it lapped at the trunks, devouring them in plumes of smoke and flame.

From a distance, Alessia spotted a clearing with griffins bolting around. As they drew closer, she noticed ash peppered their feathers, but they were mostly unharmed by the heat of it from what she could discern.

Where are the riders?

Downhill, soldiers hunkered down with their shields covering them. Molten rocks glowed against the dirt and gray of ash.

"There!" She urged the griffin lower, and among the sound of tumbling rocks and snapping trees, she cried out, "Ruan! Kian!"

Golden shields shifted, and through the cracks that formed, she saw a familiar face peer out. Ruan.

Relief flooded her, but it didn't last long, for she heard the groaning of trees. "You need to get to the skies. Your griffins are still in the clearing, get to them now! Whoever doesn't have a mount, call out, and we will grab you. This clearing is going to be consumed in fire any moment."

Fear threatened to constrict her heart so tightly, she thought it'd burst. But Alessia didn't have time for that, not as the mountain shook again.

Alessia whipped around to face Zryan, and his face paled by the second.

"This isn't right." His eyes flicked to the mountain. "I know this feeling."

She ground her teeth as he spoke in riddles. "What are you on about?" Unease crept up her spine and stiffened every muscle in her body.

If Zryan was less than confident about the situation, none of this boded well for them.

10

Zryan

Zryan blinked, a piece of ash stuck on the end of one lash, and stared up at the erupting mountain. While clouds of hot ash and embers raining over the land, blistering skin and setting trees ablaze should have been terrifying enough on its own, it was the thrum of magic below that truly made his blood run cold.

He knelt and pressed the palm of his hand to the earth. Beneath the soil, magical ley lines traveled through Lucem, all connecting at one starred point beneath Mount Pyrsos. The apex of where most assumed fae life had begun. While the ley lines had hummed before, now they raged with chaotic amounts of energy. Zryan lifted his head and looked up at Alessia.

"Whatever she is doing is happening right now. We're too late to stop it." His fear and concern was reflected in his wife's face. His wife, whose marriage-ending words he hadn't even had a moment to reflect on or register. Not while his kingdom was in such disarray. His personal hell would have to wait until a later date.

As if to echo his words, the ground shook once more, and the mountain rumbled harder, a large spew of ash and rocks spraying into the air. Soldiers ran toward the clearing with the griffins, shields raised over their heads to protect them from the flesh-searing flakes.

"We have to move back!" Alessia shouted, then a blinding light flashed from the mountain.

Zryan grabbed his velvet cape and brought it up, ducking his head into the dark folds of it. He still had to pinch his eyes shut at the light that shone through the thick fabric. It lasted for both an eternity and a mere fraction of time, the ground shaking harshly enough that Zryan pitched forward onto his elbow, and he heard a soft mutter of pain from Alessia as she, too, was knocked off her feet.

Just as abruptly as it had started, it ended. The world was silent and still; the brightness retreated to the normal sunshine of the day. The mountain itself settled, the imminent eruption suddenly stilled. Whatever had happened must have been from the ley line activity. Which meant either Phaedora had succeeded, or she was dead.

Zryan dropped his cape and looked up. Smoke still clouded the skies, leaving the land overcast, burning trees dotted along the landscape adding to the plumes. Before he could ask Alessia if she was all right, Ruan was at her side lifting her back to her feet.

Zryan climbed to his own, quickly scanning both his wife and son over to ensure they were unharmed. They appeared to be whole.

"What was that?" Ruan questioned.

Zryan shoved a hand over his short-cropped hair for no reason other than to soothe himself. "Nothing good.

Phaedora has drawn heavily upon the ley lines, which can only mean whatever she is doing requires more magic than even the book itself possesses." Their eyes met, and a silent understanding lay between them. What if she had made something with that power? *Would they be able to defeat whatever it was?*

He lifted his hand to squeeze his son's shoulder, near to his neck where the armor didn't extend. He masked his own doubts and bolstered his confidence. Now was not the time to be showing weakness, no matter how inefficient or ill-prepared he felt for what was to come.

There was a good chance that when this was through, his family would lay in tatters. He could not have Ruan going into this battle doubting their proficiency as a ruling body.

"We're going to go into the mountain," Zryan declared.

"How?" Ruan growled. "What about the barrier?"

"I have a feeling, with the amount of power that was unleashed, that it's down."

"Zryan, we can't risk it," Alessia cautioned.

"We'll send a griffin through." Kian's voice sounded behind them as he landed, his gold griffin snapping its jaws.

Ruan growled but nodded at his brother's suggestion.

"Are you okay?" Alessia was quick to ask.

"I'm fine." Kian climbed from the saddle, releasing his mount's reins and moving to stand with them.

Sighing, Zryan nodded as well. "We'll use mine." He brought his fingers to his lips and whistled. Feroces, hearing his beloved master call, trotted over. His front claws dug into the earth, and his fierce eyes darted around to the others before landing affectionately upon Zryan.

He was from a long line of fierce steads that had served

him well. All of them loyal, dedicated mounts who let no one but their sovereign king fly upon them. Zryan brushed his hand over Feroces' beak and into the white feathers of his head.

"Father, you don't have to," Kian said. "We can use another from the infantry."

They all knew how much Zryan loved his griffins.

Zryan shook his head. "No, it should be mine if we're going to chance it." He wouldn't ask the sacrifice of his soldiers. He stepped away from Feroces. "Go to the mountain!" he called to the beast and pointed. Smacking his hind quarters, he watched the griffin take off, loping with a strong, even gate. He was as graceful on the ground as he was in the air.

As a family, they shifted to watch the griffin, waiting to see if he would continue unheeded or if he would turn to ash as so many others had. Zryan's blood pounded in his ears, his doubt starting to circle as he waited to see if he had killed his favorite stead.

"It's down," Kian sighed in relief.

Zryan's head whipped to look at him. "What?"

"It's down," he repeated.

"He's past where the other soldiers were when they were ashed," Ruan added.

Zryan's own sigh of relief was issued, and he nodded. "Then let's go check out the interior of the mountain."

"Carefully," Alessia interjected. "Let's not just go rushing in there and trip another trap or get ourselves all blasted to bits by that psychotic woman and her book." Her face was lined with apprehension and fury. Filled with a motherly instinct to protect, she was ready to kill.

"Of course not, Mother." Ruan leaned in to press a kiss to her cheek, a defiant glint in his dark brown eyes belying the truth. He'd like nothing better than to stampede into that mountain and hack away at anyone and anything in arm's reach.

So bloodthirsty.

Zryan whistled for Feroces to return, and when he had, he swiftly mounted, joining the rest of his family. Together, they headed toward Pyrsos, a small contingent of soldiers trailing behind.

At the mouth of the cave that led deep into the mountain, they dismounted, leaving their griffins behind to carefully make their way inside. No sound echoed up to them except the soft drip of water and the crunch of their own sandaled feet over the ground. The heat inside the tunnels was overwhelming, leaving Zryan's throat parched and his cheeks flushed. Sweat beaded along his hairline, and he swiped at it with the back of his hand.

Darkness encased them as they made their way deeper into the earth, but as they neared the bottom, a light shone, inviting them into a large cavern.

Its vaulted ceilings were high, though not open to the sky. That portion of the mountain lay above. Along the far corner, a large river of lava flowed, disappearing into the stones. Flowing to places unknown. Etched into the walls were hooks and shelves, bearing not only tools for smithing but the possessions of Calor himself. A makeshift bed sat in a small hole dug into one side of the rock, while chairs and a table made up a dining section in the other.

But the largest, most prominent thing in the cavern was Calor's workstation that lay just a few feet away from the lava stream. Far enough away to be safe from the heat, but close enough to be of use during his fabrications.

Swords and armor lined the free walls of the cavern, while spare sheets of metal and rods leaned in a corner.

Once upon a time, Zryan had made his way into this cavern to find Calor, a nobleman turned recluse from Ludari's day, and beg him to come to the palace to teach his youngest son how to become a smithy. Calor had handcrafted all of Ludari's armor and weapons, until he had finally been driven away by the bloodshed and tyranny that were a large part of his father's reign.

The cavern was empty except for Calor, seated on one of the chairs at the small table near the cabinets along one wall. Not even his apprentice, Mal, was present. The recluse sat with legs crossed beneath him on the chair and his eyes focused on something far in the distance, vague and empty.

Zryan knelt before him, waving his hand in front of his face. Calor did not even blink.

He felt a presence at his back and looked up to see Alessia. "Do you think you can get into his head?"

"Get out of my way."

When he moved, Alessia took his place, tipping Calor's face up with her fingertip so that she could look into his eyes. She stared intensely at him for a moment, making the connection that typically let her invade someone's mind. But instead of planting something there, she hissed, wincing in pain, and jerked back.

"Alessia!" Zryan reached out a hand to her, but she shook him off, standing.

"He's been spelled. We won't get into his mind until whoever did this to him lets us in."

"By the sun!" Zryan growled, looking around them. "Where has she gone?"

None of it made any sense. Someone had been in here, and he was positive it had been Phaedora. Yet the cavern was unoccupied save for the old blacksmith and the open pit of lava he used as his forge.

"Did she escape out the back side of the mountain?" Alessia questioned.

"No," Ruan was quick to interject. "We've had both tunnels covered this entire time."

"Are we sure?" Zryan asked. "Even with the volcanic ash falling from the sky?"

His eldest son's eyes narrowed, as if Zryan were questioning his very integrity as a soldier. "Yes, we are sure."

"Well, she must have left something behind. Ruan, you continue to look the cavern over, leave no corner undiscovered. I will take Calor back to the palace to be seen by a healer. Perhaps Corsica or Pokrates will be able to lift the spell on him."

"I'll come with you," Kian offered.

"And I will remain here with Ruan," Alessia finished.

Zryan wanted to protest. To remind Alessia that not too long ago, Phaedora had sent an assassin after her. But he knew it would be a waste of his breath. Instead, he looked at Ruan. "Keep a guard with her at all times." Ruan nodded, while Alessia glowered behind him.

With a careful touch, he and Kian slipped their hands beneath Calor's arms and hoisted him up to his feet. He stood and walked when gently prodded, but his blank stare never ceased nor changed.

"Be cautious." He looked at Alessia, who nodded briefly,

then he and Kian took Calor up the tunnel and carefully placed him on the back of Zryan's griffin.

After instructing the soldiers outside to go down and assist with the exploration of the cavern, as well as to circle the Pyrsos to ensure nothing had been missed, he and Kian launched into the sky, making the journey back to the palace.

Landing in the courtyard, he slid off his griffin, handing him off to a stablehand while he helped Calor to the ground. With Kian at his side, they led the recluse into the palace.

There was a hush over the palace that made Zryan's skin tingle with apprehension. Something wasn't right. He wasn't sure what it was, but something was off.

"Kian, take Calor to the healer, I need to check the throne room."

It was a gut feeling, one he couldn't explain, that led him in that direction. He walked cautiously down the marble hall, the hair at the back of his neck standing up. Nothing, however, could have prepared him for what he found waiting for him.

Seated upon Zryan's throne, legs spread wide and extended before him, elbow resting on the arm rest while the other hand sprawled in his lap, was Ludari. Former king of Lucem and the three realms. Zryan's father.

Zryan nearly staggered but managed to maintain his composure—just barely. His heart beat erratically, and there was a fine sheen of cold sweat building over his skin. This wasn't possible. Draven, Travion, and he had slain their father, sliced his body into pieces and left him scattered over the seas of the middle realm, buried in the depths by those who could control both land and water.

Ludari smirked at him, his blue eyes focused on Zryan. Rage and triumph intermingled in their depths. To his side stood Phaedora, the Creaturae held daintily in her hands, resting against her chest. Her lovely face beamed with pride.

"Father!"

Zryan's heart sank, and he tensed, turning in the direction of the voice he would recognize anywhere. *Brione.*

"No," he rasped, swallowing against the scream of rage and fear building inside of him. His daughter knelt to the side of the throne room, bottom propped up on her heels. Around her delicate wrists, they had clamped heavy irons which chained her to the floor. "Are you okay?" he asked, taking a step toward her.

"Do not move," Ludari boomed, his voice, as always, echoing across the room with barely any effort.

Zryan froze, muscles tensing, and slowly, he looked back to his own throne, currently seized by his worst nightmare.

"Hello, Father." Zryan's voice was surprisingly steady, even flippant, as he met the other male's gaze. He squared his shoulders to stare him down, even as the memories flooded back.

Ludari, leaning down toward him when he was a little boy, letting him know what a disappointment he was. How Zryan changing himself into a peacock or a griffin was nothing in comparison to what he could do, to what his brothers could do.

Ludari, striking him with the back of his hand across the face, drawing blood as he spat words of disdain. He was shameful. Weak. He would never make anything of himself with all his dandy ways. He was as useless as his mother.

Ludari, standing over the lifeless body of Zryan's mother.

Her beautiful green eyes grown clouded and dark as they stared unseeing up at the ceiling.

Every bit of the rage, shame, and pain from his youth rushed back all at once, swirling around Zryan like a tornado capturing every bit of debris it could, anchored down or not. Lightning crackled at his fingertips and flickered up and over his bare arms, tickling the skin and making his body itch to throw it. He brought his hands together before him and formed a large ball of the blue snapping energy, prepared to throw it at the monster seated on his throne.

"I wouldn't do that if I were you," a smooth voice purred from the side of the throne room.

Carefully, Zryan glanced over, the lightning still sizzling in his hands. A tall, lean male with coal-black hair falling to his chin and an angular face stood over Brione, a blade to her throat. A growl formed somewhere low in Zryan's stomach, rolling up through his chest and ripping through his throat. "Step away from her right now," he warned.

The bright-eyed male tutted and shook his head. "I'm afraid you are not the one calling the shots here."

A deep, throaty laugh echoed through the chamber, bouncing off the walls. Ludari leaned forward, a show of dominance, though as Zryan eyed him, he could see through the show to the weakness that lay beneath. Ludari was not at full strength yet. Phaedora had used the book to bring him back to life, and there was still a lot of healing to be done in a body that had been dead for as long as his had. One whose soul should have been lost to the afterlife and unretrievable. Was that why Phaedora had needed the powers of creation in Pyrsos? Because the resurrection spell in the Creaturae wouldn't have been enough on its own. Not for someone whose spirit was not present in one of the realms.

"You're not the one in control here, Zryan; you never were. I was always going to find my way back." Ludari reached out his hand to rest it on Phaedora's back. "There are some who recognize true strength for what it is and will not tolerate having a farce ruling the kingdom."

"Funny," Zryan drawled, eyeing Phaedora disdainfully. "I thought it was simply that she hadn't had a good lay in over twenty-eight hundred years."

Phaedora blanched at the snide comment, clutching the book more tightly to her. "You have no idea who I've been with or what I've done since you so callously cast me away."

Ludari snorted, settling back against the throne once more. "My son, little better than a pleasure slave." His blue eyes, which were so much like Draven and Travion's, settled upon him, contempt in their depths.

It was hard, not letting Ludari's withering opinion of him settle back into his bones. Not to take every rebuke and condemnation to heart. What should he care what this demon thought? This vile creature who'd had enough of his wife bearing him sons and decided she was of no further use to him, who had strangled her in her own bed chambers. Tightened his hands around her throat and squeezed until he'd crushed the very life out of her.

He'd taken the only being to love him, at least until Alessia came along. Crushed the only spot of joy and peace Zryan knew in the world.

It had driven Zryan to usurp him. To free his brothers and aid them in slitting his throat and driving a twelve-inch blade beneath his ribs and up into his heart.

"Better a giver of pleasure than a mule's asshole," Zryan sniped back. From the corner of his eyes, he watched the tall male who stood over Brione, wondering if there was a way to disarm him and set her free before Ludari could take him out. "You're on my throne. I'll kindly ask you to leave before I have to make you."

Ludari snarled and snapped his fingers at Phaedora. At his side, she muttered words from the book and flung out her hand, and a wave of magic hit Zryan squarely in the chest. His body flew backward and directly into the column behind him; his back spasmed and cracked, air rushing from his lungs as he dropped to the floor.

His ears rang, and his heart fought to find its natural rhythm. Groaning, he propped himself up on his hands just as Ludari began to speak.

"You have two choices, *my boy*." He said "my boy" the same way one would talk to an animal they did not care about. "Take your place beside Phaedora and accept my rule . . . "

Zryan climbed to his feet. "Oh please, do tell me what the second option is."

Ludari smirked, in that way he did when Zryan attempted to be mouthy and would then make him pay later in so many more ways than he could have ever imagined. "Or run. Otherwise, I will have Mal slice that knife through your precious daughter's throat."

Phaedora squawked. "But could we not just keep him?" Zryan watched her half turn toward Ludari. "You promised me—" Her words halted at the withering glare Ludari cast her way, and like a weak, obedient mouse, she shrank back into her place, lips closing.

As if he had not been interrupted, Ludari returned his gaze to Zryan. "So, what will it be?"

Zryan looked to Brione, who knelt on the floor with such grace and composure, her head held high even though there was a silver blade resting against the column of her neck. Her bright green eyes peered back at him with such bravery, it made a lump form in his throat.

His sweet little girl. How could he leave her?

She must have seen it in his eyes because she gave a miniscule shake of her head. "Go, Papa," she murmured. "I'll be okay."

Zryan gritted his teeth and returned his gaze to Ludari. "*My* throne is not yours. You may momentarily sit upon it, but I will never let you live."

Ludari let his head fall back, dark auburn swatches reflecting the light overhead, and laughed a deep-belly laugh. When he was done, he stood. He made an impressive figure: tall, broad shouldered, and typically covered in solid muscle. He was thinner than he used to be, and Zryan could only assume the muscles had not yet grown back in. "You may have been able to manipulate people into doing your dirty work for you once upon a time, but trust me, boy, I do not make the same mistake twice, and you will find my guard will not be down again."

"And Zryan," Phaedora added. "Please do thank Travion for me. Bringing his wife back from the dead helped me work out the final kinks to the resurrection spell."

Zryan hissed, but before he could say anything, she lashed out with the book, clearly having made her choice in who she served, and murmured words he could not hear.

The force that hit him, like a solid wall, drove him back

through the very doors of the throne room and sent him skidding several feet down the hall, until he crashed into one of the marble statues of himself. It crashed to the floor, a shattering noise following it. When he managed to open his eyes, breathing through ribs that felt broken, he found the carved copy of his own face lying there, staring up at him.

"Father?" It was Kian, kneeling down to carefully help him to his feet, despite the wince of sharp pain lancing through his side into his back.

"Ludari," Zryan breathed out, "is back."

11

Alessia

Outside the mouth of the cavern, Ruan mounted his griffin. The beast shook its head, gold and black feathers expanding as he did so.

"I just don't know how they escaped under our noses when we had the only two entrances covered. No one could have emerged from the top while the eruption occurred." Every muscle in his forearms tensed, and Alessia knew he longed to throttle the answer out of Calor. She did too, but it would do no good since he was spelled and she couldn't undo the ensorcellment without the book. Trying would only cause a blinding ache to throb behind her eyes.

"I'm going to make one more pass around the mountain to see if Kian and I missed anything."

Alessia doubted it. However, if it gave her son peace and something to do without pacing a trench into the mountainside, so be it.

She nodded and watched as the griffin's wings beat at the air, lifting the pair from the ground and toward the clouded sky.

There had to be something they were all missing. With a heavy sigh, Alessia stormed into the depths of the cavern once again.

Jagged stone walls and a smooth floor greeted her. The only light present was from the fae-light sconces illuminating the space, but it couldn't reach the deep corners. It wasn't that Alessia doubted Kian and Ruan's thoroughness, for she knew they were both meticulous. However, there had to be some way Phaedora—or whomever else had been with Calor—escaped.

Alessia assessed the walls, wondering if there might be a passageway behind them. Not trusting the light in the cavern, she reached forward, beginning to pore over the walls with her eyes, then patted them down with her hands.

She walked along the wall until she came to a table and had to step back. Eyeing it, she leaned down to inspect it. There was a small drawer with a bronze knob, and she reached for it, pulling it out.

Alessia expected to find notes, inkwells, and perhaps an odd collection of crystals given that it was Calor. Instead, there was a gold cuff with Phaedora's family crest welded to it, a pearl hairbrush, and a glass bottle. She lifted it, barely reaching her nose when she smelled the strong scent of lilacs.

This wasn't a quick stashing. Phaedora had been *living* here?

Rage blossomed within her chest, squeezing her lungs. She ran to Calor's wardrobe, sliding his ragged togas aside, and spied elegant dresses in shades of gold, pink, and light blue. A piece of paper fluttered from the dresses and Alessia snatched it from the ground.

If you're reading this, Alessia, I'm coming for your home, then your husband, then your children.

"You bitch," she hissed. She crumpled the paper in her grasp and threw it to the ground. Phaedora was only toying with them. That much was clear given she'd had time to leave a petty token behind. Now infused with the need to know how comfortable Phaedora had been here, she searched every nook, every cranny, until her efforts and drive had her breathless.

"Mind telling me what that was about?" Ruan muttered beneath his breath as he approached. He must have returned during her frenzied search.

When she turned to address him, he was only a few feet away, but his eyes weren't focusing on her.

"Phaedora was living here. Or she planted things to make it look that way. But I highly doubt she had enough time to extract everything." Alessia curled her fingers into fists. Calor would suffer for aiding Phaedora.

Ruan's brow furrowed, but his eyes focused on a spot behind her on the wall. "Wait," he growled and moved forward, his palm flattening against the stone mere inches from where she'd been. "I didn't see this before."

Upon further inspection, a small piece of stone jutted out. It didn't look out of place, but when Ruan shoved against it, the wall of stone shifted back, allowing enough space for them to move forward but not travel anywhere. As he did so, something glimmered into existence.

Instead of the wall giving way to a stairwell or another room, a veil shimmered before them, rippling like a pool of water.

Of course it was a veil!

With a portal, it was easy for one to slip under anyone's detection.

"I wonder where it leads to. One way to find out." Ruan extended his hand, and Alessia went to bat his hand away, but before she could, the veil pulsed, zapping him and sending a shockwave through the cave.

Alessia fell to the ground, catching herself just before her head smacked against the stone. She shook her head and focused on Ruan's prone body.

Panic and fear wound their way through her. Was he alive? Breathing?

He groaned, letting her know he was, in fact, still with her. Then Ruan swore.

She crawled to him, reaching beneath his head, and turned his face toward her. *No blood.* But blood meant nothing. Ruan could have easily broken a bone, snapped his spine, anything.

He blinked rapidly, and she surmised she would have to keep him from falling unconscious.

"Ruan," she said firmly, "you will stay awake. By the sun, I demand you stay awake!" She shifted her hand over his plated chest and felt as it rose and fell quicker than before.

He was stubborn, like her—both a blessing and a curse.

She couldn't help but smile as he sat up and stared angrily at the wall where the veil had been.

Had been.

"I'm awake," he coughed out, rubbing at his eyes.

Alessia darted to her feet and stared at the jagged space where the portal had been moments ago. "Damn them. They knew we'd find it and laid a trap out. Wherever the veil led, they didn't want us following. Likely their main hideout, if this is their workshop. I can only imagine where they are now."

Ruan joined her, and just as he was readying to reach the stones, footsteps drew nearer.

"No need to wonder. I know where they are," Zryan's grim tone came.

Alessia spun around to face him. No light shimmered within the depths of his gaze. Kian stepped up beside him, frowning.

"Where are they? Have you assembled the military then?" She crossed the distance between them, and the pause after her words had her heart sinking deep into her gut.

Zryan shifted his jaw. "Ludari is alive."

Alessia had only felt the icy fingers of dread like this once before, and it was while she was huddled in her cell in the depths of Ludari's palace, wondering when the next assault would come. When he'd force her to inflict torture on his prisoners—including his sons.

Ice ran through her veins again as she stared at her husband. "What do you mean?"

"That magical pulse? It was Phaedora. She used the book . . . "

Zryan may have said more than that, but Alessia's heart pounded so rapidly within her chest that it deafened her. She swallowed once—twice.

"Let me get this straight. Ludari lives again, and they have the book?" Ruan bit out.

Alessia gritted her teeth as she half growled and half screamed. She should have killed her in that alley. She should have driven a blade into her heart. She should have tried to end her there. And as much as she cherished her children's lives, a kingdom where Ludari ruled was no mercy; it was a sentence to the darkest, most torturous of places.

Even more so because they were of his blood and posed a threat to his claim on the throne.

"And she was living here, beneath our noses." She motioned around them, her voice shaking with fury.

Surprise filtered into Zryan's eyes, and Kian growled. She wondered how he felt that his master of the arts had betrayed the family in such a way.

Family.

Alessia's gaze homed in on the mouth of the cavern, expecting her daughter to walk through any moment, but when she didn't, every inch of her froze.

"Where is Brione?" her voice came out a touch too panic-stricken for her liking, but judging by the grimace Kian wore and the guilt rising in Zryan's gaze, his hesitance to speak . . . "What have you done?" she whispered.

"I had no choice but to leave her. They had a knife to her throat, and the book—"

She struck him before he could finish and would have landed more blows if Ruan hadn't wrapped his arms around her and yanked her away. He released her once she was no longer lunging.

"You left our daughter with that monster! You know . . . you know what he is capable of, and you left her!" Her body shook as the words tumbled from her lips in a roar that tore at her throat.

Tears of rage, hurt, and despair spilled down her cheeks.

Zryan stepped closer but then seemed to think better of it, for he took a step back and shook his head. "I did what I had to because leaving her alive was better than seeing her torn apart in front of me. I couldn't live with that."

But Alessia knew that sometimes living was worse than death. Sometimes, death was a mercy, and *that* was what petrified her most.

Despite her fears, fury blazed within, and she cast her gaze upon Zryan. He'd heard her, but the disgust and rage simmering beneath the surface must have bubbled over, for he looked away from her.

She tamped her feelings down and leaned on the one thing she could do right now: rule.

"Here is what we will do. We will head back to Edessa with our infantry and join up with the harpies and soldiers who stayed behind for cleanup. There is no use trying to fight while we're all exhausted and likely famished. Eden's family manor is in town; we will camp there and come up with a plan."

Ruan nodded. "Kian and I will gather the troops and head out." With that, he and Kian left the cave.

Alessia didn't want to linger behind, and she certainly didn't want any alone time with the foolish male standing there.

"I'm sorry I had to leave our baby girl behind."

She couldn't look at him, but she could only assume there was visible anguish, for his voice was rough and he sounded utterly broken.

A moment ticked by, and she thought of answering him, but she couldn't bring herself to form any words.

So, she left the cave.

And while Alessia didn't fault him for his inability to predict the future, she most certainly faulted him for his lack of action. He didn't strike Phaedora down when he should have. Not in the alley, but so long ago.

She was wicked then and worse now.

Now that she thought about it, Phaedora had promised Naya Damaris something. What if she'd promised to resurrect her husband—Eden's father?

By the sun. How large was her web?

What did she promise her followers?

What had she done already?

Damaris Manor was a sight to behold. Four alabaster columns supported the upper balcony, and swirling foliage embellished the marble trim outside. A stately house for certain, boasting what Lelantos had done for Lucem as a member of Zryan's council.

She swallowed the bitter taste growing on her tongue. It seemed everyone who aided Zryan or was in his company soon fell victim to misfortune.

Alessia pinched the bridge of her nose and cast her gaze upon a nearby cherry tree full of pink blooms, and behind it, a wisteria vine along a trellis, its purple flowers cascading downward.

The head of the household staff emerged from the black double doors and wound their way down the iron-railed stairwell.

A wiry female with hair the shade of coal and eyes the hue of a lake stared at her. "Your Majesty, to what do we owe the pleasure?" She glanced to the side to see Zryan and stammered, "Majesties, I'm sorry."

"I wish it were a pleasure, but it isn't. I'm sure by now you've heard of the attacks not far from here, but what you don't know is that the palace has been seized." She tried to find the right words to say, but there were none other than the simple, "Ludari is back."

The female, whether she was old enough to remember or simply knew history, paled a great deal and motioned toward the door.

"Come in. We will do whatever we can to help, but I'm afraid our stores are low, as we only keep a maintenance stock for when her Ladyship decides to show."

Alessia smiled tiredly. "We mostly need a place to rest, but eating would be great too."

"My name is Danae, should you need anything, Your Majesties. Let me show you in." Danae led the way up the stairs and inside the manor.

Naya Damaris may have been a wretched female, but she knew how to keep a manor. One word came to mind as Alessia walked through the foyer: lavish. Murals were painted on coffered ceilings, and if she wasn't mistaken, the trim was lined in gold, lending warmth to the inside. However, cold emanated from the marble flooring, contrasting with that feeling.

"This way. I'm sure her Ladyship wouldn't mind you using her room." Danae wound her way across the foyer to a grand staircase and up to the second floor.

Paintings taller than her decorated the wall, but Alessia focused on the housekeeper as she turned down another hall.

Danae stopped abruptly, and Alessia nearly collided with her.

The housekeeper smiled as she stepped back, bowing her head. "Here we are, Your Majesty. Make yourself comfortable, and I'll do my best to gather things for as many of you as I can."

"Thank you," she murmured and stepped inside. A four-poster bed sat in the middle of the room, furnished with powder-pink sheets. *So very Eden.*

Alessia crossed the room, searching for a water basin. She found it at the vanity in the far corner, and as luck would have it, a pitcher of water too.

Just as relief swept through her, something rolled out from beneath the bed. She stiffened, half expecting someone to spring forth at her with a blade in hand.

Yet all she saw was a bat-eared goblin smiling up at her with needle-like teeth. They looked most apologetic, especially as their ears drooped downward.

A series of gurgling purrs left them, and then they mimed sweeping.

They were cleaning? So they opted to remain behind?

Alessia shook her head and took up the water, pouring it into the bowl. In the mirror, she saw as Zryan stepped into the room but didn't meet her gaze. His eyes were on the floor, but she could tell by the way he held himself, with much less confidence than usual, that he was still feeling her earlier barbs.

"I was about to suggest calling my brothers."

"Already on that, this isn't something to keep to ourselves." She withdrew the blade tucked away in her armor and pricked her fingertips. Blood trickled into the water, staining it. She murmured the spell, concentrating on Draven and Travion until their faces came into view.

"This had better be a good call, Alessia," Travion drawled. His brows were drawn inward, concern swirling in his gaze.

"Afraid not," Zryan said from behind her.

Draven only swore, but he motioned impatiently for them to continue.

"Ludari is alive." No sooner had the words left Alessia's mouth than Draven slammed his fists down onto his table, and his face loomed dangerously close to the bowl.

"In the Veil, *now!*" he roared in a fury so tangible that Alessia felt Zryan stiffen behind her.

Travion said nothing, only nodded, and his call ended.

She pushed away from the vanity, not sparing a glance at Zryan as she briskly left the room with Zryan hot on her heels.

If they could band together, perhaps they had a chance after all, but the fight couldn't be in Lucem. Not while the suns shone, posing a threat to Draven's life. And Midniva had just suffered so greatly.

There was a way the three realms could win, but they *all* needed to work together.

Together.

12

Zryan

The Veil was as twisted and eerie as always, even more so since the spirits Ludari had trapped there long ago had been dispersed during Naya's attack on Lucem. Light and shadows mingled through the vast emptiness. The path leading to the gates into each realm, as always, shifted out of view the moment eyes were laid upon it.

Draven and Eden were already waiting by the time Zryan and Alessia appeared on their griffins. The black kelpies at the head of Draven's chariot whinnied uncomfortably, while the griffins only eyed them with a keen predator's gaze.

His oldest brother carried the appearance of a storm cloud, blue eyes so stormy, they almost appeared black. His gray velvet cape swept along the nonexistent floor of the Veil as he climbed down from his chariot, offering a hand to his wife, who wore a light purple gown threaded with vines of black and a soft gray cape of her own lined with fur.

"How has this happened?" he growled, storming forward.

Zryan held up his hand as he hopped off his griffin, his

broken ribs screaming in pain at the sudden action. Though he said nothing, he could see the way Eden's eyes flickered with recognition. "While I am sure you're ready to join Alessia in the finger pointing, let us wait until Travion is here to help you."

Beside him, Alessia stiffened more—if that were possible—and moved to stand before her brother- and sister-in-law with her hands on her hips.

Before Draven could react, the sound of horse hooves sounded through the Veil and disappeared without an echo into the dense expanse. Travion and Sereia appeared as if out of the shadows themselves, both riding their own majestic mounts. Travion was dressed in a pair of dark blue trousers with high riding boots and a double-breasted jacket, his auburn hair—just a shade lighter than Draven's—tumbled in wild abandon. His bride, the newly queened Sereia, slid off her horse as it came to a stop, legs clad in her own pair of tight slacks, knee-high brown boots covering most of them, and frilly white blouse clutched to her chest by a dark brown leather vest etched in gold symbols of Midniva. She looked more pirate than queen.

"Travion is here," Draven drawled lowly. "So, speak."

Travion quirked a brow at their eldest brother. "Well, hello to you as well," he jeered, then turned his attention to Zryan and Alessia.

"We knew Phaedora was using power from the ley lines for something and that she had closed herself off in Mount Pyrsos. However, when Ruan attempted to get into the mountain, his scouting party was turned to ash." This announcement was met with grumbles and curses all around. Zryan took a slow breath, mindful of his ribs, before he continued. "Today, the mountain began to rumble and spew ash. We thought it was about to erupt, but then there was a strong disruption in the ley lines, and I knew it could only be creation magic at work."

"Where is Ludari now? Where did you find him?" Travion cut in.

Zryan huffed. His brother never just allowed him to finish with his thoughts. "He sits on my throne, with Phaedora and the book beside him."

"What?!" Draven spat with incredulity. "Did you just stand up and move out of his way?"

Zryan flinched internally. Of course Draven would think he didn't have the courage to face Ludari alone—after all, he'd required the help of Draven and Travion to take Ludari down the first time. "No," he said with casual irritation. "While we were investigating the mountain, he seized the throne."

"The throne and our *daughter*," Alessia added.

Zryan didn't bother looking at his wife, not needing to see more of her absolute disappointment in him reflected on her face. "He forced me out using Brione against me. They have her chained in the throne room. And somewhere in the palace, Lord Seducere's daughter also remains." Ludari held too many captives at his fingertips. Too many nobles and servants that he could use to force Zryan to heel.

"But he was just brought back?" Sereia's voice sounded out, one of her hands moving to rest over her abdomen, where her own death blow had been dealt just a few weeks prior. "He can't be at full capacity yet. If she used the resurrection spell, it heals you enough to come back, but it doesn't finish the work."

Zryan was reminded of Phaedora's parting words to him. *Please do thank Travion for me. Bringing his wife back from the dead helped me work out the final kinks to the resurrection spell.*

"He's not. Even in his strength, I could see weakness. He will take time to be back at full force," Zryan answered her.

"Then what are we waiting for?" She looked amongst them all. "Let us go now and end him *and* Phaedora once and for all!"

"No," Travion said simply. "We cannot."

"But why?!" she hissed, angry confusion flitting over her face.

"The Creaturae," Draven cut in, and Travion nodded. "Ludari and Phaedora are the two most skilled people with the book, and between them, we will never be able to take them down as we are."

Sereia made a noise of frustration.

"Perhaps I am missing something here," Eden murmured. "But if he is so powerful with the book, how did the three of you manage to kill him the first time?"

While the realms knew of the defeat of Ludari and that it was his three sons banded together who managed to do it, the details were scattered, and history tomes did not tell it all.

Zryan remembered walking into his mother's chambers, looking to speak with her, only to find that his father had killed her, stolen the life out of her because he was done with her. No longer wished for her to bear him children and saw no other reason to keep her at his side.

It had been the last straw for Zryan. While he hadn't found it in himself to fight for his own sake, the death of the mother, who had shielded him when she could, cared for him when he was little, and raised him to adulthood, had left Zryan not caring what his father did to him so long as he was able to end his life in return.

"I shifted into a woman and snuck into the dungeons. It was easy to seduce the guards there, and while they were distracted, steal the keys." Zryan had watched others. Noting the way they interacted with each other. How their eyes followed the ones they were most interested in. Because he kept as out of Ludari's way as possible, Zryan had often been forgotten about, and it had left him plenty of time to learn how to read people. He had known exactly the female to shift into to capture both of the guards' attention. Known just the words to say, the touches to offer for them to be completely besotted. "Once Draven and Travion were out of their cells, it was easy to overpower the guards who protected the Creaturae."

His brothers had doubted him at first—after all, he was the son their sire kept out of the dungeons. How did they know he wasn't letting them out for some new game of Ludari's? But when Zryan told them of their mother's death, they had seen the hatred in his eyes, heard it in his voice, and understood that their youngest brother, who they were meeting for the first time, was indeed looking to take the tyrant down.

Draven's shadows carried them unseen through the palace, and once they had snuck into the room where the book lay, the three of them were easily able to overpower the guards inside. Fire, lightning, and wind assailed them until there was nothing left but the three brothers and the Creaturae. Once they'd possessed it, Zryan felt invincible.

What was taking on his tyrannical monster of a father after that?

"And without the book, he was just any other fae." Draven's face was dark, pinched at the lips and mouth. He, too, was clearly reliving the bloodshed of those days.

"Once he was dead, we spread his body parts over the seas of the middle realm, purposefully burying them deep in the sea floor to prevent something like this from happening," Zryan finished, only for Travion to curse loudly, turning to the side as if searching for something to kick.

"That is what Phaedora was doing with the beast attacks," he snarled, turning back to them. "She was collecting his parts."

"Are there no guards on the Veil into Lucem?" Sereia asked, looking between Travion and Zryan. "How was she able to just sneak them into the realm?"

Zryan sighed, doing his best not to wilt under this new attack on his competence. "Since Draven and Travion took over the middle and dark realms, there has been no need to have a guard at the gates to the Veil."

"Arrogance," Alessia supplied, "is what it was. After Naya's attacks, soldiers should have been placed there. Protections set up."

You could have asked for it too! he wanted to snap. Instead, he threaded a hand through his hair and offered his family a shrug, as if to say, *What can we do?*

Alessia snorted and turned away.

"Whatever should have been done, this is the situation we face now," Draven cut in. "We need to get eyes and ears into the palace so that we know what he and Phaedora are planning."

Eden looked up at her husband, face contemplative, then she looked across at Zryan once more. "Can you not simply transform into someone other than yourself? A servant or a guard? And just sneak back in under his gaze?"

Zryan shook his head, wishing that it were that easy. "No, unfortunately, Ludari has the annoying ability to see through my transformations. I am of no use in that department."

A silence fell over the group then, and for a moment, Zryan had a horrible feeling they were all thinking the same thing: he was of no use in most departments. He failed to protect his kingdom. He failed to protect his children. They were in this situation to begin with because Zryan's scorned lover wished to take revenge on him and his family and see herself on the throne. Whether she thought to do that with him still or to take her place at Ludari's side, he was uncertain.

"I could send Yon," Sereia offered.

"No." Draven shook his head. "I will send Channon and Systries. Ludari is not aware of the humans that morphed into weres once they moved to Andhera. And most Lucemites have not gone beyond their own realm, let alone stepped foot in mine. They will be our safest bet."

Alessia

Draven was right. Most Lucemites could only imagine what lurked in the dark realm, and it plagued their nightmares. But they didn't truly know what creatures existed there aside from fabricated tales.

The element of surprise was on their side.

Alessia nodded. "I agree. The wolves will be our best bet."

Draven didn't wait. He turned sharply on his heel and disappeared into a mist beyond the Veil. Moments later, he emerged with two males flanking him. "Go, be swift, and *don't* die."

Although the words held no amusement in them, Alessia snorted in response. She hoped it wasn't their goal to perish on a mission.

"Report back as soon as you see or hear anything. Do you understand?"

Channon nodded curtly. "Of course, Your Grace." He shot

his fellow were-wolf a look, then the two of them jogged forward, their naked bodies blurring before shifting into the hulking, furred beasts.

"Zryan, Alessia," Eden's soft voice came, tearing Alessia's attention from where the weres had run. "Be as safe as you can. And by the moon, do not try to do this by yourselves." There was a stern quality in her tone, and Draven grunted by her side.

"Eden is right. Don't be foolish." With that, he turned away and climbed into his chariot. His wife, however, stared intently at Alessia.

"Take care, Alessia." She rounded the chariot and stepped in beside Draven, then they, too, left through the Veil.

Travion cursed under his breath and reached for Sereia's hand. "Don't be an idiot, Zryan" were his parting words before the middle realm's rulers mounted their horses and retreated through the dark.

Everyone assumed Lucem's king would fumble his way through, and part of Alessia wanted to throttle his brothers for their lack of faith, but she had her doubts too.

Zryan stared at the ground, his hands balled into fists at his side, then he seemed to shake off whatever he was thinking, and his casual facade slipped back into place. "We should head back to the manor." Though he was trying to appear at ease, he didn't look at her and didn't bother to wait as he climbed atop his griffin.

Her heart sank, and guilt warred with anger.

Why must I be conflicted?

She glowered and strode toward Zissi. His keen eyes watched her, and she felt judged, not for the first time in this bloody veil. Why had Eden looked at her so closely? Was she trying to scold her?

Alessia shook her head. Scolded by a child.

Perhaps there would be time after the war to suss through it, and if not, she would cross that bridge when she got there.

By the time Alessia caught up with Zryan, he'd just landed. The troops that didn't fit inside the manor had gathered and created makeshift shelters.

As she dismounted from her griffin, Ruan strode up to her, freshly baked pita bread in his hand. The smell should have been welcome, but instead, her stomach roiled, and she had to swallow roughly.

"Not right now." She waved it away just as Kian approached. "Everyone seems to have settled in for now." Alessia assessed the lawn, heard the soft chatter of soldiers and the squawks of griffins.

She spotted her husband removing his gear from Feroces, and once freed, the griffin flexed his wings in appreciation. Alessia sighed and walked up to him, and his eyes briefly met hers. "Signal to the boys and follow me," Zryan said before walking toward the back of the manor. Doves cooed to one another in the wisteria, and little sparrows chirped without a care.

Alessia didn't question what for, only assumed that they would discuss the latest developments with Ruan and Kian.

She spun around, waving to them, then made her way down the path Zryan had gone.

Alessia shouldn't have been surprised at how immaculate the grounds were, yet she was. Stone pathways led to a private patio that overlooked rolling hillsides, and white fencing contained a few horses, one of which Alessia recognized as Eden's mount.

Zryan folded his arms and peered down. They were surrounded by clover, and bees hummed as they traveled from flower to flower.

"Draven has sent us some of his were-wolves to use as spies. We're going to wait until we hear word from them as to what our next plan of action will be." He paused when Ruan made a noise of complaint. "Since the masses don't know about the weres, this is our safest bet. Unfortunately, all we can do is wait at this point."

Ruan kicked at a tuft of grass. "I don't like it, but it's better than rushing into the unknown. Still, I'd like to personally ensure Ludari can never be pieced back together again." He growled lowly and started to pace.

Kian jammed his fingers through his hair. "If I could get to my workshop, I could gather some of my creations, but . . . "

Even with his shop being far enough away from the palace that they wouldn't notice, Alessia didn't believe for a moment that security was lax at the moment. They'd know soon enough once the were-wolves returned.

"We can revisit that idea once we know more. As heartbreaking as it is that your sister is trapped in the palace with that monster, we must have faith in her abilities. She is as capable of a warrior as either of you." Her daughter didn't possess an affinity that aided in battle; rather, her ability was to soothe and *heal*. Alessia didn't want to think of how Ludari would try to break her or how much pressure she could endure until she snapped.

She knew all too well what it was like.

What he could *do*.

Alessia shuddered and turned on her heel. "Get some rest, boys, and eat. We'll need every ounce of strength we can muster. I don't know what Ludari has in store for us, but it will be like nothing that you have ever faced before."

She left them, not wanting to debate, not wanting to discuss anything more about what they couldn't do. About how her daughter was being held captive and she could do *nothing*.

Every step that led back inside the manor was much like running through water. Her limbs felt sluggish, and her chest tightened. There was a buzzing along her skin that she knew far too well. *Panic*. Alessia hadn't felt this way in centuries.

The more air she tried to suck in, the harder it was to breathe. She lifted her hand and rubbed over her heart; it felt like a blade was piercing her skin.

She drew in a deep breath and placed her hand against the cool wall.

Feel it. Cool beneath your hand. You're here now.

Not in a dank cell. Not staring down Travion as Ludari brought him forward so that *she* could punish him and break him down from the inside.

"Your Majesty, are you well?" Danae's gentle voice came.

Alessia swallowed but didn't smile as she glanced at the female. "I just need rest. That is all." She withdrew from the wall and crossed the foyer to the stairwell. A bath was more than needed so she could scrub the scorpion blood from her skin, and the layers of sweat and dirt too.

She pushed the door to the bedroom open and crossed into the bathing room. A porcelain tub faced the windows, and despite the lack of a mistress in the home, freshly picked flowers adorned the vases on the wardrobes.

Perhaps this was all that she needed.

Alessia tried to exhale, but her chest was too tight, and instead, she growled in frustration, loathing that she was being weak.

She forced herself to the tub, turning the faucet on. Small mercies, the water ran hot, and steam caressed her neck, then cheeks.

Undoing her leathers, Alessia let the bulk fall to the floor, and when she stood bare, she caught a glimpse of a female in the floor-length mirror. She approached the looking glass and reached out, touching the stranger's face. High cheekbones and eyes as dark as the night stared back at her, but there was no warmth, laughter, or life etched in her features.

"Where have you gone?" she whispered, but rather than hear someone respond, a small fluttering tugged her attention downward.

Alessia froze.

She dropped her hands to her abdomen and pressed into the flesh there.

No.

She turned sideways and truly looked over her body. Tall, nearly coltish if it weren't for her proudly earned muscles. Her long legs led to a shapely bottom, a thin waist, but her lower belly was beginning to swell.

Alessia hadn't noticed. Hadn't cared to inspect, and

certainly hadn't had time to consider her cycles in the past few weeks.

A strangled noise escaped her as she rested her hands over her abdomen. With each victory, each battle, she had charged into Zryan's arms and celebrated their winning as they came undone together. However, amid the chaos, she'd forgotten her herbal tinctures.

Why now? Why, when they were in the middle of a war?

Why, when she was readying to leave for good?

"By the sun! This isn't a good time, little one." She choked on a sob as she pulled away from the mirror and stepped into the warmth of the tub. Leaning forward, she turned off the water and fell back into the depths of the heat.

Ebony hair floated, covering her breasts. "If you are meant for this world, you will survive and be stronger for it." Her heart ached knowing that the chances were small. She'd battled giant scorpions, and whatever torment awaited them at Ludari's hands would make that battle seem like child's play.

She closed her eyes, letting the heat of the water soothe her as much as possible. When she could fully breathe again, she picked up a bar of soap and cloth, then scrubbed her skin until it turned rosy.

After she finished, she drained the tub and snagged the robe waiting for her on a hook. The door to the main room opened, and she heard a heavy footfall. It wasn't Danae, nor any of the other female staff members.

She wrenched her eyes shut and took a deep breath, counting the steps. By the time the individual was three steps into the room, she knew exactly who it was.

And then his face came into view. His green eyes were

bright again, and his full lips twisted up into a smile. If she were to be critical, as she often was, she would still agree that he was a handsome male, which was precisely why he was so often in trouble.

Zryan's angles were all sharp, stately even, but he was broader than his brothers, and more muscled too. With his carefree air, he was tantalizing. Even Alessia knew that.

And by the sun, he had her by the heartstrings. She wished he didn't. Fates above, how she wished he didn't.

If he knew, if he had an inkling of the life growing inside of her now, Zryan would send her away.

She pulled the robe around herself more tightly and lifted a brow.

"What a treat after a treacherous day," he murmured quietly, letting his gaze drop to her cleavage.

Whether it was the high of battle earlier in the day or the knowledge that, for the fourth time, they'd created a life together, Alessia wanted him. As much as she wished to run away, to leave behind the hurt, embarrassment, and weight of their love, it wasn't all terrible.

In their younger years, he'd been her everything. The sun itself.

Zryan must have seen it, because he crossed the distance between them and lowered his head.

Alessia lifted a hand, pressed her finger to his lips, and glanced up at him through her lashes. "This changes nothing. Okay?" she whispered as he moved in closer.

Zryan hesitated, as if contemplating whether that was all he wanted, then his arms encircled her, and he lifted her onto his hips.

She draped her arms around his neck, wanting to feel

every inch of his body searing onto hers. "The bed," she rasped when his teeth grazed just below her ear and his fingers dug into the curve of her bottom.

Zryan complied and carefully laid her down. He stood at the side of the bed, wearing far too many layers, and though she could easily access him, she wanted him bare to her.

Alessia sat up and unbuckled a part of his armor. It clattered to the floor, and she motioned for him to step back. "Undress for me." She breathed the words and watched as fire ignited within his gaze. The same inferno that spread within her. "All of it, Zryan."

He wasted no time undoing every buckle as he shed every last scrap of clothing. She shifted forward and ran her hand down his backside; his rigid length leaped as she touched him.

Fates. She wanted him inside her, filling her to the brim.

"What do you want, Less?" He reached beneath her chin, tilting her head up. "I'll give it to you."

"I'm going to suck you, Zryan, and then you're going to pleasure me with your mouth." He rumbled in agreement as she lowered herself to his erection and slid her lips down his tip, then his girth, until he pressed into her throat.

She couldn't take him all; he was too much.

Alessia withdrew only to move along his length again. She gripped his upper thighs and drew him closer. His hands dove to the back of her head, gently moving her as she pumped him with her mouth.

Zryan groaned, and the muscles in his thighs strained. When Alessia thought he was nearly there, she pulled away and sat up.

It occurred to Alessia that perhaps Zryan would notice

the slight swelling of her belly, but the chances were low. Not that he didn't know every curve of her body, but if she hadn't noticed, why would he?

She pushed open the robe, baring herself to him, and spread her legs wide, opening herself to her husband. "Zryan, I want your mouth on me."

His member leaped in response, and she nearly writhed in place, nearly told him to forget his mouth and just impale her.

He knelt and yanked on her legs none too gently, until her knees rested on his shoulders. "I want to hear you, Less. I want to hear what my mouth does to you." She was on the verge of telling him to stop using his tongue to speak when he descended on her.

Instead of penetrating her with his fingers, his lips encircled her ball of nerves, and his tongue flicked over it in quick, repetitive strokes.

Fates. He knew what she liked and how she needed it.

Alessia pressed her head into the blankets and closed her eyes, focusing on the waves of pleasure each stroke of his tongue inflicted.

"Faster, Zryan," she moaned, reaching down to thread her fingers through his hair. Her hips jerked as she yearned for more friction, then he sucked the sensitive flesh, lashing it with his tongue. Alessia gasped as bliss coursed through her, heating her in the most delicious fashion. "By the sun, Zryan!"

"Beautiful, Less," he groaned.

She nearly convulsed as completion roared through her veins, but she wanted more, hadn't had her fill yet. "I need you inside me. *Now.*"

This would not be a gentle lovemaking. Nor would this be a quick tupping. What it would be, Alessia wasn't certain, but she did know that they both needed it.

Zryan crawled onto the bed, hovering over Alessia, and nudged her entrance with his tip. He pressed against her tightness, moaning into her neck at the slight resistance. "So wet and tight."

He thrust once, and she gasped as he filled her completely.

Alessia raked her nails down his shoulders to his back and butt as he ground into her sensitive flesh.

Zryan rolled them over without breaking their connection, and she sat astride him, hands braced on his chest as she rose and fell in a rhythm that pulled moans from the both of them.

When she felt the quickening of pleasure, she pulled him up so he was sitting. He struck her just so, and she ground against him just right. His mouth sought hers, and she cried out as the first wave crashed on her.

"Zry!" She grabbed onto his shoulders, grinding herself into him as he pumped into her. His breaths grew ragged, and he grabbed her butt, squeezing to the point of pain. A beautiful, intense pain. "By the sun, don't stop." She threw her head back, gasping as she forced herself down just as he thrust upward.

With a groan, Zryan spent himself just as she spasmed around him in another glorious rapture of bliss.

Entirely boneless, she draped against him and felt his lips brush against her neck.

"This time, I'll join you in the bath." He chuckled, pulling her onto his chest as he lay down. His fingers drew lazy circles on her back.

And, just as she'd hoped for, their union had blotted every worry from her mind.

All there was, was them. In this bed.

For now.

14

Zryan

Zryan stood staring out the window of the study, looking down over the courtyard of the Damaris family home. Hannelore had just left with one of the other harpies to meet Channon at the farthest corners of the palace grounds in hopes of passing on whatever information the were-wolves may have discovered.

Two days had passed since Ludari's return. Two days of sitting in this home waiting for word from the palace, from the capital itself. Forces had amassed in the city; some of his own guards and people had turned against him. Others were pulled into the fray against their will. Rumbles had sounded in the depths, enough for Zryan to know that Phaedora was up to something within the palace walls, but no word had come from Channon yet.

"They might be dead." Ruan's voice sounded from behind him, strained in a way that Ruan typically wasn't.

Yesterday, Hannelore had returned with the news that Channon and his cohort had managed to sneak their way into the dungeons, only to find that neither Brione nor Alvia were down there. Nothing had been seen or heard of them since the confrontation with Zryan and Ludari.

He hadn't heard his son enter the room, but then, his attention was on the courtyard below, not the room around him. "They could be," he said. "But I don't think so."

It wasn't merely foolhardy hope on Zryan's part. It didn't make sense for Ludari to have killed them. With Alvia's particular set of powers, she was of too much potential use as he tried to rebuild his kingdom. And Brione . . . Brione was there to keep her parents in check. Which was also why they needed to get her out. Once she was free, Zryan would no longer be handcuffed into good behavior.

He could attack.

"Don't *think* so?" Ruan countered, aggressive the way his mother was. Neither of them wanted speculation. They wanted truth. Cold hard facts.

"He's only just returned after twenty-five hundred years. He doesn't have the support he used to have. It would be foolish to give up the grip he has over us." Zryan turned from the window to eye his son. He was a master of battle. He had truly earned his title as the Prince of War. But he also preferred to go in and forcibly beat or slice his way through his enemies. He did not enjoy so much the slow, strategic way of winning a battle over the enemy.

Ruan huffed and shifted in place, his hand unconsciously moving to the hilt of his sword, the grip squeaking lightly under his hold. Zryan studied him, eyed the strong, angular features that matched his own in many ways. The clench of his jaw, the fall of his hair, the broadness of his shoulders. But his dark eyes were those of his mother, and the rage they could fill with was all Alessia too.

Bloodthirsty. Harsh. Unforgiving.

"Have faith in your uncle's guards. They will find your sister, and once we have word and better intel, we will be able to get her out."

Ruan shook his head, rubbing at the back of his neck. "I hate waiting."

"Don't we all." Zryan turned back to the window, eyes lifting to the skies as he waited for the first glimpse of blue harpy wings.

Zryan had been impatient as well in his early years. After the fall of Ludari, when he and his brothers sat together on the throne of Lucem trying to repair the atrocities their sire had committed, Zryan had wanted to see a happy and peaceful kingdom immediately.

He'd thrown many balls in celebration, invited more nobles to the palace than had ever been there before. Gone down to the dungeons to free the captives his father had locked away for no other reason than being a potential threat to his own reign by way of their connections with others or the natural power flowing through their veins.

He'd been impatient to heal all of the wrongs. To prove that he was a different king, a *better* king than his father.

He had been impatient to make Alessia love him. To have her eyes fill with trust when she looked at him. For her face to split with a smile at the sight of him.

By the sun, she had made him work for it.

When Zryan had first seen her, fresh out of the pits of those dungeons, he'd thought he was seeing the true face of the sun for the first time. Not because she had looked stunning, malnourished and half-crazed from so much time in the dungeons. But because there had been a fire in her eyes not even all Ludari's tyranny could extinguish. A fire that ignited something within Zryan, that awoke a part of him that had never so much as stirred before. He had never wanted to lose that feeling.

But she hadn't trusted him, hadn't trusted anyone. She was like a hell-cat dropped on hot coals who needed to be approached slowly and carefully. With her family dead, killed by Ludari, and their lands given away to another noble family, there hadn't even been any place to send her to recuperate.

Zryan had dealt with her like one does a wild animal: with all the gentle caution necessary. Little moments at a time, spanning days, weeks, months. Spirits . . . the victory he'd felt the first time she glanced at him and her face had relaxed a fraction because he was near.

He had fought so hard to earn her trust. To live up to her faith in him. To be worthy of the love she had given him.

Zryan's eyes pinched shut at the memories, fresh pain lancing through him. Was it any surprise she was done? That she wanted to walk away? Their intimacy the other night had not filled him with hope that Alessia would change her mind. He understood all too well what it was like to need the feel of another person's skin against your own. To simply want the closeness of someone else near, even if you felt nothing for them emotionally.

A shout from outside brought his eyes open once more, and he found to his surprise not only Hannelore and the other harpies but Channon and Systries, standing in all their naked glory on the cobblestone of the courtyard.

Knowing something important had taken place, he turned on his heel and made his way down through the manor to the steps outside, Ruan hot on his heels. Someone had alerted Alessia and Kian, because they, too, drifted out into the courtyard, Alessia from somewhere in the gardens, Kian from the stables.

The harpies and were-wolves bowed at the sight of the royal family. Zryan waved this formality away and looked to Channon, his long blond hair tumbling around his shoulders in such fine gold, it made him think of the soft sunlight of evening here in Lucem, not the darkness of Andhera where the boy had been born and raised.

"What have you learned?" he asked the were.

"Just as we thought, she's not in the dungeons, sire. She's being kept off the side of the war room in a small closet of sorts." Zryan nodded. The chamber where they kept extra papers, quills, and ink so that it was all at hand when needed. "She is heavily guarded, never left unattended. The soldiers appear to be made up of Lady Phaedora's own guard and those of your retinue, who've pledged allegiance to the returned king."

Zryan scoffed. *Returned king.* "He's already proclaimed himself king, then."

Channon and Systries nodded. "His claim is that, since you wrongfully inherited it, the throne reverts back to him now that he has returned from the dead. There are some . . ." The guard paused as if unsure how to speak the words to the sovereign. "Some, it seems, who agree with him."

Zryan did not let his outward appearance show his annoyance or his feelings of betrayal at these words. He had failed in many ways, especially when it came to his marriage, but he had always been a good king. Fair. Honest. Perhaps a little ridiculous. A little aloof seeming. But always there for his people and building a better, brighter Lucem. One free of tyrannical rule. To think any would want to return to the hellscape of Ludari's rule was befuddling.

How many thought that way?

"Not everyone knows a good thing when they have it," Zryan stated with far more confidence and casual airs than he felt. Apparently, it was believable though, for Ruan snorted at his side. "What of Seducere's daughter?"

"Allowed to wander freely, though she is watched carefully by guards and the apprentice," Systries answered.

"The apprentice?" Kian asked.

"The apprentice to the smithy from the mountain. He visits Calor in the healer's wing."

"Mal Dolus," Zryan muttered, scowling deeply. The dark-haired minion who'd held his daughter at knifepoint.

Alessia swore none too quietly. "Can you get us in?" She bypassed everything else, getting directly to the matter at her heart.

Channon nodded. "We can."

"We'll have to be careful, Your Majesties," Hannelore added, looking between the king and queen. "The palace is heavily guarded."

"We can get past guards," Ruan stated confidently.

"No." Alessia shook her head. "You're not going."

"What?" Ruan snapped.

"She's right," Zryan stepped in. "You and your brother will stay here. Your mother and I will handle this."

"That doesn't make an—"

"Ru . . ." Kian cut him off. "We can't have the entire royal family in the palace at one time." Kian looked from his brother to his parents.

Ruan growled but conceded. "Fine. We will wait on the outskirts of Celeia to help with any potential chase you're facing once you've escaped the palace."

Zryan could live with that. He looked to Hannelore and Channon. "Let's talk extraction."

They went under cover of dusk, when the sun had set as far as it would and the land was covered with just a hint of darkness, like the sun had passed behind a cloud. It wasn't enough to afford them full coverage, but it helped their dark cloaks blend into more shadows as they moved through the streets toward one of the hidden passages into the palace that Zryan was counting on neither Ludari nor Phaedora being aware of.

It was something he and Alessia had made sure to add into the build of their home, a hidden way out in case it was ever needed. Only the royal family and Amyntas were aware of it, and Zryan refused to believe his chamberlain would have turned on him.

Channon hurried down the back street in his large wolf form, giant paws scraping almost soundlessly on the stone. He sniffed around the area of the wall Zryan pointed out to him, then let out a soft yip when all was clear.

Together, Zryan and Alessia slipped out of the alley they were tucked away in and moved to the portion of the wall that Channon guarded. Behind them, Systries followed, and overhead, the harpies watched from perches atop nearby homes and the palace walls themselves.

Zryan pressed his hand to an innocuous part of the wall that looked no different than any other, but it was one that he knew well. As he murmured a soft spell, magic hummed beneath his hand, and the bricks twisted out of the way to reveal a staircase into the ground.

He looked over at Alessia, then, letting his magic crackle over his fingertips, he held his hand up like a torch and led the way into the tunnel. Slowly, the four traveled through the dark tunnel with only Zryan's crackling hand to light the way. The tunnel itself led beneath the palace grounds and came up outside of the throne room. If all went well, both Ludari and Phaedora would be asleep due to the hour.

When they reached the end of the tunnel, Zryan pressed his ear to the wall, listening, then he murmured the spell to open this wall as well. Unlike outside, the bricks did not turn out of the way to create a hole; instead, one small section slid aside. Peering out into the hall, Zryan saw that, for now, it was empty, and stepped past the large statue of a pegasus that blocked the opening from general view.

Once he, Alessia, and the wolves were in the hall, Zryan moved quietly in the direction of the war room, listening for any approaching guards or servants. Just as he was about to step into another section of hallway to take him to the small cupboard his daughter was meant to be kept in, Alessia grabbed the armor at the back of his neck and stopped him in place.

He froze and watched a guard pass by, then let out a breath when the soldier didn't see them pressed tightly to the wall. Zryan looked back at Alessia. "Thank you," he whispered.

Alessia nodded and motioned him forward.

When they stepped into the new hall, it left the war room in view, but there was no one around. And as they came to the small closet itself, there was still no one. Trepidation filled Zryan's bones. He knew even before he opened the door that Brione was not there any longer.

There were signs that she had been there. Scraps of paper with recipes written down. New tonics and mixtures he was sure his daughter had come up with to aid all sorts of ailments and problems their people could be suffering from. He wanted to gather them all up, to keep them protected in his pocket as parts of her. Instead, he turned back to Channon and Systries.

"Where is she?!" he hissed.

"She was here when we left this morning," Channon whispered back.

Suddenly, voices from down the hall caught their attention, and everyone stiffened.

"Come, you know I am the smartest choice."

Zryan's eyes narrowed. He recognized that voice. *Mal.* Without telling Alessia and Channon what he was up to, Zryan left his wife and the wolves to move down the hall toward the voices, which were just around the corner.

There, tucked into a door frame, stood Alvia, blond hair spilling down her back in silken waves, her soft, rounded features pinched with worry, and her teeth chewing on her full bottom lip. She was beautiful, all soft curves and warmth, the kind of body a man could melt into, and Zryan wanted nothing more than to see her curled into the arms of his youngest son, blessing him with all the love and support he deserved. No matter what his family said, Alvia Seducere was meant to be a part of their family.

So long as she was not a traitor.

"I know nothing of the sort," her soft, but firm, voice floated down to him.

Mal's tall and lean form loomed over her, his dark hair falling like a veil around his features. "Ludari will only use you. Phaedora will see you as a threat," he purred, low and manipulative. "I can protect you. Together, we can use our abilities to better purposes than serving this tyrant."

Aliva's blue eyes flitted up to Mal's, and the softness that had been within them disappeared to be replaced by coldness. "*Now* he's a tyrant? That wasn't what you were saying when you helped to drive King Zryan out. Or when you held a knife to the princess' throat."

Mal tutted. "That was simply self-preservation."

Zryan's entire body hardened at the mention of his daughter and the part Mal had played. He stepped into the hall, letting his hood fall off his head to reveal his features.

"Is that all it was?" he growled.

15

Alessia

Alessia's fingers flexed the moment Zryan rounded the corner. He snarled, and though his body was hidden by a cloak, she knew his muscles were coiling, readying for him to leap into a fight. As much as she wanted to restrain her husband, hearing the male snidely remark about holding Brione at knifepoint boiled her blood.

If Zryan tore his arms from their sockets, she'd delight in it, but given the chance, she'd do it herself.

"Mal," Alessia hissed as she darted around Zryan and yanked a dagger free from her waist. She moved faster than a viper, quicker than her husband had anticipated, for the blade met the traitorous male's neck before Zryan had the chance to stop her.

"Oh," Mal chuckled. "Your daughter has your fire." He purred his words, which only further stoked the inferno within Alessia.

It took every ounce of strength in her to not slit his throat on the spot.

Alessia narrowed her eyes and curled her lip at him. She

laughed, and it sounded a little unhinged even to her ears. "You may boldly prod at my family, and even me, but I don't need a blade to silence your tongue. I just need your mind."

Her husband growled, "Alessia," but she didn't pay any mind. She would rip what she wanted from Mal if it was the last thing she did.

Mal glanced to the floor for a moment, the only chink in his armor indicating he was rethinking his stance, perhaps even worried. "You don't want to do that because I happen to know where they're holding your precious daughter."

Alessia turned her attention to Alvia and lifted her brows expectantly. At this point, she wasn't certain whether the female was truly on their side or not. When one's back was against the wall, they were willing to do anything to save their hide, but where was her loyalty truly?

She *had* called Zryan king still . . .

"He does know where she is. They move her frequently, but I swear to you, Your Majesties, she is well cared for, and they haven't harmed her at all." Alvia's voice was soft, if not a little strained given the circumstances.

Mal's throat bobbed, shifting Alessia's blade slightly. "That is true. I do know where they have her right now, and it isn't up here." He lifted a hand and pointed to the floor. "The dungeons. And it's heavily guarded by those loyal to Ludari, so you'd find yourself well in over your head if you barge down there." Mal grinned at her, and his eyes danced with mischief.

Alessia couldn't tell if this was yet another trap.

"If you scramble my mind, I may not be able to get you to the dungeons safely," Mal added and nodded solemnly.

Alessia exhaled sharply as she pulled her dagger away

from his throat. "You will show us. Or his lightning will seem like a relief when I'm done with you." She thumbed in Zryan's direction.

The blond female fidgeted with her fingers, and Alessia sighed, then stepped toward her. "Run. Get to safety and don't speak of this to anyone." Despite the situation, there was a flicker in Alvia's eyes that she recognized: resilience and strength. And at that moment, Alessia trusted Alvia. She motioned to Mal. "He is not the alliance you need and will surely only end in your undoing if you continue to deal with him."

Alvia nodded, then her brows furrowed as she fled down the hall.

"Before I paint the floor crimson with your blood, bring us to our daughter." This time, Zryan crossed the distance between the two of them, and an electric current pulsed around his fingertips and wrists.

Mal held his hands up in surrender and shrugged a shoulder. "The way is fairly clear. The only sticky part is, the stairwell to the dungeon is heavily guarded, as is the vicinity of her cell." He stepped forward, but when Zryan edged ahead, he thought better of it and shrank backward. "No one wanted to chance you rescuing daddy's little girl."

When neither Alessia nor Zryan reacted to his bait, Mal sighed and strode down the hall.

Alessia held her arm out, blocking her husband from advancing. "If there are guards everywhere, how are you to sneak us past them, anyway?"

An almost bashful expression formed on Mal's face, and he placed a hand to his chest, bowing ever so slightly. "I have my ways. Now, we really must be going." Mal continued on, glancing left to right before heading down the hall. Then he turned toward the east wing.

Despite how many forces Alessia knew to be circulating in the palace, and knowing how well-guarded it truly was, few were making their rounds on the first level.

By the time they reached the stairwell to the dungeon, true to Mal's word, more soldiers appeared. They held spears in hand, ready to use them if need be.

Mal motioned for Alessia and Zryan to hang back, which she loathed. She rolled her eyes and bit her tongue. Zryan squeezed her shoulder in silent assurance. Every movement from the deplorable male was a mockery, but what other choice did they have? Running him through with her dagger would do nothing but ensure their demise.

How had their lives come to be in his hands?

He was a lowly apprentice, and he'd dared to speak to *them* in such a manner.

Mal would pay dearly for his treachery.

A moment later—whatever he'd muttered to the guards at the top of the stairwell, they meandered off—he crooked a finger toward them.

Alessia darted across the open way and into the stairwell with Zryan close behind her.

"Stay as close to the walls as you can." He jogged down the stone steps, then halted just before the bottom one. Two guards were at the bottom, but when Alessia glanced down at Mal's back, he held up six fingers.

Six that he saw.

There were probably more that he didn't see.

Mal waved to the guards, chuckling as he stepped down.

"Why, hello. I was sent down here to fetch as many of you as possible there seems to be—"

He cocked his head and glanced up the stairs. Alessia's rage flared to life, not for the first time in his company. Was he purposely giving them away?

"Something is going on upstairs! All guards on duty report to the first level, now!" The male guard charged up the flight of stairs in a flurry.

Zryan flattened himself against the wall as much as he could, as did Alessia. She didn't breathe as one nearly ran into her.

Mal turned around and flourished a bow. "You're not the only one with tricks."

"What was that?" Alessia hissed and stepped down until she was level with Mal. She had her assumptions that it was a mind affinity, like she had, but would he divulge the entirety of it?

Grumbling, Zryan moved ahead of them. "We don't have time for this! We don't have a key, so what good was that little game of yours?"

Alessia wanted to press because suspicion was growing inside of her and she didn't trust this wicked male as far as she could throw him.

Still, Brione was down here.

Mal lifted a hand, and from his middle finger dangled a single key. "*You* don't, but I do." He smiled down at the key as he brought it in front of his face.

Zryan charged forward, baring his teeth as he readied to throttle him. Unfortunately, he only grabbed Mal's wrist and squeezed until he released the key. "Where. Is. She?"

Mal turned on his heel, his eyes wrenching shut as he

rubbed at his wrist. "This way, Majesties." He led them down row after row of empty cells, and the farther away from the stairwell they grew, the more the space relied on the fae-lit sconces illuminating the darkness.

"Ah, there is the ray of sunshine," Mal proclaimed as they rounded a corner. He bumped into Zryan, who stiffened as though he was fighting every urge to throttle him into the ground.

Brione rushed to the front of her cell, glaring at Mal. "You deplorable—"

"Brione!" Alessia rasped her name in relief.

Mal brandished the key which had Zryan staring down at his open hands. "You wretched little—" His eyes darted to Brione, and whatever words were left on his tongue shriveled, for he moved forward as Mal unlocked the cell door.

When it opened, Alessia ran in, and Zryan was at her back. "You're all right!"

Her arms encircled her daughter—or at least, they should have, when the cell door slammed behind them.

The image of Brione in her arms fizzled away into nothing. Alessia stared at her hands for a moment, then glared in Mal's direction. She knew precisely what this was: a trick of the mind, an illusion. Instead of creating a nightmare in one's mind, Mal could craft them for everyone to see and believe. Now she understood the distractions he'd created were tricks of the mind and ears.

Laughter spilled from Mal as he leaned against the iron bars and grinned at them. "You two aren't as clever as you think. Did you honestly think I'd usher you down into the pits of the palace and help the three of you escape? You should have destroyed my mind when you had the chance."

Brione slammed her fists against her cell, not one but two over from where they were. "You are the scum of the realm. Two-faced, spineless—"

"What a beautiful mouth." Mal shook his head and stepped away from Alessia and Zryan, meandered toward Brione, and unlocked her cell. "I owe your parents no loyalty, but you, I'll spare." He opened the door and motioned for her to step out.

"Get away from her," Zryan roared, but in here, he was as useful as a caged human.

Brione lifted her arm to strike Mal, and he caught her wrist.

Alessia launched at the door, her fingers curling around the bars as she shook them. It was useless. She knew the wards on the cell, knew their ability to snuff out one's power, to render their affinity useless. She *should* have brought him to his knees earlier. "Brione, don't fight him. Get out of here. Wolves are waiting for you, and they know what to do!"

With a dip of his head, Mal tugged her in closer but didn't lower his voice. "The guards are preoccupied with what they think to be an intruder. You'll have enough time to escape through the south wing, to where I assume your precious wolf friends are hiding. Run and don't try to save anyone else, or you will most assuredly die by Ludari's hand." Mal pushed her away from him and nodded toward the stairs.

Brione spared them one glance, then darted away.

Relief for her daughter flooded her, but that relief was a temporary thing, for the walls of the cell were not a comfort to her. No, they brought back the trauma from centuries ago.

Since Alessia had met Mal, all he had done was talk. In the room, through the hall, down into the dungeon and in front of the cells, but now that he had successfully imprisoned them, he was silent.

Mal only smiled at them and walked away.

His steps echoed inside her mind, reminding her of the days in the old palace's dungeon. She had learned Ludari's gait over time, and those of the guards who'd taunted her most. With so many years spent as a captive, it became a habit for her, listening to the footfalls, listening to their particular gaits.

Alessia's heart pounded in her ears, sounding more like the heavy footfalls of Ludari. She half expected him to crouch down in front of the door, grin at her, and pull her out for one of his games.

But Ludari wasn't there.

No. No. No. No. No. No.

Her throat ached, and when she rubbed at it, she realized she was screaming.

Behind her, Zryan's voice finally cut through the sounds of her unraveling mind. "Alessia!" He grabbed her by the shoulder, and if she hadn't played his voice over in her head, she would have used her affinity on him.

"I cannot be trapped in a dungeon again," Alessia said hoarsely. She rubbed her throat as if she could feel a collar encircling her neck.

"I will get us out of here." His voice was full of determination as he searched for a weakness in the bars. Alessia knew it was futile.

There was a reason Alessia didn't search for a weak spot, and it was because she and Zryan had used the Creaturae to fashion holding cells that needed no chains. Just a key and the wards to render a magic wielder useless. Gone were the shackles and collars Ludari had used in his old palace.

Zryan wouldn't be able to shift or call on his lightning, and no matter how hard Alessia tried to delve into someone's mind, she wouldn't be able to.

"By the sun!" she screamed, staring down the row, wishing she was free so she could wring his bloody neck. "I vow, I'll kill you. I'm going to kill you when this is through." Phaedora was first on her list, but Mal was second, and she vowed he would suffer.

From several rows down, she heard a prisoner cackle. "If he doesn't kill you first," the male voice sang.

That was a distinct possibility. A reality Alessia may have to face, but not one she was willing to accept.

16

Zryan

Brione was safe. All three of his children were free from the reach of his father. No matter what happened to him now, he could rest easy in that. Ruan would know to take the reins of the kingdom; he and Kian, along with Brione, would meet up with their uncles. Together, they would defend Lucem and find a way to take down Ludari and Phaedora.

Alessia.

After the first tenuous moments, she had removed herself from the bars and settled down on the stone slab that ran along the back of the cell. She'd pressed her head into the wall and shut her eyes. Perhaps blocking out the cell around them. Perhaps blocking him out as well.

Zryan pressed his forehead into the cell's iron door, feeling the cold of them against his flushed skin. He could easily have sat down and accepted his fate if it were not for his wife. He couldn't simply leave her in Ludari's clutches. He'd promised her she would never have to face anything like that again. He couldn't break that vow as well.

Pushing away, Zryan began to pace back and forth along the three walls of iron, eyes following each bar top to bottom. Looking at where they connected to the ceiling. Where they were buried in the earth. He gripped each one tightly, rattling it with all his strength. And when he had finished his first round of it, he tried again.

There had to be a loose bar. One area where his guards had not kept up maintenance. One weak spot where something had slipped and he could potentially use his ability.

Everything was sound. While it should have filled him with immense pride, the anger began to build inside him. How could he have landed Alessia back in prison? How could he have brought her back into Ludari's hands?

He should have come alone.

Zryan gripped the bars before him, shaking them with all the force in his body, straining to bring forth his magic to the point that sweat beaded from his hairline.

"Agghhh!!" he screamed, muscles shuddering with effort, his veins popping, and something wet dripped onto his hand. Still, nothing came. Not even a hint of electricity. He glanced down at his palm at the second drip and saw the spots of red collecting there.

He lifted his hand to swipe at his nose, blood smearing across his knuckle and finger. Zryan sniffed and ignored it, kneeling instead. Closing his eyes, he pictured the small body of a mouse. Took a deep breath and gritted his teeth, telling his muscles to shift. For his size to change and hair to sprout along his body and his form to alter into that of a tiny being that could slip between the bars to freedom.

When nothing happened, he grabbed the bars once more

and began to shake them, letting out a frustrated howl.

"Enough!" Alessia snapped behind him, her voice quaking in a way he hadn't heard in a long time.

Zryan slumped forward, his head pressing once more into the bars as blood dripped down his lip and along his chin. "There has to be a weakness." His voice rasped, weary and horse.

"There is none! We built these," Alessia said wearily. "And made them so no one could escape. So that no matter their affinity, they couldn't break the wards. Spare your energy."

He shut his eyes, listening to the silence of the dungeons. Nothing but the weighted quiet of being surrounded by the womb of the earth. There was a chill that made the hair on his arms stand up and a dampness that seemed to make the chill settle even further into his body, reaching his very bones. Was this what Draven and Travion had felt all their days? A cold that wouldn't leave them? A chill that settled in like a brutal knife beneath the ribs?

Children. They had been just children when their father had led them down here and left them in the dark. Meanwhile, he had lived atop in the sunshine. Growing up with their mother's arms around him. Forever under Ludari's scrutiny. Forever disappointing and never measuring up. Deemed too weak, too pitiful to be of much use. To be of any threat. Only good once his one hundredth birthday had dawned, and he'd been deemed of age to wed. To be sold off, in a way, to bring Ludari more power.

Zryan's worth had only been the book. Wedding Phaedora so that the book would come into his possession.

But at least he'd had his mother. At least he'd had a

glimpse of love. Some kindness in a world of harshness and disdain. Draven and Travion hadn't even had that. And Alessia . . .

Zryan opened his eyes and looked over his shoulder at his wife. She sat rigid on the stone bench, her body nearly vibrating with an anxious energy he was now just seeing. Her tanned skin had paled, a grayish hue to it that spoke far more than her silence did.

He stood, swiping at his nose and face with the corner of his cape, cleaning himself up before he went to her. "Are you okay? I know this can't be easy." He kept his voice soft, unthreatening.

"I am fine," she said slowly.

"Less . . ." Zryan sighed. "You don't have to preten—"

"I said, I'm *fine*," she snapped, her eyes opening to glower at him.

The weariness within Zryan increased, settling into his bones as deeply as the chill had. He nodded even though he could see the pain swirling in the depths of her dark eyes. The chaos that was building inside of her.

Instead of saying something else, Zryan took a seat beside her. Far enough away that he wouldn't brush her skin and potentially agitate her further, but close enough that, if she chose to, she could lean into him for warmth and comfort.

Not that he expected that.

They sat silently, nothing but a light *tap* from somewhere in the dungeons to keep them company. Eventually, the soldiers returned. Chattering filled up the silence, but not clear enough for them to hear what was being said. Now and then, a guard would walk down past their cell, eyeing them with a smirk, as if they had done the capturing themselves.

Zryan merely wiggled his fingers at them each time, blowing a kiss to one and a wink to another. Let them take pride in his current position. He wouldn't show them the frustration inside of him. Wouldn't let them see the hopelessness he felt.

He never showed it. Had learned how to hide his despair behind a facade of bravado. Learned how to make everyone believe he worried about nothing, cared about even less. If no one expected anything from him, then they couldn't be disappointed in him. And if they expected nothing out of him, they paid less attention to him. Leaving Zryan to his own devices. Leaving him to form plans that could overthrow them.

A light pressure on his shoulder surprised Zryan. He looked down and found that Alessia was asleep, her head resting on his shoulder, her arms around herself. He pressed a kiss to the top of her head and gently shifted her so that her head rested in his lap, and he was able to drape his cape over her form. It allowed more of the cold to sink into his body, but her fingers pulled the cape more snuggly around herself, and that brought a smile to Zryan's lips.

Carefully, he stroked his fingers through her hair, brushing soft strands from her forehead and tucking them behind her ear.

She was still the most beautiful sight he had ever beheld. The fiercest flame that had ever come into his life. He couldn't lose her. He knew he had taken for granted that she would simply stay. That even though they were broken, she would remain at his side, and he would still have time to somehow fix what he had destroyed.

Zryan's heart clenched, pain lancing through him at the

thought of Alessia completely pulling away. Her words came back to him. *Don't for one moment believe I'll be by your side when the dust settles.*

His eyes shut, fingers still brushing through her hair, and he leaned his head back against the stone wall.

When Ludari had been dead, and his parts strewn about the waters of Midniva and beyond, Zryan had taken it upon himself to go back down into his father's dungeons and release everyone that was down here.

He had watched, over the century of his existence, how those who were deemed traitors—meaning they had vocally opposed Ludari's tyranny—were killed, and later, once the Creaturae was in his possession and the Veil between realms had been formed, exiled to the dark realm—as if that were a mercy. Those who were deemed too powerful and thus a threat but too good to be done away with entirely were sent to the dungeons. Just as his brothers had been. Brothers he had only ever heard secondhand stories about. His mother refused to speak of the children she had been unable to save.

Zryan had been there the day that Alessia and her family were brought in. Listened to Ludari list their supposed crimes and slit their throats there in the throne room. He'd watched the horror and the rage come over their daughter. Watched the way she had bravely stepped forward to inflict her gift, her nightmare, upon Ludari in revenge. She may have succeeded if she hadn't been so unnumbered. If the captain of the guard hadn't brought the butt of his sword handle down on her head, knocking her unconscious.

He had wanted to stand up and speak on her behalf. To somehow save her from the dungeons. But he had stayed silent. Ludari never listened to him. Never took any of his words for worthy. So instead, the unconscious girl, not even of age, was dragged off to the depths of the dungeons.

But he never forgot her. That spark of fire. The courage that flowed through her. She would have taken on the king of Lucem without hesitation. No concern for herself.

Zryan's fingers sank more deeply into Alessia's hair, rubbing gently at her scalp. The memory of Alessia's bravery stayed with him. Shaming him and his own cowardice. Reminding him of his daily failure.

He had wanted to be braver. To find some hidden strength within his core to take on his father and end his reign. But he hadn't been strong enough. What could his electricity do against Ludari's ability to strangle him with vines or fill him with sharp, piercing thorns? To create sneaking, living buds that released plumes of poison?

Zryan pinched his eyes tight against his inner demons, regret filling him to the brim. Why had it taken his mother's death? He shouldn't have waited. It shouldn't have required that kind of fury to lead him down into the basement. He'd had the ability to sneak in there at any time.

But there had been so much fear.

"Papa?" His voice was little and afraid. He winced as he heard the warble.

"I said, come here!" his father snapped, pointing to the place before him.

Tentatively, Zryan moved toward him, fear shuddering through his small body, making his fingers tremble. He tried to remember what mother had said. Don't show your father fear. Stand straight. Head up. Meet his eyes. He hates it when you shirk and flinch.

So, he tipped his head up, teeth clenching hard enough to squeak inside his jaw just so his chin wouldn't tremble. He stopped in the exact place Father indicated. It wasn't good to be off even a slight inch.

"Your mother claims you've come into your powers." It was a statement, not a question. Zryan nodded. "Show me."

His thin chest rose with a deep breath as he tried to steady himself. He'd only just realized what he could do, and when he was too nervous, it didn't work so well. But he'd had good luck turning into a rabbit as of late. Perhaps that would be the best one to try.

Zryan shut his eyes, blew out the breath slowly, and concentrated on the image of the bunny in the menagerie. Tried to think of its warmth and softness. The feel of its fragility in his hands. How it made him feel strong to hold it.

His body began to shift, form shrinking, ears elongating, teeth sharpening. When he was almost done, almost shrunk into the form of the little gray rabbit, he looked up at his father, hoping to at long last see pride in something he had done.

Instead, there was contempt. It made him falter, and he paused halfway between little boy and rabbit. A malformed monstrosity of skin and fir.

Father hissed and shook his head. "Pitiful," he muttered. "What are you even supposed to be?"

Zryan released the magic in his body and quickly reverted back to his child form. "A r-rabbit."

His father's scorn only increased. "A rabbit," he said with disdain. "What use is a rabbit to me in battle? What use are you to me in any situation?"

Zryan shrunk back, forgetting his mother's words, and the anger in his father's eyes flared. "I can do any animal!" he hurriedly shouted, trying to take that look away.

It didn't work, and his father struck him hard, making his ears ring and the taste of blood flood his mouth.

"Useless. Get out of my sight."

Shrinking further in on himself, Zryan turned quickly and ran from the throne room, holding in his sobs until he was out in the hall. His mother was there to pick him up and soothe him in her arms, shushing him quietly as she carried him back to their chambers.

A hiss left him as a sharp stinging sensation spasmed through his palm. He opened his hand and looked down. Red half-moons scoured the flesh of his palm, blooming with blood. He hadn't realized he was squeezing his fist so tightly.

His eyes drifted down to the sleeping form of his wife once more. By the sun, moon, and sea, he would do whatever he needed to get her out of here. Ludari would not take Alessia from him, even if he'd already lost her. Somehow, he would get her back to his brothers and to their children.

A whimper slipped from Alessia's mouth, and all other thoughts halted, his attention zeroing in on her. His eyes took in the way her face had become pinched, her lips tight as she shook her head a little. Her fingers, which had gently held his cape, were now clutched around it to the point of whiteness.

She whimpered again, murmuring something he could not understand but which he recognized as fear mingled with pain. He knew the dungeons would only take her back. That being in this prison would do terrible things to her memory.

When her cries became more like screams, he sat her up, giving her a gentle shake to wake her. "Less, wake up. You're—"

Her eyes snapped open, a feral light burning in their

depths. Before he could react, she threw herself at him, hands going around his neck, and the weight of it carried them both to the floor. The force of the fall made his ribs scream in pain, his entire body going rigid with it, giving her the advantage as she locked herself in position. Alessia was atop him, all of her weight bearing down onto the tight grip around his throat, cutting off his breath.

Blood pounded in his ears, and his lungs strained for breath. "A . . . less—" He tried to get the words out but only succeeded in releasing what little breath he had left. His hands lifted to her waist, and he shoved hard, getting a leg propped in the right position that he was able to roll them.

He had to slam her shoulders into the ground harder than he wanted, but the shock of it snapped her out of it. He saw the moment the wild gleam faded and sanity returned. Alessia frowned up at him in confusion. Regret flashed for a moment in her gaze, then she was smacking at him, pushing him off of her.

Zryan slipped to the side, falling to his bottom on the dirt floor of the dungeon. A cough raked through his chest as he sucked in much-needed air. Alessia, looking mussed and still more fragile than he'd seen her in a long time, climbed to her feet. She put distance between them, her hands brushing loose hair back out of her face.

"Are you all right?" she asked in a clipped tone.

"Are you?" he wheezed. When she shot him an angry look, he sighed. "I'm fine. Nothing that won't heal in time." His fingers rubbed at his sore neck just so he wouldn't touch the aching ribs at his side. He really should have asked Eden for some healing magic when he'd had the chance.

But only the worthy deserved aid.

17

Alessia

Soldiers stood before her, stripped down to just a cloth hanging from their waists. Their ribs jutted out, and dark circles lined their eyes. Starving. Just as the cruel king preferred his foes, weakened and unable to fight back.

These poor males had refused to serve and refused to take an order from the tyrant. He had razed their homes, and if they'd had any living family, either infused them with a plague so horrendous that they ended their own lives or saw that they were torn asunder by mountain lions.

Ludari leaned in toward her ear and rasped, "Now, finish them off with terror." When she balked, he withdrew a knife and held it against her throat.

She reached out toward the males, reaching for their minds, and when her mental fingers caressed the strands of their subconscious, she yanked on them, infusing them with poison. Everyone had a deepest and darkest fear, and Alessia's talent was using that to make them crumble.

These poor souls were far too weak for such torment, and one by one, they fell to the ground . . . dead.

Alessia sucked in a breath and stared down at her hands, frowning. The memory of her fingers wrapped around his throat, squeezing, made her stomach lurch.

How many had she slain because of Ludari? How many had she tortured? She balled her hands into fists and hunched over.

Alessia forced the rising bile down and shook her head. Part of her wished to inspect Zryan's neck—and his side, which he kept favoring—but the dregs of her torment twined with reality. She was back in a cell, back in Ludari's hold, and Alessia knew there would be no escaping for them this time.

Nevertheless, she didn't want to hurt her husband. She may have been furious with him, but if this was their end, she didn't want to go out fighting against him. No. Alessia wanted Zryan to know that through hurt, through their trials, she loved him, and by the sun, sometimes she wished she didn't.

He needed to know that too. The last thing she wanted was for him to remember her screaming that she wouldn't be by his side in the end.

As she opened her mouth, the sound of sandals clapping against the floor brought her attention down the way.

It wasn't Mal. He had a particular glide in his walk that reeked of playful arrogance. Nor was it any of the guards, for they had sloppier footfalls. No, this one was heavier, full of confidence.

She knew exactly who it was.

Ludari.

She darted to the front of the cell, glaring at him. He was currently shrouded in darkness, but she didn't need to see his face, which looked so much like Travion and Draven's. No, unfortunately, she knew him by the slow approach, the slight drag in his heel. And it made her stomach revolt, although there was nothing to spew.

Zryan growled, rising from his seated position, and stalked toward the bars. But his father didn't spare him a glance, not at first.

Perhaps if she were a youth again, not as damaged by life, she could have seduced her way out of the cell no differently than Seducere's daughter could. But Alessia was far too sharp and lacked a gentle heart that could fuel her actions as well as words.

She had been honed into a weapon. A tool to use. And after Ludari's reign, she had been left scarred beneath the surface, changed and hardened over time.

When she could no longer use that as an excuse, it was her failing marriage that further wounded her into disrepair.

Ludari's cruel gaze fell on Alessia, and he chuckled. "Some things never change, I suppose. Still as feral as ever." He assessed her, like one inspecting their livestock, and nodded to himself. "There have been times I've considered bringing you to heel because I recall your magnificent ability to dole out punishments." He sighed and reached forward as if he were going to reach through the bars but thought better of it.

Good. Because he would have had a broken arm to contend with. Especially as he brought up their history together when she'd fought so damn hard to forget it.

Alessia had been tempted once to erase said memories, but in the end, they did make her who she was, for better or worse, and it allowed her to judge specific situations in a clearer mindset.

When one compared themselves to a tyrant, it was easy to convince themselves they were not evil, and not nearly as twisted as they thought.

"Don't speak to her." Zryan attempted to shove Alessia back, as if he could shield her from Ludari at this point.

She wanted to laugh. She wanted to scream.

"Too bad you're broken."

She hissed. His words sparked fury and sadness. It was his fault she was broken, for that was what he did. He played with things until they broke, then threw them away.

"It's amusing, though. Your life has come full circle. You were both under my thumb once, and here we are again." Ludari scratched at his temple, confusion rumpling his brow. He drew even closer, his eyes roving along her body in a way that made her shiver. His gaze lingered on her abdomen. "What an utter waste," Ludari hissed, turning his attention back to her face. "Never did I expect you to fall for such an invertebrate, Alessia Pagonis." He stepped back, motioning to them. "But you won't be walking away from the palace this time." Ludari folded his arms and paced in front of them, stroking his chin as he drew out this pointless discussion.

Alessia's blood boiled, and she could see Zryan warring with the fact that he couldn't leap out of the cell and end his father. But would he? She hated that she doubted him with everyone else, but would Zryan freeze given the opportunity to take Ludari out by force?

She didn't know.

Zryan was no spineless fool. However, he *did* hesitate; he tried his best to think through a situation and find the best solution. Often, it was not the most violent option, which

Alessia opted to take nine times out of ten, but that was how she had been raised, how she had been used.

Her husband took a situation into consideration and mused over how he could manipulate it to his benefit.

How unfortunate there was nothing to manipulate here.

"Yes, I'll just let you into my home, take my family from me without so much as a fight." Zryan's voice had a casual lilt to it, but Alessia knew better. There was nothing relaxed about him, and he wasn't as detached as he was letting himself seem.

"Spare me, Zryan. You're pathetic as ever." He waved him off as if his words were no more than theatrics. "You couldn't usurp me before without the aid of your brothers, and you certainly wouldn't be able to now." Closing the distance between them, careful not to step into arm's reach, Ludari stared down his son, grinning.

Zryan glared back at him, each line of his face hardened, and though his back was against the proverbial wall, he didn't shy away.

How could she ever have thought he was anything like his father all those years ago when she'd been released from prison? When it came down to it, Zryan had no likeness to his sire, and though her memories weren't the sharpest when it came to her years of imprisonment, Alessia recalled seeing his mother when she was brought before Ludari.

Brilliant green eyes that were full of life and love. The same sharper angles, with dark hair tumbling down her back. *Like our Brione.*

No. Zryan was nothing like his father. And that was a blessing.

"Let me out and I'll show you what I'm capable of," Zryan ground out.

His father seemed to consider this, then only laughed. "You could try, but in two days, you'll be dead. Your execution will be most splendid." He clapped his hands together and rocked on his heels. "So, whatever grand gesture you'd like to perform or escape you'd like to attempt, make it quick."

Zryan cried out in frustration, which seemed to please Ludari. His attention switched from his son to the cage that confined the pair of them. "This is brilliant craftsmanship. I like these . . . especially since it renders you both entirely useless. Far more pragmatic than chains, in my opinion." With a chuckle, he turned on his heel. "Enjoy the last of your moments together."

Then he left them.

She watched until his figure faded into oblivion, and as it did, Alessia could feel the threads of her sanity unwinding.

Her chest tightened to the point that she couldn't breathe and her vision blackened around the edges. With every new breath she drew in, it was as if her lungs were being crushed. She wheezed, squeezing the bars that were the only thing keeping her standing.

Dead.

Dead in two days.

This time, when her stomach revolted, she allowed the contents to spew forth and onto the floor.

By the sun . . . Dead!

"No, no, no. This cannot happen." Alessia fell to her knees and pounded her fists onto the dirt bottom until her knuckles bled and throbbed. Had she broken bones? What did it matter?

Muffled shouts came from somewhere, but Alessia didn't *care*. Let Zryan shout, or whoever else was down in the pits with them. Let her screams deafen the guards!

She dragged her fingers down her face. "Not like this." Her shoulders shook as she sobbed none too quietly. Dying like a cornered rat in a cell hadn't been on her list of ways to die. Nor had being strung up like a common thief before the masses. She didn't know what Ludari had planned, but she could assume the worst, and she did know that whatever humiliated them most was the route he would take.

It was Ludari's way to break someone down until they believed they were no more than dirt beneath one's fingernail.

With the book, anything was possible. With the book, they could be dusted, they could have every bone broken at the uttering of a spell.

Alessia was meant to die in battle.

Not this way.

"I did not fight to survive for this!" She screamed until her throat was raw, and when she started raking her nails down her face, feeling the sting of them, Zryan rushed forward.

"Alessia! By the sun, listen to me!" His voice was hoarse, and she opened her eyes to look up at him, wondering if he'd been shouting at her before that moment.

She gnashed her teeth together, loathing the feeling of coming undone, but she couldn't stop it any more than a burst dam could stop the rush of water. With each outburst and each display of weakness, she grew angrier, hating herself all the more, loathing that he had to see it and despising him for watching.

"Don't touch me. Don't look at me!" But he didn't relent; he stepped into her space again, and her muscles froze.

Alessia didn't want to hurt him anymore, but he wouldn't leave her alone. With a defiant cry, she shoved at him again, but this time, he was a wall against her, and his arms enfolded her.

Tears spilled down her face as she sobbed angrily.

"I hate you." All the hurt, all the emotion she had pent up over the years rained down and came out through her hoarse voice. "I hate your broken vows, the way you dishonor me, after everything I gave you."

Her heart.

Their children.

A new home.

A new life.

It wasn't enough. Somehow, she wasn't enough, and perhaps it was because Ludari's poison had been in her all these centuries.

Zryan loosened his grip on her and stepped away, retracting in every sense of the word. He averted his eyes, his chest heaving with as much emotion as hers, but he didn't say a word.

"Why do this to me? To us?" The words tumbled from her lips before she had the chance to stop them, raw and ragged.

18

Zryan

Why do this to me?

Alessia's words hung in the air between them, the *why* like an arrow piercing directly through him. Sharp and calculated.

Was this where she wanted to discuss everything that had come between them? Where she wanted to hash out the travesty of their marriage? All the ways in which he had failed her. All the ways in which he had proven himself to be a bad husband and terrible father. All the ways he had—

Zryan halted. He hadn't even realized he'd begun pacing. That his feet were carrying him back and forth across the cell as he let the words bounce around inside his brain, wounding each part of him the more they circled.

He paused in his steps because he *had* been a good husband. He had loved her with everything in him. Had adored her. Had wanted no one *but* her. And he *had* been a good father. He'd helped to put his kids to bed. Snuggled with them when they needed comfort. Carried them along beside him through his days overseeing the kingdom.

But he'd had one quick moment of negligence. One terrible, awful moment. He had made a mistake that couldn't be taken back, and she had pulled away from him. Cut him off from his child in his worst hour. Cut him off from her.

Zryan spun to face Alessia and at last admitted the one thing he should have admitted so many years before. "Because you *left* me!"

Alessia, with her wet cheeks and red-rimmed eyes, stared back at him as if he had grown a third eye in the center of his forehead. "What are you talking about?" Her tone was incredulous. "I have never left you. Despite everything, *everything*, I've been here at your side this entire time."

Zryan shook his head with vehement insistence, his hands fisted as he took up his pacing once more. The emotions inside him were too strong to keep still. So much riotous chaos swirling around, making his stomach tight and his shoulders taut. His heart beat erratically, to the point that he thought it would stop beating altogether, simply shatter in his chest. "Your body was here, Less, but not your heart. I watched the emotions bleed out of you when it came to me. By the *sun*, Lessie, I needed someone." He turned on her once more, needing her to see the pain inside him as he spoke. "You may be okay on your own, I know you were down in the depths of those dungeons for so long, you had only yourself to depend on, but I *needed* someone. I needed *you!*"

She flinched back a little as if he had struck her, surprise but also confusion warring on her face as she shook her head in denial. "I didn't, not until—"

"You did!" He cut her off, because if he didn't now, he would never speak his mind. Never admit to her all the pain in his heart. All the reasons why he had strayed away from the absolute love of his life. But he needed to say it. Realized that he had desperately *needed* to say it for so very long. Had, in fact, wanted to talk to her about it. About what had happened that day. Wanted to know why she hadn't been able to overcome it. "The day Kian was hurt, you started looking at me differently. Treating me differently. For sun's sake, Alessia! You kicked me out of his bloody room when I deserved to be there at his side just as much as you!"

Alessia paled at his words, and a part of him wanted to stop. Wanted to take the words back and simply accept all the blame. To admit all the ways he had destroyed their marriage and leave it at that.

But the dam was open. The words were flooding out, and there was no stopping them now. "It was like all my failures had rushed back. Every horrid word of doubt and disdain my father spoke of me was coming true in your eyes. You looked at me like I was less."

Her lips fell open, eyes conflicted. A little piece of him dared to hope when he saw what looked like the desire to comfort him flare up inside her gaze, but then she squashed it down. "I was angry and upset. Our son had nearly died. It wasn't about you. Not *everything* is about you!"

His teeth clenched, and he shot her a furious glance. He was well aware of that fact. That, try as he might, many things were actually not about him. Because he wasn't *worthy*.

"It didn't end with that night, Less." He shook his head, moved to the bars of their cage, and pressed his forehead against them, fingers curling around the iron to squeeze. "You started sleeping in other chambers, went so far as to have your own rooms decorated simply so that you could flee from my presence." The pain of those days rushed back, fresh and unhealing. A new wound to scour his heart. "Only occasionally would you offer me any affection at all, and even then, it was like you thought you needed to do it, not that you wanted to. And I . . . *starved*. Fool that I was, took it. Because at least I was able to hold you in my arms again, even if just for a moment."

His forehead pressed into the bars even more, the pain of it better than the agony in his chest.

"Zryan . . ."

"When we found out that you were pregnant with Brione, I thought perhaps it was a chance for us to rebuild. To grow closer over another child, our first daughter." His head turned to look back over his shoulder at her. "Instead, it felt like a final cut, and you just pulled away from me even more. And I don't know why . . ." His words became soft, fading off in his pain.

"You didn't know why?" Alessia was incredulous, and she shook her head, laughing bitterly. Slowly, she stood, clearly needing to find higher ground once more. To even the ground between them. "*You* pulled away. Do you know how many times I had to watch you flirt with someone else right in front of me? Any beautiful noble's daughter or strapping soldier that came through." Her voice was bitter. "You used to tease me, Zryan. Your eyes would light up when I walked into the room, but there was none of that. Just distance. You still looked at our children with light and adoration when you saw them, or when you'd pick up Brione and soothe her cries, there was a gentleness and love there. But you didn't look at me like that anymore. I felt as if I were nothing but the breeding mare to bear your children."

"What?" Zyran spun on his heels, horror and anger intermingling inside of him. "Me?! You hadn't properly looked at me in *years*!" The volume of his voice rose with every word. "If I had withdrawn at all, it's only because—" Zryan cut himself off.

Turning back to the bars, he caught them once more, squeezing with all his pent-up rage. He wanted to scream. To point fingers. To be all you, you, you, but he was starting to realize how meaningless it was. What good would come of trying to place blame at her feet? Only he controlled his actions, whether responses or not to hers. No one had thrown him into the bed of another. That had been all his own doing.

Tears sprang to Zryan's eyes, and he pressed his lids shut. The air between them was heavy with emotion. Thick with unsaid words and despair. Was there even hope of fixing any of this? Did it matter if things were fixed? Perhaps what mattered now was that he was honest with her. Completely and utterly. That he lay everything bare before her and not attempt to hide.

He straightened from his slumped position, finding courage that he did not know he had, and turned slowly to face her. She stood in the middle of the cell, her arms wrapped around herself, holding her emotions in. Or perhaps holding herself together.

Zryan pressed his back against the bars, feeling the strength of them bite into his shoulders and back. Accepted their sturdy support.

Despite the millennia that had passed between them,

Zryan could still see the young fae he'd first let out of the dungeons. Still saw her wariness as she explored the new world Draven, Travion, and he were creating. Zryan had wanted no one at his side as badly as he wanted Alessia Pagonis, and it was as true now as it had been then.

He found calmness within himself to continue. "I didn't intentionally go looking for someone else's arms," he said softly. He wanted to look away, but he forced his eyes to remain on hers. He couldn't shield himself from her pain any longer. No more blinders. No more denial. "I simply felt so lonely. I had you and the children. But at the same time, I didn't feel like I was truly a part of our family anymore. I felt outside of it. Shoved aside because I had proven I wasn't worthy to be a part of it." He swallowed roughly against emotion welling up inside him and noticed Alessia do the same.

"When it happened, I was so desperate for affection, it no longer mattered where it came from. I don't even remember her face," he admitted, shame washing through him. It prickled along his skin, making his body heavy, pulling him toward the earth. "I just remember staring up at the ceiling when it was over, wishing that it was you lying beside me and hating myself even more for what happened."

"Then why did you keep doing it?" she asked, voice hard as flint but tinged with pain.

Zryan shook his head and brushed the back of his hand across his wet eyes. "Because I am weak. Because I thought I had lost your love entirely, and I needed affection to come from somewhere." He laughed bitterly. "My father is correct, I am *weak*. And I am pathetic." Zryan shook his head.

"Spirits, Alessia, I *know* I betrayed you. I know I did so

much to hurt you, over and over again. I honestly do not understand why you've stayed this long. Why you continued to stand beside me. I didn't deserve it. And I knew what I was doing each time it happened, yet each time, I would tell myself that you didn't love me anymore. You had abandoned me, so it could be excused. I could find the affection I needed elsewhere. I could find comfort for all my pain in someone else's arms. Convinced myself it was okay because you didn't look at me with love anymore. You didn't want me, but someone else did." His voice broke, and he bit at his bottom lip.

Alessia had turned partially away, her shoulders heaving —not with sobs but with quick draws of breath as she tried to steady herself.

"I did stop," he said finally, tears pricking his eyes again.

Alessia froze, then slowly turned her head to look at him. He could tell she didn't believe him. "Lies."

"I swear, it's the truth. I haven't been with anyone but you for a number of years now." He swallowed and brushed fingers along the bruised flesh of his throat. "I couldn't live with myself anymore." A choked laugh left him. "I know what you're thinking. Why now, after all this time?" He shrugged. "I don't know. Only that my guilt finally began to outweigh my own selfishness and I couldn't take what I was doing to you anymore. I ran out of excuses. And watching my brothers marry has only been a further reminder of the wrongs I've committed."

Alessia scrubbed her hands over her face. He could only imagine the thoughts rampaging through her mind. He wanted so badly to go to her. To wrap his arms around her and hold her to his chest. To give her the comfort he'd been able to give her in the early days of their love.

"I'm sorry, Lessie," he whispered, unable to speak louder past the ball of emotions lodged in his throat. "I should have come to you when I first felt you pulling away. Should have asked what was going on inside your head. Should have said it hurt when you pushed me aside." He pinched the bridge of his nose. "I should have ignored my own self-doubts and simply talked to you. *Fought* for you." He had to stop, to swallow against the tears that threatened to come. "I'm sorry I gave up on us."

19

Alessia

The failure of their marriage wasn't entirely Zryan's fault.

Alessia could list every one of his flaws, bring up every transgression, but as he listed her failures off, it dawned on her that they'd both let arrows fly. Each one wounding their marriage. Each one hurting the other. The biggest issue had, in fact, been when they ceased talking to one another about minor issues, which bloomed into larger ones.

Before long, there was a chasm between them, and it was far too wide for a bridge.

But, spirits! Listening to the raw anguish, seeing him on the verge of tears, this was just another dagger to her heart, and one that she'd needed to wake up. She *hated* baring herself and being vulnerable, but closing herself off was what got them to this point in their relationship to begin with.

In the end, she was no better than him. He hadn't been the only one who'd escaped into another's arms. Simply because Zryan had thwarted a few trysts didn't mean she hadn't been successful.

She clenched her fists and closed her eyes. This was more than difficult to put into words, to speak without blaming him when it was just as much her fault too. She saw that now. *Now,* when they were slated for execution in two days.

Alessia drew in a deep breath, calming herself, centering her thoughts. "I have stayed for all these years because I do love you. Despite the hurt, betrayal, and disappointment, I love you. Even when I hate you, I love you, and I loathe that while you're my greatest strength, you're also a weakness." As soon as the words tumbled from her lips, she felt the rawness of her emotions wear her down.

He weakened her every time he looked at another. Each day when his attention was on something or someone else. Even as he lifted little Brione into his arms, his attention was on their child and not her.

While it was a selfish want, Alessia only needed to know that they could survive the hardships too. But when the very one who was like the sun in her life pulled away, she was left cold to the core.

The familiar loneliness returned, and she relied on herself. Zryan was right. She was fine on her own, but she didn't care for it. Far too many shadows plagued her mind without the brilliance of her sun.

Zryan stilled, and in the quiet, he scarcely breathed. Alessia wished that he'd open his mouth, cut through the silence, fill it with laughter. Whatever would erase the hurt they'd both caused in the cell.

"I will own my wrongdoings, and you own yours, but I don't know where to go from here." She dropped her hand to her galloping heart. The sound of it pounding in her ears deafened her. "I can't do this anymore, though. I was angry when I said I wouldn't be here when the dust settles, and I shouldn't have said that." She paused, glancing to the side as a rat scurried into a hole in the foundation. "But it's how I felt. If this is what it is to be—" She laughed; it sounded hollow to her ears, which only encouraged tears to fall anew. "It doesn't matter. We'll be dead in two days."

"I can't do this anymore either," he said, ignoring her other words. Zryan closed the distance between them and used his finger to tilt her head up. "I want to be your husband. I want to be the one you come to when you feel vulnerable, and if I hurt you, let me know instead of bottling it inside. I want to be *safe* for you, Lessie." A strangled noise escaped him as he leaned his forehead against hers. "By the sun, when did I stop being that for you?"

She reached up to squeeze his bicep, hoping to soothe his aches as much as her own. "I stopped being safe long ago, so I cannot answer that question. All I can say is that I am sorry. Truly."

His arms encircled her, squeezing gently. "As am I. More than you know."

With a sigh, she leaned against him. They'd needed this, and it released tension she'd been holding for . . . by the sun, how long?

"For however long we have left, let's try."

Zryan nodded and dipped his head so he could tuck his face into her neck. "I vow to try."

And she believed him. Because why lie when their time was running out? This was their end. A small fluttering brought her attention to the little life she carried. Fates, she wanted to tell him and give him a reason to fight again, but he would only hurt himself on the iron bars.

More than that, if they did escape the dungeon by some blessed miracle, she wanted him to try for them. Not because of their unborn child, but for *her* and because they vowed to work on things *together*.

If it was meant to be, there would be time, and Alessia would give him the very sun in the sky like he'd done for her years ago.

"I don't suppose the guards will bring us a pot to piss in." She eyed the floor angrily, the familiar pressure of her bladder spasming. Even Alessia knew it was foolish to think Ludari would allow them a shred of dignity.

He wanted Alessia and Zryan to feel like bottom feeders.

Zryan chuckled as he withdrew from her. "I promise not to watch." He jerked his head toward the corner and walked to the front of the cell, pressing his palms to the bars.

With a sigh, Alessia retreated to the far corner to relieve herself. The next two days would be long ones, and if she knew the tyrant at all, he'd draw the process out as much as possible.

When she was done, she returned to Zryan's side. Guards chuckled down the way, dragging a prisoner by their arms. Instead of hurling them into the nearest cell, the fae brought the individual near them.

Calor's slender face came into view, his eyes wide with panic, but he possessed a faraway look in his gaze, one that she was familiar with. He was spelled, perhaps for a second time.

The guards threw him into the cell adjacent to theirs without a care, and he tumbled to the ground, mumbling.

"Calor," Alessia said as she crawled to the front of the cell, pressing her face to the bars. "Calor!"

"Leave him. He belongs there," Zryan said, not sparing the fae another glance.

Calor didn't answer anyway, only mumbled more.

Fates save us all.

Alessia woke with her head bent at an awkward angle on the dirt floor. She wasn't certain when they had fallen asleep, but Zryan's body pressed into her from behind, keeping her warm. She groaned as she sat up, rubbing at a knot in her neck.

Since Mal had deceived them, no food or drink had been brought to them, and neither had a pot in which to relieve themselves. Instead, they'd had to use the corner like animals. Luckily, it was cool in the dungeon, otherwise the heat would have worsened the growing stench.

"What I wouldn't give for some lamb pie right now," she muttered as her stomach rumbled in protest. However, it was the dryness in her throat that was most bothersome.

Alessia rolled over onto her knees, wondering what fresh terror awaited them today. Would Ludari visit, taunt or pull them out of their cell to play a few games?

All Alessia needed was to be in front of him, lock eyes for a moment so she could ensnare his mental threads, then he would belong to her.

She would make him crumble, and this time, she would ensure Ludari was never pieced back together.

It was a dream, of course. A good one, for once.

Zryan reached for her, pulled her down into his chest, and she simply stayed there, absorbing his heat.

"Mead sounds good too," he added, chuckling, but he cut himself off and carefully adjusted her as he sat up.

Alessia followed his line of sight out of the cell and watched guards leave their posts. She quirked a brow, unsure why when it was far too early for them to switch, and no one was running as if there had been a breach.

Perhaps it was Ludari beckoning them for some game in the courtyard. Oh, what wretched choices would he force the guards to make, driving each one to choose between their brethren?

She sagged against the iron and shook her head. "If I had slit Phaedora's throat the last time we saw her, this wouldn't have ever happened."

Zryan rubbed at his side and grimaced. "If I had known this was what she had in store for us, I would have let you. But she was once a pawn too." He leaned against the wall and glanced up at the rough stone of the ceiling. Hardly any light touched it, but every once in a while, a flicker from one of the fae-lights danced across the darkness. "I never loved her. She was a distraction from my father's wickedness, and the first chance I had to step away from what *he* had forced me into, I took it." Zryan used his foot to nudge her, as if he was trying to pull her from brooding over the several ways she would end Phaedora.

"Nevertheless, let me have my hatred for her. She may not have been vile to you then, but she is now, and we meet our end tomorrow because of her."

Alessia sighed shakily and sat, then lifted her hands to

cup her face. No tears came; those had dried up yesterday. Exhaustion and lack of water had deprived her of that.

Silence spread between them, but rather than the typical tension that vibrated around them, it was a comfortable quiet. As comfortable as they could be considering their circumstances.

A new set of footsteps brought her attention to the aisle. Alessia turned in time to see the gauzy white fabric of a dress.

At first, her heart seized within her chest. Phaedora had finally thought to visit them, then. The notion riled Alessia, and she wondered if she could tear a piece of her armor off to strangle her with, but as the female drew nearer, it was clear that this wasn't Phaedora.

Her shoulders sagged a fraction.

It was Alvia.

What in the great mountain's name was she doing down here?

Alessia scrambled to her feet and peered through the bars as the young female drew nearer. "Are you mad? What are you doing down here?" Anger rose in her. She would not have the blood of Seducere's daughter on her hands.

"Alvia, you should be upstairs. This isn't safe," Zryan muttered from where he sat.

Zryan had always been a source of positivity that Alessia could look to when she felt her worst, but even he was depleted of such energy. That didn't bode well for them.

They had both resigned themselves to death.

Alvia's impossibly blue eyes rounded, and she pulled a key from between her cleavage and waved it. "It is safe enough if you know how to work your way around guards."

"You have the key," Alessia breathed and reached for it, but the blasted female was just out of reach.

An ugly part of her wondered if this was no more than a trick. It was a tactic Ludari would use. Release them, only for them to be hunted like mice scattering.

Zryan moved to his feet, and he focused on the silver glinting in Alvia's hand. "You've come to release us." There was no question in his tone, but he and Alvia shared a long look, one that didn't inspire hatred or jealousy in Alessia. No, she felt one thing blossoming in her chest.

Hope.

Zryan

Bright eyes filled with hope and courage stared back at him through the bars of his cell. Zryan felt his head shaking against his own will.

"This is too dangerous," he said, though part of him was saying to be silent. To not try and talk her out of something she had already started. But she was someone else's child. Someone's daughter that he had brought into his home at an unsure time. She was in this situation because of him and no one else.

Alvia smiled softly. A smile that was sad as well as sweet. "You are right, Your Majesty. This is too dangerous. But what is even more dangerous is allowing Ludari to remain on the throne. While I have not heard all the stories, I know enough to realize no one is safe while he is here and in control." She paused, perhaps debating whether to be frank with her words. Zryan nodded to encourage her. "You decided for me who I would marry; at least let me choose how I may die."

Beside him, Alessia snorted, and when he cut her a

glance, she was looking back at him, her brow cocked as if to say, *She has you there.*

He sighed but nodded. "Very well."

Alvia nodded too and moved to the lock, but before she could unlatch the door, footsteps sounded from farther down in the dungeon, and another guard came into view. He took in Alvia, and then the space around them, clearly noting that his other comrades were gone.

"What are you doing down here?" He reached for the hilt of his sword.

Alvia spun, key tucked away in her hand. "I simply wanted to see how the king and queen were doing."

"Former," the guard corrected her, brows furrowed in suspicion as he stepped closer.

Alvia's body changed, taking on a more relaxed stature as she took a step toward him. "Oh, of course!" A trill of laughter slipped from her. "Thank you for reminding me." With his eyes on her and her casual glide, Alvia had managed to get within reach of him.

The guard was surprised when her hand fell to rest over top of his, and for a moment, he pulled his sword farther from its scabbard—then he paused. His eyes took on a dreamy, heated cast as he leaned over her more.

"Aren't you a pretty little thing," he purred, head dipping as if he meant to kiss her.

Alvia stepped into his body, wrapping her arms around him, and as she did so, she spun them on the spot. "I am, aren't I?" she cooed, pressing her body against his so that he was forced to take a step back, then another, and another, until he was close to the cell.

Zryan did not hesitate. He reached out to wrap his arms

around the guard's neck. Pulling him tight against the bars, he used the extra leverage to press his forearm into the guard's throat. The guard struggled, kicking out with his feet, but Zryan only pressed harder until he heard a snap of bone, and the guard's body went limp.

With the thud of the body to the floor, Alvia was already at the latch, key inserted and twisting it. As the metal creaked and the door swung open, Zryan felt a rush of relief fill him. They once again had a chance to come out of this alive.

Stepping out of the cell, he took a deep breath, feeling the flood of magic once more. It rushed through him, like a dam had been broken. A rush of energy flooded his veins, catching his breath and releasing on a shudder. He brought his hand up and watched the sizzle of electricity flicker around his fingertips. It felt good to be back to himself again.

"Thank you," he said to Alvia.

She merely nodded, then looked to Alessia. "Tobias is upstairs. He's going to help us get out of here."

So, she meant to come too. Zryan pressed one hand to the middle of Alessia's back and set his other on Alvia's shoulder. "Beautiful, let us get out of here now before someone else comes along."

With quick steps, they made their way through the dark dungeon and up the stairs. At the entrance onto the main floor, they halted, Zryan peering out carefully. Just as Alvia had said, Tobias was there waiting for them.

"Your Majesties!" he said softly, relief showing in his eyes, and a smile split his lips.

"Tobias." Alessia looked pleased to see her guard had stayed as loyal as she thought he would. Loyal, and alive.

"Let's get you out of here." His eyes shifted from his queen up to Zryan, who nodded in agreement.

"If you can get us to the throne room, there is a hidden door to a secret passageway that runs beneath the castle and out onto the streets," he informed him.

Tobias' eyes lit with surprise. "I can do that." The guard took a moment to look around them, stepping farther into the hall to make certain they were safe, then he waved them out of the staircase to the dungeon. "Let's go, and keep it quiet."

Zryan wanted to remind him of who he spoke to, but instead, merely pushed Alessia and Alvia ahead of him so that he could take up the rear, a crackle of lightning ever at the ready. Their steps were quick yet quiet as possible, slipping down the hall and up another set of stairs toward the throne room.

Tobias halted on the staircase, checking the hallway before allowing them all to proceed. As they crept down the passageway, another section opened up before them, and he held up a hand once more, pressing a finger to his lips. He stepped out into the hall perpendicular to them, and soft murmurs were heard as he spoke with the guards who were passing.

Zryan pressed to the wall of the staircase, his heart hammering in his ears, waiting to be discovered. Looking behind him to make sure no one was approaching from the lower level. A commotion had started, voices belonging to soldiers who had perhaps realized they were no longer in the dungeon.

"We have to *go!*" he hissed, glancing up at Alessia on the stairs above.

She met his gaze, then took Alvia's hand. "We're going to run," she told the fae. "Don't stop until we get to the large statue of a pegasus on the east-facing wall. Understood?"

Alvia, looking far paler than before, nodded quickly. Zryan felt a moment of pity for her, and shame. She should not have been in this position, but here she was.

Alessia held up her hand, raising first one, then two, then three fingers. As the third lifted, they all burst into the hallway, and the two guards Tobias was attempting to be rid of looked up in shock. Tobias reacted quickly, striking out at the first one as they saw him, and Zryan lashed out at the second with a bolt of lightning. Alessia was already pulling Alvia down the hall along with her, her protective instincts in full swing.

As the guards collapsed, Zryan and Tobias chased after them, their sandaled feet slapping loudly on the marble, echoing down the corridor. Silence no longer mattered; getting to the secret passage in time did.

Zryan rounded the corner, and he saw that Alessia had the secret passage open. She was just about to push Alvia through when five guards rounded the opposite corner and came into view. Zryan cursed and ran toward them, lightning crackling. Beside him, Tobias raised his sword.

The guards saw them coming, raised their weapons, and prepared for the attack. The sound of blades clanging rang out, and Zryan released his lightning. It bounced off the walls and ceiling, connecting with the soldiers and making their bodies freeze as it coursed through them. Heads falling back and spines arching, they howled in agony before collapsing.

"Alessia, *go!*" he shouted, looking back at his wife.

"Not without you!"

Before he could growl at her, Tobias had his hand on his chest and was pushing him toward the passage. "Both of you, go now!"

Zryan moved, both he and Alessia ducking into the darkness of the staircase. "Are you coming?"

"Yes, he is," Alvia cut in, pushing on Tobias to encourage him to go into the passage.

"You as well, my lady," Tobias uttered.

The fae shook her head, looking down at the three of them on the descending staircase. "No, someone has to create a distraction. I have more potential use than Tobias, so they may keep me alive." She looked at the guard as if to apologize.

"Alvia," Zryan started.

She shook her head. "Go, Your Majesties. And get this tyrant off the throne." She pulled the secret door shut, enclosing them in darkness.

Zryan felt a protest well up on his lips, but then took a deep breath. He had to focus on the kingdom in its entirety. Not one fae but many. Zryan called his electricity to him once more and stepped past Alessia. He took her hand and led them down the passageway and back out onto the streets of Celeia.

"Do you know if the wolves or harpies stayed?" Alessia asked Tobias as they scurried away from the wall around the palace and down a narrow alleyway.

"I believe so, Your Majesty."

"Do we search for them?" she asked Zryan, her eyes on him.

Zryan looked up into the air, trying to search the building

tops for a sight of them. "I don't think we have time. All we can hope is that they see us."

Together, the three of them slipped down another street, passing behind a smaller home. From a window, a young child spotted them, squawking at the sight of the adults passing by. Zryan held a finger to his lips, and the small child giggled and waved.

They rounded the corner of the home and found themselves in a deadlock with a number of soldiers. Scrambling back around the corner of the house, they ducked down, peering around at the guards. They were knocking on doors, hauling people outside. Zryan watched, disgust and fury rising inside him as they dragged a fae and his wife into the streets.

"Who do you swear fealty to?"

"King Zryan and Queen Alessia." The male held his head up high, only for the soldier to backhand him.

His wife cried out, moving to help him up onto his side.

"Would you like to change your mind?" the guard asked.

The husband tipped his head up, as if about to be stubborn and hold his ground, but his wife threw her hands up before him. "Yes! We swear fealty to King Ludari!"

The guard smirked and drew his sword. With one swift swing, he cleaved both of their heads from their shoulders, the heavy orbs falling to the ground to roll. Screams rang out in the air, those crouching in their doorways looking on with horror.

"I suggest everyone be quick to choose the right answer and not require a change of heart!"

Zryan rose to his feet, lightning crackling and a growl low in his throat.

However, the swift flap of wings and the scrape of claws stopped him from stepping out into the open. Looking back, he found a large were-wolf skidding to a stop before them. Its body shuddered and quivered, and then the wolf became a blond-haired man.

Channon straightened, chest heaving with pants. "Your Majesties, you're free!"

"We had some help," Zryan muttered, looking him over in all his nudity. And here Draven commented on how much Zryan liked to be naked when he was surrounded by this all the time. "How did you find us?"

Channon pointed upward, where a harpy crouched low on the rooftop of a house, her eyes darting around them, keeping watch.

"She spotted you from the air. We've got eyes throughout. If you follow me, I believe I can lead you safely out of the city."

Zryan stiffened. "I'm not going anywhere until we deal with that lot out there."

"Sire—" Tobias started, but it was Alessia who stepped before him.

There was anger in her eyes. Hatred for what she had just seen.

"I want to stop them too, but it will only continue if we're captured again."

Zryan's hand squeezed tight at his side. It felt like cowardice. To tuck tail and flee. To leave his people to defend themselves while he went safely away. What kind of a king was he if he just left them? Alessia's hand came to his cheek, and his eyes fell to hers.

"We will stop them, Zry. But we need the numbers to do it."

Zryan sighed but nodded. Leaning in, he pressed a quick kiss to her lips. "Let's get back to our children and figure out how we end this."

With Channon once more in wolf form, and harpies overhead keeping an eye out for approaching threats, the three of them ducked down alleys and hurried across streets, quickly making their way across Celeia. Zryan had to admit, it was an efficient way to do it, the nose of the wolf and the eyes of the harpies to guide them.

When at last they came to the edge of the city, Hannelore was there to meet them, their griffins at her side. The harpy smiled coldly and nodded her head in greeting. "Your Majesties, I have been instructed to bring you back to Edessa."

Zryan took the reins of Feroces, looking back at the city. Behind him, Channon and Hannelore conversed quickly, then the were-wolf darted back into the city, disappearing down a different street, and he was gone. Back into the thick of it to snoop and eavesdrop. The only hidden weapon they had at the moment.

Mounting his griffin, Zryan pulled on the reins, and Feroces launched into the air, taking them high above the city walls so that he could see down into it. Smoke billowed in some areas, while shouts came from others. His people were under attack, and it was up to him to find a way to end it.

21

Alessia

From the sky, Celeia almost seemed peaceful. The sun's rays bathed the stone buildings in a golden glow, casting hard shadows. Alessia wondered how many of the people knew that Ludari was back, that this quiet they now faced would end at any moment.

Zissi squawked at Feroces as he pulled ahead and started to descend as Edessa came into view. The clustered buildings grew farther apart, and the land surrounding the homes was more expansive.

Damaris Manor's marble structure stood out against the lush, green lawn and floral landscaping. From above, it seemed almost over the top, too vibrant, too much, but it was beautiful nonetheless.

The griffins touched down on the lawn, and Alessia quickly dismounted. Before she could turn around, Brione launched forward, wrapped her arms around her neck, and squeezed. *Safe*. Brione was safe and alive. She'd sent her to safety, but still, breathing in the scent of her daughter's hair, seeing her stand before her with tears in her eyes . . . It warmed her to the core.

"My sweet," Alessia murmured, cupping her face.

"You're alive," Brione's voice cracked. She assessed Alessia, as if making certain she wasn't imagining it. "But how?"

Alessia reached up, squeezing her daughter's shoulder with just as much relief as Brione felt. "We are." She sighed heavily. Exhaustion threatened to pull her down to the ground, that and the lack of hardy sustenance. However, there was little time to waste before the true battle began.

There was no time for weakness.

"It was Alvia Seducere and Tobias who aided us." Zryan nearly grinned. However, his eyes gleamed with a certain level of pride. Behind him, Tobias climbed off Feroces, where he had been riding behind Zryan.

Alessia wanted to roll her eyes, but Alvia had done well, and she deserved the praise.

Ruan approached, his dark brows narrowing in confusion. "Sudecere's daughter?" He snorted, his hands gripping onto his waist. "And how? By exposing her breasts to them—showing some leg?"

It must have rankled him beyond belief to know that he couldn't be in the palace, forcing guards into submission as he controlled the situation. That a noble's daughter could do what he couldn't.

Alessia cut him a glare, and just as she was readying to speak, Zryan cleared his throat.

"Mind your tongue. Without Alvia, we would have been executed as Ludari planned."

Brione stepped away from Alessia, then embraced her

father too. "I was afraid he would speed up the process. I knew he'd planned for it, but never did I believe Mal would have deceived you so cruelly." Anger flared to life in her eyes, and the gentleness faded, reminding Alessia more of herself than she cared to admit.

She *did* want to gut the trickster male, but his time would come. Their primary focus was Ludari and his possession of the Creaturae.

Ruan muttered under his breath, and Alessia wondered if he was still reeling over Alvia "While you were occupied in the dungeons," he started, only softening his tone when Zryan glowered in his direction, "Kian and I gathered a militia from Edessa. We didn't dare venture into Celeia, so our numbers are small, but they're willing to fight as best they can."

"With the pooled resources of fine metals in the town, I've been able to craft weapons for them too," Kian supplied as he joined them.

"The weres and other harpies are stationed in Celeia. They're assembling ambushes should any advancements on *us* begin." Ruan flexed his hands on his hips. His jaw muscles leaped as he relayed the information.

More waiting. More waiting. He hates it as much as I do.

"We should call Draven and Travion," Alessia said as she turned to face Zryan. "They need to know—"

"I already did." Ruan dropped his hands to his sides as he closed the distance between them. The gold cuffs on his bicep depicted his rank as general, and beneath the red fabric and gold vambraces, Alessia knew there to be scars from battle. Hard earned ones, and they were why he'd earn his position in the royal army.

She should have known Ruan would have handled things efficiently.

Nodding, Alessia motioned for him to continue.

He bared his teeth like a sneering lion. "We weren't certain if we'd need to storm the palace to retrieve you. And without an ample headcount at our ready, we had no other choice." Ruan sucked his bottom lip into his mouth and wore on it. "Draven is readying his troops at once to march against Lucem."

Alessia's heart sank. *Against Lucem.* This was her home, had always *been* her home, yet war would rage on again after only a matter of months. However, this time, the kingdom would likely be decimated. Her people, their homes, their lives . . . destroyed.

"We need to call him again, at once," Alessia offered.

At least they could all agree upon that.

Inside the manor, the scent of freshly baked bread wafted through the air, accompanied by the distinct warmth of *lamb's meat pie.* Alessia's stomach churned with the need to eat but also threatened to revolt as the scent of *baking* offended her senses.

She ventured across the foyer and pushed into the study. The last time she'd seen the interior of this particular room, it had been when she called Eden, right before her mother burst into the room and everything went dark.

Much like the landscaping outside, there were plants everywhere. In the study, in particular, there were small trees potted near the large bay window and propped next to the bookshelves were shrub-like plants.

Zryan strode past her and toward the bowl in the corner of the room. A full pitcher sat propped there, and he poured the water into the bowl, pricked his finger, then, as the blood rippled, he spoke the spell.

Draven's face came into view. His brows lifted, the only surprise he let filter through. "I see you have escaped." He brushed a finger across his lips, then turned to look over his shoulder. "Seurat, send a message to Ailith, and fast. She's to remain in Andhera at the Veil." When he turned his attention back to them, his eyes flicked to the side, catching Zryan's attention.

"What are you thinking?" Zryan said as he stood over the bowl, his hands resting on the table.

"I cannot fight in Lucem with you, and by the moon, I'll not leave you to face him without me." Draven spat, then drank from a goblet. "You'll bring the fight to Andhera. He doesn't know the terrain, and neither do the Lucemites under his control. What my army doesn't cut down, the wilds certainly will." His voice grew low at the end.

Alessia flexed her fingers, trying to come to terms with the idea of taking her own down. She was certain a good portion of them didn't want to fight but would be forced. However, she knew many had sworn their allegiance to Ludari with all their being. Not just because they'd been held at swordpoint.

"Very well," Zryan muttered.

"We need to prepare. There is no way Ludari hasn't sent someone on our trails already," Alessia rushed. "Be ready for us, Draven. And you may want to send for Travion sooner rather than later."

"I will handle Travion and Sereia," was all he said before the image darkened.

Behind her, Ruan entered with Brione and Kian close

behind. He briskly crossed the room and sat down at the desk, unfolded a map, and motioned for everyone to close in.

"This is where I sent the harpies. The wolves are dispersed in Celeia should any of Lucem's forces push through with ease. We cannot afford to disperse any more than what I have. Am I missing anything?"

Zryan frowned at the map. He and Alessia had vanquished their fair number of threats, planned and charged into battle, but their son was brilliant when it came to strategy. If Alessia were to point out any flaws, it would be that he lacked empathy, and that clouded his judgment when it came to battle.

"So, if they travel through Celeia and take the path to Edessa, what of the citizens?" No one could risk sending an evacuation decree, for Ludari would know their plans and know troops were coming. How many would suffer?

This, of course, was nothing Ludari would consider. He didn't care who died in his name. But Ruan? Alessia frowned, hoping she'd see some conflict in his gaze, and for a moment, she thought he'd hardened over the years, to the point that perhaps he shared more in common with his grandsire than she cared to admit.

However, his shoulders sagged. "I fear for anyone in their direct path."

An eruption of activity outside the study shifted Alessia's attention to the door. She frowned as a harpy came into view. Hannelore tucked her wings closer to her body as she strode into the room, eyes blazing with fury and muscles taut with tension. "Celeia is under attack. We're doing our best to address it, but I should warn you, there are . . . creatures I've never seen before." Confusion swept across her face as she looked down at her hand, which was coated in fine dust.

"Soldiers made of clay are storming through, tearing into our harpies. And what they aren't taking down, the army is burning down. They're destroying the capital in search of you. Whatever it is you plan to do in Edessa, get ready to fight, because they march for us." Hannelore dipped her head in a curt bow. "Now, I'll return to Celeia, but know that I'll force a retreat if it's worse than when I left it."

Ruan cursed under his breath but nodded. "I trust your foresight. Go quickly and fight well." He pounded a fist to his chest and stood.

"It is time to get everyone ready and into their places," Zryan offered.

There would be no respite for them. Come what may, they'd fight until they couldn't anymore.

Alessia parted from her family and took charge of a squadron of soldiers. She frowned as she spotted a few militia members. She only hoped they would fare well during the fight, and though it saddened her that they were here, it gladdened her heart to know they were loyal to her, to Zryan.

"We will move to the eastern part of the road, so if they seek to use the woods to ambush us, we'll cut them off." She led them into place and stared up at the towering oaks. Their leaves danced in the soft, warm breeze, unaware of the mayhem about to be unleashed.

Now, they needed to wait.

Time seemed to still.

Alessia dug her fingers into Zissi's feathers, hoping to soothe him as he clawed at the ground. He wanted to fight as much as she did, and that wish would come true soon enough. She withdrew her sword from its scabbard, laying it across her lap as she stared ahead.

Zryan and his troops were beneath tall oaks that offered a decent amount of coverage from the sky. The soldiers with griffins hung back, readying for takeoff at a moment's notice.

Alessia drew in a deep breath. Then a strange noise echoed across the land. The ground shook, then, faster than she could register, one of the clay creatures emerged from the woods nearby, followed by a swarm of them.

Lightning purpled the sky—Zryan's signal—then he roared. "We fight! Forward!"

Zissi took flight, and Alessia's grip tightened on her sword as he climbed into the sky. Looking down, her heart sank as a horde forced its way down the road, into the forest abutting it then tumbling through the overgrowth.

So many, too many!

These creatures were unlike anything she'd ever seen. They were roughly the size of a male, though taller, with no detailed features. Their fingers were the most defined part of them, for their eyes were two gaping holes and their mouths a small slit.

"Down!" she cried out to her griffin, and he obeyed, allowing her to strike several of the abominations down. There was nothing to them. No organs, no sinew; they simply crumbled to the ground.

Every time she rushed forward, a whoosh of air resembling a moan escaped the creatures right before her sword shattered them.

And they kept coming, using their body mass or weapons

they'd picked up during battle to decimate whatever was in their path.

Alessia forced Zissi to the sky once again so she could reassess the situation. An army of clay approached, and she realized they weren't meant to be efficient fighters, for their advantage was in numbers.

That was something Alessia and Zryan didn't have in Lucem.

22

Zryan

Not only were the clay figures beyond numbering, but they were huge. Towering over all of them by almost an entire head. Shoulders broad, bodies thick, limbs long and crushing. While they could be shattered, there was also a strength to each strike they doled out.

Zryan found himself surrounded as he waded into the fray, his lightning spider-webbing out around him, connecting with the attacking figures. The blue-hued tendrils of power zapped over their bodies and halted them in their tracks. A low, eerie moan slipped from their lips as if they were somehow in pain, then the creations shattered. Zryan released a triumphant *whoop* and pushed through his small band of soldiers, the ground solid beneath his feet and the sun bright and burning overhead. He found the next batch of creatures to dispatch, their open clay maws like an endless void into darkness.

It spoke of emptiness. Of nothing. It chilled him despite the warmth of the day.

While the creatures attacked, they did not seem to think. There was a mindlessness to their actions, these large clay creations pulled from the earth. Good for destroying but not filled with ingenuity. *Golems.* He had heard stories of such things, but not since Ludari's days had they been created.

Beyond him, Zryan could see Ruan doing the same thing. His own lightning struck from the clouds above to pierce the amassed groups of clay creatures, rolling over them and shattering them in its wake.

However, just as Zryan and Ruan were both ready to step farther into the fray, the clay fragments began to clatter and shake, drawing together in large piles. He watched in horror as the pieces tumbled over themselves, stacking higher and higher until they formed the basic shape of a golem. With a quick sheen of light, the creature reformed into something much larger than before, equaling four or five of the smaller figures combined.

Zryan cursed under his breath, striking at two with his sword to shatter them as he turned on the giant figure towering over him. He gripped his hilt in both hands and ran, angling his sword so that, as he leaped into the air, he was able to stab it into the chest of the golem.

The sword sank into its hard surface, but instead of shattering, Zryan hung there, trapped in the suddenly thicker essence of the creation. The golem let out a low rumble of discontent, wrapped its large hand around Zryan's midsection, and pulled him and his sword free. It threw him through the air and into an oncoming wave of clay figures. As his body smashed through the golems, tumbling head over heels, the clay figures crashed to pieces beneath the weight of his impact.

Zryan collided with the earth and finally rolled to a stop. His head was spinning and his ears ringing. His side screamed, pain lancing through him as he gasped for breath. Each inhale sent more pain ricocheting through his body, drove his ribs farther into his abdomen where they were not meant to be. He pressed a hand to his side and forced himself to breathe slowly, to ground himself. There would be time to heal those later. The more pressing matter was the battle currently raging around him.

As if to prove the point that present matters were more pressing, he heard the clatter of clay pieces as everything he had just broken with his body drew together to form yet another large figure.

He pushed up to his knees and saw Alessia descending upon the golem he had attempted to take out. Her sword cleaved into the top of its head just as Brione attacked from below, joined by several of the militia. Their assault was successful, and the creature cracked in half, crumbling as it hit the ground.

Beyond, Kian was warring with several of the creatures, his golden arm glinting in the sunlight, smashing through clay figures with ease. And with each broken creation, the pile of shattered clay gathered around him.

Zryan's eyes shifted beyond him, to the sea of figures still coming, to the manors he could see going up in flame as Ludari's forces reached them. It infuriated him to see the devastation, to know that it was happening solely to hurt him. So his father could make a point. That the longer Zryan fought, the more people he would bring down with him.

Cursing, Zryan climbed to his feet. There had to be a way to destroy the golems. He spun, hearing the shattering of another, and found that Ruan had brought down one of the large beasts. The hope that this would be the end of them was quickly squashed as the pieces from his swept across the ground and began to gather with those from Zryan's.

"Spirits," he hissed, watching the monstrous figure that took form. He barely came to its knee, and it swept out at a group of soldiers without much effort, sending them careening through the air to collide with the great oak trees beyond.

Yelps and cries echoed through the air, mixing with the sounds of battle that rose from the field.

This wasn't working. They were only making matters worse for themselves.

"Ruan!" Zryan shouted, trying to get his son's attention. But he was gone, out of sight.

Zryan brought his fingers to his lips and whistled sharply. From a safe space in the woods, Feroces appeared, soaring through the air. He dodged past the flying fist of the monster golem and landed before Zryan. Zryan grabbed his reins and leaped onto the back of the griffin. Feet sliding into the stirrups, he kicked at his hind quarters, and his mount launched them into the air.

Above it all, Zryan was able to see the battle taking place. A number of the militia lay strewn across the field, brought down by clay golems or their own countrymen, who were bringing up the rear. Those who were fighting for Ludari were now dressed in a shade of blue that had always been preferred by his sire. They, too, lay across the field, limbs torn free by angry weres, arrows pierced into their backs by the ruthless harpies fighting from the air.

The trouble was, whether they killed all the Lucemite

soldiers or not, the golems were only getting larger and stronger the more they broke them down.

A loud crash rumbled, and more screams pierced the air as one of the giant golems pushed its way through a nearby manor. Floors crumbled, and the roof caved in. Zryan could see the fae inside tumbling from upper levels to the earth below, only to be buried by brick and mortar or crushed beneath the weight of a giant clay foot.

His people were dying. Edessa, following in Celeia's wake, was being razed to the ground.

"Ruan!" Zryan shouted once more, searching for his son. He found him at last, thanks to the streak of his lightning cutting through the air to web over a number of Lucemite soldiers. Their screams rang out, and they collapsed.

Snapping his reins, Zryan steered Feroces in the direction of Ruan, calling out for his son once more. This time, Ruan heard him and looked up.

Zryan landed quickly before him, leaping off his griffin to come up within speaking distance. "We have to retreat." Ruan's lips opened, but Zryan cut him off. "We can't do anything about the golems and haven't the time to figure out how to kill them. We're losing civilian homes and what militia you've managed to gather."

Ruan's eyes swept away from him and out over the battlefield. Bodies strewn everywhere, crumpled wings of downed harpies, soldiers in crushed armor alongside those of the civilian fae who had joined in on their fight. "To the Veil," Ruan said at last.

"If we retreat now, they may think it is due to lack of options rather than where we are purposefully headed."

Ruan's eyes snapped back to his, and he nodded. "Then

that is our plan. You take the east bank; I will take the west. Call everyone to retreat to the Veil."

Zryan nodded and reached out to clamp his hand around his son's wrist. Ruan reciprocated the action. "Let's get our people to safety."

He moved to climb back onto Feroces just as Ruan climbed onto his golden griffin. As they launched in different directions, Zryan knew he could trust his eldest to get the job done. Soaring over the battlefield, he began shouting for retreat. Over his shoulder, he heard the trumpet sounding, letting everyone know to pull back.

He found Alessia and Brione in the midst of it. "Retreat!" he shouted. "Head to the Veil!"

Alessia looked up to catch his eyes and nodded. She began shouting herself, directing what little was left of the forces back and away from the fight, helping to lead everyone in the right direction.

Zryan flew down to the head of the battle. Calling a great force of lightning to himself, he gathered it until it was so bright, he could barely see, then he released it on the opposing force all at once. Like an explosion, it created a wall of light and fire, blinding everyone within close range and effectively stopping their enemy long enough for his troops to pull back.

"Feroces, to the Veil!" Trusting his beast to get him there, he shut his eyes, letting them reorientate themselves after the blast.

When he opened his eyes once more, it was to see fae soldiers, militia, and harpies all fleeing in the direction of the Veil. Amongst the horde, he was pleased to see Channon and Syrsties had made it to them from Celeia. To his left, Ruan flew atop his steed, blasts of lightning leaving him to cover their retreat.

Zryan extended his hand, aiding his son in this endeavor. Beyond, the clay monsters crumpled and shattered, then regathered only to grow larger and stronger. It was a frightening and endless battle, and he cursed the cleverness of Ludari for creating such an army.

The road to the Veil was blessedly short, and soon, their troops were making their way through the gateway and into the unknown land beyond. "Brione! Kian!" Zryan shouted as he landed. "Make sure to be on the other end to guide them through to Andhera!"

Hannelore swooped down beside him. "I'm on it, Your Majesty. Someone should be there to aid them as they step into the night realm for the first time."

Zryan nodded and waved her off. "Go, and many thanks."

The harpy, who bled from a wound at her temple and looked more rumpled than he had ever seen her, nodded and took to the air once more, flying through the gateway and into the Veil beyond.

Zryan looked over at Ruan. "Are you prepared to stand with me until the end?" he asked. "We need to provide enough cover to hold them off."

Ruan's lips slid into a deep smirk. "It would be my pleasure." His hands drew together, and as they did, electricity crackled between his fingertips, forming into a ball that he then wound back with his arm and released into the oncoming hordes.

Lightning exploded in the midst of them, leaping out and snapping over anyone nearby. They froze, seized, and sank to their knees, smoke drifting up from them.

While his son concentrated on the soldiers, Zryan lifted his arms into the air, searching for all of the energy he could find in the sky. It crackled through the air, making the hair on his arms stand up and his cape cling to his back. He waited, until it was so sharp, it stung his skin, then he released it from the clouds. The lightning rained down on the clay golems like a wall of light and power.

The crash boomed through the air, a wave of sound that knocked fae off their feet and smashed the golems into tiny bits. It was enough to knock both Ruan and him to one knee. Zryan looked back over his shoulder to see that the last of their forces were slipping through the gates.

"Run, *now!*" Zryan shouted, and together, they leaped to their feet and turned for the gateway. Whistling for his griffin, Zryan ran. His sandaled feet slapped against the ground, his side burned with white hot pain, threatening to crumple his legs and steal his breath. But he continued to put one foot in front of the other until Feroces caught up, nudging him with his head.

Desperate for relief, Zryan grabbed his reins and swung himself up into the saddle, a cry of agony slipping from between his lips as he seated himself. He leaned over the feathered head of the griffin, allowing Feroces to carry him through the water-like ripple of the Veil and into the Veil realm itself.

Zryan gasped in short breaths and concentrated on holding on as the griffin galloped along the path, following the others who had fled. As the gateway into Andhera appeared, Zryan held his breath, accepted the new veil, its wet yet dry sensation passing over him as he slipped into utter darkness.

23

Alessia

etal clashed against metal as soldiers fought on. The screeching of swords was deafening, but it was no worse than the crackling lightning or quaking from the thunder rolling across the land.

Sweat trickled down her face, stinging her eyes as the blazing sun beat down on them.

Zissi screeched as he landed in front of the Veil. He galloped across the turf as Alessia wielded her sword and brought it down hard on one of the clay soldiers.

The being burst into shards and fell to the ground in a useless heap. *Not for long, the bastard. It'll just grow!*

Pain blossomed from Alessia's thigh, and she glanced down as a Lucemite glared up at her, an evil gleam in his dark eyes. He withdrew the sword from her and arced it high, readying to deal a killing blow.

Her heart sank to see one of her own with such hatred in his eyes for her.

Alessia hesitated but for a moment before she raised her

sword high, then let it fall as fast as Zryan's lightning. The steel bypassed the slow block on the soldier's part; her blade bit into the armor and, with ease, cut through the male's neck.

She gritted her teeth as the air touched her wound, and tears sprang to her eyes and spilled down her cheeks as she cried out and forced Zissi toward the Veil. The soldier's death sparked no joy, for this wasn't a clay creature nor an abomination crafted by Ludari. He had been a Lucemite—one of her own—and that pain stung more than any blade ever could.

"Move! Now!" Alessia caught sight of Brione herding those on the other side into the Veil, and with a nod, she barged through the portal, into the space in between the realms.

Shadows swarmed in the Veil, and something in the distance groaned. There would be no resting here, no collecting themselves.

Zissi lunged, beak snapping as he sprang for the troops who shouldered past him. He was ready to attack any offender, even allies who were too close. Alessia tightened her hold on the reins, redirecting his attention.

Through the mayhem, Brione's gaze met hers, and without a word, she motioned toward the other side of the Veil. Her daughter nodded curtly, then pushed her way to the front of the line just as Alessia did the same.

Zissi passed through the barrier, immediately stiffening as they crossed into Andhera. As ready for battle and as aggressive as the griffin could be, Andhera was a foreign place with an energy of its own. For a realm thought to be dead, it seemed to breathe more than Lucem or Midniva.

The air was cold to her, but in comparison to Midniva's winters, it was mild. Still, there was very little light, especially as they entered the woods. With the shift in lighting, all she had to go by was the absence of the howling specters and the temperature shift. Soon, her eyes adjusted, and above them, gnarled trees loomed, blotting out any hope of moonlight.

The abrupt switch from bright sun to night left Alessia entirely reliant on her mount, and even Zissi took a moment to adjust, his steps unsure as he tested the ground. But when his stride quickened, she knew his eyes had adjusted.

Zissi wasn't the first to stumble, nor the last. The grunts and curses following told Alessia that the soldiers were having a difficult time as they passed through the Veil.

There was hope that this would be enough of a setback for the royal army under Ludari's control. And, without the aid of wolves as well as harpies, they wouldn't fare well in these parts. They'd want to battle, to fight and maim or kill the beasts that prowled the woods.

Even Alessia knew it wasn't about slaughtering them all but stilling them until they could pass through.

She sucked in a breath and glanced up. The limbs of the trees wove together at the top, creating an eerie canopy, but that wasn't the worst of it. From beyond the clearing, something—a creature—hissed and rumbled. She had crossed into Andhera enough times to know that chimera and manticores ran rampant through these parts. They were as much guardians as they were a plague on the terrain, for they destroyed whatever was in their path, slaughtering and devouring what they could.

"Alessia!" Zryan cried out as he charged through the throng of fae. "The chimera, they're going to—"

Flames leaped from the darkness, temporarily lighting where the fire had originated from. A goat's head with black horns emerged from the middle of the chimera—one of three heads, but the most problematic one by far. To the left was a lion's head with a thick, black mane. And lashing out from behind was its tail—or should have been. Instead, it was a viper with fangs that dripped with venom.

"Push forward, soldiers!" Alessia barked, trying her best to lead the way. Roars emerged as the chimera pounced on their prey, and though she couldn't see it, she could hear limbs tearing, screams filling the air, and the absolute terror from their small army.

An eruption shook the ground as the clay creatures swarmed into Andhera, and mayhem ensued. Soldiers fought against the chimera, slowing the progression to the other end of the woods.

Fire licked at the ground, hungrily consuming the dry wood. If they were trapped in here, they'd all burn to death.

Turning Zissi on his haunches, Alessia forced him through the mass of fighting fae and clay and through a ring of fire. She cut down several of the golems, and they crashed to the burning ground in a heap of ash.

The last thing Alessia wanted to do was allow the beast to grow and gain power, but their sheer numbers were too much.

She grimaced, waiting for them to reassemble, but as precious moments passed, they never shifted, never took the shape of a giant.

Fire. Fire ends them.

Alessia spun Zissi around, and the griffin charged through the battle. "Push the clay into the fire! Build a wall of it to stop their advance if you must. It stops them from reassembling!" She screamed until her throat felt as though it would bleed.

The stragglers that forced themselves ahead Alessia took it upon herself to corner against the growing wall of flames. When they tried to advance on her, she brought her sword down, shattering them, or Zissi reared and struck them down.

At one point, it seemed futile to fight against them, for the clay nearly engulfed them, but once the fire lapped away at the shattered pieces, dust filled the air, and there was less and less battle to be found.

When the last one had finally been obliterated, the chimera appeared dazed by the loss of their food, and when they sniffed the ground, their attention was fully on the remaining troops.

"Do *not* engage if you can avoid it," Hannelore shouted as she swooped down. Dried blood caked the side of her face. "Their numbers far outweigh ours. Our goal is to escape!" She flew away toward Brione—to instruct her, Alessia hoped.

Behind Alessia, a tree fell from the fire eating away at the trunk. Zissi bolted forward, and she circled him around, calming him the best she could.

Lightning struck not far from her, and she jerked her head to the side. "Zryan! How do you kill them?" But he didn't reply, for he had leaped at a chimera that lunged at him with the lion's mouth open, geared toward devouring him.

"Take out the goat head!" Ruan growled as he severed a head, the lion's mouth readied to bite him, but he ducked under and quickly sliced off the viper. With all but one head gone, Ruan spun around and impaled the lion. "You need to burn their bodies. They have far too many hearts and will revive the moment you turn your back on them!"

Except they couldn't waste time simply sitting in the woods, battling and kicking the dead into the flames.

"Fight only what you must! We have to get through." Alessia encouraged Zissi forward, and he galloped down the path. Without the hindrance of the clay people, it was easier to move, but chimera lurked to the sides, watching and waiting for the moment to strike.

"Move forward!" Just as she was screaming, were-wolves and were-panthers burst onto the path, lunging and grabbing ahold of the beasts. The troops surged forward, running when they had the chance and fighting when they had to.

Eventually, the web of gnarled branches above gave way to a clear sky, and the moon bathed the ground in light. Although dim in comparison to the sun, Alessia could see the bare ground, and if her eyes didn't deceive her, the exit to the woods.

"Get your people out of here," Hannelore barked as she swept into view, her wings keeping her aloft. "Even Draven runs through and doesn't fight unless attacked. They will all die here if they fight."

As if she didn't know that! Alessia scowled, bit her tongue, and reminded herself that Hannelore knew the lay of the land better than she, and that her ultimate goal was to make sure they all made it out alive. Still, she wasn't keen on taking orders from her when she was trying to do the same— save her people.

Ruan must have ordered the riders to take flight, for

griffins took to the air, and moments later, Zryan ran up to her. Blood trickled down his bicep, and Alessia quickly assessed him for other wounds. Finding no immediate ones, she allowed herself to relax a fraction.

He handed her a bow and quiver. "Get in the sky with the others. We need aerial support." And while that may have been true, his voice shook with an unspoken fear for her well-being, and his too.

"No, I can help on the ground."

Zryan's jaw flexed. "Get in the air."

On the verge of pressing Zissi forward, she paused and reconsidered her stance. They had limited troops on griffins, and while there were also harpies, they needed all the help from above that they could get.

"Zryan." She said his name sternly. "You will get out of this with our sons, understood?"

His gaze softened a fraction, and he nodded before leaping back into the fray.

Zissi launched himself into the air, his wings beating against the cool air. With the aid of the fires, she could see the chimera lurking just on the edge of the woods.

She slung the quiver over her shoulder and pulled free an arrow. Nocking it, she aimed for the snake head on a chimera that was just emerging from the woods. As the arrow hit its mark, it alerted a nearby were-panther, who turned and mauled the lion's head. Soon, a harpy joined in, and together, they took the beast down.

So it went for far too long, but they were nearly at the mouth of the woods, and that was all they needed.

They just had to survive it.

24

Zryan

Their one blessing was entering Andhera during the day, when the yellow moon hung in the sky. While the darkness still fell over the land, casting everything in shadow, it was like a clear night in Midniva when the moon shone brightly. For the average mortal, daytime in Andhera may not be that bad; for a Lucemite who was used to sunshine at all times, the moonlight was like having a blanket thrown over their head.

As the griffins took to the air at last, with the harpies helping to provide support from above, the rest of their infantry ran down the main road that led through the woods. They moved swiftly but cautiously, the darkness just as much a threat as the beasts. The chimera were not pleased that their prey were escaping, and one launched itself at a soldier who tripped and fell. Zryan unleashed a strike of lightning at the beast, sending it scrambling back. He was pleased to see another soldier bend down to help his fallen comrade to his feet, looping his arm over this shoulder to help him.

"You take the right flank, I'll take the left," he called out to Ruan, who nodded. Between the two of them, surely they would be able to keep the beasts from attacking.

Father and son parted, their own griffins handed off to other soldiers so that they could remain on the ground to provide cover. Zryan cursed his brother's land. Cursed the yellow moon above that kept everything clear but still hidden. Cursed the chill in the air that made him shiver. Cursed the beasts that sought for one thing, and one thing only—blood.

How Draven had made this his home, he would never understand, and he also realized he had never thanked his brother for the sacrifice he'd made. At least not truly. Not with full acknowledgement of what it must have been like to come to this realm and survive.

His own panting breath was all that he could hear over the footfall of everyone running, the eerie quality of Andhera seeming to make the sound echo through the trees. Every beast must have been aware of their presence here.

From the woods, Zryan saw the glow of yellow eyes and did not wait to see what it was before he released a bolt of lightning. It crashed into the trees, causing the wood to spark and the horror that was there to be exposed. Humanoid face set in a fur mane that trailed down into a mangy lion's body with long legs and powerful paws. Topped off with a black scorpion tail.

It was a revolting monstrosity that filled Zryan with disgust and a sudden and distinct fear of winding up beneath its sharp talons.

"Manticore!" he roared, warning those before him.

The weres ran on the outskirts, howling when they

spotted a beast, letting either Zryan and Ruan or one of the harpies know when and where to fire.

A fae screamed in pain and terror as one of the creatures leaped unspotted from the woods, tackling him to the ground. Before Ruan or Zryan could react, Hannelore swooped down out of the air and was upon it. She landed on its back, a hand fisted in its mane, and pulled its head back. As its throat became exposed, her sword glided across, spraying black ichor out over the fae below.

He was wounded, but he was alive. Hannelore helped him to his feet, and keeping an arm around his shoulders, she aided him along.

As their party burst out into the open fields of Andhera, emerging from the thickness of the forest, Zryan released a breath of relief. Openness did not mean they could not be attacked, but it did make it easier to see the beasts before they were upon them.

No longer running for their lives, Zryan paused, a hand to his side, and hissed through his teeth. The pain was white hot and staggering once more, the harsh panting of his breath not helping. Ruan seemed to recognize his father's need and called for the soldier riding Feroces to land.

"Here, mount up." Ruan held the reins out to him.

"I am perfectly fine," Zryan said, fighting for his typical nonchalant attitude. Ruan only glowered at him and thrust the reins into his hands.

"Mount." One clipped order, then he turned and continued on the path toward the castle.

Grumbling under his breath, Zryan listened to his son and climbed atop his griffin. He kept himself to the ground, but no longer needing to overexert himself was a help.

The road from the Veil to the capital city ran along rolling hills of dark grass and sharp jutting rocks. Small clumps of gnarled trees with white glowing flowers tucked into dark purple leaves set along the hills, sometimes on their own, other times beside small stone huts. Their glowing windows should have been a small shot of welcome in the darkness and yet somehow made the land feel more isolated and cold.

They had been traveling the main road for half an hour when they crested a hill and the capital city of Arcem came into view. Zryan's shoulders slumped in relief. He was exhausted and starving. The need to simply be safe within a castle's walls and for a moment, not concerned with his or his family's safety, was strong within him.

The city was made up of stone manors, shops, and smaller homes, all built on the slope of a hillside that led up to where Castle Aasha sat on a high cliff. The castle pierced the sky like a wound, slicing through the darkness. The castle was built from black stone, with sharp turrets and high walls that surrounded it. The cliff it sat on the edge of looked down over a vast pit. Absolute darkness dwelled in that pit, so dark, it always made Zryan's eyes feel as if they were being plucked from his head. It was the entrance to the afterlife itself. And while those who died in Midniva and Lucem did not always pass instantly on to the afterlife—sometimes they ended up as revenants wandering the hills of Andhera— anyone who fell into that pit did not come back. The final death waited for them at the bottom.

Zryan suspected some of the harpies had flown ahead to warn of their approach, for as their haggard looking band of warriors passed through the gates of Aasha, Draven and Eden were already there waiting in the courtyard.

Eden's eyes fell over them quickly, and before anyone could say anything, she began calling to the castle staff for aid. Medical care and chambers for all. There was mention of baths and food, all of which sounded perfect to Zryan. But first, his brother.

Zryan dismounted, grunting when his knees almost buckled, but straightened up and found his fallback cockiness. Striding to Draven and Eden, he gave a sweeping bow. One that made his body scream, but he only brightened his smile.

"So kind of you to welcome us into your humble abode."

Draven eyed him coolly, assessing and scanning over his form. "You look like shit. I'm surprised you're in one piece."

Zryan pressed a hand to his chest. "Is that any way to—"

"Here so soon?" another voice cut him off, and Zryan looked over toward the stables to see Travion and Sereia exiting. "We weren't expecting you to arrive for at least a day."

"Yes, well, our sire decided to decimate Celeia and Edessa with forces made of clay and dirt. We hadn't much of a choice in the matter," he said dryly. Gone was his cockiness as weariness flooded back in.

Travion's brow furrowed at this news, but his attention was stolen by the sound of a soldier retching behind them. Zryan turned around and actually took in his infantry for the first time. A ragtag group of soldiers, civilian militia, and real and bronzed griffins. Everyone looked harried and beaten. They were covered in ash and dirt, blood spattered over them, and a number looked pale and shaken to their core from what they had just ridden through.

"They've had a proper welcome to Andhera, I see," Travion muttered, stepping up beside him.

"You've no idea." Sighing, Zryan turned back to Draven and Eden as his family came to stand around him. "We are in desperate need of baths, beds, and a meal."

"Of course!" Eden stepped forward, gripping Brione's hand and tugging lightly as she waved them all in. "Draven." She looked at her husband. "Let's get them inside before we pester them with questions."

Zryan was not surprised to see the way Draven dipped his head in acknowledgement of her words. He wouldn't say his brother had been cowed into obedience, but he looked to his wife for her softness and care.

"Go in," Draven said to him. "I'll see to it that our stablehands care for your griffins."

Kian stepped up to them. "Have them treat the metal steeds the same, only no food required."

Draven nodded and motioned for them to enter through the main doors of the castle. Passing him, Zryan clapped his brother on the shoulder and squeezed. "Thank you," he whispered.

"We'll kill him," Draven murmured and returned his squeeze with a look of determination in his eyes.

Zryan nodded and made his way up the steps and into the dark castle.

Inside, the castle seemed even colder, though Eden had done quite a bit to add warmth to its halls. Where once there had only been stone and flaming sconces on the walls, there now hung vivid tapestries that depicted all three realms. It added life—a sort of life that had not been there before.

A small band of tiny, haggard looking goblins, giant eyes

and ears far too long for their heads, scampered along the walls, chattering away in a language Zryan did not understand. They were not much bigger than rats and were scaly things with only bits of hair on top of their scalps. When the castle had been built, the goblins had moved in, and Draven had never seen fit to cast them out.

"Zryran, Alessia, my maid Loriah will lead you up to the chamber that we have for you. Fortunately, since I've arrived, we've actually set up bedchambers."

Zryan chuckled, then winced. "Well, I am pleased to hear we won't be sleeping on the floor."

Eden, perceptive as always, noticed the wince. "You're injured." It was not a question.

"My ribs," he said with an aloofness he did not feel.

Eden nodded. "I will be up shortly to take care of that, once I make certain everyone has been squared away." Her words did not broker argument, and Zryan did not have any wish to do so.

"Appreciated." Then, alongside Alessia and a small ragtag group of goblins, he followed the young maid, who seemed to glide along the floor rather than walk. While she was a solid presence, there was also a quality to her that almost made her seem transparent.

Revenant.

Someone who had not slipped into the afterlife for whatever reason: unfinished business, a thirst for adventure, or perhaps a failure to love. They were dead, but they were not gone. Not whole, but present. Spirits who could come and go and choose whether or not to be solid.

Draven had given them all purpose. New jobs. New unlives. A chance to live a new role until they felt they had completed the life they had missed out on and were able to pass on through to the afterlife. Typically, it was humans who wound up here. Most fae lived so long that, once they passed, there was nothing left to hang on for.

The room that they were led to was dark and welcomed them with a chill in the air. But Loriah floated over to the sconces, lighting them before moving on to the fireplace, where she soon had a large fire crackling away. The four goblins that had followed scurried in after her.

With the light, Zryan was able to see the large four poster bed in the center of the room, dark golden bedding covering it, framed by lighter golden curtains. It looked lush. Welcoming. Warm. Two of the goblins were bouncing over its comforter, doing something that looked almost like a dance before colliding together and rolling over until they hit the pillows. Zryan wanted nothing more than to shoe the tiny creatures away and collapse beneath the covers to seek oblivion for a few hours. Instead, he turned to look his wife over.

He ignored the maid, who was working on bringing in a large tub to set before the fire, a number of other revenants following behind with buckets of steaming water. He took Alessia's hands, clasping them tenderly between his own, and pulled her closer to him. There was a wound at the top of her head that had bled down the side of her face, and there seemed to be a gash in her thigh, but blessedly, beyond that, she seemed unscathed.

"By the sun," he rasped. "Even covered in dirt and blood, you're still the most beautiful sight I've ever seen." Saying the words released tension in Zryan he did not know he had been holding in.

They seemed to affect Alessia too, for her dark eyes welled, though tears did not fall. "Spirits, Zryan . . ."

He said nothing else, just pulled her against his chest, one hand pressing to the small of her back, the other lifting to cup the side of her face, drawing her lips to his. She tasted of fire, a welcome match for the lightning that coursed through his own blood. The heat of her returned kiss was everything he needed to add balm to his broken spirit.

Through the scent of smoke and ash, Zryan could smell Alessia. Vanilla and jasmine. He knew that she bathed in it, coating her honey skin in the warm scents that always made him want to lap her up.

The sound of someone clearing their throat pulled the two apart, their breath mingling in the tight space between.

"While I am very happy to see the loving moment between the two of you, I do suggest we get you both healed and cleaned before you commence with any intimacy."

Zryan and Alessia turned together to look at Eden in the doorway. She bore a small smile on her lips, true happiness in the depths of her eyes as she beheld them.

"Tis true," Zryan agreed. "I wouldn't want to dirty the sheets with grime when I can dirty them with love making."

Alessia snorted and gave him a soft swat. It shouldn't have hurt, but it nearly made him double over. The joking atmosphere of the room disappeared, and Eden hurried over.

"We need to get you out of your armor so I can see exactly what is going on."

As he dropped to the edge of the bed, Alessia and Eden both began to unstrap his armor, dropping it carelessly to the floor as they stripped him. Another goblin squawked in protest as it was nearly crushed by his heavy golden chest piece. "It's nothing but some busted ribs."

To prove his point, his side bloomed with angry looking bruises that stretched from hip to breast and spanned to his back and stomach.

"Zryan!" Alessia hissed at the sight of it. "You *idiot*! Why have you left it so long?!" She was furious, but it only made Zryan smile. It had been a long time since she had shown such concern for him so freely. "Stop smiling, you fool!" she snapped. "You could have died."

"I was fine." He grunted as Eden moved to his injured side and pressed her hands to either side of him. It made his muscles spasm as pain lanced through him; he hissed through his teeth and shot her a glare. Eden was unfazed and began to pour magic into them by way of heat that eased the pain a little.

"And what if you'd been struck and your ribs punctured your lungs?" Alessia asked, arms crossed beneath her breasts.

His eyes fell to them and took note of how generous and glorious they were. So proudly on display. "But that didn't happen." He hissed again as he felt several of the bones snap back into place, scraping against each other. Relief flooded him shortly after as the bones settled back into place and his breathing eased.

"Yes, well, not for a lack of trying on your part." Her forehead was creased, concern pinching the corners of her lips.

Zryan sighed and reached out to take her hand, squeezing it gently. "There wasn't time. Between Brione, the dungeons, and then Edessa . . ." He shrugged.

She grumbled but nodded.

Eden finished and stood up. "There, you should be entirely healed by morning."

"Thank you," he said to her.

"Of course." Eden squeezed his shoulder, then turned to Alessia. "And now, your turn." As she worked on Alessia's thigh first, Eden chewed on her lip.

"What is it?" Alessia asked, studying her face.

Zryan could see something was weighing on her mind, though she didn't speak it.

"I have a friend." Eden paused, squaring her shoulders as if she had to brace herself to say the words out loud. "Her family lives just down the lane from my manor." She looked between Zryan and Alessia. "Do you know if she is okay? Were all the homes destroyed?" Her hands were clenched before her. "Did anyone in the area get out?"

Zryan and Alessia shared a look. There had been so much devastation. The likelihood that her home was not one of the ones that had been demolished was very slim. Eden had already lost her father because of him, and then her mother due to her fury with Zryan. He hated to think that her close friend was now also gone. "Unfortunately, it is hard to say who made it out okay and who did not. We tried to pull the battle away from Edessa as quickly as we could, but there were several homes lost in the process."

Eden's lip trembled, but she stood straighter and nodded. "I will try making contact once I am finished here." And that was all she said on the matter, turning to finish up with Alessia's injuries before she excused herself.

Alessia shook her head. "The chances her friend . . ."

"I know." Zryan stood and pulled Alessia into his arms,

pressing a kiss to the bridge of her nose then at the corner of her forehead. He tucked her in against his chest, taking comfort in the ability to hold her once again so freely.

"You take the bath first," he murmured. "I'll sit back and enjoy the view."

25

Zryan

He only watched for a moment. In the end, after chasing the goblins from their room, he had fallen asleep lying on the bed, and it was the warm, slightly damp press of Alessia's hand to his cheek that woke him from the oblivion of slumber.

Groggy, he opened his lids to leer up at the vision looming over him. Dark wet strands of her hair fell around her shoulders, honey skin gleamed warmly in the glow from the fireplace, and love shone in her eyes.

By the great sun above, it was what he had desperately dreamed of having for so long. This was the Alessia he had first won over. This was the Alessia that brought him to his knees in desire and made his heart swell with tenderness and ferocity.

"Bathe," she commanded him, her voice soft but firm.

It was a tone that made his blood heat and his member threaten to stir. Zryan nodded and sat up, his hand slipping around the back of her neck. "Of course, my love." She met him halfway, her tongue delving into his mouth, grazing against his before she pulled back, teeth tugging lightly at his bottom lip.

Zryan groaned and stood, no longer tired or aching. Only wanting to feel her skin beneath his fingers and taste her on his lips. Reading this in his expression, Alessia pointed to the tub that now held fresh, steaming water for him. He nodded, but not before his hand brushed lightly over the heated space between her legs.

Striding across the room to the fireplace, Zryan unhooked the leather baltea from around his waist, letting the groin guard drop to the floor. He then unbuttoned the woolen tunica as well and let it fall to his ankles, then slipped out of it. This left him in nothing but his sandals, which he bent down to unlace. Once he was free of them, he kicked them aside and stepped into the metal tub.

This time, the hisses escaping his lips were not from pain but from the sting of heat. It was a shocking difference from the cooler room but soon had him melting into it as the warmth spread through sore muscles. Letting his head fall back against the rim, he closed his eyes, soaking up the feeling of the water around him.

"Don't take too long," Alessia's voice carried across the room. "I may have to take care of myself otherwise."

Zryan's eyes snapped open, and he pressed his cheek to the edge of the tub so that he could look over at her, sprawled elegantly on top of the bed, draped only in a linen towel. "You will have to do no such thing while I am present."

Their eyes connected, promise residing in both. And suddenly, Zryan no longer cared about the heat of the water warming his aching muscles. No longer wished to sit and soak in its depths. He wanted only to meet Alessia across the room and join with her in a way that had not happened in more centuries than he cared to count.

He ducked himself beneath the water, wetting himself entirely. When he came back up, he shook the water out of his eyes and reached for the soap. His fingers scraped through his hair and scratched at his scalp as he washed the dark strands. When he'd rinsed it clean of suds, he worked quickly on washing the blood and grime from his body, happy to see the dirt settling on the bottom of the tub that was no longer upon his frame.

With eagerness, he hopped out of the tub and plucked up the linen towel that had been left for him. Drying off quickly and efficiently, he flung it away and set his sights on Alessia.

He had only made it halfway across the bedroom when her hand rose to halt him. With a quick flick of her wrist, Alessia pointed to the floor, and Zryan heard only his shaky breath increasing with anticipation as he automatically sank to his knees on the stone.

It had been so long since they had been in this position. Where they could meet in a place of trust and love. Alessia, powerful and commanding, holding his love and desire in her hand. And Zryan, giving everything over to her in a way he had never trusted anyone *but* Alessia with.

He watched as she stood up from the bed, her fingers hooking the towel from around her. Slowly, the linen fabric slid down her curves to puddle at her feet. Zryan's mouth went dry. No matter how many times he saw the beauty of her body before him, he would never grow tired of it. Every angle, every curve. Long legs that carried her gracefully across the floor, slinking like a deadly cat on the prowl.

"Are you ready to be my good boy?" she purred, voice low and husky. Zryan's member jerked in pleasure at the sound of it, and he lifted his chin to gaze up at her. A warm hum spread through him.

"Only until I get to be terribly, terribly naughty." His lips slowly spread into a salacious grin that lit a fire in Alessia's eyes.

Her nails scratched lightly up his throat and beneath his chin. "I want your mouth on me Zryan, like I am the last and only meal you will ever have."

The demand sent a shiver of desire coursing down his spine, and without hesitation, he wrapped his fingers around the back of her thigh, lifting her leg up to drape over his shoulder, exposing her for his exploration. Both hands slid to cup her bottom, holding her steady as he leaned forward and buried his face into the warm mound at the apex of her thighs. He inhaled deeply of her scent, need spiking in his bloodstream and heading directly to his length that now stood rigid.

His tongue swept along the seam of her core, then darted between to circle the bud of nerves that waited there for him. Slowly, he teased her, waking up her body with gradual glides, feeling the way her body began to grow languid and soft, almost inaudible murmurs left her lips.

When Alessia was as pliant as he wanted her, his tongue increased its pressure, lapping at the pearl with more intention, lips sucking at it to make her jerk with pleasure against his mouth. He growled happily, taking each whimper, each sigh, and each roll of her hips as a small victory. He gloried in what he was able to do to her, all of it adding to his own desire that was quickly mounting inside him.

Nipping at her lightly, he lowered his head to lap along her core, tongue delving into her depths, stroking against the slick sides before he returned to the pearl nestled so divinely between the folds of her sex. His fingers tightened on the rounded flesh of her bottom as he lapped greedily, ringing another cry of pleasure from her.

When Alessia's back began to arch, her fingers buried tightly in his hair, pressing him more roughly against her, he knew that she was close. He continued his actions, tonguing her bud until she was crying out roughly, the sounds of ecstasy ringing off the stone walls.

Zryan lapped her gently through it, then as she came down, pressed his cheek to her thigh and gazed up at her. His eyes heated with the need that burned deep inside him, a hunger to be joined with her. But his lips glistened with her fluids—proof he'd brought her to completion, and this filled him with a languid pleasure that warred with his own desires for physical pleasure.

Chest still heaving, Alessia ran her fingers through his hair and to the base of his neck. Her other hand came up to cup his jaw, and she brushed her thumb over his lips, capturing her own essence upon the pad of it. She then pressed her thumb into his mouth, and he accepted this gift, gently licking her clean.

Alessia murmured, desire still brimming in her eyes. "Bury yourself in me," she rasped.

Zryan did not have to be told twice. He rose from the floor. Fingers still dug into the flesh of her bottom scraped down to her thighs, and with ease, he hoisted her up onto his hips. "Help me," he murmured against her lips.

He hissed as her long fingers circled around his member,

giving a few deft strokes down over the hardness that was desperate for her. When she guided him to her entrance, he wasted no time and drove himself up into the welcoming heat. Zryan moaned harshly as the tightness wrapped around him, shaking him to the core with how perfect they felt locked together.

Their lips met in a feverish need that made him growl as he lifted her up, pulling her almost entirely off of him before he pulled her back down just as he thrust up, piercing her to the hilt. Alessia gasped into his mouth, her teeth biting down on his lip, and he moaned back.

Needing a surface to support them, Zryan closed the distance to the bed and pressed Alessia's back to the wooden post. Her legs tightened around his waist, and her hands gripped his shoulder and clung to his hair. The pain of her nails in both only increased his pleasure, sending tingles coursing through each nerve ending.

He rocked his hips slowly into her, hands running down to her knees then back up her thighs to her ass, gripping the rounded flesh.

"More," Alessia growled, her breath heaving with her need.

Zryan looked at her through his lashes, drawing his hips back to plunge deeply into her once more, slowly, but with force. "Is that a command, Your Majesty?" he cooed, and by the sun, he hoped so.

In response, Alessia yanked back harshly on his hair, pulling his head back to expose his throat, and bit him there where his jaw connected to his neck. He shuddered, pleasure racing through him, and thrust deeply into her again, eliciting a grunt of enjoyment.

"Yes," she whispered into his ear, breathy and panting.

Zryan groaned and began to rock into her with deep, even strides that drove him mad with the friction and left Alessia whining in happiness as he stroked against the spot inside her. Her nails bit into him as she pressed into the post herself, giving herself purchase to meet his thrusts with needy ones of her own.

Feeling their pleasure mounting, Zryan pulled them away from the post to drop them down onto the end of the bed. He laid Alessia back against it, remaining on his feet with his knees braced on the edge of the mattress. He scraped a hand up over her stomach and curled it around her breast. His fingers rolled the hard bud at its peak, bringing more cries of happiness from Alessia as his thrusts within her increased, striking each time against that ridged spot inside her.

His head fell back as he began to feel overwhelmed. His skin was too tight to contain everything coursing through him, his pleasure so heady, he swore he could taste it. When Alessia began to clamp around him, he leaned forward, driving his hand beneath her hips to angle her up into him more as he pushed them over the top. His mouth latched onto hers as she cried out raggedly, muscles spasming around him and sending him over the edge.

Zryan moaned deeply, dragging his lips along the edge of her jaw and burying his face in her neck. As the shudders between them slowed, the only sound was their own breath coming quick and needy.

Zryan moaned happily, nuzzling along the edge of Alessia's throat. "Spirits above and below," he whispered. "I love you."

Alessia brushed fingers down his cheek. "I love you too."

He lifted his head so that he could look down at her, something inside him still needing to see the proof of it in her eyes. When he saw it glowing back at him, he dipped his head to kiss her once more. Zryan gripped her properly and stood, bringing her with him. Carefully, he turned on his heel and sat himself on the end of the bed with Alessia straddling his lap.

Slowly, his hands brushed up over her back, just as her own hands traveled across his shoulders and down his biceps.

"Did you mean it?" she asked him. "Everything you said in the dungeons?"

Her vulnerability shook him to the core, and he leaned in to kiss her, making it slow and loving. "I meant every word," he whispered, pulling back just enough that they could look into each other's eyes. "I don't want anyone but you, Less, I never really did. I just want it to be you and me."

"I promise to let you have me."

That was all he needed. That was all he had *ever* needed.

Their lips met once more, a new heat building that spoke of vulnerability and love. A desire to simply be connected. This time, as Zryan sank into her silken depths, their bodies pressed together on the bed, hips gliding slowly but purposefully. Their mouths only broke for short breaths between. His hands explored every curve, relearning familiar lines, just as her own fingers brought his skin alive.

When their pleasure mounted, they came together, shattering in a way that was as beautiful as it was passionate. Deep inside Zryan, a broken piece slid back into place, healing a hurt he'd carried for a long time.

When it was done, they lay in a tangle of limbs. Fingers

brushing over skin, lips pressing soft kisses to cheeks and jaws. Simply sharing space. Sharing time.

Zryan wished to never leave this moment with her. But unfortunately, reality came crashing back in as was needed. A knock sounded on the door with a call to dinner. Zryan pressed his forehead to her shoulder and grumbled.

"Perhaps I can foist this onto Draven and Travion, and you and I can simply escape into the dark."

Though he could not see her, he knew Alessia was offering him a knowing smile. "You would never turn your back on your brothers, or your people."

The fact that, despite everything, she still knew that of him pleased him greatly.

"True." He lifted his chin. "I am a terribly selfless man." He winked at her and brought her hand to his mouth to kiss the back of it, even as she rolled her eyes at him.

26

Alessia

lessia's body still hummed from fading desire. Despite everything, she smiled because, for the first time in more years than she cared to count, she felt whole. A war may have been at their door, but united with her heart again, and her family, it was empowering.

Zryan had left for supper as soon as his Andherian clothes were delivered, and the garb posed a new distraction for her, one that had her *considering* foisting the war onto Draven and Travion.

She turned to the privacy screen in her room and reached for the dress hanging there. Her fingers brushed along the heavy velveteen fabric. Gold vines stretched from the waistline to the high collar and wove along the wrist-length sleeves.

Even with the hearth blazing, it was still a touch too cool for her thin Lucemite skin. *Thank the fates for this.*

She pulled the dress on, muttering about the buttons in the back. "Loriah," Alessia said softly, then jumped as the female appeared before her. She hadn't expected the summoning to happen so bloody fast.

The revenant drifted forward, her pale skin lacking the glow of someone alive. Dark, silky strands of hair lay flat against her back in a single braid.

"How can I assist you, Your Majesty?" she bowed her head, keeping her eyes low.

"The buttons, I cannot do them myself."

Loriah nodded, then closed the distance between them and started to button the back. She moved quickly, then stepped away. "Is that all?"

Was it? She frowned and reached for her hair, which fell freely around her shoulders. "I'm sorry that we bring war to Andhera." As much as she wished it had remained in Lucem, there wasn't any hope for them there.

Loriah's eerie pale gaze met hers. "No one blames you, and we will do everything we can for you, and our king and queen." She pressed her thin lips together and glanced away as if listening to something—someone. "Will you be needing me for anything else?"

When Alessia shook her head, the girl vanished. But she wasn't left alone for long, because the door burst open, and in swept Eden and Sereia.

Eden's cheeks were rosy and her eyes a touch too bright, as if she'd sampled too much wine already, and Sereia sipped from a teacup.

"Can I help you two?" Alessia murmured, dipping down to pull on her ankle boots. She laced them, and when Eden still hadn't said anything, she quirked a brow and stood. "If this is about supper, I'll be there—"

"Did you tell him?" Eden licked her lips as she strode forward, the scent of pomegranate wine heavy on her breath.

"Tell who what?" Genuinely taken aback by the question, Alessia looked to Sereia, who also looked confused but sipped quietly at her—Alessia sniffed the air—whiskey?

Eden ran a hand down her violet gown. Silver roses stretched from the skirt toward the bodice, and the fabric hugged her breasts, then gave way to sheer sleeves. In less than a year, this sweet, naive fae had turned into a queen.

"The baby," she whispered and met Alessia's gaze.

"Oh shit," Sereia blurted, then turned around to shut the door. "There is a baby—Alessia, you're pregnant?" she whisper-yelled, her eyes widening.

Alessia's shoulders slumped a fraction, and she sighed. "So, you did know." She looked to Eden, who lifted a fine brow. "When we met in the Veil. Which means you aren't the only one."

The fire popped loudly, sending an ember shooting across the floor like a terrible omen. She lifted a hand to her face, dragging her fingers down her cheeks. "Ludari likely also knows, and he will use it against Zryan." Brione most likely knew as well, and it made her reassess all their interactions. Why she'd been more worried about her well-being as of late.

"You need to tell him," Eden pressed as she crossed the space between them and took Alessia's hand in hers.

She searched the other queen's eyes and shook her head. "No. I cannot. What is the point in telling him when we don't know what the outcome of this will be?" She clenched her teeth, willing her tears to cease forming. "When we were in the dungeon, we had it out with one another, and we made promises to change the way things are. If he knows the truth, how am I to know it's for me, for us, and not for the baby?" It was selfish perhaps, but Alessia needed for this to be about their marriage, for their union, not because they'd created another life together.

"You can only hide it for so long," Eden said softly.

"She is right, though," Sereia offered. "What if something happens to either one of them during this war and we do win? I don't think Zryan would forgive himself."

At least Sereia understood her perspective.

Eden dropped her hands, then boldly reached out to Alessia's abdomen. It was intimate, and Alessia fought against shoving her away because, unborn or not, she wanted to protect the life growing inside of her. Still, she knew Eden meant no harm and only nodded for her to continue.

Warmth spread from Eden's fingers through the fabric of the gown, and she smiled widely as she pulled back. "Well, you have a strong life force growing inside of you. I believe if anyone can survive this madness, it would be you." She stepped closer, and though she was shorter than Alessia, she tried her best to press her forehead to hers. Alessia dipped her head, fighting back a smile.

"You inspired me once when I needed it most, now let me inspire you." She lifted her hands and placed them against Alessia's face. They were warm and full of life. "You are one of the greatest warriors I have ever seen, with more heart and courage than most. At the end of all of this, remember one thing: we have one another, and we will fight to the end, together."

Alessia wrapped her arms around Eden, then eased away.

Tears threatened to spill down her cheeks, but she forced them back. "Thank you. I needed that." She turned her attention to Sereia as she neared. "Let us do this together, then."

"But first, we eat," Sereia said with a grin, lifting her cup. "And drink. We may as well die with food and drink in our belly."

With a laugh, Alessia motioned for them to head out.

When they arrived in the dining hall, the table had been laid out as if this was a banquet and not potentially a last meal. Still, as heavy as that thought was on Alessia, it warmed her to see everyone together. Bathed, smiling, and filling their bellies.

Her gaze settled on Zryan, and she had to swallow a sound of surprise. She'd never seen him in Andherian garb, and though he'd dressed in their room, he'd flung the overcoat onto the floor. He wore a white linen shirt, and somewhere between the last she'd seen him and now, he'd rolled up his sleeves to mid-forearm and unbuttoned it until it dipped toward his chest.

Pants. By the sun. Had she ever seen him wearing pants? Still, even from where she stood, she could see the way the fabric clung to his muscled thighs. Oh, she preferred this garb to the easy togas of home.

He turned around to face her as Sereia and Eden made their way to the table. His eyes brightened as he drank in the sight of her. "Well, there is one good thing about the restriction of Andhera's clothes, and that is the way it looks on you." Zryan stood and pulled out the chair beside him.

She crossed the room and sat in the chair offered to her. "I was thinking the very same thing." Alessia slid her hand beneath the table and gripped his thigh. "It's a good look on you."

"It seems we're not the only ones who think the more clothes on you, the better." Travion chuckled.

"Anyway," Kian interjected. "As I was saying, I should go back to the palace and see if I can collect my creations now that Ludari marches for the Veil."

What had they been discussing while she was in her room? Alessia frowned and peered down at Draven, who sipped at his goblet of blood. His brows furrowed as he contemplated it.

"Why in the sun's name would you do that?" Alessia grabbed a roll from a basket and shook her head. "That is foolish."

"Are you an idiot?" Ruan turned to his brother beside him and shoved at his shoulder.

"Your mother is right." Draven ignored the outburst and leaned into the crook of his chair. "Why risk it when you can have whatever you need here?"

Kian seemed to consider it. "It would be impossible for me to complete all the pieces before the battle begins."

"Well, what do you need? If it's workers, the revenants don't sleep, and you need only ask for supplies, and it will be done."

"So be it. After supper, I'll curate a list and begin working."

Alessia sighed, knowing she had to eat, but the desire to had faded. She stared down at the small roasted bird in front of her and frowned.

Zryan leaned in toward her and brushed a kiss against her temple but didn't utter a word, and for that, she was grateful.

Not eating wasn't in her best interest, so she grabbed her fork and simply listened to the chatter around her.

After everyone had left the dining hall, Alessia escaped into the gardens. It wasn't her first time here, but it was the first time she'd seen Eden's improvements. While the grounds were well kept and beautiful in a dark, haunting sort of way, they were full of new life now.

With the fading of the day moon, she had to squint to see the finer details. Purple leaves clustered on the ground with green stems protruding from them, and light purple blossoms emerged from the top.

Behind her, someone approached, and Alessia turned as Zryan rounded the corner. His lips turned up into a playful smile, and she spread her arms wide.

"My lord, I am without an escort. You shall tarnish my reputation," she said teasingly. Then, as his arms encircled her, pulling her body against his, she leaned into him.

"There will be no tarnishing. Just very thorough lovemaking." He hummed as he looked around the garden, searching for an ideal spot. "Perhaps on the bench."

Alessia shook her head.

"As if my brother hasn't done the very same thing." Zryan scoffed. "Don't let him fool you. He is still a son of Lucem."

"I don't want to talk about Draven's sex life." She pushed away from him, but it was in play instead of rage, which had grown to be commonplace over the centuries when she wasn't cross with him. "I was thinking," Alessia started, crossing her arms under her breasts. "Ludari in his wildest dreams couldn't imagine a place like this."

Zryan was quiet, but he moved to stand beside her, assessing the garden with a new appreciation.

She lifted one hand and motioned beyond the gardens. "And that, without you releasing your brothers, this never would have come to be." And her, too. He'd helped her from the dungeons as well and brought the sun into her life in so many ways. "Because we are free, we have a family. Not just you and I, but all of us."

This would be the time to tell him, to let him know about their new child, but as much as Alessia was a warrior, she was a coward in that moment.

She bit her tongue and instead focused on Zryan. His eyes glimmered with unshed tears, and a smile that was reserved for her only—vulnerable and *sweet*—crept over his features. He said nothing but dipped his head to capture her lips in a tender kiss.

If this moment could stretch a lifetime, it would be bliss.

27

Zryan

For the first time in days, Zryan slept through the night. Though the darkness in Andhera made it seem strange, no sunlight peeking through the window, he'd had Alessia tucked into his side. There was a comfort and peace from her presence that Zryan hadn't felt in a very long time.

When the night had worn off and he'd donned the Andherian slacks and shirt, this time for warmth rather than necessity, he sought the nearest servant to ask after his family. Most were just stirring, but Kian had awoken early and already set to work.

Refusing breakfast, he made his way down to the castle smithy, and found his son amongst a sea of revenants. The sound of hammers ricocheted off the stone ceiling, and the heat within instantly dampened Zryan's shirt. He found Kian next to Draven, working on a piece whose framework was considerably large. Both males were shirtless, their forms glistening with the sweat of their efforts. Hands coated in grime, they had clearly been at work for hours.

"Doesn't anyone sleep in this castle?" Zryan joked, eyeing his son.

Both Kian and Draven looked up, the former with a small grin, the latter with a dry look.

"I slept," his son said. "But I woke early, and it didn't make sense to wait. Then when I got down here, Uncle already had everything ready for me."

Draven nodded. "The revenants and I worked all night to source the materials Kian needed and prepare."

Zryan looked around them. It was impressive what they had managed already. Many revenants swung hammers, molding bits of metal into shapes that Kian desired. Others placed pieces over the open flame, like a kebab roasting on the fire. The hiss of hot metal being dipped into water melded with the hammering, and white steam puffed into the air.

"What are you working on?" he asked, rolling up the sleeves of his shirt and moving to stand with them over the piece.

"We're building the frame for a large serpent-like creature with wings," Kian responded.

Draven continued to work on a hinge at one of the joints along its length as Zryan looked between the two of them. "A serpent with wings? How will it move on the ground?"

"Well, much like a snake, it will slither." Kian swiftly hammered a nail into place, the gold metal of his left arm gleaming in the firelight.

"We were discussing giving it legs as well, so that it can climb structures if we send it down into the city streets," Draven added.

Zryan nodded, musing over this information as he gazed

around at all that was happening. Many seemed to be working on legs, while another batch of revenants were crafting sharp, pointed tails. Another set appeared to be shaping claws. *Scorpions?* he wondered. If so, they would be as large as the manticores they had spotted in the woods, and knowing Kian, just as deadly.

"Very well." Zryan turned back to Draven and Kian. "How can I help?"

His respect for Kian only mounted as the morning spanned into afternoon and they continued to work. There was a brief period where they halted their actions to eat and drink—something that the revenants did not require, and so they hammered on—but other than that, Kian was a relentless taskmaster.

When one portion would be finished, he would hand Zryan something else to bend into shape or heat over the scorching flames of the forge. Zryan's muscles ached even more so than they had from the battle. His fingers were growing numb from the reverberations of the hammer on metal. He wanted desperately to call off and say that he was done, but Kian did not stop. Kian was a force to behold as he moved from fire to water to each new creation.

Watching his son create before his very eyes filled him with a pride none of his own successes had ever brought. Kian was tireless, and even when his hammer slipped and he hit a thumb, or the fire got too close and singed his arm, he merely swiped the offending part along his slacks and continued on.

He had never felt prouder to be Kian's father.

"I must say, son," he began as Kian took a momentary break for a drink of water. "If you carry this level of focus and stamina into the bedroom, Alvia Seducere will be a very happy wife."

Kian stared blandly over at him. Draven, who was hammering feather-shaped sheets of metal onto a wing frame, kept his head down. But Zryan was sure he had seen the hint of a smile on his brother's lips.

"Don't look so displeased, it's the truth," he insisted.

"Father . . ." Kian started, then stopped, as if searching for his words. "Why?"

Zryan lifted a brow in question. "Why what?"

"Why are you attempting to betroth me to someone I don't even know? And unasked, might I add."

"Haven't you heard?" Draven drawled. "It's your father's favorite pastime." His gaze flicked up from his work, pinning Zryan with a cold stare.

"And look how well *that* worked out!" Zryan trumpeted happily, pointing at Draven. "Even after I told him he didn't have to, he still married her within only a couple of months. Madly in love, the two of them!"

Kian rolled his eyes and shook his head. Downing more water, he set the skin aside and picked his hammer back up, beginning to hammer a piece of metal over top of an anvil, deftly shaping a curve into it. "I'm not looking for love."

Zryan shook his head. "Whether you want to admit it to yourself or not, you are." He stepped around the flying serpent with legs and stood before his son. "You are deserving of it."

Kian looked up at him, something within his gaze that he was trying to shutter. Perhaps his own self-doubts or some unadmitted desire. "She and I are not alike at all."

"As if that matters!" He pointed at Draven, who snorted and went back to work.

"That was different. They were forced together under special circumstances that helped them to get past their differences. Alvia and I are . . ."

He slipped his hand over Kian's, stopping his next swing. "I think you could be wonderful together if you would just give it a try. I know getting to know new people is not your favorite thing. I swear, sometimes I think you were cut from your uncle's mold." He sent Draven a sideways glance. "But it is worth it when it's for the right person."

"And what makes you think she is the right one?"

"Because she is beautiful." Both Kian and Draven snorted, but he continued anyway. "And she is strong, and courageous. She has already proven her loyalty to this family in spades. Alvia did not need to help your mother and me escape, risking herself in the process. In fact, she could have come with us, but she stayed to cause a distraction so that we could leave."

Kian's expression was becoming softer, a more contemplative look in his eyes. Zryan fought the smile that wanted to spring to his lips.

"I think it's worth giving it a try. There could be something special between the two of you."

Kian sighed, hammering some more at the metal sheet, then he grunted. "Okay. Fine. Should we all survive this horror and come out the other side to a semblance of normal society . . . I will attempt to court Alvia." He looked back at Zryan. "Now will you get back to work?"

Zryan laughed, clapped him on the shoulder, and returned to his portion of the beast. A hum of happiness settled in his bones as he thought of the possibility of one of his children being happily squared away.

His happiness carried him through to the end of the day, when Kian finally set down his hammer and proclaimed himself to be starving. Zryan, long since having lost all feeling in his muscles, nearly dropped from fatigue. Instead, he nodded his agreement and tossed down his own hammer.

Blacksmithing was a torture device, he decided, and for the life of him, he could not understand how this was Kian's happy place.

When they came out into the hall, it was to find Travion leaning on the opposite wall, a bottle of dark liquor held in either hand and a third tucked under his arm.

"Come," he said to Zryan and Draven, handing them each a bottle, and led them down the hall and out into the night.

Zryan cursed as he stubbed his toe on something in the dark but followed his older brother. "What exactly are we doing?"

"We're getting away from all the twittering happening inside that castle, and the three of us are going to sit and bemoan our circumstance before we face off against our tyrant of a sire yet again."

He'd brought them out on a large, round stone patio on the outside of the castle, one which looked down on the gardens. In the center of the patio was a fountain that trickled shining silver water from each level until it splashed into a wide pool at the bottom.

Zryan dropped down on the edge of the fountain and stared into the water. There, in the shallow depths, were deep red fish that darted about. They were beautiful, if not dangerous, with a wide slash of mouth and sharp teeth in each of their heads. He lifted his already uncorked bottle to his lips and took a long swig.

The liquor, whatever it was, had a taste of black mulberries but hit with a fierceness that left him wheezing for breath as it burned down his throat and settled like living flame in his belly. "By the spirits of the afterlife!" Zryan choked out. "What is this?" He glanced over at his brothers.

Travion chuckled, taking a swig of his own and then making a face just as pinched. "It's an Andherian delight."

Draven, who had settled back against the railing of the stone patio, sipped his casually, clearly used to the bite. "Seraut makes it as a hobby. He calls it shine and distills it from fermented mulberries. However, it has more of a kick since Eden arrived. I think between the two of them, they've concocted some strange berry none of us are aware of." He shook his head and took another drink. "Thanks for the belladonna." He waved his bottle at Travion.

Their middle brother grinned. "Didn't think it would be half so fun if you weren't getting sloshed right alongside Zry and me."

Zryan took another drink, more prepared for the kick this time. "What chances do you think we have, now that we lack the element of surprise?"

Ludari had not seen it coming the first time around. Zryan had never stood up to him. Never defied him. Ludari never expected him to go into the dungeons to free his brothers. Or that together, they would overthrow his guards and steal the book.

"A chunk of ice's chance in flame." Travion grinned and held up his bottle in salute.

Zryan saluted him back and took another sip.

"Andhera balances the scales a fraction," Draven commented, staring out over the darkened landscape.

"A lot of good it will do us." Travion seemed too calm for the great chance of death that hung over them all. But Zryan knew it was bravado, the same he used to hide his own fears and concerns.

He stared at his brothers. Two fae he hadn't known until well into adulthood. Who were still closer to each other than he had ever managed to get with either of them. But he loved them, which he wasn't sure he'd ever told them.

"I'm sorry," he said at last, which made both sets of eyes turn his way.

"For what?" Draven asked.

"Losing the book." Zryan shook his head. "I thought we had it perfectly guarded, but I should have learned from Ludari's mistake. If it is in reach, it is not safe." He took a large swig of the burning shine.

Draven took his own drink, then shook his head. "And just as you lost it, so, too, did I. It was there in the throne room, and when I should have secured it, I took for granted it would remain where it was. And Travion, well . . ." A sardonic smirk came to his lips. "He gave it away."

Travion grunted, his first sign of displeasure since they had gotten out here. "Who of us hasn't lost it, and who of us wouldn't give it up to save a loved one?"

Zryan frowned, thinking about it. "I think . . . at this point, if I gave it up to save Alessia, she would only kill me afterward." He wasn't sure what it was, but he simply knew his wife would not thank them. Not when their children were at risk. Either one of them would happily give up their lives if it meant their children would be safe. "And I . . . well, I think perhaps I owe it to all of you to offer myself up if the time should come."

His brothers stared at him as if he had lost his head.

"What do you mean by that?" Draven growled.

"Only that, of all of us, I have suffered the least. It's my turn." He lifted up his bottle to them and took a deep drink.

"Zryan . . ." Travion began, a frown on his face and something foreign in his voice. Concern for him, perhaps?

Zryan held up his hand to stop him. "I have my family to protect, and both of you have only just married." He looked down at the bottle he rested against his thigh. "I don't want either of you to lose that." He knew that pain all too well, and he didn't want either Draven or Travion suffering such a loss. He looked at Travion. "You've already had to watch Sereia die; you don't deserve that again."

Travion rubbed at his face. "I still see it in my dreams. I don't believe a thousand years will take it away."

"And you," Zryan said, turning to Draven. "You've given up everything for us to come to this land and settle it. Your spot of happiness has been too brief, I want only more of it for you."

Great emotions welled up inside Zryan, tightening around his heart and clenching his stomach. His throat squeezed, and his eyes burned a fraction. Silently, he thanked the cover of the darkness and hoped Draven's eyes weren't too keen.

"Do you know," Draven began, "what I saw when I passed through the Sollicitus Cave?"

Zryan had only heard briefly of what transpired between Draven and the cave. Sollicitus was more like a tunnel that ran beneath the cliff Draven's castle sat upon. Due to its proximity to the opening to the afterlife, it could toy with and warp the mind of anyone passing through it. Sometimes to the point that they died from the pain and agony it brought out in them. Sollicitus was used when someone of Andhera's court needed to pay for a crime but death wasn't warranted.

Draven had gone through once he'd realized Naya Damaris tricked him into killing an innocent vampire and his son, fooled by Naya into believing they were guilty of something that had really been her. Eden's mother was a psychotic hag Zryan was happy still sat in torment in Travion's dungeons.

"What?" Zryan prompted.

"This." He breathed out and took a large gulp from his own bottle. "Ludari, back to life, and so big, he was able to sweep you up in his hands." Pain filtered into his gaze, and he stared somewhere in the distance, between Zryan and Travion. "I watched him kill first you, Zry, throwing your lifeless body at me. And then he picked Travion up and bit him in half."

Zryan had never seen so much strain in Draven's form before. There was a hard, pinched quality to his face that Zryan knew came from pain.

"And then I lost Eden in a sea of fire. She was just gone. No matter how hard I searched, I couldn't find her. There was nothing left to do but give myself up to the flames. It was my nightmare, losing all of you. And now we face it all over again."

Travion cursed lowly, as did Zryan.

"We won't let that happen," Travion stated.

"We'll send Ludari back to the afterlife and make certain he stays there this time," Zryan added.

Draven nodded, though his features were still pinched. "It was easier before," he said. "When I didn't mind dying. But now . . ." A sad smile flitted over his lips.

"Eden," Zryan finished for him. Draven met his eyes and nodded. "The thought of dying is much easier when you're not leaving behind the one being in this shitty world that brings you joy."

"And peace," Draven added. His shoulders loosened as he lost himself in some memory. "She brings me peace that I never had before, and I can't bear the thought of breaking her heart by dying."

Draven looked as if he couldn't believe there was someone who loved him so greatly that their heart would break at the loss of him.

"It does put things in perspective," Travion muttered. His bottle was half empty, and Zryan realized he had some catching up to do.

"Do you mean you won't be so eager to throw yourself against the sword and die?" Zryan asked.

"Sereia would never let me hear the end of it if I died on her."

Draven snorted. "Yes, please, do not wind up a revenant haunting my halls so I have to deal with the both of you for the rest of my immortal life." A strange look crossed

Draven's face. "Which reminds me, I have someone to introduce Sereia to when this is all over."

Travion muttered an "okay" around the mouth of his bottle.

Zryan chuckled, listening to them, and drank deeply of his liquor. It burned his throat, adding fuel to the fire already in his belly, but it was warm, and now he welcomed the bite.

28

Alessia

The day moon descended on the horizon and the night moon rose, replacing its brighter sister with the dimmer blue. If Ludari came at night, he would regret it. However, Andhera would benefit in many ways. It was the darkest period in a sunless realm, which would be enough to throw Lucem's royal army off.

It wasn't as if Lucemites lined up to visit the nightmare realm when it was dangerous just to pass through the Veil.

Alessia chewed on her bottom lip as she stared down at the map of Andhera. She wasn't the only one in the study. The entire family had congregated there, minus Eden.

Draven leaned over the map. "It should go without saying, a great deal of their army will die in the woods. With no wolves or harpies to aid them, and no knowledge of how to properly kill a chimera, their survival rate will be dismally low." He withdrew from the table and crossed his arms, fixing his gaze on Zryan.

Alessia frowned. "While true, the clay creatures pose a genuine threat. Their sheer numbers could overpower us without access to a great deal of fire. More than that, do we really want to reduce Andhera to ashes?"

Draven frowned at this.

Kian pointed at the map of the city below the castle. "I'll have some of my creations here, and along the battlement too. As an extra line of defense, and should any of those golems get close enough, they'll rain fire down."

Tension wove its way through the room as if it were a living thing, and quiet settled over the group, save for the sound of the crackling hearth. It wasn't just Alessia mentally preparing for battle; it was everyone.

Eden walked through the doors, striding quickly to the table. "The city is being evacuated as we speak. Only the families closer to the castle are left to move out. They're being escorted to Initium."

"Good," Draven muttered. "We will use Aasha as a fortress. So don't be afraid when the fight comes to her. This is what she was made for." He dropped his arms, a new rigidness visible, and it wasn't until Alessia turned to glance at the doorway did she notice a windswept harpy.

"What is it?" Draven pressed.

Ailith, Draven's general, bowed her head. "There is activity in the Veil. The chimera are restless, and new fires have started. I'm assuming the first wave has passed through. I advise everyone to get to their positions at once, for the battle will begin within the hour."

Alessia's heart thrummed wildly, adrenaline coursing through her veins as the time for battle approached. Despite how she reveled in defending her home and loved ones, this one hit far harder and differently.

She loathed fighting against her people.

"Return to your station. We'll handle the rest here." Draven jerked his head toward the door, and as his general left the room, he sighed. "You heard Ailith. Prepare for battle."

"Alessia and I will head down to join the front at the forest's edge. Hopefully, we can contain the fight there long enough to give the remaining citizens time to get out," Zryan offered.

Draven nodded in silent thanks, and with that, nearly everyone filed out of the room to prepare.

All that remained were Zryan and her children. Alessia approached Ruan, and he dipped his head for her to kiss his cheek. "Be safe," she murmured, then she moved to Kian and placed her lips to his temple. "Be brave." Then she lifted her hands to cup Brione's face and kissed her forehead. "Be strong. And we will see one another when this is through."

Her heart constricted at the thought of losing one of them. But Alessia trusted their abilities, their strength, and their tenacity.

She strode toward Zryan and placed her lips to his, savoring the feel of them, committing the moment to memory. "It's time we fight, my darling."

Although the mood was dour, Zryan's eyes glimmered with happiness, and a hint of a smile curled the corners of his mouth.

With that, everyone left the room.

Alessia secured the bow and quiver to Zissi's saddle, then shoved her sword into the scabbard. Zryan was beside her, checking his straps, when the horn blared. From where she stood, she could see the flames in the woods stretching toward the sky.

More activity.

"The army has arrived!" someone shouted.

Alessia quickly mounted her griffin and glanced down at her husband. "I need to get there."

The words were barely out of her mouth before Zryan mounted. "Not without me." He gathered his reins up and hissed to Feroces. "Together, Less." He nodded, locking eyes with her, and in his gaze, she saw more than his voice could project.

If we die, we die together.

A hint of a smile touched her lips. "Together."

United, the griffins launched into the air. It was dizzying at first, being in the night sky with no true light to guide their way. Though the night moon gave off as much light as it could, it still wasn't what Alessia was used to.

Andhera's landscape was dark, and all Alessia could see were shadows moving where soldiers scurried into place. It made the torches of the evacuating citizens stand out all the more. A small, dotted, fiery trail weaving out of Arcem.

Soon, she and Zryan arrived at the battlefront. Andhera's army waited at the mouth of the woods, weapons drawn and bodies poised to launch into an attack.

Zissi landed and forced his way through a throng of weres. Their teeth gleamed in the dim light, and deep growls resonated in their throats.

The harpies held swords, grim determination lining their features.

When the woods came into view, she halted her griffin and turned to look at Ailith. The general bowed her head in recognition but didn't utter a word.

Anticipation coiled around Alessia's muscles, as if at the drop of a pin, she would bolt into battle. She wanted to, yearned for this war to be over, and wanted a semblance of normalcy to return so they could piece the realms back together.

An explosion erupted, chasing away the dark with a flash of light that shook the ground. Not lightning but fire.

"Alessia," Zryan called to her left. He held his sword, and his eyes were full of grim determination. "I love you."

Her throat tightened as she spoke the simple words. "I love you." And she meant it with every drop of her being. There was more she wanted to say, but as the first fae soldier emerged from the woods covered in dark blood, Ailith's war cry rang out.

"Now!" The harpy took flight, swinging her sword around to crash down on a bewildered soldier.

Desperate to escape the death trap of a forest, the Lucemites dove for the ground, bolting to the side to evade the Andherians. If they thought they could escape this madness, they were wrong and should have never sworn their allegiance to Ludari.

Alessia drove her griffin into the charging fae. She withdrew her sword just in time to block a strike to her side. Zissi craned his neck, snapping at the offender, and his powerful beak crushed the soldier's throat.

She had no time to consider the fallen Lucemite as her

mount whipped her around to another attacker. This time, a spear narrowly missed her abdomen. She searched for the one who had thrown it and caught sight of the perpetrator.

He stood hunched forward, sword in hand, and charged.

Except, just as he was readying to leap at her, lightning rained down from above, sank into his body, and sent him crashing to the ground, convulsing.

Zryan.

She glanced around for him. He found her across the melee and saluted before turning to face the writhing mass of bodies surging toward them.

From the corner of her eye, Alessia saw movement, but it was too late as a figure leaped at her, forcing her from the saddle and onto the ground. Her sword lay a few inches from her, but her attacker drew his, tip pointed down.

Not willing to go without a fight, she writhed between his legs, trying to gain momentum. He was stronger and didn't budge.

"May the Old Ways—"

"Rise?" Alessia sneered as she stared up at him, reaching for the strings of his mind. A small barrier resisted her touch, but she pressed on, whispering to his mind that his enemies were behind him. Creatures from Andhera, fanged, with rotting flesh. Not truly there, of course, but his mind said differently.

The soldier lurched backward, as if repelled by her. His mouth twisted in horror as he shrieked. "Get away!" With his sword raised high, he ran into his comrades, landing blow after blow on his confused allies.

It wouldn't last long, but long enough for Alessia to get

back on Zissi. She rolled over, groaning as her side protested, grabbed her sword, and swung herself back into the saddle.

A new sound wove its way through the shouts of soldiers, growling of weres, and clashing of swords. It was one she'd grown familiar with recently: smashing clay.

Horror snaked its way through her, and she searched the vicinity. Golems burst through the mouth of the forest, and weres forced them to the ground, shattering them. Harpies took their swords to them, and they burst into tiny shards.

Every single piece that collected on the ground was another piece that could create a *giant*.

"Stop! Stop shattering them!" Alessia cried to the Andherians. An arrow whistled from somewhere, striking her in the shoulder. She grunted and rocked backward.

Griffins that were not allies flew above. She grimaced and yanked the arrow free. "If you take them down, you need fire!"

Frustration grew inside of her. Alessia pushed Zissi forward, then urged him into the sky. He swooped toward Ailith, who had just struck a rider free from their griffin.

"Tell your troops to use fire to obliterate the golems. Striking them down isn't enough, you need fire to end them completely, otherwise their parts will gather together to form larger versions. Use the chimera if you can." Zissi banked to the side, then dove for the ground.

As if to prove her words true, the shattered pieces closest to them rattled into one large pile, and soon, a golem the size of six formed.

Zryan remained aloft on Feroces, calling lightning down to strike and pass through Lucem's soldiers, and while the

Andherians seemed to be controlling the numbers flooding in, it was the golems that posed an issue.

There were too many, and now the bloody things were piecing themselves back together. "Zryan!" Alessia swooped down toward him. "They've taken out too many of those abominations. There isn't enough fire here to reduce them to ash."

Zryan's gaze lowered to the ground, and he frowned. "Not unless we want to burn the entire forest down." Even as they spoke, the golems were shuddering, reassembling to a monstrous size. "We should head back to the city."

Alessia nodded. "At this rate, we don't have long until they arrive." Reluctantly, she turned Zissi around, and they started their quick journey back to the city.

Massive golems, easily double the size they'd battled prior to Andhera, stomped down the road toward the city, unfazed by the weres nipping at them. Arrows ricocheted off them, falling to the ground as if they were mere toys. Others stuck but seemed no more than toothpicks in relation to the creatures.

When they hovered over the city, Zissi descended until he landed on the cobblestone streets. Alessia forced him into a gallop, and he raced through the narrow pathways, only halting when a figure emerged from around a building.

Zryan landed beside her. "You're bleeding," he said with a growl.

She ignored him because bleeding was not her concern.

Ruan held a hand out to still the griffin. Worry filtered into his dark eyes, then anger. "What news do you bring?"

"The city is being targeted by those abominations. Bigger than before, so be ready to douse the land with fire!"

Ruan looked beyond her, to the road that wound into the city. She glanced over her shoulder and saw what he did: several giant shadows bounding down the road.

Metal glinted in the sky, and Alessia for the first time noticed Kian's beasts had been imbued with life, waiting to guard, to attack and obliterate whatever came into their path.

They would need all the help they could get.

29

Zryan

Just within the border of the city, an army awaited their foe. Were-wolves, -panthers, and -tigers prowled down the streets, hiding in dark alleys and preparing to launch at anyone wearing Ludari's colors. Metal scorpions the size of manticores scuttled along the outskirts of the city, acting as the first line of defense.

On the rooftops, the second wave of harpies crouched, arrows notched on their bows, ready to fire as soon as they were given the signal. And above that, Kian's newest creations slithered through the skies on large black wings. They slinked through the darkness like serpents down a waterfall, hints of moonshine glinting off the gleaming metal of their backs.

Zryan pressed a hand to Alessia's back and leaned in to kiss her temple. He hated to see her go, to know she would be flying into this chaos and out of his direct line of sight. But neither of them could properly fight if they were too concerned with protecting each other. "Be safe. This is far from over."

She nodded and took his hand, squeezing it. "I'll see you on the other side." Alessia mounted Zissi and launched into the air.

The crashing of large footfalls over the hills shook the earth beneath them, dragging his eyes away from Alessia's receding form. He turned and saw five large clay golems heading their way. In front of them, General Ailith flew with what was left of her harpy forest squadron, heading for the city. At the feet of the large clay creations ran more of smaller golems in droves, along with the Lucemite guard.

Zryan squinted, trying to see through the darkness. Somewhere out there was Ludari. He knew his sire wouldn't miss out on this finale. That he would want to be here to quash the last bits of life from them. But where was he?

As the first giant golem reached the city, one of Kian's scorpions went out to meet it and was instantly trampled by the weight of the abomination crunching the metal to bits. General Ailith landed atop one of the homes, yelling instructions to her troops, and burning arrows flew in response. But it was not enough. The monstrosity was too big. It bellowed a long, low sound like a sad whale, which shuddered through Zryan's chest. Its steps were slow and almost clumsy, but each one carried it twenty feet.

Buildings crashed to the ground, brick and stone shattering as its foot swept out. Troops scattered out of the way of falling debris, and Ailith shouted for another rain of burning arrows. These slowed it down, its hands batting at the thick arrows sticking from it. But as its clay fingers swept down over its chest, the arrows fell to the ground like matchsticks snapping.

"We need something more!" Zryan screamed. This wasn't going to be enough.

A whistle rang out from somewhere behind him, a sharp sound that he somehow recognized as belonging to Kian despite the distance. From the sky, one of the slinking serpents dove upon the clay creation, a streak of fire rumbling from deep within it. As the blast struck the golem, it let out another low moan, the flames licking over it.

For a moment, Zryan held his breath, waiting. When the golem began to crumble, large chunks crashing to the city streets below, a cheer went up.

It was the last sound of joy Zryan heard for a long time.

Through the crumbling of the golem came an endless wave of more. They descended upon the city and those waiting inside, like the ocean tide rolling in to wipe away every last speck of dry sand.

The scorpions attacked, taking down the first line of them, but the golems continued to come, rushing over the shattered pieces beginning to slide together, and heading deeper into the city. The harpies fired more burning arrows down on the smaller golems, and this time, it worked. They exploded and crumbled into dust as the fire licked over them.

But there were so *many* that they just kept coming, rolling over the scorpions, passing through the flaming arrows, and crashing into the weres. Sharp teeth and claws dug into clay, powerful jaws crushing them with ease. But it was a seemingly endless wave.

And all around them, the bits that weren't burnt began to collect into piles, larger golems rising in the midst of the city.

Zryan cursed, calling lightning from the sky. He let it

erupt onto a street full of them, catching any bits of hanging fabric that he could alight. "We need something to start a fire!" he shouted down to Hannelore, whom he recognized battling her way through Lucemite soldiers.

The harpy looked up, twisting her sword around and driving her blade into a fae behind her. "Hay from the stables!" she called back, eyes lighting up.

"Get the message back to the castle," he ordered.

Whipping around to decapitate a soldier who had attempted to sneak up on her, Hannelore shouted a "yes" and then launched into the air.

Zryan turned back to the battle just as the ground began to shake to the point that the earth itself split open. From the depths, tree roots grew and spread. They wrapped around the were forces, hauling them down into the pits. Wild, thorny vines crept up and over the edges, large black blooms sprouting.

Zryan grew rigid, trepidation flowing through him. He knew what this was. He knew *who* this was.

"Retreat farther into the city!" he screamed, just as the blooms opened and thick clouds of poisonous spores released into the air.

Spirits . . . Terror seized him, blood thundering in his ears. Where were his children? Where was Alessia? Frantically, he looked over the streets and around him, but he could find no one.

"Retreat!" he shouted again, watching several fae soldiers and harpies alike walk into the plumes, clutch at their throats, and fall to their knees. Ludari was taking out his own forces along with Zryan's, but he didn't care so long as he won.

Suddenly, a tornado ripped down out of the sky, whipping up the poisonous air and several of the vines, yanking them away.

Zryan looked back and found that Travion and Sereia had arrived. Sereia steering a chariot pulled by a black kelpie, its horn glinting in the darkness, and Travion controlling the whirlwind of destruction.

Leaping onto Feroces' back, Zryan flew him down to the streets to meet up with his brother. "Try not to take out the golems!" he shouted as he flew his griffin over the racing chariot.

Travion looked up, a wild look of pleasure on his lips. "We're planning to make them bigger on purpose."

"What?!"

"Combine them so there's fewer to deal with, then lead them to the castle."

"What are you thinking?" Zryan shouted. Had he lost his mind?

"Draven is waiting to rain fire down on them along the wall!" Sereia shouted back. "Now let us get on with it." She slapped the reins of the chariot and pulled ahead, bringing them closer to the battle with the golems.

Trusting that his brothers had a plan that would work, Zryan directed Feroces up into the air. It was dark, which would make it difficult to find him, but Zryan *would* find Ludari.

They soared through the sky, darting past flying serpents, who continued to bombard the golems with blasts of fire, over warring groups of weres and soldiers as blood ran in the streets, and evaded the reaching grasps of thorn-covered vines reaching into the sky.

There didn't seem to be a part of the city not overrun by the clay creations, their numbers so insurmountable, Zryan knew there was no hope of defeating them, no matter how much fire they found.

Where was Ludari? He searched the darkness for his sire. He had to be somewhere in the darkness, watching this terror as it demolished the city around them. He hadn't been at the front of the battle, which meant he had to be somewhere at the back. Safe. Out of harm's reach.

The thought disgusted Zryan. He needed to find Ludari. He needed to bring the harm directly to him. Kill him and take control of the Creaturae.

The book was the only way to bring this to an end.

It was the screams of agony that directed Zryan to Ludari's whereabouts.

Ludari sat astride a brilliant white pegasus, its stark beauty a shocking contrast to the darkness all around it. Zryan recognized it as his own steed. Behind him, Phaedora rode the mare he had gifted Brione simply because he'd known she'd love it. She sat prim and resplendent. Both beautiful and absolutely useless. Here only to gloat as a victorious queen overlooking what she presumed would be their fall.

The screams had come from the abominations that surrounded Ludari like a protective wall. Monstrous horrors that made Zryan's blood run cold.

He'd found the manticore, and with the Creaturae, warped their already distorted figures into something beyond nightmares.

Their humanoid faces had only grown more grotesque, large fishlike eyes protruding from their head, giant gaping mouths with rows upon rows of teeth. The luscious manes that had once surrounded the heads had given way to flesh-covered spikes, razor-like horns breaking through the pale skin at the top. Massive paws now ended in claws that were more like scythes, unable to be retracted.

Instead of one scorpion tail at the back, there were now two, which had doubled in size and now seemed to be able to shoot their acidic poison rather than just stab. The poison dripped from the tips, so full, they looked ready to burst.

The screams that issued from the soldiers they overtook were blood curdling. Zryan watched as a were, shocked out of his tiger form, was beset upon by one of the monsters. The beast snarled and chomped its way through his stomach, going for the most vulnerable part. Its thick claws pierced his thighs clean through to the ground, effectively pinning him in place while it ate him alive.

Zryan felt sick to his stomach. Unable to do anything to help him, he did the next best thing. He raised his hand into the air, calling forth as much lightning as he could contain in one hand, and he unleashed it down on the ground beneath him.

The bluish-white fingers of lightning crackled over the ground, piercing through the beast and were, causing a loud boom to echo over the hills as it exploded.

Two of the beasts nearby also went down, which was good, but it also gave his position away.

Ludari looked up into the sky, and even in the darkness, he saw Zryan. Barely a glance had passed between them when Ludari threw out his hand. Blade-like thorns flew through the air toward him. Zryan pulled Feroces harshly to the side, the projectiles just missing them.

In return, he sent a bolt of lightning straight down toward Ludari and his entourage, but his aim was off in the swift movements, and it struck slightly to the left of them. Their mounts reared, threatening to spill them onto the ground, but they held on.

And this time, when Ludari unleashed his thorns, Zryan felt the impact in the armor along his side and the fire in his shoulder and bicep as two made contact. Another grazed his cheek, leaving a streak of pain and clipping his ear. Below him, Feroces faltered.

Zryan cursed, one hand tightening on the reins while the other gripped onto the crook where wing met back as his griffin fell from the sky.

They hit the ground with a sickening crunch of bone and feather that Zryan felt collapse beneath him before the impact with the rocky terrain sent Zryan tumbling head over heels, his world reeling, his body screaming, and everything in him out of control. It was the drag of his armor and sword against the ground that finally brought him to a stop. His lungs screamed, and he inhaled sharply, dragging air into lungs that felt near collapsing from a lack of oxygen. Zryan clawed at the earth below him, dragging himself into a semi-upright position on his hands and knees.

The pain in his body was unlike anything he'd felt before. But it was the state of Feroces that left him hollowed to the core. Gasping through the pain, he crawled over to the form of his griffin. Feroces screeched weakly, his body broken and thorns protruding from his feathers all over his underbelly. His wings were torn and crumpled, and one of his legs entirely twisted.

Zryan felt wetness on his cheeks as he gingerly pulled the

griffin's feathered head into his lap. Frescoes blinked quickly, eyes swiveling, then screeched brokenly once more.

"I'm sorry, old friend," he rasped. Drawing the dagger from his belt, he slid it quickly across the creature's throat and watched the light fade from his eyes. Zryan bowed over him for a moment, pressing his forehead against the silken feathers atop his head.

Zryan stood, pulling thorns from his bicep and shoulder, and slowly straightened his protesting body. He watched the retreating form of Ludari heading into the besieged city beyond him.

Giant golems crashed through the homes of Arcem, demolishing any that came into their path. Howls rent the air along with screams of agony. One corner of the city flashed with lightning as Ruan, thankfully still alive, battled. And beyond, around the walls of the castle, liquid fire poured down on top of the heads of golems, lighting larger fires that caught on anything around them.

The desire to destroy filled Zryan, and finding resolve he didn't know he had, Zryan stripped his armor, let everything fade away, and shifted. His hands became large paws, claws extending from his fingertips. His body began to slouch, dropping him to all fours, and from his now fur-covered hind end, a large scorpion tale emerged. The last pieces to sprout were large, leathery wings from his back.

Zryan crouched low, then sprang into the air, wings beating heavily, quickly carrying him higher. Flying himself rather than upon his griffin was a whole other feeling, but there was no time to think about the rush whipping through the air brought him. Instead, he chased after the retreating form of Ludari.

It was the group of soldiers acting as further protection behind him that Zryan reached first. His claws tore through the shoulders of one, piercing his body as he leaped from him and onto the next. His teeth sank viciously into a throat, and his tail whipped to sink into the back of a fourth.

This time, as agonized screams rose into the air, Zryan's claws and rage were the reason behind them.

30

Alessia

The ground trembled to the point that Alessia crouched low and readied to make a grab for it in case it split in two. However, it wasn't the ground beneath her feet that was a threat. As screams rang out, she watched in horror as rocks tumbled down from the castle, and then, with a deep, tired groan, the cliffside gave way and tumbled into the pit below. A moment later, a portion of the fortress wall crumbled away with one of the spires.

Draven. Eden!

A flash of panic wound its way through her. Unsure of where her family was in the madness, she could only hope they had been far enough away from the cliff. But Eden and Draven . . . they were holding the castle. Alessia had to get to the top, and she prayed to the sun, moon, and stars that they were all right.

Dust and rocks flew into the air, knocking into friend and foe. Alessia ducked low as a boulder bounded by, but the fates were on her side as it careened into an approaching golem, shattering it just as it lifted a spear.

She blew out a breath and staggered toward Zissi, who had pounced on a soldier and torn into the male's neck with his beak. Blood and sinew dripped to the ground as the griffin swung to face her.

With a groan, she turned to mount her griffin, but a body collided with her, forcing her to the ground. She'd expected the tip of a sword to drag across her throat, but a fist collided with her jaw, stunning her.

"Not . . . today." She reached down to her hip and grabbed her dagger. In a quick move, she drove the blade into the attacker's side. When they shifted to round on her, she withdrew it and dragged it across their throat. Blood sprayed down on her, and she spat it out, shoving at the body as they tried to staunch the flow of blood.

It was too late. Nothing but a healer or the book could save them, and neither was in their reach.

"Mother!" Brione shouted as she ran headlong toward her.

Aside from a thick layer of dust coating her daughter's face and sweat gleaming on her brow, she was whole and unharmed. Relief passed through Alessia, but they needed to move quickly. "You're coming with me."

Alessia mounted Zissi and regretted using her injured arm to lift herself into the saddle. There would be time to moan over flesh wounds later; now was not that time. She also didn't want Brione to waste her affinity on something as minor as a non-life-threatening injury.

Lightning rained down, ricocheting off nearby buildings, burying into the ground, and attackers too. Either Ruan or Zryan were alive and well; all she could do was hope the others were as well.

"I have a feeling the battle is going to culminate in the castle," Alessia said over her shoulder as Zissi took to the air. She didn't want the enemy to infiltrate the castle, and she would do everything in her power to stop them. "Grab the bow and arrow, shoot down any foe." More than primed to fight, the griffin sped forward, beating his wings quick enough that the cool air stung her eyes.

Brione shifted behind her, and from the corner of her eye, she saw an arrow pointing downward. The bow creaked, then the twang of the string let Alessia know an arrow was loosed.

In the sky, Alessia scanned the ground in search of Zryan, and she spotted him before Ludari and Phaedora. A throng of soldiers and large monstrous beasts created a barrier, and beyond them, a manticore launched itself into the fray, claws tearing through armor as if it was nothing.

Zryan.

And still, the clay creations stormed through the city, bigger than she'd seen them before. Arcem would be destroyed in no time with those beasts crashing around, destroying, killing, and *growing*.

Flames leaped higher, devouring the homes and structures until they turned Arcem into a beacon in the night.

"Change of plans," Alessia declared as she urged Zissi to climb higher. "Don't hesitate to shoot a foe." Although she didn't have to say as much, for Brione knew. "But be careful of the one-tailed manticore."

Brione aimed true and fired an arrow straight through the neck of a soldier poised to strike the manticore's side.

Zryan inclined his head toward the sky, roaring his appreciation before bowling into the other threats. Ludari sneered at his son, rounding his pegasus away from the fight. Phaedora sat primly astride her mount, surveying the destruction below the castle with a calm satisfaction, and Alessia's blood boiled.

She wanted to see that wretch's face as she drove a sword into her heart, watch the life fade from her eyes and the smirk drop as she realized it was Alessia ending her life.

And Ludari . . . as much as she yearned to kill him too, that glory would go to the brothers—again. They deserved it.

But now, they needed to stop them from getting any closer to the city.

"Brione. I'm going to drop you down with Phaedora. I'm going for Ludari—"

"No! He will kill you." Brione swore behind her and angrily rummaged inside of what she assumed to be the quiver. "I'm out of arrows."

The sound of steel sliding free of a scabbard reached Alessia's ears, and she nodded. "Perhaps. But not before he can use me as bait." It was who Ludari was, and if she could play a part in his demise, she would.

This time, she wouldn't hesitate to reach out to his mind. If she was quick enough, she could bring him to his knees.

"Don't let Phaedora run away, Bri. Do everything in your power to stop her, even if that means killing her." She reached around to grab her daughter's arm, squeezing it, then Zissi dove, swooping in toward Phaedora.

"Now!" Alessia cried and Brione leaped from the saddle, jumping to Phaedora's mount just as she was taking off.

Her pegasus struck the air nonetheless, climbing higher even as Ludari shouted for her return.

"You'll meet your end soon enough, Phaedora!" he

sneered, urging his mount to run up the hill. His eyes weren't on the sky, nor were they on the road before him; they were fixated on the book in his grasp.

Oh no you don't.

Zissi swooped down, front claws opening, and just as Ludari looked up, the talons gripped him, lifting him from the pegasus.

Ludari roared in fury, but too heavy for the griffin to sustain carrying while thrashing, Zissi released him, and Alessia unsheathed her sword and launched from the saddle, tumbling to the ground.

The breath was knocked from her, but she wasted no time getting to her feet and racing toward Ludari as he bent to scoop up the book.

Alessia jammed the butt of her sword into his head, knocking him down. She danced away from him as he lunged and kicked the book with all her might before he could pick it up.

Ludari was larger than her. That didn't mean he was quicker, but his muscles had regenerated since she'd last seen him, and should he grab her, she wouldn't fare well.

Zissi sped off toward the pegasus, herding it away from its momentary master. Alessia cursed her mount, only because now he was chasing his foe and left her unable to take off.

"Alessia, take a look around you. There is no way to survive this war. You're all dead." Ludari sprinted forward, but with no weapon in his grasp—not that he needed one.

Alessia ducked as he clapped his hands, sending shoots of grass into the earth, but they sprang forth again like spears. She sucked in a breath as she dodged them, trying her best to trip him over his own creations and avoid being stabbed in the process.

He faltered once, and she pressed forward, launching at him with her blade drawn. If she hadn't been so focused on taking him down, she would have noticed one of his flowers rising beside her, but it was too late when she realized the purple petals were opening to expose the white mouth and the barb it shot at her neck.

She dropped to the ground, writhing in pain before the feeling in her limbs vanished. Dread washed over her. Death by his hands wasn't how she ever wanted to part from this life, but if she could distract him long enough . . .

"Oh, Pagonis. A fighter until the end," Ludari said with a chuckle. He came to stand over her, grinning down at her prone figure. "You always wanted a glorious death, didn't you?"

Blood trickled down his temple, onto her chest, and she scowled at him. She refused to answer, refused to let him hear her voice quaver.

Shouts rang out from down the road, followed by the rumbling sound of a collapsing building. But Ludari's gaze remained focused on her, and she saw as a new plan unfolded in his gaze.

Unable to fight him off with her hands, she growled.

"Feral beast," Ludari said, gripping her by the shoulders and sitting her up like she was no more than a doll. Then he picked her up and threw her over his shoulder. He rose and walked toward the discarded book, picked it up, and searched for a new mount.

"Zissi," she rasped, but it was no use. The griffin was too far, too homed in on his prey. Alessia's eyes rolled into the back of her head, but she heard the manticore roar, heard as Zryan's voice struck the air.

She felt the electrical current coast along her skin, but Ludari only laughed. Unable to open her eyes, she could only surmise, as her body jostled, that he'd found a mount.

"Time to play, Alessia." Ludari shifted, then something slammed into her skull, and she knew no more.

She awoke to Ludari's sandal nudging her. Her limbs tingled; feeling had returned. However, Alessia didn't dare move. The less he knew about her well-being, the better. If she could take him by surprise, perhaps she could knock the book from his grasp. Her eyes scanned the vicinity, and she noticed they were on top of one of the battlements.

The spire blocked her view, but she assumed beyond it was the pit to the afterlife. Her stomach sank. *So close to true death.*

"Good, you're awake."

Bricks shook loose, clattering to the ground as if Aasha was readying to dump more of herself into the depths.

"Indeed, if it means I get to watch you die." Alessia laughed, then sucked a breath in as he grabbed her by the braid, wound it around his fist, and hauled her to her feet.

"You'll be the one—" His words were cut off as Draven charged down the walkway atop the wall leading to them, his face pinched as he took stock of the situation. Just behind his shoulder was Eden, and her eyes met Alessia's.

Are you okay?

Alessia nodded curtly.

Eden's attention was at once trained on Ludari, her hands extended as though readying to use her ability at any moment.

Alessia tried to keep weight on her feet, but the tingling numbness made it difficult for her to judge her movements. She could hardly feel as her foot rocked back and forth on the stone. *Bloody useless.*

"Ludari, I'll only ask once. Unhand Alessia," Draven ground out as he halted before him.

"Draven," he said, and something akin to pride entered his voice. Although Alessia was willing to bet it didn't reflect on his face. "I am most impressed with what you built here and mastered. You and I both know who you have to thank for that."

Draven bore his fangs. "Don't think for one moment that I am going to thank you."

"Now that is an imperfection I cannot look past," Ludari hissed.

There was a flash of movement from the corner of her eye —a griffin? It landed beside Draven, beak open as it screeched. Then, where feathers once were, there was soon flesh. *Zryan.*

Ludari tensed as the numbers grew, but he held the book more tightly to his side, and his grip on her loosened a fraction.

She allowed her body to sag, and with the new distractions, he lost his grip on her, and she tumbled to the ground. Her hand immediately went for her boot, and she retrieved the hidden knife there. Faster than a viper, Alessia rose onto her knees, wobbling from their numbness, and embedded the blade between Ludari's ribs. But he was quicker to react than she was in getting away.

Ludari yanked the blade free, tossing it aside before he grabbed her single-handedly and held her up.

"Say goodbye to your wife, Zryan, and your unborn child."

Tears filled her eyes. This wasn't how he was supposed to find out. They were meant to be wound together, joyful and full of love. Yet she'd known he would use it against Zryan to bring him to his knees. "I'm sorry, Zryan. Just *kill him*," she shouted.

31

Zryan

He was too late.

Zryan saw Alessia going for Ludari, wanting to cry out for her to stop, but his manticore throat and tongue were unable to speak the words. He'd been in the midst of transforming back to his own form when Ludari knocked Alessia unconscious and threw her over his shoulder.

"No!" he screamed, throat aching from the force of it. He couldn't let him take her, not again.

Before he could transform once more, a blow to the head sent him stumbling forward. He staggered, head spinning, then twisted around. A soldier lifted his sword and slashed toward him.

Zryan spun out of the way, falling to his knees to avoid the blade. It brought him within a hand's reach from a discarded sword. Rolling, he grabbed the sword and swung it to drag across the male's stomach. A large red line formed on his clothing, then he crumpled.

Not bothering to climb to his feet, Zryan simply remained

in position as his head and body shuddered, rippling into something larger. *Faster.*

His white-feathered head stretched into the sky, beak opening to release a screech, then he spread his wings and launched into the air.

Below him, the city was ablaze, homes and golems alike burning so intensely, even the dark skies of Andhera were lit up. Several of the large clay monsters still rampaged through the streets, leaving devastation in their wake. More still attacked the walls of the castle. Kian's flying serpents rained fire down upon them, helping the harpies who fought to protect the walls.

Beyond the walls, a portion of the castle had collapsed, giving way beneath the crumbling cliffside that had taken hits from the earthquakes. The devastation was unparalleled. It would take years for Draven to return his realm to its former glory.

As he neared the wall itself, he spotted Travion and Sereia battling below. Zryan didn't want to waste the time, but he also knew what it would take to end Ludari. He swooped down, landing between them. His claws tore through one of the clay figures, shattering it, and in the meantime, he transformed his head back from a griffin's.

"Travion!"

His brother slashed through a figure; behind him, Sereia tossed a mound of hay upon it and waved the burning torch she carried across the pile. It went up in flames. But at the sound of Zryan's voice, they both turned to look at him.

Travion's brows shot up, but it was Sereia who swore at the deranged sight of him and jerked back as if slapped.

"What's going on?" Travion asked.

"Ludari has Alessia, and he's headed to the castle. He flew by pegasus to the battlements when last I saw him. I need you to meet me up there. None of this will end until he's dead and we have the book."

"Get up there, we're on our way."

Zryan didn't wait for any more words; he crouched and jumped into the air, wings beating hard to lift himself back up into the sky. Each flap brought him a little closer to Alessia. A little closer to ending the male who'd broken both of them in many ways.

Ludari and Alessia were easy to spot on the battlements, Draven and Eden facing off with them. It was a relief to see his brother already there; his presence would make it easier to surround Ludari.

Zryan's paws touched down on the stone, the griffin wings receding into his back and the fur shedding away to reveal bare skin. Standing in all his naked glory, Zryan felt the cool breeze raise goosebumps along his forearms and watched his wife embed a dagger into Ludari's side.

It wasn't enough. Ludari growled, tossing aside the blade and hauling Alessia up into his arms. There was a heavy scowl on his face as he turned them quickly, facing Zryan with Alessia clasped to his chest, the Creaturae opening in his other hand.

And then Zryan's world shattered all over again.

"Say goodbye to your wife, Zryan, and your unborn child."

Pregnant.

Alessia was pregnant.

He couldn't breathe for a moment. Everything around him seemed to slow down as his brain fought to catch up on what those words meant. *Why hadn't she told him?* Why hadn't she stepped back from the battle so that they could protect the life growing inside her? Protect at least one of their children from all this horror.

Their eyes met across the stone bricks of the battlement, her eyes pleading for him to understand and her lips begging him to kill Ludari.

Zryan knew what she wanted. Knew why she had kept this from him. She wanted him to act. Wanted him to do so without any hesitation or any regrets.

But he couldn't. He couldn't risk her life, or that of their unborn child.

Zryan tore his eyes away from Alessia and met Ludari's gaze instead. His eyes were cold, full of contempt but doused with a heady hint of triumph. He knew that he had surprised Zryan with the announcement of the baby. That he had undermined him.

"What is another child, right? Aren't we all expendable?" Zryan kept his eyes on Ludari, not Alessia, who was pleading with him to act. Nor on Draven, who he knew was slowly drawing shadows around him to disappear into them. "At least, that was your view on *your* children."

But Ludari would not be distracted, and his mouth raced through the ancient dialect of a spell. The entire castle shook, the battlement cracking away from the fortress walls, leaving a large divide between them and Draven.

"Sorry, Zryan, but you won't be able to depend on him."

Draven let out a bellow of frustration. "Zryan, rush him!"

"Do it," Alessia seconded.

His heart pounded in his ears. His hands crackled at his sides. Every ounce of anger he felt for his father rushed through him, amounting to something that could not be contained, and deep in his heart, he knew he had to do whatever was necessary for this to stop. This went beyond him. Beyond Alessia. Even beyond their children. No one in the three realms would be safe until Ludari was dead.

Quickly, he gathered lightning to himself, pulling it from the skies at such a rate, no one in this vicinity would remain. He saw, rather than heard, Ludari's lips moving with yet another spell. He would need to be faster than him. From the corner of his eye, he could see Draven backing up, preparing to leap the large divide.

Zryan drew his arm back, but just before he released the amassed collection of electricity, a gleaming gold griffin appeared behind Ludari, carrying Travion and Sereia.

The griffin dove, its paws knocking at the back of Ludari, forcing him to release both Alessia and the book as he stumbled off-kilter. Draven, using his vampiric speed, ran for the large crack in his castle walls and leaped over it. And Zryan reabsorbed some of the lightning into himself so that it rippled and wound around his arms and across his body.

He thought of nothing else as he looked at Ludari and ran, the palms of his hands colliding into Ludari's chest with enough force to drive him backward several feet. Zryan's lightning crackled, small bits coursing over Ludari's chest, shocking him.

Ludari hissed, showing his teeth. "What do you think you're doing?"

Zryan didn't respond, he only smirked and rushed Ludari again, another hard impact to the chest to send him backward, another shock of electricity coursing through him, and this time, a swift fist to the jaw.

Ludari's face jerked to the side, blood forming at the corner of his mouth. When Zryan rushed him a third time, he was ready. His fist connected with the side of Zryan's head, making his ears ring. But it didn't stop Zryan from pushing him back once more, this time to the edge of the battlement itself.

He forced himself into Ludari's proximity, wrapped his fingers beneath the armor at his shoulders, and threw all caution to the wind. The only thought in his mind was ending this once and for all.

The two of them fell over the edge, straight for the wide-mouthed pit below.

A scream echoed their descent, but Zryan focused solely on Ludari.

Ludari's face twisted in surprise, then fury. As they fell, his hand extended, his abilities calling for a root or a vine, something to keep him from the pit. Zryan tightened his grip on Ludari's armor and released the lightning in his veins. It spread over Ludari and himself, causing his sire to thrash in agony. But still, his hand remained out.

A large root shot from the earth and wrapped around Ludari's wrist, jerking him to a nearly neck-breaking stop just as they reached the edge of the pit. The force of it knocked Zryan loose of his hold, and he felt himself slipping down Ludari's body. At the last possible moment, his hand caught around Ludari's ankle, and he tightened his grip, body dangling from that point.

Ludari was limp, blood oozing from his ears and from his nostrils, and Zryan wondered if he was dead. He reached for the other ankle, intent on crawling up him, when Ludari's eyes opened and pinned him with a cold stare.

"Utter waste of my time." He rasped and kicked out at Zryan's face.

The blow caused his body to swing out, free arm flailing, legs kicking. It was only the claws he extended from his fingertips into Ludari's ankle that kept him from falling. Ludari howled with pain, and the sound was seconded by the metallic screech of a griffin. Zryan looked up only long enough to see the golden creature diving toward them and the dark-clad figure of Draven scaling down the side of the cliff much faster than he should have been. Rocks and dust tumbling after him.

Another kick collided with Zryan's face, snapping his head back. Pain raced down his neck and tightened his back and shoulders. He growled and, kicking out with his own legs, swung his body back around, pulling himself up enough that he could drive claws into Ludari's calf. They sank in deep, causing him to cry out, and Zryan took delight in the sound.

"Hold on!" Travion shouted from above.

But Zryan didn't need him; he didn't need any of them. He was going to end this once and for all. He climbed up Ludari's body, one fist full of claws at a time. As he reached eye level, Ludari snarled, and something sharp pierced Zryan's side, lodging deep beneath his ribs, desperately close to his heart: a thorn from Ludari's hand.

He coughed, something burning and thick in his lungs. But he looked Ludari in the eyes and pulled him close. "I may be pathetic," he hissed, coughing a little, "but I *will* be the last thing you see before you die."

Before Ludari could respond, Zryan pulled one set of claws out of his shoulders so that he could slice them through the root around Ludari's arm, then his other hand moved to slice him across the throat.

For a moment, they seemed to hang there, suspended in air, blood soaking the front of both of them.

Then they plummeted.

Ludari gurgled against the blood filling his throat and weakened from the loss of it.

Zryan closed his eyes and pictured Alessia. Pictured sweet little hands and feet bundled all up in her arms. He thought of Ruan. Kian. Brione. He smiled and spread his arms out.

Then sharp talons surrounded his shoulders, his body whipped to a sudden halt, and he felt himself being lifted into the air.

He wheezed, coughing up wetness from the heaviness in his lungs, and peered up to see the golden griffin above. Before he could blink, he was out of the pit and landing on the edge of it, where Draven was.

"You fool!" Draven hissed, dropping to his knees beside Zryan's crumpled form.

He could only laugh, which ended in a deep cough, the taste of copper filling his mouth. "Seemed"—another hacking cough cut him off—"like a good . . . idea." More coughing overtook him. He knew now that he was drowning in his own blood, that the thorn Ludari had driven into him must have pierced his lung.

Somehow, it seemed fitting that it should happen here, with his brothers around him.

"Do we have time to get him to Eden?" Travion rushed off the griffin, skidding over the ground as he came to their sides. "I didn't realize any of that blood was his!"

Draven shook his head, then lifted his wrist to his mouth

and ripped a large gash in it with his teeth. This, he brought to Zryan's mouth. "Drink!" he growled. "This will give you enough time."

Zryan shook his head, but Draven forced the bloody wrist to his lips, making it so that he had no choice but to accept the fluid. He coughed more, gasping against the liquid fire pouring into him from his brother's wrist as well as the blood steadily filling his lungs.

Draven pulled his wrist away, hoisted him into the air, and carried him to the griffin. "Let's get him to her."

Bless the strength of Kian's mechanical beasts, for it bore the weight of all three of them.

Alessia

Zryan!

Alessia forced herself upright, her limbs tingling, but the feeling was trickling back into them. She ran to the edge of the battlement, staring down into the gaping hole. Heart and chest constricted, and tears sprang to her eyes. Was he gone? Had they been too late? There was no returning for a body lost to the pit. Just as she'd given up hope, a griffin soared into the sky, metal gleaming in the moon's weak rays.

Three riders sat astride the creature and at once. She eased down the side of the wall, comforted that her husband was alive and Ludari was finally *dead*.

She swallowed roughly, dragging her gaze to the crack running along the bricks of the walkway. If Eden could banish the lasting effects of the poison in her system—the thought vanished the moment Kian's metal griffin touched down and Zryan was hauled from its back by Travion.

Her heart thumped wildly in her chest, and she forced herself upright, wincing as her ankles rolled a few times.

"Zryan!" she screamed as Eden knelt before him and placed her hands on his side. Her husband didn't call out to her, didn't wave off her concern. She sucked in a breath, trying to stop the growing panic and ease her worries.

They had just repaired their relationship.

They had made amends, and they were going to have a new baby—

Alessia assessed the divide between them, wondering if she could make the jump without plummeting to her death.

"Alessia, he's all right—or will be," Draven called out finally, when he'd pulled away from his prone brother. He extended his hand as if calming a wild griffin. "Eden has mended the worst of it." He turned on his heel to peer down at the battle still raging and frowned. "I am needed down below. Eden will remain up here, but Travion, you're coming with me. We need to end this."

Sereia glanced from Alessia to Travion. "I'll be with you shortly." She watched as Travion and Draven left them. "I'm coming to get you, Alessia."

From the corner of her eye, she saw a flash of white wings. She turned to face the pegasus as its hooves struck the air, and the mare lowered so she just hovered above the stones.

Brione grinned down at Alessia as she shoved a bedraggled looking Phaedora off. The blond fae struck the battlement and tumbled so that she was only a mere foot away from Alessia.

Phaedora.

"I need your sword!" Alessia called to her daughter, and with a nod, Brione threw it down. She caught it with one hand, urging her body to obey, for this was what she'd wanted since the beginning.

Brione's gaze flicked to where her father lay. "Papa?" she asked Alessia.

Her daughter was torn as Alessia took a step forward, worry etching itself on her features. "Go to him, Bri. I have this." Reluctantly, Brione urged her mare away. Alessia drew in a sharp breath, growling as she advanced on Phaedora.

She lifted the sword, intending to lop her head off, but the bitch spun away, grabbed a handful of rubble, and threw it at Alessia's face in a desperate attempt.

"You're done here, and you will join Ludari in the afterlife. I will punt you from this fucking ruin myself." Alessia charged, dropping her sword as she tackled Phaedora to the ground. She screamed as Alessia landed a hard punch to her jaw, and though the wicked fae's eyes rolled back into her head, she didn't lose consciousness.

Phaedora surged forward, sending her forehead into Alessia's.

Alessia faltered, rocking back, but not enough to send her to the side. Using her anger, she leaned forward and grabbed Phaedora by the shoulders to hold her down. The other fae, not a soldier in any form, swatted at her, tried to scrape her exposed skin, and clawed at her like the desperate thing she was.

Alessia laughed and shifted her hand to Phaedora's throat and squeezed as she flailed around. "I'm going to enjoy watching the life fade from your eyes."

No sooner had she spoken the words Phaedora threw her arm to the side, too fast for Alessia to realize what she'd done. Before she could block it, the wretch brought a brick against the side of her head.

Pain radiated through her skull, and she fell to the side, unable to focus. *Don't you dare give up, Alessia. You are not done yet. Get up!* She groggily rose to her knees, swaying before she climbed to her feet and faced Phaedora. "You bi—" Icy pain radiated from her abdomen, and when she dared to glance down, the dagger she had used on Ludari protruded from her belly.

"No," she whispered at first. How could her little warrior survive *that*? "No!" Alessia staggered backward, and in the distance, she could hear another screaming.

Sereia had made it onto the battlement and was racing toward them, sword in hand. But she was *too late*. Tears sprung into Alessia's eyes as she bent down to scoop up her sword. Orange flames from below rose higher and higher; despite the rocky terrain, fire was engulfing Arcem, chasing away the chill in the air.

"Goodbye." Alessia raised her sword, and just as she spun it forward and thrust it into Phaedora's chest, so, too, did Sereia from behind, piercing her through the neck. The fae dropped to the ground, dead.

As soon as it was done, Alessia's hand fell to the blade jutting from her, and she went to grab it, but Sereia reached out to stop her.

"Not yet, let me grab Eden—Brione . . ." Sereia glanced over her shoulder, then back to Alessia, to where the blade was. "Alessia."

"Don't," she bit out, not wanting to focus on the reality that, more than likely, she'd lost her child. "Get her now."

Sereia eased her down, careful to not shift the dagger. She

squeezed her shoulder, tears glistening in her eyes too. "You'll be okay."

Alessia rested her head against the bricks and closed her eyes, wondering if those words were more to reassure Sereia than they were for her. She groaned as a new wave of pain wracked her body. The muscles in her abdomen contracted, and she clenched her teeth.

Stay with us. Stay!

Since realizing her predicament in Edessa, she hadn't allowed herself to truly bask in the truth—that she was with child. There hadn't been time to dream of what they'd look like or who they would grow into.

However, now she mourned for the loss of a child she could never hold in that way. A life unlived. But they'd know, for a brief time, that Alessia had loved them as fiercely as she could. She regretted they'd never hear Zryan's whispered *I love you.*

Alessia reached down to her belly. A pool of fresh blood lay there. "We'll be together soon," she murmured. "My little one."

Someone ran toward her, but her eyes were far too heavy to open. "Alessia, I'm going to remove the blade," Eden said as she knelt beside her. "Your baby is fading, but they're alive. So you need to be strong for the both of you, okay?"

Still alive.

She fought to open her eyes, but all she could manage was a small smile, which was cut short when the blade was extracted. Pain, white and hot, coursed through her. Alessia screamed.

"Zryan," she whispered. "Where is Zryan?"

"He's all right. Brione is with him, finishing his healing."

Eden's voice was full of tension. "Sereia, help me get this armor off of her." Piece by piece, the leather was peeled away, until Alessia's torso was bare to the chilled air.

Hot liquid spilled down her side. She knew it was blood. Leaving her faster than Eden could get her hands on her.

"What can I do?" Sereia asked, her voice shaking.

"Hold her hand, keep her awake as much as you can."

Darkness beckoned Alessia though, and she was tired of fighting. Exhausted from battle, from confronting her emotions.

She felt as Sereia took her hand in hers, and she squeezed as hard as she could. "Don't you dare fade on me, Alessia. We have yet to toast our victory. Together, we rid this world of that bitch. I refuse to drink to that alone."

Alessia tried her best to curl her fingers around Sereia's, but she could only assume it was a feeble attempt. "Can't . . . drink," she gasped out.

"Well, I can patiently wait for a good celebration," Sereia said, squeezing her hand again.

A new warmth spread through her as hands slid across her stomach. Her muscles contracted again, and this time, she grit her teeth.

"Try to breathe," Eden coaxed. "Your body is trying to save itself by—"

"No." Alessia fought to open her eyes and glanced down at Eden. The other fae's eyes were wide with worry. "That's not an option."

Eden didn't argue, only nodded. "Take a deep breath. The next few moments are going to hurt."

What was more pain if it meant saving the life of her little warrior? Alessia's head fell back against the stones, and she gripped tighter onto Sereia's hand as a searing pain wound its way inside of her. She gnashed her teeth together to keep from screaming but couldn't help it as her cries bled into the nightmare realm.

It felt as though the blade was twisting inside of her. And it wasn't just *her* that was upset, for the little one inside of her seemed to thrash with quick kicks and flutterings. But each tiny protest brought with it a little more hope.

How long Eden worked on her, she didn't know, but when the feeling of hands left her skin, Alessia was ready to succumb to the pull of sleep.

Eden shifted beside her. "I have done all I can, Alessia. Now, it's up to your body and the child."

Sereia loosened her grip on Alessia's hand, and she released a shaky breath. After this, Alessia would have to make it a point to be warmer toward her sister-in-law. She'd never been truly unkind, but distant and cold for how she'd treated Travion.

This changed things. It changed everything.

When Alessia opened her eyes, Eden was removing her cape and using it to cover Alessia's bare torso. "Thank you," she croaked.

"Don't try to rise yet, you're still healing." Eden glanced over her shoulder at the sound of hooves.

"Alessia. Spirits, no!" Zryan's voice carried as he raced forward and dropped to his knees.

"Mother!" Brione cried out as she rushed to her other side.

"Be careful!" Eden cautioned, blocking Alessia with her hands. "You will undo her healing."

Zryan made a noise of frustration and slid his hand

beneath her head. He pressed his forehead against hers. "Less, my Less." Tears sprang to his eyes and fell down his cheeks.

She groggily lifted her hand and cupped his cheek. "You did it," she murmured and drank in his features, not that they weren't already committed to her memory. She traced his sharp jawline, covered in blood and dust. "I knew you could."

Zryan peppered soft kisses along the bridge of her nose. "You're okay," he said, but it sounded like a question to her. He looked away and at Eden. Alessia couldn't see her face, but when he turned back to her, there was a hint of sadness that hadn't been there before. "We'll be okay." He gingerly dragged his knuckles down her hip, the closest he likely dared to get to where she'd been healed.

"I'm so proud of you," Alessia said through a sob and lifted her hand to rest at the back of his head. He had done it —faced his fears, tossed his self-doubt aside, and conquered Ludari. And nearly died in the process. "But don't ever do that again." Her voice took on a sharper tone. "I couldn't bear losing you."

A strangled noise escaped him as he pulled away. "And you're one to talk. I'm going to have words with you later about that, but for right now . . . rest. The both of you need rest." Zryan's gaze slid to Brione, and her eyes widened sheepishly.

"Well," Sereia said. "For that to happen, she probably shouldn't be on the rooftop half-naked. Although, fighting in the nude doesn't seem to faze anyone here."

Alessia laughed, then groaned, regretting it. She started

to relax, then nearly bolted upright, but Zryan pushed on her shoulder. He looked down at her in confusion.

"The book?" she rasped.

Brione rapped her fingers on it. "I have it."

"Good. Now we can finish this," Alessia murmured.

Eden cleared her throat and extended her hands to Brione, who deposited the book in her grasp. "Well, someone will, but *you*, my dear sister, won't be."

To that, Alessia snorted. But if anyone was to end the battle in Arcem, it deserved to be its ruler.

Zryan

His body ached, muscles screamed with a weariness that went beyond exhaustion into something else entirely. His torso felt stretched, skin too tight from healing, and his lungs still burned. While Eden had sealed the holes in him created by Ludari's thorn, she'd not had the time to drain all of the blood from his lung or even bring him to the point where it didn't feel like a hearty sneeze wouldn't undo her repairs. Coughs still wracked his form, body desperate to dispel blood that had pooled where it was not meant to be. And, by the sun, moon, and sea, he did not wish to leave Alessia's side. His hand beneath her head, his eyes locked on her face, his other arm curving protectively around her stomach and hip . . . He couldn't bear the thought of leaving her—of leaving *them*.

Yet the chaos was not over. The war against his sire had been won, but the battle had not ended, and Zryan could hear the destruction from the giant clay golems booming out through the night. Draven's kingdom was being demolished, and Zryan couldn't sit back and let it continue. Not when his brother had willingly accepted this destruction to protect them. To give them the advantage.

He leaned down, pressing his forehead to Alessia's. "I have to go end this," he whispered. "Please be still and listen to our daughter. I will return to your side as soon as I am able."

Alessia gripped his shoulder tightly, looking up at him intently. He waited for her to speak—something encouraging or loving perhaps—and then, "You may want to put some clothes on."

He laughed, the pressure hurting, but he didn't care. They were alive. She loved him once more, and all of that joy meant much more to him than anything else.

"Let them all see and be envious." He grinned down at her and brushed his fingers along her jaw. "I will be back." Zryan looked to Brione, who hadn't gone very far. "Call for some of the revenants; they can help you get her inside and settled."

"I'll look after her, Papa."

Zryan smiled, leaned down to kiss Alessia quickly, then stood to embrace his daughter. When he felt he could leave them, he turned to Brione. "I need your cape."

Brione nodded. "Of course." She removed the cape from her shoulders and handed it to him.

Zryan wrapped it around his hips and knotted it at his waist. "The fur lining is quite nice against my skin."

Brione blinked, making a slight face. "You may keep it."

Zryan chuckled, kissed his daughter on the forehead, then turned to Eden.

Together, they climbed onto the pegasus Brione had abandoned and lifted into the air. The battle below still raged, none of the Lucemite soldiers realizing that Ludari had fallen, and there was nothing to stop the clay golems from rampaging against the city except fire that only wrought more damage.

Draven and Travion were easy to find. A dark-clad figure in the midst of fire, feeding the flames or shifting them with the wave of his hands. A conductor orchestrating a deadly concerto. The other figure wielding wind like a weapon. Slashing through groups of golems, shattering them as if wind itself were a weapon.

Their pegasus dropped down between them, prancing away from the large flames washing their skin in heat.

"Draven!" Eden called out, and somehow, despite the noise and chaos around him, he turned at the sound of her voice. She held up the book, and Zryan watched the look of relief wash over his face.

Zryan slid off the silken white creature and lowered cautiously to the ground. His torso stretched, his injuries complaining, but he held together. "Let's get this done!" he shouted over the roar of the fire. "Travion!"

As the three of them came together, Draven took the Creaturae from Eden and opened it. As one, their eyes fell to the pages as he quickly leafed through it.

"There!" Travion's finger came out, tapping down on a page.

Zryan leaned in. An incantation to undo a creation. "Care to do the honors?" he asked Draven. It was his home after all.

Draven nodded shortly, chest expanding as he inhaled deeply and began to call out the incantation, the ancient dialect pouring off his tongue smoothly.

Zryan held his breath, eyes fastening on the largest group of golems, waiting to see if the incantation would work. They raced toward a group of Anderians standing their ground, ready to defend themselves and what remained of Arcem. Over top of them, a large golem swung its arm out toward a huddle of harpies raining arrows down on Lucemite soldiers.

For a moment, the world stood still, and nothing happened. Then the golems shattered into tiny speckles of dust, which exploded in large clouds before falling to the earth. Still. Gone.

Cries of shock rang out, and General Ailith directed her harpies and weres in around the remaining Lucemites, blocking a retreat and calling for surrender. A filthy looking Ruan and a ragged looking Kian helped to enforce the containment. The soldiers conceded without hesitation, throwing down their arms and lifting their hands into the air.

Draven slammed the Creaturae shut and swept a hand out to recall the fire that raged around them. Travion lifted his hand into the air, and storm clouds formed. Soon, a soft, chilly rain fell from the sky to douse the rest of the embers.

As for Zryan, he let his shoulders drop and his body relax truly for the first time in years. There was so much to do still. Decisions on what to do with the Lucemites who had transferred their loyalties over to Ludari without thought. Repairs to be made to both Andhera and Lucem—though perhaps the book could aid in making that go more swiftly. But in this moment, none of that mattered; they had the book back, Ludari was gone, down into the afterlife with no body to resurrect, and Alessia loved him.

"I'm going to be a father again," he announced.

Draven and Travion turned to look at him.

"What?" Draven asked.

"Alessia is pregnant." He grinned broadly, and he was pleased when both of his brothers smiled happily for him, moving at the same time to slip an arm around him in a hug of congratulations.

Zryan hummed contentedly in the back of his throat, squeezing his brothers back.

When they parted, Eden moved to Draven's side, and he and Travion eyed the pegasus. "I'm taking it back up," Zryan said to him.

"You and your fancy skirt don't belong on it. Walk back." Travion reached for the reins, only for Zryan to slap his hand away.

Travion looked affronted, but Zryan grabbed the reins instead. "My wife was stabbed, and so was I. Me and my fancy skirt *are* taking this pegasus back up into the castle."

Travion chuckled. "Go." And slapped him on the ass.

They were a ragged looking lot who sat around Draven's dining hall. None of them had bothered to bathe or change yet, their eyes all threatening to shut on them and their bodies bearing an assortment of bruises, cuts, stab wounds, and fractures that Eden and Brione were far too tired to deal with at this time.

Morning would come soon enough, and as of this moment, no one was going to die from their injuries.

The revenants, whom Zryan thought were striving to return some semblance of normalcy to their castle, had prepared a massive feast as the royal family straggled back into the castle, collecting in the throne room to examine each other and assure themselves that everyone remained relatively whole.

Now, they sat around the table heavily laden with food. Zryan's children were together, Ruan tearing into a thick lamb roast while Brione's head rested on his shoulder. She lazily brought grapes to her mouth, munching on them as if the effort was more than she could take. Her other hand rested on the table, threaded with Kian's. He, too, seemed ready to doze off into his cup but was attempting to cut his own meat one handed.

Across from them, Sereia sat sideways in Travion's lap taking turns feeding herself and then him, a little smile of devious delight on her lips. Part of Zryan half expected her to suddenly pinch him, just to see him squirm. Travion gazed back at her, accepting what bits of food she offered him, face radiating satisfaction.

While Draven sat at the head of the table, the only one not looking ready to fall asleep—something Zryan hated him for—Eden sat just perpendicular to him. Her eyes were lined with weariness, her chin resting propped up by her chin, elbow on the table. Despite the exhaustion lining her face, there was a small smile on her lips.

Zryan wanted nothing but the whiskey in his glass and the ability to crash into the bed awaiting him upstairs—so long as that wasn't the part of the castle that had tumbled into the pit. But for now, Alessia leaned into his side, their chairs so close together, they were nearly one. He had wanted to get her into bed right away, but she'd fought him on it, saying that Brione had worked with her heavily, and that while she needed to be slow and careful, she and the babe should be fine.

He kissed her forehead, his hand sliding gently over her abdomen to cup the slight bump that could be felt there. Zryan couldn't believe he hadn't noticed it while his face was mere inches away.

The quiet of the dining hall was interrupted as a revenant appeared between Draven and Eden. Both of them looked up to him. "Your Majesty, your guest has arrived."

Draven's brows lifted, then his gaze shifted down the table to where Sereia and Travion sat. "Send him in."

The revenant disappeared, only for the dining hall doors to fly open and another figure to glide in.

He looked solid enough, and the way he had used the doors, flinging them aside to bang against the walls, would make one think he'd needed to come into the room through them, but the near glide of his booted feet over the stone floor gave him away.

Revenant.

A sharp gasp rang out, and a chair scraped across the floor.

Sereia was on her feet, disbelief and tears in her eyes. She had grown pale, but there was hope spreading over her face. "A-Adrik?"

The revenant chuckled and opened his arms. "Hello, Captain."

The new queen of Midniva ran into her former first mate's arms. There was laughter and tears, and Zryan was only slightly disappointed she hadn't run straight through his ghostly form. Travion joined his wife soon enough, his and Adrik's hands clasping each other's wrists in a quick shake.

"How? I don't understand!" Sereia said, looking between Adrik and Draven. "When we first arrived, I had hopes I would find you here, but when you didn't show up, I assumed you'd passed on."

"Adrik has been on the outskirts of Andhera with a scouting patrol. I had wanted to call him back for you, but there wasn't time. I thought it best to wait until after the battle was fought and won to reunite you," Draven explained.

Sereia looked as if she might argue for a moment, then her face softened. "Thank you, Draven." They shared a silent look of understanding between them, and Sereia turned back to her first mate.

Zryan smiled, watching his brother. "You've grown soft, Draven," he taunted. "I thought you'd hold that grudge forever."

Draven had hated Sereia with a passion, never forgiving her for refusing Travion's first proposal in such a drastic manner—diving from a cliff into the sea and running off to join a pirate ship. Whenever she would show up in Midniva to wind up in Travion's bed again, Draven had been sure to let her know of his disapproval.

Draven shrugged his shoulders, but his hand slipped around one of Eden's. "It is my duty to help revenants find their purpose in their unlife and find the peace that will help them pass on. Adrik needed to see his family again."

Eden eyed Draven with a little shake of her head. Like all of them, she knew that it had been more than that. Draven had a softer heart than he tended to show the world. "Plus," she quipped, a smirk spreading over her lips, "he likes coming to the castle whenever he can. I think he's sweet on Dhriti."

Zryan laughed, thinking of the former pirate chasing after Eden's personal harpy guard. "Now *that* is something I would like to see."

Happy, he leaned back in his chair and pulled Alessia carefully into his lap to hold her. She was nearly as tall as he was, so it wasn't an easy thing to do, but somehow, they managed it so that she could lean her head on his shoulder and drift off a little.

There was a lot to be done. So *much* to be done.

But for tonight, he was going to hold his wife and simply be happy for everything he had.

34

Alessia

A full day had passed since the battle, and Eden loomed over Alessia with furrowed brows as she ran her hand along the slight swell of Alessia's abdomen. She'd listened to her sister-in-law's strict orders to rest, not necessarily for her sake but for the child's, since they'd taken the worst of the injury.

As much as Alessia wanted to join Zryan as they truly ended the war, she knew her limits, and she'd pushed herself as far as she could go.

"What a stubborn little mite," Eden whispered as she withdrew her hands. "I mean that in the best way, and it's no surprise considering the family." She laughed softly and stepped back as Alessia sat up.

"Thank you," she sighed. "It is a rather mulish family." She rolled from the bed, the cool air of the room brushing against her bare body. Every muscle still screamed at her, sore from use and the demands of fighting.

Alessia crossed the room to the privacy screen and let her fingers drag along the sheer black gown hanging from it. It was befitting of Lucem and not Andhera. She'd be returning today to pick up the pieces of her shattered kingdom and punish those who had willingly acted against them.

"Alessia," Eden said softly. "Do you think when you return, you can check on Aurelie for me?" Her voice shook with worry, and when Alessia was through drawing the gown over her head, she turned to face the other female. "I can't leave Andhera until the dust settles here, and I just—"

"I will. It's the least that I can do for you." She crossed the distance between them and wrapped her arms around Eden. "Thank you, for everything." Alessia brushed a soft kiss to her temple and withdrew. "Now, before we both dissolve into tears, let's go meet with the others."

Zryan led Zissi into the courtyard. The rubble, for the most part, had been cleared away. Smoke still permeated the air, tickling the back of Alessia's throat. It would take time for Andhera to recover, just as it would for Lucem, but they were all alive.

Ruan, Kian, and Brione had left for home along with Ailith and her troops the night prior, refusing to rest until the kingdom was *theirs* again.

The Lucemites remaining in Andhera, who refused to swear fealty to Zryan, to her, were sent to the dungeons, to either feed the woodland beasts or the king. The others returned home with Ruan and Kian.

Draven walked up beside Alessia, his expression unreadable, but then he extended his hand and cupped the side of her face. "*We* did it, Alessia. And don't for one moment think otherwise." He offered one of his small smiles to her and stepped away. "Be well, and don't be strangers."

Everyone had had a hand in winning the war, but she *had* felt as though she missed the grandest part of it all—when the roar of victory rang out. Regardless, it was over now.

She walked up to Zryan and leaned into his warmth. "Let's go home and truly finish this."

He nodded and helped her mount, then tucked the Creaturae into the satchel. "And Draven, what do you think of a quarterly blackout in Lucem? So that you may return to your old land and terrify the masses?"

Draven lifted a brow, and he surprisingly seemed to consider the offer. "Once a year, we may celebrate in Lucem, but no more than that. We will talk once our kingdoms are settled."

Zryan chuckled, his arms reaching around Alessia so he could grab the reins. "I will take it." His breath fanned out over her neck, and she leaned back into him. "Be well," Zryan offered before Zissi took flight.

Alessia hadn't had a chance to survey the damaged city, but as her griffin soared above, her heart sank. Several buildings had been reduced to ash, and those that weren't dust were rubble. Although she'd been at the very top of Aasha and had seen the damage herself, it looked worse from afar.

Andhera would rebuild and thrive once more, Alessia had no doubt of that.

When they reached the Veil, neither chimera nor manticore stirred, and she wondered if they too were tired of fighting, or perhaps their numbers had dwindled during the battles. Without a spare thought, they left the darkness of the nightmare realm.

As they emerged into Lucem, she had the good sense to close her eyes and wait several moments before opening them. She almost wished she hadn't.

The ground had turned black from where flames licked at it, singing the once lush grass. There were several uprooted trees with their limbs snapped and foliage burned.

"By the sun, our home."

"We can and we will rebuild," Zryan said by her ear.

"Before we return to the palace, I need to do something for Eden."

She didn't need to say another word, for Zryan redirected Zissi toward Edessa. The last time they'd been close to the manor, mayhem had been unleashed and from the sky, and there hadn't been much left around the home. But Eden needed to know, and it was the least Alessia could do.

The moment they hovered over what once was the building, she swallowed roughly. Only one pillar remained standing; the rest of the manor had fallen in on itself, exposing the interior to the outside.

Zissi landed, and Alessia quickly dismounted, darting across the lawn and inside. "Is anyone alive?" It seemed a foolish thing to ask considering the state of the home. Marble hung precariously above her, but she pushed on to where the stairs once had been.

She brought a hand up to her mouth as she spotted a light pink skirt sticking out from under the rubble, and when she bent down, she saw the crushed body of not one but two fae. The brunette's arms encircled a male youngling with a mop of brown hair.

"Alessia," Zryan's ragged voice came. "There is nothing we can do for them now."

And she knew that, but it still stung as though they had been *her* friends, for they were Lucemites, and they should have been protected.

"I know," she murmured and left the destruction. It was a truth that hit her hard. This was only one of many heartbreaking instances in Lucem.

The wages of war were death.

Warm rays touched the palace, lending the white stone a golden hue. If she wasn't so heartsick, it would have been a relief to be in her homeland. But there had been so much devastation everywhere. She lifted her gaze beyond the palace spires and saw the sun glinting off something metallic.

A serpent with wings flew toward them, its slinky frame seeming to slither through the air.

Ruan sat astride the beast. Dark circles lined his eyes and the typical smirk was gone. How he could even sit upright was beyond Alessia. "Just in time. We have the palace surrounded, and the rest of the soldiers are in the courtyard. If anyone is thinking of escaping, they won't make it far."

"Remain in the air but send a few harpies down with us. I think they need a little reminder as to who their king and queen are," Zryan said, and Alessia could hear the grin in his voice.

Electrical currents raced along his forearms, tickling the hairs on her arms but not harming her. Although the sky was bright, the air crackled with pent-up energy, and as a large bolt raced toward the ground, Zryan drove the griffin down to the courtyard.

The beast landed in front of the soldiers, screeching as if daring anyone to come forward and defy him.

A murmur rang out among the soldiers. Their swords were drawn, but they didn't rush forward, nor did anyone flee—yet.

Zryan slid from the griffin, and Alessia reached down, grabbing the book before she, too, dismounted and walked to the front of the line.

Harpies landed in the courtyard, folding their wings behind them as they waited for the word. Despite the battle in Andhera, they still seemed primed for a fight.

Zryan stood before what once was a fraction of their army, his eyes full of hope, but the hard lines in his face, his taut muscles, said he was everything but relaxed. "We understand that Ludari forced some of you to serve, and others went willingly. But we are here to offer a choice: surrender and swear fealty to us so that you may live, or pay for your treachery."

"And we will find a punishment befitting of your crimes." Alessia rapped her knuckles against the leather cover of the book.

Swords clanged to the ground and sandals scuffled on the stones as soldier after soldier took a knee. If there were any that thought to run, Alessia didn't see them or hear them.

When every head was bowed, she took a step forward. "Each and every one of you will do public penance by rebuilding our kingdom. Understood?"

As one, the troops pounded fists against their armor. "Yes, my queen!"

Thank the sun and sky. She couldn't muster any energy to fight.

"Stop!" Brione's voice rang out as she charged forward, chasing a slender male.

Recognition slowly clicked into place. *Mal.* He rounded the corner, but Brione was close behind him.

The earth rumbled as the metal serpent lowered to the ground, its tail thrashing in an attempt to slam into the fleeing male, but all it did was create a barrier. A useful one.

Mal faltered, and Brione slammed into him, tackling him to the ground. Before he could use his affinity on her, Alessia ran for them.

"I swear to you, I'll have you again like this, *princess.* Just as breathless but without the scowl." His green gaze danced with heated promise, and the more he grinned at Brione, the more Alessia wanted to ensure he'd never speak again.

"Until I figure out what use a pawn has to us, you'll endure a fraction of what the three realms have." Alessia reached out to his mind as quickly as she could and frowned at the missing strands there.

Most had a loom she could pluck strings from, but Mal had very few to spare. She'd seen this once, when someone's memories had been erased and they were but a shell of themselves. There was a thicker strand that presented itself to her, and as she struck it, Mal shuddered on the ground.

His eyes glazed over, seeing but not *seeing.* His mind was lost to the nightmare she'd unfolded on him.

Fear of being forgotten. Fear of being nothing. Fear of emptiness.

Alessia nodded toward her daughter. "Brione, see to it

that he's locked in the dungeons. I don't think there is a way he could even try to escape from that."

"I will aid her, Your Majesty," a familiar voice said by Alessia's shoulder.

She froze, then turned on her heel to face the guard. *Tobias.* Dust clung to his blood-flecked face, but his warm eyes remained on her, and he offered her a crooked smile. Relief flooded her, and though she wanted to embrace him, she only nodded.

"I'm pleased to see you made it back from the dark realm," she said, but the words held more emotion than she could physically convey.

"And you, Majesties." Tobias bowed his head, then approached the other side of Mal and grabbed him by the elbow.

"Ruan and I will see to the soldiers. Head inside with the harpies." Zryan leaned in to brush a quick kiss to Alessia's forehead.

She smiled, pulled away, and motioned for the Andherians to follow her.

After the palace had been cleared and secured, Alessia padded outside into the gardens. She wasn't alone, for her family sat on the marble benches, sleepily gazing up at the sky or at a flower. The only one who appeared less drained was Alvia, and she sat with her hands folded in her lap next to Kian.

If it hadn't been for her quick thinking and willingness to

put her life on the line, who could say what would have happened to the three realms?

Everyone had earned rest, and it would come soon enough, but she wanted to embrace this moment.

Striding up to her husband, Alessia snaked her arm around his neck and slid into his lap. He embraced her, leaning his face into her neck. How fitting for them that war had brought them together not once but twice.

"I know that I don't just speak for myself but your father as well. I am beyond proud of all of you," Alessia said, glancing at each of her children.

"Now that we have the book back, what is going to stop someone else from trying to take it?" Ruan grunted and roughly rubbed at his face.

There was always that fear, and it was a natural one given the *very* recent happenings.

"I will build a box this time," Kian interjected and looked between her and Zryan. "But with the book. And let it be known that whoever opens the box, mayhem like they've never seen will be unleashed."

Ruan snorted. "Do you think that will stop them?"

"Who wants to destroy the realms on purpose?" Alessia shrugged. Phaedora had unleashed chaos for a reason. She didn't believe that the female had wanted to bring the realms to ruin, for where would she live to rule? In hindsight, Alessia wondered if the fae thought she could wield Ludari no differently than the book. But the tyrannical king had not been one to be controlled.

Brione hummed and bumped her knee into Kian's. "What will you call it?"

"Phaedora's Box," Kian said with a chuckle. "I think it's

only right that an object so menacing bears the name of someone who is equally sinister."

Alessia laughed, and soon, everyone was chuckling.

Was sinister. Not anymore. Not ever again. The threat of Ludari and Phaedora was over, and if there was one good thing that had come from it all, it was how it had brought everyone together as a family.

United.

Epilogue

Zryan

A shrill cry rang out in the room, breaking the silence that had fallen over it not too long ago. Zryan groaned, and beside him, Alessia stirred. Rolling over on the plush feather bed, he pressed a kiss behind her ear.

"Sleep, I'll go."

She murmured her understanding and went back to sleep.

Zryan threw the coverings off of himself and padded tiredly across the room. Rubbing at his eye with the heel of his hand, he stood over the gilded crib and looked down at the crying infant. A tiny fist flailed in the air, somehow worked free of the swaddling.

"You were just put down, little one," he rasped groggily.

The servants had pushed for the newest little royal to be cared for in the nursery at night, so the king and queen could rest, but there was something about having their first child in hundreds of years that had made both Zryan and Alessia want to forgo that.

He reached into the crib and plucked the small bundle up.

The tears still sounded, shaking her tiny chest. Resting her against his chest, her small bottom cupped in his hand, he shooshed her quietly and gently rocked her back and forth.

She settled quickly enough, and Zryan understood the need deep in his own bones. To wake suddenly, no heat from anyone else's body near, staring up at the ceiling entirely alone. He rubbed her back as she snuggled in once more and moved to the window, staring down over the palace gardens.

"You've been born into an interesting time, sweet Aesira," he whispered to her, turning his head to look at her.

Her eyes were open, big and dark and staring up at him, entirely awake. He chuckled and shifted her into the crook of his arm so that they could more easily meet each other's gaze.

"We've found a new era of peace," he murmured. "The kingdom, as well as your parents."

Aesira blinked up at him, eyes far too bright with awareness for the hour. Zryan rubbed his thumb over her sweet, rounded cheek and pressed a kiss to the small tuft of auburn hair on her head.

She was a miracle, their little warrior, who had survived more than any babe should long before she had even been born. Along her shoulder, she bore a silver scar, a sign of the attack that had come upon her by Phaedora's hand. A sign of her strength and her fight to survive.

Aesira squawked, and he chuckled. "What? Does my scruff scratch you? Perhaps you shouldn't wake me up in the midst of sleeping."

"If you're just going to talk, you may as well do it here in the bed," Alessia grumbled and threw the covers back.

Zryan grinned and turned away from the window. "Apologies, the princess is wide awake."

"Of course she is." Alessia pushed up a little to rest more against the headboard and beckoned them over.

Zryan crossed the room and crawled back into the bed, handing Aesira over into Alessia's outstretched arms.

Sprawled upon the mattress once more, he rested on his side, a hand beneath his head, and gazed upon his wife and daughter. The sight made his heart clench with amazement and also expand with so much love. More love than he could even imagine.

None of this had felt possible a year ago.

Yet here it was. Here *they* were. And Zryan knew that he could face anyone, and anything, so long as he had Alessia at his side.

Come what may, they would make it through to the other side.

"I love you," he said adoringly.

Alessia dragged her eyes away from admiring her daughter and smiled softly. "I love you too."

ACKNOWLEDGMENTS

Thank you so much for reading the Immortal Realms trilogy! It has been a labor of love and one that we've enjoyed. We built not one, but three epic realms that we hope you've enjoyed.

First, we want to thank our beta readers, Carla and Lou, for helping polish this novel. You stuck it through to the bitter end with us and we appreciate that so much. You are the best of the best.

To Meg, our splenderific comma goblin, you're always there for us, fixing our blasted commas and other nonsense. Thank you also for working with us on our crazy deadlines. You have helped us more than you can even understand.

To our loved ones, who are patient and understand when we need to duck our heads and write all the words so we can crush a deadline. You're the real heroes here!

To the Midnight Tide Publishing clan; you're all so amazing and talented. Thanks for being a big support system for everyone—including us.

Donna, our loyal Patron supporter, a huge thanks to you for believing in us.

Finally, to our readers who have followed along on this journey with us. Your love of our characters and this world we have created is the driving force behind our writing. We wanted to give you a final epic conclusion to the three brothers' stories, and hope we have done that for you.

Until our next endeavor,

Happy Reading!

Elle Beaumont & Christis Christie

P.S.

Should you ask for more . . . We we have some plans.
wink, wink

THE OFFICIAL PLAYLIST

Want to listen along while you read and immerse yourself into the world of Wages of War? Listen to the playlist below!

SCAN FOR SPOTIFY PLAYLIST

1. Darling, I Want To Destroy You by AFI
2. Together Right by Finger Eleven
3. Castle by Halsey
4. Every Beginning Ends by Noah Cyrus
5. Words As A Weapon by Birdy
6. Lifetime by Three Days Grace
7. Torpedo by Jillette Johnson
8. Someone To Talk To by Three Days Grace
9. If I Were A Boy by Julia Sheer
10. Empty by Letdown

ABOUT ELLE BEAUMONT

Elle Beaumont loves creating vivid and fantastical worlds. She lives in Southeastern Massachusetts with her husband and two children. When not writing or chasing around her children, she enjoys making candles. More than once she has proclaimed that coffee is the lifeblood and it is how she refrains from becoming a zombie.

Stay up to date and receive some free books by signing up for her newsletter! ellebeaumontbooks.com/newsletter

Join Elle's Facebook group and hang out with her facebook.com/groups/ElleBeaumontStreetTeam

For more information visit
www.ellebeaumontbooks.com
Follow Elle on social media!

facebook.com/ellebeaumontbooks
instagram.com/ellebeaumontbooks

MORE FROM ELLE

Demons of Frosteria

Frost Mate

Frost Claim

Immortal Realms Trilogy

Seeds of Sorrow

Tides of Torment

Wages of War

The Hunter Series

Hunter's Truce

Royal's Vow

Assassin's Gambit

Queen's Edge

Secrets of Galathea

Brotherhood of the Sea

Bindings of the Sea

Voice of the Sea

King of the Sea

Standalones

The Dragon's Bride

The Castle of Thorns

Slaying the Frost King

Anthologies

Emporium of Superstition

The Darkest Lullaby

ABOUT CHRISTIS CHRISTIE

 Christis Christie lives on the east coast of Canada, in Nova Scotia. She gets most excited about diving into a new fantasy world while writing, but also loves a good supernatural plot. Tiss, as she is affectionately called by her friends, enjoys being creative in any way she can, so if she's not writing then she's crocheting or she's embroidering. Her favorite animal is the sloth, and her favorite retellings are anything Beauty and the Beast related.

Follow Christis on social media!

facebook.com/ChristisChristieWrites

instagram.com/tiss.writes

MORE FROM CHRISTIS

Standalones

Spun Gold

The Dragon's Bride

Sanctuary of the Lost

Of Loyalties & Wreckage

Of Love & Ruin

Of Hope & Blight (June '24)

Immortal Realms Trilogy

Seeds of Sorrow

Tides of Torment

Wages of War

Reaping Series

Ephesus

Anthologies

Emporium of Superstition

MORE BOOKS YOU'LL LOVE

If you enjoyed this story, please consider leaving a review!

Then check out more books from Midnight Tide Publishing!

The Stars Would Curse Us by Stephanie Combs & Valerie Rivers

The Iris were sent to us from the stars, but their rule is controlling and oppressive. Every season, we send our brothers and sisters to the marriage drafts . . . but the selected never return.

Aella

My world falls apart when my best friend and I are drafted to compete for the hand of Esterra's most eligible bachelor, the devastatingly handsome Iris prince. As an elemental fae, it should be the greatest honor, but the competition is filled with violence. I question my true purpose as we fight to survive in games rigged against us.

Arianwen

Life should be simple—go on my rite and return to marry a man I've never met—but when a handsome stranger falls from the sky, everything is turned upside down. Secrets and lies unravel, leading me to question everything as I find myself pulled into a rebellion.

My heart longs for a better world, but am I willing to forsake duty
in pursuit of it?

We both face choices:

LOVE or DUTY

LOYALTY or ADVENTURE

FIGHT or SURRENDER

Is fate truly written in the stars, or have they abandoned us?

Now Available

The Songs That Beckon by M.A. Brown

Their grief binds them

The Song calls them

The Darkness wants to claim them

Three people, drawn together by shared tragedy must struggle together through love and loss to save all that they hold dear from the rising darkness.

The first in a dark and dreamy duology filled with prophetic dreams, dusty books and pining looks.

Available Now

Bound Island by G.D. Roman

◆Until the Knots of Avalon break.◆

Brye, Lenna, and Tara have lived their entire lives on an island surrounded by mists and protected by magical bonds. Nothing could be more perfect. Until one night, when magic begins to fray at the seams, and their lives change forever.

The Healer - Brye's healing abilities are her pride, making her the best match of the season. If only someone were interesting enough for her. Until she catches the eye of Prince Gareth, the least interesting one of all.

The Mist Maiden - Lenna has lived her life in the shadow of her sisters. Until Beltane, when her magic explodes. Now, she has been chosen to be a Mist Maiden, protector of Avalon. A role she was never destined to play.

The Warrior - Tara knows that she is meant to be more than being someone's mate. A warrior through and through, Tara strives for the extraordinary. No matter the cost. Even if that means she might have to sacrifice her growing feelings for Aiden.

As Avalon slowly becomes an island lost in the mists, will the sisters strengthen their bonds and save their home, or will they break apart forever?

Available Now